PRAISE FOR *KEEP YOUR CRO*

D0175569

"...There's a reason the characters, ar keep that crowbar handy...!"
-Tony Monchinski, author of *I Kill Monsters* and the critically acclaimed *Eden* novels.

"KYCH is a rollercoaster ride of action, adventure, suspense, horror, gore, and personal relationships at the end of the world as we know it. If this is only the first book in the series then hold on to your socks, the rest will blow them off!"
-James Jackson, survivalist/weapons advisor and author of *Up from the Depths*.

"...S.P. Durnin manages to bring a shining light into the quivering darkness of the apocalypse...!"
-Michael S. Gardner, author of *Downfall* and *Betrayal*.

"...The humor is great, the survivors are fun to follow and each truly speaks with a voice of their own."
-Stuart Conover, via ScienceFiction.com.

"...I found myself hooked into the book early on and kept getting mad that I had to stop reading it to do things like work at my day job, sleep, and tend to other annoying but necessary interruptions."
-Richard Baker of Zedprep.com

"...a high-action story of survival, love, betrayal and sacrifice. If you enjoy the zombie genre then you'll definitely enjoy this book!"
-Tiffany Clark, via Zombie and Post-Apocalyptic Fiction Fan Club.

"...keeps you intrigued from start to finish. SP Durnin's writing style is compelling and he clearly enjoys creating vivid characters and story sequences..."
-Patrick S. Dorazio, author of *The Dark Trilogy*.

"...S.P. Durnin takes you on a wild ride through the Zombie Apocalypse, all the while showing us both the best of people, and the worst of people. If you like Zombies, you will love this book! "
-Cedric Nye, author of *The Road to Hell is Paved with Zombies*

IS COMING

KEEP YOUR CROWBAR HANDY

SP DURNIN

A PERMUTED PRESS book

ISBN (trade paperback): 978-1-61868-314-4
ISBN (eBook): 978-1-61868-315-1

Keep Your Crowbar Handy copyright © 2014
by SP Durnin
All Rights Reserved.
Cover art by Roy Migabon

PERMUTED
PRESS

For Tonia... Love you, wife.

ACKNOWLEDGEMENTS

I wanted to take this opportunity to thank some people even though they already know who they are—those who through aid, advice, and support (which sometimes entailed putting a swift boot upside my butt-cheek) got the crowbar swinging: Tony (The Beast) Monchinski, Sara (Baconhugs!) Beverage, J.L.Bourne, Bowie V. Ibarra, Michael (Our Benevolent Overlord) Wilson, Bobbie Metevier (who didn't lynch me after editing this novel!) James R. Jackson, Michael S. Gardner, Roy Migabon (for an awesome cover!) Shawn (Walking Corpse) Riddle, and John (The Camel Spider) Brewer.

Also, special thanks to my Beta (reader) Corps: Tim (Good Stuff) Wendt, Keith (Jitterfreak!) Rogers, Anthony (X!) Masten, and Leslie B. Foster (See? Told ya you'd make it into the book, kid.)

You guys kick ass.

-S.P.

I'm sure—in the years to come—there will be people who claim they know what caused it all.

I can also tell you that each and every one of these big-brained, pencil-pushing assholes is full of it.

They'll say it was the government. Maybe a terrorist attack that went horribly wrong and started the whole mess. They might tell you it was "divine retribution" for our sins or "Mother Nature" striking back. They might even say, "Hell was full, so the dead started returning." I'm sure some will claim it was caused by a space-borne virus which survived for millions of years in an absolute vacuum, then fiery entry through the Earth's atmosphere, which brought humanity to the edge of extinction.

All bullshit.

Nobody knows why it started. To be frank—at this point—nobody gives a rat's ass. Why isn't really important when your every waking moment is spent trying to survive.

So, before you decide to ask, "Why?" (Which would cause me to slap you repeatedly about the head and shoulders), you need to realize that a better question would be, "Why not?"

So, I won't tell you what to believe about our actions.

I'll leave the moral arguments up to you.

Hopefully, because of our sacrifices, there will be a generation left alive to condone or condemn them...

—excerpt from, *The Chronicles of Jacob O'Connor: Year Zero*

PROLOGUE

Tracy Dickson's shoes were crippling her.

Mostly because she'd broken the heel off one of her pricy Manolo pumps about two minutes and half a block prior. She silently cursed—for the forty-eighth time—Mike Barron's parents for ever doing the dance of the two-backed beast that caused a miserable jerk like him to be spawned in the first place and took off the now-ruined heels to mince her way down the street.

She'd believed everything people had told her about Mike. That he was charming, sexy, driven, great in the sack, and an all-around swell guy. She'd spent the entire day getting ready for their second date. Having her hair done at Penzone along with the truly agonizing bikini wax. Doing both her finger and toenails at home because she'd blown her extra cash on the bikini wax. Picking out the right little black dress and spending about an hour primping before Mike cabbed over to pick her up.

At dinner everything was great. Tracy, Mike, Carly, Nathan, and Shannon ate sushi and sipped Dom at Arrow, one of the bistros in the Market district that all those city-beat, local-printed papers rave about constantly. Mike was attentive, listened to her when she spoke, and seemed genuinely interested in what she had to say.

She believed this, because his eyes didn't glaze over every time she began to talk.

They strolled, half buzzed already, about five blocks downtown to the Rim. It had become *the place to go* ever since the grand opening about three weeks prior. It boasted the best martinis anywhere in town and the sweatiest, heaviest bass-thumping, all-but-screwing-your-brains-out-on-the-floor, rave-style dance music this side of the Mississippi.

Shannon's father had developed half the neighborhood over the last three years, so she had *carte blanche* at most of the clubs within that six block radius. Owners and bartenders treated her like the heir apparent, and rightly so. No one wanted to piss off the landlord by treating his daughter like the rest of the sheeple. So their group breezed past the queue, through the velvet ropes under the envious eyes of those stuck outside for at least another hour, and into techno-neon heaven.

Tracy enjoyed the next couple of hours. The bass was heavy enough to pulverize your bones. The Jaeger flowed freely, and Mike confirmed that he could dance almost as well as anyone in the place. The fact that he did it with his shirt half off, showing his perfect Bowflex body was in no way unappealing either.

The night didn't turn sour until Tracy was coming back from the ladies room with Carly. As they made their way past the bar, they noticed Mike sprinkling powder into her martini and casually tossing the empty capsule down the back of the booth's curved seat. Tracy knew Carly had seen what he'd done from the look on her face. Tracy's jaw all but hit the floor and she made a beeline for Mike with murder in her heart, fully intending to stab him in the jugular with her eyeliner. After recalling the tales of prison hos she'd read about online, however, Tracy opted for a different course of action. Instead, she acted as if she was going to take a sip, paused and hurled the contents of her glass in his face.

Things turned ugly after that.

In no small way due to the fact that when Tracy asked Carly to confirm what they'd both witnessed, her friend told Tracy to stop causing a scene. Discounting the fact that Mike Barron had just tried to dose her with the current date-rapist's drug of choice.

Tracy screamed that Mike was a fucking rapist.

Mike yelled that Tracy was an uptight bitch.

The bouncers tossed them both out for throwing beer bottles at each other and a joyous time was had by all.

Mike turned and began to walk back uptown as he planned to visit another club. He was sure he could salvage the night due to its abundance of coeds usually drinking away their tuition...

Tracy began walking the other way in the vain attempt to catch a cab downtown at 1:22 a.m. on a Friday night. If she hadn't been so focused on being Barbie-doll perfect, she would have remembered to grab her cellphone when she left her two-bedroom apartment, run downstairs, and dived into the cab earlier.

It wouldn't have mattered really. It's not like she could've called a cab. She could only *just* afford her crappy little place and didn't have much to spare. She'd been forced to take a job pushing make-up to do so. She had to work before her parents would open up the near limitless coffers of the family accounts to her. You need to know the value of a dollar, they'd said.

What a crock, she'd thought.

Tracy was certain she could bat her eyes, jiggle a bit, and talk her way past the door guy. If all else failed she could always give him oral. But she shuddered at the thought of crawling back to the others to beg them to loan her cab fare. So fighting the sting of betrayal, she continued westward, feeling like the last person on earth in the empty streets, but with her dignity still partially intact. Two blocks later, while trying not to step on broken glass, she noticed the homeless guy staggering out of the alley just ahead. He moved stiffly, like he'd just guzzled a fifth of Thunderbird and wasn't prepared for the kick that comes with downing far too much cheap rotgut. Tracy swerved to one side to let him continue on towards wherever he was going to sleep it off, but the man stumbled towards her again. She angled left to get out of his path and again the drunk oriented on her, continuing to advance.

This was the last straw. After learning the guy she'd believed to be Prince Charming was really just a slimy toad in a silk shirt, getting the brush off from her supposed friends, and walking barefoot for the last three blocks, Tracy was in a truly bitchy state of mind.

"I don't have any change, so fuck off!" she said.

The homeless guy kept coming.

"Look, asshole," Tracy fumed, "I've had a *really* shitty night so..."

Then the smell hit her. It was like putting your nose about six inches over fresh road kill.

What the hell did this guy do? She thought. *Shit himself and roll around in rotten hamburger?*

He drew a few steps closer before Tracy noticed things about him that didn't add up.

She could smell the horrible funk preceding him. It was *really* bad. No matter how drunk he was, how could he stand it? His jaw was hanging slack, but his eyes were focused on her. His clothes were covered in filth and grime, but that looked a lot like a Ralph Lauren suit he was wearing. Tracy frowned at the thought of someone giving a three thousand dollar suit to the Salvation Army thrift store. She was all about helping her fellow man, but that was going just a bit too far.

Then he started to moan. A dry, rasping, painful sound. It sent a chill up her spine. He reached for her, and Tracy decided it was time to take steps.

She swung back her purse like a major league hitter and slammed it across his face. Usually, when someone went into hysterics, a good, sharp slap in the pie-hole sobered them up quick. Reasoning the same would work against somebody smashed out of their mind on malt liquor, she put some authority into her swing.

The impact knocked the vagrant to the left, away from her and head first into the front of a brownstone. There was a definite crunch as his face met the bricks and Tracy winced.

Then he turned towards her again.

She gaped at the ruin of his face. The man's nose was obviously broken and all but smashed flat against his upper lip. She also saw the stumps of at least four incisors shattered so badly that they were little more than bumps in his gums. There was little blood, and what did seep came from where part of his cheek and lip had been scraped away. It looked like foul, half congealed, dark honey. Bone showed on his right cheekbone where a good amount of flesh had been sloughed off, but the vagrant showed no sign he even noticed. What she'd mistaken for oil or maybe sewage all over the left side of his suit was actually blood from a crater-sized hole in his neck just over his jugular. She saw all this as, with the same rasping moan, he pushed away from the wall to come at her again, arms outstretched.

Bare feet forgotten, Tracy backpedaled until her butt hit the door of a rust-toned Chrysler displaying a pair of expired meter tickets. The vagrant closed the distance between them, the remainder of his lips pulling back from broken teeth in a feral snarl. She jigged to the left and attempted to catch him off balance, but his reflexes didn't respond fast enough for the move to work, and she almost hit him square as she dodged right again. His hand caught her forearm, and Tracy felt the first icy fingers of panic clutch at her. He was trying to pull her arm towards his mouth. She grabbed her attacker by the throat, digging her fingernails into his skin and the tissue beneath in an attempt to cut off his air. This did no good. He began to snap at her like a mad dog.

Tracy realized this lunatic wasn't going to come out if it. Her fingers were so deep in his neck she couldn't see her nails anymore. His flesh felt cool and faintly slimy, not the way someone's skin should normally feel. She reached full-blown, freaking-out panic. The blood running down her wrist was like cool syrup and stank of rot.

She kneed him in the nuts.

This was bad for two reasons. The first was that the force of her patella slamming into his genitals didn't seem to cause any discomfort and served to bend him over, almost knocking her to the sidewalk.

The second was the vagrant bending over caused her to lose her grip on his neck and ram her right hand into his mouth, allowing him to sink what was left of his teeth into her palm.

Shock held off the pain for a few seconds as Tracy watched him try to bite deeper into her flesh, but the gap in his teeth prevented him from taking out the chunk. She *was* able to see the blood from her hand slide back over his bloated tongue, however.

Then the pain hit. It was so intense Tracy almost vomited up the overpriced sushi she'd consumed earlier in the night. It felt like...like someone had tried to take a big fucking bite out of her *hand*!

Raw survival instinct kicked in, and in a move born of desperation she brought her left leg up, silently thanking her mother for forcing her through years of ballet, and kicked him in the chest. The blow caused the vagrant to take three tottering steps backwards, before he tripped over the trash can that blocked the basement stairs to the brownstone's lower door and fell. He disappeared down the concrete steps, followed by the trash can, finally coming to rest with a wet twak sound, just past the floor drain at the bottom.

He didn't get up again.

His skull had lost its battle with the second to last step and grey matter was smeared across the landing. It coated the back of his already-destroyed Ralph Lauren suit, blended with the filth, and created a foul paste that would make it necessary for the police to use a shovel to pry him from the sidewalk and into the body bag the next morning.

Tracy never knew any of this. She had already bolted down the sidewalk, aware of nothing but her avenue of escape.

She never knew the vagrant's name was Carl Davis. She never knew he'd been on his way home from work two days earlier and decided to take a shortcut past the river walk where he and his wife first met. She never knew he'd jumped down the bank when he saw someone struggling out of the water to try to help them. She never learned the woman he'd been trying to help had torn out his jugular before he shoved her rotted form back into the river. She never guessed that as he had lain in the mud dying, Carl hoped he'd pushed the horror far enough back into the current so that it wouldn't be able to claw its way back. She'd never suspect his wife was waiting to tell him that, after almost two years of trying, they were finally going to decide what color to paint the nursery.

Tracy ran twenty-two blocks like a demon was howling at her heels. She never looked back.

The pain in her hand was blinding. All she could think of was to get home. Maybe it wouldn't be that bad. She could clean it out, apply some Bactine, and keep her hand covered for a couple of weeks.

She finally made it back to her building, her eyes still wild with panic, but her hand had begun to go cold. It helped with the pain and she was able to open the security door, then make it into the elevator before beginning to cry.

It seemed an eternity before the elevator made it to the fifth floor. The heavily scratched and scuffed mirrors on its doors showed discoloration under her eyes that Tracy couldn't account for. The vagrant hadn't punched her or connected with her face, but she was beginning to resemble a raccoon. Her lower lids had begun to get puffy and more than a little purple. Well, hiding that was the least of her problems. She could tell people she'd been bitten by a stray dog, and she could cover a couple of bruises with some creative eye shadow.

She leaned against the wall as she walked to her door, cradling her wounded hand to her stomach while searching her bottomless purse for keys with her other. The pain was horrible, but was losing its sharp edge. With any luck, her plan to sterilize and cover the bite would allow it to begin healing and keep her from the ever-embarrassing visit to the emergency room.

Dropping her purse inside as she entered, Tracy double locked her door and scurried to the half bath where she spent an agonizing twenty minutes cleaning her hand. Scrubbing the wound was far more painful than the liberal application of peroxide that followed. After her vision cleared, she smeared topical ointment to the now barely seeping bite and wrapped it with gauze. The pain was less now. Maybe cleansing it aided her body in deadening the nerves or something. Or she could be in shock.

She remembered that people going into shock should be kept warm and awake, so she wrapped up in her terrycloth robe before putting the kettle on to make some holy java goodness.

Her hand barely hurt at all now, just twinged a bit as she filled the mug. The smell of coffee was divine and she sat on her threadbare couch holding the mug just below her nose, inhaling the smoky richness, trying to calm down. So much had happened over the last six hours. Mike had turned out to be an ass, her *friends* had been revealed as backstabbing socialites, and she'd been mauled by a cracked-out executive bum.

Tracy leaned back and closed her eyes. Luckily, she had the weekend off. She would pull herself together, then face the world Monday a bit worse for wear but still ready to make it sit up and beg for its mother. She'd make *damn* sure word got around about Mr. Mike-fucking-Barron too.

The pain had faded to something just a bit more uncomfortable than a healthy sunburn and was losing intensity, being replaced with a cool numbness. Before she knew it, Tracy was beginning to nod off. She knew she shouldn't and decided to get up for another cup of coffee.

In just a minute or two...

* * *

Tracy drifted into the mercy of sleep minutes later, mug forgotten on the cushion next to her left hip.

Her arm fell off the couch into her lap, blood seeping through the gauze that was already tacky and half congealed.

She was already getting cold and the shapely legs she'd hoped to wrap around Mike Barron's well-muscled torso in animal pleasure had turned a disturbing shade of yellowish-gray. As time passed, she drifted deeper into REM sleep and beyond. Past any anticipation of well-planned social revenge, beyond any urges of sexual abandon, then finally into coma.

Over the next few minutes her breathing became less and less pronounced, then finally stopped altogether.

Ringing silence permeated the apartment, and the aroma of expensive coffee warred with the odor of a body just beginning its fall into the first stages of decay...

CHAPTER ONE

Jake was convinced that customer service made up at least *one* of the lower levels in Hell.

This belief was reinforced by the snide and disgustingly self-centered woman at the Supercenter pharmacy desk, currently bitching at the top of her lungs like a Russian drill sergeant. It seemed because she thought she was the by-God center of the universe, everyone in the world needed to realize how important her broad-beamed, Bible-thumping ass was and give way to Ms. Anna W. Bessendorfer of the lakeside Bessendorfers.

Jake wished she would just waddle back the way she'd come, walk out into traffic, and get hit by a fucking bus.

She'd pushed her way to the counter, past a single woman with her obviously sick toddler and the eighty-eight year old Mrs. Jennings, who'd been waiting almost forty-five minutes, to demand the prescription she'd called in during the ten-minute drive from her home.

The counter attendant, a young, Asian woman with a nametag that read "Kat" (whom Jake thought was *very* pretty, even with the odd hairstyle—streaks of what looked to be deep blue that went well with her exotic features) looked as if she'd rather be anywhere else on the planet. She attempted to explain to the ranting hag that it would take at least another two hours to have her airsickness medication filled. Twice now. Half the pharmacy staff had either called off or not shown up for work and they'd been behind since opening.

The single pharmacist, a Mr. Joe Pavek, looked as if he'd just run the entire three miles from there to midtown as he worked at breakneck pace. Sweat rolled down his forehead and his hands moved non-stop, filling order after order with robotic precision. Joe didn't envy Kat one bit right then. He understood that being polite and helping people was what they were there to do, but the insufferable Ms. Bessendorfer was beginning to grate on his nerves, as well.

"I understand your frustration ma'am," Kat said for the umpteenth time, trying heroically to keep anger out of her voice, "but we're really backed up due to being short staffed today and—"

"Does it look like I care about your problems?" Ms. Bessendorfer interjected snidely with a raised and oh-so-carefully penciled on eyebrow. "I need to catch a flight to our New York headquarters in less than two hours and I still have to stop by the office to pick up the quarterly reports. I don't have time for this! You people need to stop whining about how far behind you are and take fewer breaks!"

Does this broad realize how pretentious she sounds? Jake wondered, shaking his head and looking down at the faded CBGB t-shirt he'd opted for this morning.

He didn't have any clean button-ups.

The woman's attitude made him sick. One of the things his parents had impressed into him at a young age was that you were respectful to the elderly, especially those in obvious need of help. The fact that this ridiculous hag had all but shoved the aging Mrs. Jennings aside really irked him. He caught himself wishing for that missing piece of the Mir Space Station to come crashing through the roof and squish her like a bug, but he realized she'd still be an inconvenience to the pharmacy staff who would have to mop her up off the floor.

Kat soldiered on. "Ma'am we're working as fast as..."

"Don't *ma'am* me! I pay your salary! Without people like me you'd be out of a job, you ungrateful little stain!" Ms. Bessendorfer huffed.

* * *

Anna Bessendorfer had dealt with people like Kat before, people who just didn't understand that she had better things to do than stand around listening to the simpering of those who couldn't make something worthwhile of their lives. Well, that was never going to be Anna W. Bessendorfer. She was on the fast track at Beautyquest, where she'd worked for the past eight years, monitoring the quality of everything from shampoo to sea-salt infused foot scrub. She owned her own four-bedroom, two-bath home which she shared with no one but her dog, Baby. Her friends all said the dog was spoiled, but there was nothing wrong with letting your pet sleep in the bed with you, was there? Baby got lonely and whined if Anna didn't let her do so at night.

Anna was also in charge of the evangelistic committee at her church, where everyone just loved how excited she was about Jesus and bringing new members into the congregation.

So what if two (or three) times a week she drank herself into a pale ale infused stupor and catted around with everyone possessing external genitalia? She was doing good work. Her rewards in this world and the next were assured, so she didn't have to be treated like everyone else. She was above the petty, little problems other people had and didn't care if they knew it.

"Do you have any idea what I do for a living?" Anna fumed. "I'm the one who approves the eye shadow you're wearing! I need that medication immediately! I can't be unsightly for tomorrow. There's far too much riding on making a good impression with the board. Possibly a promotion! Now you get back there and get my order, or I'm going to the store manager to let him know how incompetent you are!"

She drew one of her newly printed business cards out of the garish purse at her side and shoved it under Kat's nose. "Do you see this? That says Beautyquest Team Co-coordinator. That means I monitor people like *you* every day, and let me tell you something. If any of them did their job the way you're attempting to do yours, they'd be out on their narrow ass in the unemployment line!"

She sneered at Kat, giving her the once over, looking as if she just found a roach in her corn flakes.

"Do you realize how much I make?" Ms. Bessendorfer demanded, shaking her I'm-So-Important card in Kat's face. "I could probably buy you and every pathetic thing you own with about a week's salary!"

The lovely Asian's eyes narrowed dangerously.

"Tell you what, *Mizz* Bessendorfer," Kat grated, causing Joe the pharmacist to look at her worryingly, "why don't you..."

"Do you mind?"

Both women jumped as Jake plucked the business card from Anna's hand.

* * *

He was the one who'd offered to drive the near homebound Mrs. Jennings to pick up medication that took the edge off the pain from her recent knee replacement. Actually, Jake had insisted. He wasn't about to let her try to take a bus or pay outrageous cab fares, because Gertrude Jennings had never been behind the wheel of a car in her life. He'd walked beside her as she'd driven the "silly little scooter" as she called it, so she wouldn't feel ashamed asking for help to get groceries from the higher shelves, or out of the freezer cases either. Jake didn't mind doing things for her. Like him, Gertrude Jennings had no family. Her husband had passed away years before and they never had children. Jake did have a younger brother, but they hadn't seen each other in years. When their parents split, their mother had taken Eddie to Boulder with her. Over the following year letters and phone calls began to come farther and farther apart, until finally they stopped altogether. His mother had remarried and changed her last name. Eddie was about eight at the time, so it wouldn't have been too difficult to convince him that he should have a new name too and Jake's search had come to an abrupt end.

His father wasted away after he left home, finally succumbing to depression after his son took an internship with Britain's SAS as a civilian journalistic consultant. Jake flew the eleven hours back to bury him and had been one of seven mourners at his father's wake. It was held in the dive bar over which the senior Mr. O'Connor had lived.

Afterwards Jake finished out the last five months of his assignment and returned to Buckeye Country—a bachelor's degree richer but totally alone.

He'd never been so depressed in his life.

Except for a couple of friends he'd stayed in touch with, Jake had no one. The next few years had been a series of assignments that kept him on the move. Nairobi, Alaska, Texas, the West Indies. He'd practically lived out of his suitcase until begging off the higher visibility jobs, opting instead for steady work as an editor/ghostwriter. It provided him some stability and, hopefully, the chance to get a life.

When Jake moved into her building, Gertrude made supper and brought it to him that first night, when he couldn't find a stinking pot amid the boxes to make himself a bowl of Ramen noodles. Hell, he couldn't even find the damn Ramen.

After that, he'd made a point of taking her along when he hit whatever grocery Supercenter was having sales that week. He wouldn't let her try to lug her trash outside, winter or not. She'd fuss every time she'd catch him as he ran out past her in the hall, jacket in one hand, current week's rewrites in the other, holding a stale bagel from his cupboard in his mouth to make his deadline. Those evenings sure enough, she'd ambush him at the landing refusing to take 'Thank *you, but*—' for an answer and Jake would be eating roast chicken for dinner. Or pot roast with potatoes. Or corned beef and cabbage, which he had a genetic weakness for anyway, being a Mick.

So, no one blamed him when he'd finally had enough of watching this self-important hypocrite shovel abuse into the atmosphere and decided to take steps. As Ms. Bessendorfer gaped and Kat looked on quizzically, he examined the card.

"Tell me, ma'am," Jake began, "have you ever heard of Murphy's Law?"

Anna gave him a quizzical look that said, *what the hell is this guy talking about?*

"What the hell are you talking about?" she asked.

"Murphy's Law states that the least desirable possibility will always exert itself. Or if anything can go wrong it will," Jake explained. "I prefer a slightly different version that states: the least desirable possibility will exert itself at the worst possible moment. Or if anything can go wrong it will, at the worst time."

Mrs. Bessendorfer looked as if she assumed he was on drugs.

That would fit with his punk-rocker shirt and combat boots, but he didn't display the wasted, malnourished, pasty look that junkies normally had. Jake was more lean than muscular. His six-foot frame looked nothing like the hulking behemoths so popular in action movies or muscle-building magazines, but his chest was deep and the cords in his arms rippled as he crossed them. He'd never been what most people considered handsome, but a narrow waist combined with broad shoulders and the weight his serious gaze carried tended to give his face a gravity that would win him many a conquest in the clubs.

Morals notwithstanding.

"I don't have time to discuss psychology with random strangers," Anna snapped, dismissing him with a wave. "I've got..."

"A perpetual case of constipation?"

She stood, mouth open at his audacity. "What?"

"I spoke clearly," Jake said. "Do you have a hearing deficiency? Along with the irritable bowel syndrome, I mean?"

Anna Bessendorfer was speechless.

"The Pepto's over there on the third shelf," he said helpfully, pointing up the aisle, past a display for the latest weight loss miracle pill. "You might want to get the economy size bottle. Better value, you know."

Anna's face began to turn red.

"Maybe you should consider calling your doctor, scheduling a colonoscopy," Jake recommended with a sympathetic look. "If you don't have your health... you don't have anything."

"Who do you think you're talking to?" She sputtered waving her arms in a fair impression of a flightless waterfowl. "What gives you the idea you can *speak* to me that way?"

Jake wasn't impressed.

"The fact I don't work here helps. It means I don't have to stomach abuse from a self-absorbed twit with an overinflated sense of self-importance. It also means I can say whatever I damn well please, just as *you* can in this country, and there's nothing you can do about it," he explained. "Also, since you think you can commit assault and get away with it, I—as a law-abiding member of the community—felt a deep personal responsibility to point out that you're opening yourself up to possibly dire financial consequences."

Anna stared at him in shock.

"Not that I have a problem with someone acting like a pompous ass," he admitted, "but seeing that you *did* basically just shove two people, one of which was holding a small child, in a public place... Well. Members of local law enforcement agencies would likely have a problem with that. And that would make it *terribly* hard to make that board meeting. Wouldn't it?"

"How dare you!" Ms. Bessendorfer ranted. "What business is it of yours?"

"It'd make a good article," Jake admitted. "I could call it, *Power Corrupts*: *a Synopsis of Self-importance in Executive America*. My editor would love it."

"Your...e-editor?"

"I have a column published nationally. Wouldn't be very difficult to make a couple of calls to the local TV stations. I'm sure they'd love to air related spots, especially with the magazine running articles on the subject." He reached into his battered leather jacket hanging on the Supercenter scooter Gertrude occupied and pulled out the notepad he'd carried since his first year of college. Flipping it open, he took the ballpoint out of the spiral that held said pad together and clicked it out.

"Could I get your side of it? It would be a good idea to match it against video footage the security office keeps, and then compare it with psychological profiles of those with the same delusions." Jake began scribbling on his pad. "You said you work for Beautyquest. Can I ask for how long? Which department? Just so we can research as to whether this kind of behavior is a symptom of job related stress, or a side effect of another malady?"

Anna Bessendorfer's expression flashed from surprise to disgust and finally settled firmly into seething anger. "You print one word..."

"And you'll what?" he asked curiously. "Stab me with your eye liner? Give me a tumor with your Blackberry? Yell and scream and throw a hissy fit and try to intimidate me? Please. I spent time with the SAS. Let me tell you lady, they've got drill sergeants that make *you* look like a fluffy bunny by way of comparison. Now, I'm not a pushy guy. But I *swear*, if you don't wait your damn turn like these people have, I will make it my mission in *life* to see that you serve time for assault. I'm sure two victims, coupled with witness testimony from the employees and a concerned bystander, would go a long way towards that end."

Miss Bessendorfer was about to escalate into a full-blown scream when she caught a glimpse of Kat and Joe Pavek from the corner of her eye. The young woman was leaning on the register counter with a predatory grin, and Joe looked like he'd just found a stray Franklin in his pocket. To her right, the toddler's mother seemed ready to begin hostilities, and Mrs. Jennings wore a look of profound disapproval. Even if she did have to ride around in a silly little scooter.

After giving Jake a look overflowing with venom, Anna swished her way quickly up the aisle and grabbed a few boxes of over-the-counter motion sickness pills. She turned back to voice a scathing remark at the little people who had just completely ruined her day because of their unwillingness to defer to her on general principals. Jake looked at her with a raised eyebrow and whatever she'd planned to say died on her lips. He had to be bluffing, didn't he?

He spread his arms as if to say, *was there something*? causing the merry Mrs. Bessendorfer to spin on her heel and set sail for the register at the far end of the Supercenter.

Jake watched her go as Mr. Pavek handed Kat Gertrude's pain medication. He hated people like that. People who would shit all over somebody just because they believed what prep school they went to or how much money they made entitled them to act like a five year old.

Kat beamed at him as she rang up the medication.

"That was brilliant," she said, as Joe gave him a thumbs up on his way back to fill the toddler's prescription. "She nearly lost it when you mentioned your publisher. I wish I could've gotten a shot of her face for the break room!"

"Yeah, well..." Jake rubbed the back of his neck with a sheepish grin. "I am a journalist, but I work freelance. I get published a few times a year, but mostly I ghostwrite and proofread novels. I don't know what any of the local TV station phone numbers are unless I borrowed your Yellow-pages, either."

"You were *bluffing*? Oh, that's priceless!" Kat's eyes and smile widening with mirth. She scribbled her phone number on one of the store fliers and pressed it into his hand. "Look, give me a call later. I'm going to see a performance at Bueno Dave's tonight. I'd love to talk when I'm not hip deep in Mary Kay psychos."

Jake tried not to blush as he folded the paper and shoved it into his back pocket. "Okay. I don't know if I'll be available though. I have to finish the cookbook I've been editing which is due next Tuesday, but we'll see what happens."

Her eyebrows rose.

"Smart, gutsy, nice to old ladies, *and* you can cook?" she marveled. "No one's that good. Are you secretly a serial killer?"

"Nope."

"An alien bent on global domination?"

Jake shook his head.

"Girlfriend?"

"Just Mrs. Jennings," he said, "but she's not the jealous type."

Gertrude rolled her eyes. Then the pretty young woman cocked her head and squinted at him thoughtfully. "Boyfriend?"

Jake chuckled. "Nope. I just don't have much luck with relationships. I think it's because I have a weakness for vintage punk rock. I never hit any clubs. That bass-loaded garbage gives me migraines."

Kat laughed as the toddler's mother swiped her credit card through the reader.

"Well, let's see what happens then," she said as he paced Mrs. Jennings past the counter. "Nice guys *are* still out there. Good to know."

"I think that's part of my problem," Jake mumbled to himself and followed Gertrude up the aisle.

"What problem is that, Jacob?" Gertrude asked. He hadn't meant for her to hear his comment and was reluctant to discuss the topic. Right up until she threatened to ram him with the scooter as they moved through the parking lot to his car.

"Being a nice guy," he said. "It's not beneficial to your social life when it comes to dating."

"I never understood what women today see in men that treat them badly," Gertrude said dryly. "When I was young, a man had to be *nice* to you. I wouldn't give someone who was more concerned with getting in my bloomers than what was on my mind the time of day."

Jake shrugged and held open the door of his Jeep for her. It was genuine US Government Issue, which he'd purchased just after his return from England. Best three hundred dollars he'd ever spent, in his opinion. Granted it had been in a box. Unassembled. But his friend Allen Ryker's father had offered to put the monster together for another two hundred. He'd done a bang up job too. In about two weeks Jake had received a call to pick it up. Allen's dad adjusted the carburetor for a minute then shut the hood, smile plastered wide across his Greek mug as Jake walked in. He proclaimed that he'd never had so much fun as he did putting the Jeep together and the olive green vehicle's engine rumbled to life on the first try.

He also told Jake he'd decided to buy a couple more to sell, along with a third for himself.

So far, he'd assembled and sold almost a dozen.

Other buyers had ordered four more too, and Allen's father was having the time of his life putting Jeep after Jeep together in a bay at Ryker's Auto Body.

"Really, Jacob," Gertrude said, "you need to find yourself a nice girl. Not like the last one. What was her name?"

"Nichole."

"I told you she was nothing but a floozy," she chided. "No self-respecting woman would wear a miniskirt that short. And made of leather? Besides, she worked in a *brothel* for heaven's sake."

"She was an exotic dancer."

Gertrude sniffed. "Don't split hairs, dear. You need someone that uses her head for more than something to keep her hair on."

True enough, Jake thought.

He and Nichole had met through Allen. Their relationship, if you could call it that, had begun that same night at a bar. Jake learned that the bar was only three blocks from where Nichole worked. She'd strutted in, moving like the High Priestess of Naughtiness, and every guy there had instantly hated him. The evening ended with a marathon of sex beginning at his doorway, through the living room, and finally ending in his bed where her fingernails left little half-moon slices in his shoulder blades. Saying Nichole was addicted to sex was like saying a heroin addict needed a fix. Theirs had been a brief, tumultuous affair that, not to Jake's surprise, ended like a train wreck. Worse yet, he knew the breakup *was* due to his lack of, what she termed, *sexual open mindedness*. What Nichole wanted just wasn't in his genetic make-up. Sappy as it was, he'd always believed that sex was a way to express affection, not just push the human body to fornication extremes. When she started talking about bringing other women home, he realized the downward spiral had begun.

Jake knew that most men would jump at the idea of a threesome with two smoking hot women, but he wasn't one of them. After two months of her pleading, both verbally and physically, he'd finally had enough and broke the news to her over dinner. She had taken it well. Kind of. He had to toss the shirt he'd worn that night. Merlot just doesn't come out of a tan shirt. Neither does mustard, as it turned out. It did however prove, without a *shadow* of a doubt, that you couldn't base a relationship on sex alone.

"Yeah well. Sometimes I think I was born in the wrong era." Jake slipped into the driver's seat and brought the Jeep to life. "Maybe I should take a correspondence course in jerkism."

"What?"

"Sure! That's what I need," he replied, grinning. "New wardrobe, crappy attitude, ditch any kind of values I have. The ladies will be lining up."

Mrs. Jennings looked at him with her *you're full of it* gaze and latched her seat belt, wincing as her arthritic hands twinged. "That would bring your supply of corned beef and cabbage to a swift end, young man."

"Forget I said it." Jake swung his Jeep out of the parking lot. "I'd never risk depriving my belly of corned-beefy goodness."

The drive back to their building was uneventful, with the exception of stopping every few blocks or so to allow yet another ambulance to go by. Jake began to frown when the fifth one almost broadsided a classic MGB, and then narrowly missed a tubby guy on a vintage ten-speed. Gertrude noticed his expression and looked around.

"What is it, Jacob?" Gertrude asked.

"Probably nothing," he said, still frowning. "I just can't remember seeing this many ambulances. At least, not in a while."

Mrs. Jennings followed the latest one's course up the ramp to the 670 freeway.

"Do you think something's happened? A fire or some kind of terrorist attack?" she asked.

"No, nothing like that." Jake shook his head and checked the surrounding skyline for smoke. "They were all going in different directions. If something that big had happened we'd definitely see the smoke, and emergency vehicles in thirty-one flavors would be streaming to the same location."

Gertrude looked half-convinced as she raised her eyebrows. "Sure about that, are you?"

Jake nodded and accelerated, bringing them back into traffic. "Reasonably sure. Those years I spent with Britain's SAS. I picked up quite a bit about how to recognize real danger through close observation of my surroundings. Well, that and my brilliant journalistic intuition."

Gertrude smiled, nodded, and gently smacked him in the back

of his head.

"Hey! Don't mess with the driver!"

"Oh, you're the driver?" she asked. "I thought you were a comedian."

Jake sighed as he pulled into the tenant parking lot behind their building. He punched his code in and the solid steel gate slid open smoothly, allowing him to move the Jeep through. After the vehicle was clear, well-disguised motion sensors inside the lot activated pneumatic hinges on the gate and the massive door closed with a pronounced clank.

That was one of the many good things you could say about their landlord, he mused, helping Gertrude out and grabbing her bags while ignoring her protest that she could at least carry the little one. He thanked the powers-that-be every day that he'd found the owner to be a standup guy.

After Jake viewed the vacant apartment, George Foster had handed him a three-page list of the current tenants' phone numbers and asked him to call any of them for an honest opinion of the building, its upkeep, or him in general before the writer made his decision. He also made it clear to Jake that drugs, wild parties, or any other shady activity would result in eviction by way of a size eleven boon-docker to the ass.

"Anyone screwing with my peace here only does it once. If you can accept that, welcome to the building. If you can't, have a nice day, quit wasting my time, and fuck you," Foster had said.

Jake signed the lease for his apartment, overlooking the dilapidated warehouse next door, right there.

When Foster asked him why, he admitted that the unit commander told him just about the same thing during his first day with the SAS. He brooked no shite, protected his men, and (after about a month) treated Jake just like one of them. It helped that the writer was CPR certified, could shoot almost as well as the rest of the brick, and didn't flinch every time a gun was fired.

Foster had chuckled telling him how his own unit cross-trained with the Limeys in '88 and that anyone who could hold his own with them was welcome in his building.

George Foster kept his property in top shape too. The building's utilities almost never went down (which was rare when renting), because he crawled around under floors and through air ducts with the repair crew so often. Nobody could get in without a pass code, which the residents made up themselves, or authorization from a resident. Then they had to get by a truly motivated ex-Navy security guard who knew all the residents by name. The elevators and stairways were kept absolutely perfect at

Foster's specific request. The one time the elevator had broken, he'd actually run everyone's errands for the two days it had taken for repairs to be completed. He'd camped out in the lobby at night, disabled the external intercom, and walked every delivery up himself. He'd gone up with every resident when they'd come home, regardless of the hour, letting them know that he was dead serious about getting the elevator running ASAP. The following day, he contracted for a new and very expensive 24-hour repair service, after giving the building's now former service provider a large piece of his ex-Navy mind. He hated taking the stairs due to the fact they made the pins in his knee ache. He was damned if he'd ask *them* to do something he hated to do *himself*.

George was approaching seventy and lived alone in a tiny two-room he'd set up in the building's basement. The man didn't spend much time there, however, probably because he didn't have any family of his own. Gertrude informed Jake once that Foster did have a brother in California somewhere, but they only saw one another every few years or so. Evidently, his brother's wife didn't like the old soldier's sense of humor.

Their teenage daughter loved it, though.

He always seemed to be around, no matter the hour, working on one project or another. George usually kept his office door locked too, which Jake thought a bit odd. Another oddity was the way the aging man somehow just *produced* things, seemingly at will from within. George had once entered his little cell and, not five minutes later, come out with an RPG for Jake to examine. The writer honestly believed Foster had a wormhole to a National Guard armory under his desk or something.

The other residents believed he kept all his best porn in the office's many filing cabinets.

George was closing up the lobby intercom as Gertrude and Jake came in. He finished tightening the last plate screw, shoved the power drill he'd been using into his ever-present, side satchel and motioned for some of their bags. Knowing better than to decline, Jake handed over the four in his left hand and hit the call button for the elevator.

"Hey, Mr. Foster," Jake said. "What's up?"

"Damn it, O'Connor, I told you how many times now? My name's George. Not *Mr.* or *Sir* or any of that other horseshit," he grated. "If ya can't bring yerself to use my name, just call me Chief. Hiya, Gertie. Still cradle robbin' I see."

"Hello, George," she replied with a smile. "Well, Robert's been gone ten years now, so I thought I might get a more current model."

Foster laughed uproariously as the elevator doors opened and they stepped inside. He tended to treat his tenants like he'd treated the men in his unit when he was still on active duty in the Navy. His bawdy humor and can-do attitude endeared him to Gertrude and the older occupants (along with Jake who admired him for his blunt, if occasionally crass humor). The rest of the younger ones took his comments in stride because he was the best landlord any of them had ever encountered, and they didn't want to piss the man off.

"I figured that," George said, as the lift rose to the fourth floor. "You always got *me* all frazzled before I enlisted. Almost swore off women altogether when I came back and learned you'd got hitched."

"What changed your mind?" Gertrude pulled out her keys as they trooped down the hall.

"Fell in forty-eight hour lust with a French girl named Claire two months into my second tour," George said with a smile. "Figured you couldn't *all* be bad after that."

Gertrude held the door for the two men as they lugged her bags into her kitchen, but shooed them both away when they tried to unpack.

"Oh, no," she said crisply. "I draw the line at males trying to put groceries away. You two will just shove things in wherever there's room, and I'll spend the next hour reorganizing the mess."

"You mean the cheddar cheese don't go up in the cupboard next ta the spaghetti?" Foster asked, straight-faced. Jake tried to cover his laugh by faking a cough, but Gertrude saw through him.

"Out, out!" Gertie grabbed the cane she kept hanging on her pantry door next to the spice rack and ump-teen different kinds of tea. "Go! I thank you, Jacob, George, but if you don't get a move on, you'll have some contusions!"

The two men ran for their lives.

After Gertrude shut her door, Foster stood in the hall smiling while Jake hugged his sides, nearly incapacitated with laughter. "Think we could've taken her?"

George shook his head, still grinning. "Not a chance. She'd a-handed us our asses."

"Kinda thought so."

"Heh. Well, I'm headin' down." George reached into his utility bag and pulled out a battered notepad. He leafed back a few pages, crossing off projects he'd completed with a grubby ballpoint. "Oh, almost forgot. Yer friend Allen left a message for ya. Said to remind ya to pick him up at Bolton Airfield at two o'clock, sharp."

Jake rolled his eyes, rode the elevator back to the lobby with

Foster, and fished the keys from his coat pocket.

"Stop by when ya get back. Got something new ta show you boys," George said. "Make them shootin' games Allen's so fond of look like a pillow fight. I'll be in the mood to maybe take it to the range I think. Some fool's coming to make me an offer on the warehouse. Again."

"Why do you hang on to that eyesore?"

Foster snorted. "It's like me. Old, tough an ugly. Besides, I might turn it into a garage fer the building one day. Thoughts on shootin' later?"

Jake shrugged. "Maybe. Al may not need any more adrenalin after today, though."

George gave him the *Look*. The one drill sergeants save for recruits who ask questions on the first day of basic training. It said, I can't believe yer dumb enough to let stupid shit like that drop out of your pie-hole. Gimme fifty more push-ups, dip-shit.

"We talking 'bout the same friend here?" George asked.

Jake smiled ruefully. "Let's just say Allen never lets a Friday go to waste without getting high."

George's expression turned homicidal. "Stoner?" he growled.

"No, no. Nothing like that." Jake assured him, then hit the bar to open the lot door. "Al's into a different kind of high."

* * *

Tracy Dickson was still in her apartment.

Rigor had come and gone over the course of the last twenty-four hours and the smell was getting more and more pronounced. A gray tinge had spread over her torso, giving her skin the dull, sickly look of a department store mannequin that hadn't seen any maintenance in the last thirty years.

Her coffee mug had tipped off the couch in the early hours of the morning, coating the rug with the tepid remains of Jamaican roast, which stained the hardwood floor beneath.

Tracy's answering machine displayed six messages, each one just a little more worried than the last, finally ending with Carly promising to come by to check on her with Nathan that evening if she hadn't heard from her by nine.

The corpse couldn't have cared less...

CHAPTER TWO

Laurel was daydreaming of a weekend off when Kat arrived.

It was just after six, and most of her customers had already come and gone for the day, so she decided to knock of a whole three minutes early. She'd been able to open a holistic, supplement store of her own and believed that finally, after years of working in national-chain mega marts, she would have it made. Cater to a specific clientele, be her own boss, set her own hours, live the dream.

Sounded good at the time, Laurel mused.

Between keeping the books, dealing with the suppliers, searching for local product, filling then shipping orders, and days that started at five a.m. (ending usually around ten at night), she hadn't possessed anything resembling a life for almost a year now.

Laurel tried to remember the last time she'd done anything other than have coffee with Kat. Her roommate/best friend/sounding board, made it a point to pull her (kicking and screaming) once a week to her favorite bar/house of java and song on the lower south side of town. The filtered bean squeezings were always top notch, nine of ten times the music was something folksy (or at least acoustically performed), and if the crowd wasn't full of people Laurel could connect with? She could live with that for an hour or two of relaxation.

Laurel St. Clair was an inch or so shorter than Kat's five-foot-ten with a shock of deep red hair cascading halfway down her back, hair which earned her countless envious complements. The only problem was it would never quite cooperate. No matter what she did, one stray lock would always work its way from the scrunchie, or out of the hair clip, and fall over her left eye. She had a dancer's build and even though she didn't possess the Out-To-Here breasts the current crop of semi-anorexic movie starlets displayed, she filled out the Saint Brigid sweater (which she'd knitted herself, thank you very much) quite nicely. Her waist was slim and it curved appealingly into shapely hips, which had a tendency to sway a bit more than usual when she got upset. A few freckles, the legacy from a Scottish grandmother, complimented her looks and as Kat phrased it, *Would make any red-blooded boy sit up and bark at the moon.* Trim and toned, Laurel had no idea she'd caused a few hapless victims to walk into streetlights and a couple of parking meters on her morning jogs. Not until the last one almost got hit by a bus. Which was why she'd changed up to her earlier five a.m. run time.

Originally from out west, she'd come to the wilderness that was Ohio a few years ago just in time to purchase a failing health food store. Laurel breathed new life into the place and had more than tripled its clientele in the first months. Two years later it was still putting food on the table.

She was considering changing her rose hip supplier when Kat all but flew in the door with an expression that was, in a word, worrying. Usually she was an upbeat bundle of smiles. The Kat who walked into Laurel's *You Are What You Eat* today, however, had the determined look of a WWI trench-fighter, fully prepared to pull the trigger and shoot a bullet across no-man's land and into the noggin of a German stooge.

Katherine Bright-feather Cho was Laurel's polar opposite. She made no apologies for her looks. Mama-san had fallen for a Native American Air Force pilot back in the day and she'd received her exotic features from both parents. Her complexion was that of mild Earl Grey tea and many people asked if her ancestors were Japanese or Chinese. Her reply was always *I'm Squaw.* Her face displayed the high cheekbones and dark eyes of her Navajo father, and her trim form moved with a panther's grace due to daily lessons in several different styles of martial arts via her mother from the time she began to walk. That, coupled with her habit of wearing midriff shirts to show off her well-defined abs, gave her the *come and get it* look. Kat's appearance made it necessary, more often than not, for her to go after guys herself, rather than waiting for them to work up the courage to approach her though. Laurel had warmed to her free-spirit nature when Kat had been looking for a roommate to split the rent while she finished her pharmacy tech certification.

They'd been best friends ever since.

"Hey Kat," she called, "how was your day in the land of the ill and ill-mannered?"

Her roommate smiled.

Laurel began to worry at that point.

"Believe it or not, I met the single most annoying fucking *bitch* in the world today," Kat said, still grinning like a cat that had just coughed up a mouthful of yellow feathers. "She was suffering from pickle-up-the-ass syndrome if anyone ever does. If that witch had spoken to me on the street that way, she'd be eating pudding for the next four months until her face healed. I'd have broken her jaw for her."

Laurel's eyebrows rose. "And this was a good thing?"

"Not really." Kat admitted, shaking her head as she grabbed an energy drink from the stand-up cooler next to Laurel's register. "It was the guy that made her take her bitchy ass on out the door that made my day."

"*Another* one?" Laurel asked. "How many does that make, this month?"

"Stop that," Kat said. "And Bernard doesn't count."

"You were playing tonsil hockey on our couch for an hour."

The blue-haired woman laughed. "You are becoming a prude. When was the last time *you* engaged in any nocturnal gymnastics of your own?"

"Well, the last one ended so *well*," Laurel said dryly. "I thought I'd take a break from drama and emotional..."

She stopped to give her roommate a narrow look. "You know, the last time you started in on how long it'd been since I'd had a date, I ended up spending a unpleasant evening in a sports bar, fending off advances from a Cro-Magnon, with a steroid addiction," Laurel said.

Kat rolled her eyes. "Bret was a nice guy! You would've gotten along great if you'd given him a chance!"

"He thought wheat-germ was a type of flesh eating bacteria!"

Kat threw her hands up in exasperation. "That's your problem, Laurel! You always find fault with every guy you meet. This one isn't intelligent enough, that one isn't sensitive enough. It's like you *want* to become that crazy lady, with twenty cats, locked up in your house, where the highlight of your day—"

"What did you do?"

Kat stopped, mouth open. "Huh?"

Laurel crossed her arms. "What. Did. You. Do?"

"Don't know what you mean."

"Kat!"

"Alright, alright!" She gave a resigned sigh. "I *might* have given that guy my number in a feeble attempt to introduce him to my best friend who needs to break out of her emotional stagnation."

Laurel put her face in her hands. "Tell me you didn't give him my name."

Her roommate gave her a scathing look. "No, I told him you hadn't had a date in six months and was desperate for some hot, monkey loving. Gimme a little credit, will you?"

"Okay. Point taken. Sorry"

"I told him about your show tonight and asked if he wanted to come."

"Aspirin! I need aspirin!" Laurel exclaimed. "No! I need a drink!"

"You keep Jameson's under the counter," Kat offered helpfully. "Seriously. This guy was a dish. Had that rugged, strong-n-silent vibe and basically pulled a knight-in-shining-armor move outta his hat. I *wish* you could have heard him take that broad apart. He didn't yell or scream or anything. He just calmly squashed her self-centered attitude like a bug."

"Really?" Laurel droned as she grabbed the bottle of Ireland's finest, along with two cups from a display, and poured two fingers into each. "Why don't you date him then?"

"Oh, he couldn't keep up. That man wasn't the love 'em and leave 'em type."

"What makes you say that?" she asked, taking a healthy swig of her whiskey. Laurel had never been one of those women who had to play with her liquor. She believed if you were going to drink, drink. If you were going to sip, get a water.

"His whole demeanor, really." Kat downed her shot and smacked her lips. "Boy, that's good. He was late twenties, and his eyes had this weight. Like he'd seen some really bad stuff, you know? I guess he may have, being a journalist. Anyway, he was there with this woman in one of the scooter carts? *Obviously* not family, and he was helping her shop for heaven's sake. How many guys can you name who do that for their own mothers let alone random senior citizens?"

"Maybe she was his neighbor?"

Kat raised an eyebrow and considered that. "The defense rests. Nice to little old ladies? That's a keeper. Besides, he had the *cutest* ass..."

Laurel choked on her whiskey and went into a coughing fit. "You're incorrigible," she said, once she got her breath back. "If a man rated you on your boobs you'd have a fit, but you'll do it to a supposedly nice guy?"

"No. *You'd* have a fit if a guy did that to *you*," Kat explained. "I'd just feel the need to educate him on my other qualities. My razor sharp wit, my love of Hemorrhaging Brain shooters, my utter sense of selflessness when it comes to hooking up my roommate with hunky journalists. You know, the minor stuff."

Laurel shook her head, smiling in spite of herself. "Fine. Help me close up. We'll hit the North Market on the way to Bueno Dave's and get some Thai."

"Why don't we ever eat there?" Kat asked. "Dave's a great chef, but I don't think I've ever seen you eat so much as a tortilla chip at his place."

"Because," Laurel replied as she locked the front door, then reached up to pull the security grate. "I know how much that puppy in the window is there. Hit the lights for me, will you?"

"What do you mean?" Kat killed the lights and made for the side door as her roommate grabbed her coat from the closet-sized (because it used to be a closet) office.

Laurel gave her a pitying look as they exited. "Dave's from Korea, right?"

"Yeah. So?"

"Canine is a staple there, you know."

"What does that have to do with any..." Kat turned slightly green. "Oh, gross! Are you shitting me?"

Laurel smiled. "I wouldn't shit you, you're my favorite turd."

Kat's face displayed the *you got me* look people show when they realize they've just fallen for it, then she grinned slyly. "There is a silver lining to playing a venue that serves Benji."

"What's that?" Laurel gave the side door a good shake to make sure it was latched.

"That guy today definitely had the mild-mannered journalist thing going." She chuckled. "Maybe if you bat your eyes and jiggle the twins, you can spend the night with The Man of the Steel. Or at least a man with wood."

Laurel chased Kat down the street to the battered, dark grey 1970s circa pickup she'd driven since high school, swearing loudly that she was going to style her roommate's hairs with a pair of garden shears.

Kat wiped her eyes, still laughing as she buckled in and her roommate pulled away from the curb. "Seriously. I pretty much hit the nail on the head with Calvin. I *knew* he was a slime ball, so you should trust me about this guy."

"Okay," she sighed. "I'll give him a chance. If he shows up. And *if* he's not a butt-head. We don't get along, I can always say I have diarrhea from the nachos or something and take off."

Laurel admitted that Kat had been right about Calvin. He'd been a gigantic mistake. Successful, educated, charming, but utterly lacking morals. Worse he was, quite frankly, a pussy hound. After they'd been seeing each other for just over five months, he'd shown his true colors when Laurel walked in on him getting it on with a blonde from his job.

In *her* apartment.

She'd stood in the doorway to her bedroom stunned for almost a full minute, while the blonde rode him like a Sit-n-Spin.

Once they noticed her, the blonde pretty much freaked out and left Calvin to Laurel's wrath. He didn't have a choice, really. He'd had the bimbo tie his hands to the headboard. She'd neglected to let him loose in the scurry to grab her clothes and dash past Laurel for the door.

Calvin had almost soiled the sheets when Laurel approached holding a large knife she'd retrieved from the kitchen. He begged her not to do anything crazy. He said he cared about her more than anything in the world, that he'd made a mistake, and would do anything to make up for it. Laurel told him that he was a *two-timing, slut-humping pig* and to get out, then cut the ropes binding his wrists. Calvin very much looked like he wanted to reply to that as he put his clothes on, (actually pulling his briefs on backwards at first), but thought better of it as she tested the edge of her knife with one thumb.

Laurel had avoided relationships like the plague since, throwing herself into her music. Most of what she played sounded much like what you'd hear at a medieval fair, but more upbeat and with lyrics that weren't so outdated you had to have a degree in Victorian studies to understand them. She managed to get gigs about twice a month at Bueno Dave's, because Dave was a fan of anything Swords and Sorcery. Many a night he held role-playing or card-game tournaments for all the would-be Dungeon Masters to get their magic on as she performed. He said it added to the ambiance of the evening and, since that night was always wall-to-wall packed, Laurel played for almost two hours every time. Granted the money wasn't all that good, usually a couple of Franklins, but she got free drinks. Besides, she'd had bookings for more than a few parties and weddings from Dave's patrons, which added to sometimes low coffers, so she really didn't mind giving up a Friday or two a month.

"Look out!"

Laurel jammed on the brakes and swerved right as a police car careened from a side street, siren blaring. It skidded into a bootlegger turn and would've slammed into her driver's door if she hadn't jumped the curb. Her truck ended up sitting on the sidewalk just shy of the doors to Darryl's Pawn and Pay. The two women sat in shock as the cops ignored them and, without a second glance, shot north to vanish around the corner half a block away.

"Are your all right?" Laurel asked after a minute, once her heart rate returned to normal.

Kat still had a death grip on the dash. "I'm good. I think I need a Dramamine, but I'm good."

Laurel slowly pulled her pickup back onto the street, dropped it into neutral, and sat idling next to a parking meter. As her breathing slowed, a fire engine blew across the same intersection, following the police car's path.

"Wow," she said, "whatever happened must have been pretty bad."

Kat grunted in acknowledgment, then released the dashboard, leaned back against the bench seat, and lowered her window. "Probably another shooting. Seems like these nuts are going postal at the drop of a hat anymore. Like that freeway shooter a few years back, wigging out...blowing people away? Personally, I think they've all played to many video games."

She joked about violence as a defense mechanism. Her parents had both been killed by a car bomb when they'd gone to visit her mother's family in Japan, just after Kat had graduated high school. Her grandfather had pulled her through the next eight months with a flurry of hard-nosed calls and emails. He'd made it clear that if she didn't keep herself together, she'd get a visit from her grandmother, who'd always wanted her mother to move the back to Japan anyway. While Kat did like Japanese food, she had no desire to move to Tokyo and become a sardine. The place was so crowded you couldn't take a deep breath without having to apologize for stealing someone's air.

Laurel shook herself and put her aged truck into gear again. "Well. Let's just hope none of the dark elves bring their crossbows tonight."

Kat smiled. "That's my girl. Just remember to keep that rapier wit in your pants when Romeo shows up."

Laurel sighed and wondered if it was too late to join a convent.

* * *

Jake leaned against his Jeep on the field butting up to Bolton Airstrip, the airport beside the outer-belt, south of the city. Bolton was far smaller than Buckeye Central's main hub, so you could actually get close to the runways. He stood there sipping a Coke, waiting for Allen Ryker to once again thumb his nose at the gods.

Allen had discovered skydiving at a young age and had jumped at least twice a month for the last twelve years. At the ripe old age of twenty-seven he'd racked up well over two hundred and thirty jumps. The fact that he hadn't had an accident and burrowed into the ground, much like the coyote in those old Looney Tunes animated shows was a testament to his ability as a jumper.

Personally, Jake thought his friend was nuts.

The seventeen jumps he'd made with Britain's SAS had more than rid him of any desire to *ever again* throw his aerodynamically challenged body out of a perfectly operational airplane.

Unless it was crashing.

He tilted back his head to watch a single engine plane bank east, move with the prevailing winds, and finish its climb just shy of eight thousand feet. He knew any moment now, Allen was going to leap out of that hatch to plummet towards the sod and concrete at over one hundred miles an hour. Allen had claimed that free-fall was as good as sex, and that the only thing that could be better was having sex while in free-fall, which was why Jake feared for his friend's sanity. He'd always been far too worried about catching a really big bug through the mouth, then having the back of his head blow out like a watermelon hit by a hollow-point, to get any enjoyment out of the experience.

He took another swig of Coke and saw a speck separate from the plane. As he always did, Jake prepared himself for Allen's normal antics. His friend had a habit of pulling his chute under what the instructors termed, "a prudent-fucking-altitude".

As Jake began mumbling to himself Allen's form continued to streak closer. By the time he could see the color of his friend's goggles, he was bellowing at the top of his lungs.

"Pull the cord... Allen, pull the cord... Oh shit, pull it-pull it-pull it...! Goddamnit *all! Pull the fucking cord!*"

Jake broke out in a cold sweat, certain he was seconds away from seeing a best-friend-flavored bag of Jell-O bounce off the tarmac. Then he saw the parachute unfurl and heard the WHOOMP as it flowered out into a massive rectangle, bringing Allen Ryker nearly to a dead stop midair.

What his—now undoubtedly crazy—friend had performed was called a LALO: Low-Altitude, Low-Opening jump. It wasn't something attempted by novice jumpers and, when done improperly, it could easily result in death. As if flinging yourself out of a plane thousands of feet up couldn't do that without adding the excitement of playing chicken with the ground. Jake swore Allen was trying to break both his legs every time he jumped. His friend laughed it off, however, and swore Jake had lost his nuts in Limey-land. Jake in return always gave Ryker the one-fingered salute, letting Al know he was number one in Jake's book.

I wonder if he was dropped on his head as a child? Jake mused, watching Allen bank gently to the right as he lined up his decent towards where the writer stood.

Al came swooping in, flared just before he touched down, almost stalled midair, hit his releases, and dropped the last yard to land gently on his feet as his chute continued on. Jake took four quick steps to the left and watched the parachute drop over his Jeep as Allen stood there, sporting what could only be described as a shit-eating grin.

"This is why you always get to buy the beers when we hit a bar," Jake grumbled, as his friend skipped towards him giggling like a lunatic.

"Don't be a sissy. I wasn't even close to burning in," Allen replied as he shed his helmet and pulled off his goggles.

Allen Ryker was an inobtrusive looking guy with a constant smile who radiated—what he himself termed—competent goofiness. He was a few inches shorter than Jake and about thirty pounds lighter, due to the fact that his parents were diminutive in stature. Still, his forearms and wrists were rock hard from ripping apart whatever piece of machinery caught his fancy at the moment. Though skinny, Allen moved with confidence due to years of both ballet in various studios and kung-fu lessons with Jake. Truth be told, he only enjoyed ballet because it gave him a great sense of balance, which was helpful in the martial arts, and he got to all but grope some really hot women on a regular basis. *Curly haired, bundle of energy* described Allen perfectly. Always ready with a witty quip when the situation called for it. Jake and Allen had been friends since before either of them had been interested in the fairer sex.

Allen had never really found his niche as a kid, so he'd ended up in both concert band and the track team. He still ran every morning but treated it like meditation. Running gave him time to settle his thoughts, clear his mind, and let the body go on autopilot. He hated people who treated running like something that should be revered, too. That was just stupid. The gimps who could talk about when they ran, how they ran, where they ran, what they wore, books about running... He didn't go for those foofy shorts or the high-tech cross-trainers, either. Allen wore sweats and combat boots. His belief was if you ran in all that ultra-comfort garbage, if you really needed to flee from something, you wouldn't be able to because you weren't wearing your special shoes. If you were used to running in boots that felt like you had five-pound weights on the ends of your legs, you could pretty much run in anything.

"How's the Beast running?" Ryker asked as they removed his parachute from the Jeep. "Dad keeps asking when you're gonna bring her in for a tune-up."

Jake shrugged. "No problems really. He did too good of a job putting her together. As long it has gas and I change the oil every few months, it's like the thing is pretty much maintenance free. Unlike the last *date* you hooked me up with."

Allen rolled his eyes. "You're never gonna let me live that down, are you? Man, I told you she was a good time. I never said she was someone you'd want to settle down with! Hell, Nichole didn't even know how to *spell* commitment."

"Commitment, no. Committed, yes."

"Face it, my friend," Allen rolled the silk into a semi-tight mess, stuffing it back into his pack, "you're just not gonna find a nice girl in a bar. That animal doesn't exist there anymore than say, unicorns do."

"Well, *that's* not at all depressing," Jake replied, bringing the Beast to life.

"They're just like guys, bud." Allen raised his voice against the wind as Jake drove for the hangar. "They're all looking for the BBD."

"The what?"

"BBD. Bigger. Better. Deal," Allen said, snapping his fingers to emphasize each word.

Jake gave Ryker a disgusted look as he brought the Jeep to a stop in front of the jump hangar.

"I hate that text lingo crap."

"BRB!" Allen said, jumping from the vehicle as his friend cocked a hand as if to slap him.

Jake relaxed in the seat and leaned his head back, trying to think of a good argument against his friends comment. Sadly, he had to agree that probably ninety-seven percent of the population believed as Allen did.

He'd reasoned long ago that there were two types of males in the Homo sapiens species: Alpha and Beta. Just like in that Ringo Starr movie, *Caveman*. Alpha males were the ones who used to go out to kill the saber-toothed tigers, skin wooly mammoths, and basically kept their tribes together through fear, strength, and dominance. The Beta males were the ones who stayed behind with the rest of the tribe and discovered new ways of doing things. Ways that would make life better, easier for everyone. One of them probably discovered fire, learned how to use it, then brought it back to the tribe.

Where it was promptly taken away by an Alpha.

He knew, without a shadow of a doubt, that women were attracted to the Alpha male type first, then settled for a Beta. Usually after realizing most of the Alphas were pussy-chasing, ass-clowns who wouldn't know what monogamy was if someone smacked them up-side the head with it and said, *Look. This is monogamy.* Alpha males tended to know what they wanted and when they wanted it, took it no matter who it hurt. Beta males knew what they wanted but, unlike the Alphas, wanted to obtain it without hurting someone else. Jake refused to take flack from assholes and was very protective when it came to people he cared about, like an Alpha. On the other hand, just because he was pretty good with all things violent, sure as hell didn't mean he liked it, which was a Beta trait.

With a few exceptions.

Anyone who raped children, beat or killed women, or flew planes into buildings to blow up lots of innocent people for religious reasons, in his opinion, didn't need to be on the same planet as the rest of humanity. He had no qualms about whipping the living shit out of bullies, either. The one time he'd had a run in with the law was when he'd beaten the tar out of two guys in college. They thought it'd be fun to date rape a German exchange student after she'd told one of the frat brothers Tequila didn't make him any more attractive. Jake had enjoyed every punch he'd thrown and the crunch of every one of their bones he'd broken.

He fished in the pocket of his battered leather jacket, grabbed his smokes and lit up with the Zippo he kept in the dash. Nicotine was Jake's one vice. He didn't do drugs. He didn't go out to the bars every weekend, get shit-faced, and start fights. He even recycled. He wasn't going to budge on his smokes however.

He inhaled a lung full of sweet nicotine, settled back again in the driver's seat, and shoved the mostly full pack back in his jacket pocket. As he did, he felt a scrap of paper and pulled it out.

It was the phone number of that girl from the pharmacy, Kat. He didn't know why she'd given it to him. Even in the asexual smock/uniform, Jake could tell she was—as Allen would put it—smoking hot. He wasn't a bumbling high-school teen or gangly college kid any more, but he also didn't have any illusions about his looks. He might be dubbed kind of handsome in the right kind of light... from across the room...but he was never going to be modeling underwear in fashion magazines. Hell, he wouldn't be modeling baseball hats. From the rear.

He smoked and stared at Kat's number, torn between the desire to see what would happen if they did go out and the gut-deep certainty anything between the two of them would end with hard feelings on one side or the other.

Jake was still trying to decide what to do ten minutes later, so he didn't see Allen come out of the jump hangar wearing his trademark Holy Jeans. They were Holy because they had holes in both knees and had gotten him laid more than a dump truck full of Spanish fly. Allen took one look at his friend and made a great show of tiptoeing around the Beast to gaze over his shoulder. His jaw dropped when he read the scrap and, with an enormous smile, snatched it out of Jake's hand.

Jake all but jumped out of his seat in surprise, almost making the question of whether or not to call Kat a moot point. His seat belt nearly gave him a vasectomy.

"And what's this?" Allen gazed at him with pride. Like a martial arts master whose student just performed the Five Deadly Fists Style flawlessly.

I'm doomed, Jake thought.

"Tell me you have plans to meet this girl."

Jake scratched his cheek. "We already made plans to hang out tonight, man. Besides, I don't want to look..."

"Desperate? You are." Allen thrust the number at Jake like a fencing foil. "Call her. Now."

Jake hedged, mind moving at warp speed, trying to think of a way to avoid the horror that loomed before him.

Allen produced his cell phone and started dialing.

"What are you doing?" Jake struggled to release his seat belt.

Allen put the phone to Jake's ear. "It's ringing."

"Damn it, Al! If you don't..."

Kat picked up just as Jake got the first words out of his mouth.

"Ah...Hi there, Kat." He gave the smiling Allen a look that was half panic, half *I'm going to kill you for this* and took the evil cell phone. "It's Jake O'Connor. We met today at the pharmacy. You probably don't... Oh. You do? Yeah, that wasn't really... Well, thanks... Actually, I was wondering if your invite for tonight was still open... Eight...? Sounds good."

Jake had a flash of inspiration.

"Would it be alright if I bring a friend? He enjoys that type of music." Allen was shaking his hands emphatically, while mouthing the words, *No, you idiot!*

Jake's face fell. "Oh. Okay. Where's... Sure, I know it. Great fajitas... Alright. Well, we'll see you at eight then. Okay...Bye."

Allen took his phone from Jake's hand with a hard look.

"You *moron*! You almost screwed the pooch on that one." He stormed around the Beast to hop into the passenger seat.

"How so?" Jake asked as they pulled out, leaving Bolton Field's runways behind. "I thought you always said it was a good idea to have a wing-man when you were going out."

"To a club or a bar," Allen fumed, "not on a *date*."

"Well, lucky for me she has a friend who's going to be there too."

Allen's eyebrows shot up. "Oh, *really*? Damn, that means I'll have to change my shirt before we go. You have anything I can borrow?"

Jake caught his friend's goofy smile and laughed into the wind as the Jeep soared down the freeway on-ramp.

CHAPTER THREE

Laurel was making herself a spearmint tea when her roommate finally finished with the bathroom. She'd long since resigned herself to Kat's marathon grooming sessions, but it continued to surprise her how long it could take the lovely woman to primp in that tiny space.

She'd been jealous at first that Kat never seemed to work at it and still looked like she'd just stepped out of a salon. Kat's mother's delicate features combined with her father's deep natural skin tone made makeup a choice, not a necessity. A few of those ultra-long primping sessions had dispelled that illusion though.

Kat had changed into a pair of black pants, which looked a lot like a pair of tights in Laurel's opinion and left little to the imagination. True to form, she was also wearing a cut off tee-shirt with Anime characters on the back and a logo emblazoned on its front that proclaimed *Team Ninja*! to the world. Said shirt also left little to speculate about and made it plain that Kat was going commando.

"You realize we're about to spend the evening surrounded by grown men who spend *their* Friday nights pretending to fling fireballs at each other?" Laurel said evenly.

"It's always the quiet ones." Kat gave her redheaded roomie the once over. "Were you planning on getting ready any time soon?"

Laurel succumbed, bypassing the impending argument, and headed for her bedroom. She pulled on a lace thong—a real one, not the kind with just the piece of dental floss up the back. If she ended up displaying it at any point, and she didn't think she would, at least it all matched. Then she pulled on the tightest pair of jeans she owned (they weren't *that* tight...Okay, maybe they were) and rooted through her closet until she settled for a leaf green, v-neck shirt with sleeves that came down to just above the tops of her elbows. It might show a little cleavage but hey, if this guy was an ass, he could spend the next week jerking it over something he'd never have. She opted for a strapless bra that didn't push-up as much as it accentuated. Laurel ran a brush through her hair, impotently cursing the damned stray lock that just wouldn't stay back, and looked at the results.

Not bad. Her hips were a little too slim and her boobs a little too big to consider her figure hourglass, but the mirror displayed a redhead that could break hearts with the best of 'em.

Screw it, she thought and strode back into the living room.

Kat didn't look pleased with her results. "You kind of forget something?"

"I don't have a belt to match," Laurel said.

Kat rolled her eyes and took on a martyred expression.

"Makeup," she said, pointing down the narrow hallway. "Bathroom."

Laurel slumped her shoulders. "Alright, but this guy should see what he's getting into. I don't do makeup often."

"I know. Sweet *gods*, do I know," Kat said, following her into the bathroom and opening the medicine cabinet. "Now sit and let Auntie Katherine work her magic."

Laurel sighed and sat down on the toilet. "So, what's this guy like?"

"Close your eyes," Kat said, grabbing a light-brown eye shadow from under the sink. "Like I said before, there's gravity to him. Not like he has to be the center of attention, but..."

"Heaven forbid. That would put the two of you at odds."

"No talking! And be nice or I'll make you look like Darryl Hanna in *Blade Runner*." Kat started applying shade to Laurel's lids. "I dunno. Call it woman's intuition."

Laurel thought about that for a minute.

"Is he cute?" she asked.

"Well! Little Miss Double Standard."

"I'm just asking!" Laurel protested.

"And I'm just messing with your head. Now, stop moving." Kat seemed happy with how the eye shadow looked and moved on to lipstick.

"Cute? No," She mused. "He's got that ruggedly handsome thing going on. Six foot, light blue eyes, kind of messy brown hair... I don't think he spends a lot of time working on his appearance. Just steps out of the shower, gives it the once over, and pulls on his pants."

"So, you've been thinking about how a guy you're setting me up with looks when he gets out of the shower?" Laurel asked. "Maybe this won't be so bad."

"Oh, I can picture that. Scrumptious, for *sure*," Kat said, remembering how Jake's shirt had strained across his back and shoulders. "You're busted, by the way."

Laurel opened one eye. "Huh?"

"I know what you're thinking."

"You do not."

Kat grinned. "Then why are you blushing?"

"I am *not* blushing."

"Are too."

"Am not!" Laurel felt heat on her face. "Okay. But it's *your* fault."

Kat laughed. "Don't blame me. Just because *you* have a dirty mind..."

Laurel kept her reply to herself if only because her roommate was partially right. She blamed it on a healthy love of fiction and, to be quite frank, a lack of any way to scratch the itch. She didn't hop in the sack with guys on a whim and had an aversion to one night stands that stretched back to her college days. Besides, it was hard to find a man. The world was full of *guys*, but *men*, the ones who wanted you for the things you had inside your head and not just in your pants? They were few and far between.

Ah well, she thought, *there's always cold showers.*

Five relatively painless minutes later, Laurel was allowed to view the results. She had to admit, she looked pretty good. Kat had applied subtle eye shadow that gave her an exotic aura, instead of the raccoon look so many women went for, then accentuated Laurel's lips with a light reddish-brown shade that didn't look glaringly out of place against her skin and healthy crop of freckles.

"Well?"

Laurel shook her head. "I bow to superior talent. I thought you were only supposed to use your powers for good?"

"I swear, when you meet this guy, you'll be thanking me." Kat laughed, tossed the lipstick back under the sink and held up her index finger. "Scratch that. You'll be thanking me *tomorrow*."

Laurel let that one go by and trotted back out into the living room for her guitar.

"Speaking of shallow," she began, to which Kat gave a mock bow, "what happens if... What's his name again? Jake? What if Jake's friend is a shithead?"

"I'll give him a fake phone number," Kat said. "Shitheads understand that. It's like a courtesy today. They preen over getting some hottie's number and when it turns out to be bogus, they tell their shithead friends how they just couldn't get along. Or how she wanted a commitment right off the bat and that would cramp their style. Or how she wasn't that good in the sack, blah-blah-blah.'

Laurel gave her a quizzical look, grabbed her keys, and made for the door. "That doesn't bother you?"

"Why should it? There are plenty of fish in the sea. Always another guy waiting to take his shot at the title." Kat grabbed her distressed leather jacket and wallet. She never carried a purse. Kat maintained that if guys could do it so could she. Laurel gave up trying to come up with a suitable comeback that didn't imply Kat was a slut.

"That's kind of slutty," Laurel said.

That got a grin out of her blue-haired roommate. "So says the Queen of Cleavage?"

Laurel stopped half-way out the door. "I knew it. Let me..."

"Don't you fucking *dare*," Kat said, pushing her out onto the stairwell and emphatically pulling the door shut. She dropped into a stance that said she meant business. "This is the best you've looked in five months!"

"Gee, thanks," Laurel said, shifting her guitar case to a more comfortable grip.

"If you even think about going back in to change that shirt, I'm going to kick you in your coochie."

Laurel started down the stairs, trying very hard not to think about how funny the word *coochie* was when someone said it out loud. "Seriously. What's your impression of this guy?"

"Roomie mine," Kat said, face serious, "I'll give it to you straight. If I were you: creative, a closet hottie, a little repressed..."

Laurel snorted and headed for her truck. It sat about fifty yards down the street because her landlord was too cheap to spring for a covered garage. Kat was silent until they reached it, earning a raised eyebrow from her roommate.

"As I was saying... if I were you?" Kat said, considering it for a few seconds. "I'd have screwed his brains out right there on the pharmacy counter."

Laurel just stood there jaw hanging open.

"I'm serious," Kat said.

"You're making me nervous."

"You should be." Kat's eyes glinted mischievously.

"Why?"

Kat shrugged. "I've been with a lot of guys... hey! No comments from the peanut gallery."

Laurel hid a smile.

Kat tossed her jacket through the window. "I don't really have problems when it comes to dating, but if I had a choice? I'd want a good guy." She nodded. "That's Jake, guaranteed."

Laurel felt butterflies in her stomach. "You don't even know him."

"Don't ask me how I know, I just do," Kat said. "Hope I end up with a guy like *that*."

They both stood next to the truck for a few seconds, and then Laurel hefted her guitar into the bed, hopped in the cab. Her roommate got in and sat quietly while Laurel started the truck and pulled into traffic.

"Now," Kat began, "that's down the line, you understand. After I've been with more guys, screwed their brains out and acted like a total slut."

Laurel broke out into helpless laughter.

* * *

Jake was resigned to the fact that the gods were sitting up there in the heavens flicking cosmic boogers in his direction.

About twenty minutes after they'd walked into Bueno Dave's, it became clear that Kat, as she insisted they call her, had designs on Allen. With his sense of humor, easy—if somewhat silly—grin, and open nature, he was bringing smile after ready smile to her face. That was not to say Jake felt ignored. They'd spoken on a few topics over a short time. When he had the chance to look back on it, the first twenty minutes felt like an interview. After which, Kat turned her full attention to Allen.

Ah, well, Jake thought, *at least the food's good. And Kat is really cool. Even if she has the hots for Al and her friend didn't bother to show up.*

"So, how was the rest of your day?" Kat asked, leaning back in her chair and taking a sip of what looked to be a Hemorrhaging Brain. Allen, always the smooth one, looked at her drink so he wouldn't stare at the way her abs moved.

"Not bad," Jake admitted. "After I got Gertrude settled, I picked Al up at Bolton, went back to my place, and finished up work on that cookbook, while *he* gamed."

"I wasn't gaming. I was shooting Nazis in the brain."

"Oh, yeah!" Kat exclaimed. "Call of Duty! Cool. I always thought the first mission was the most fun. The beachhead at Normandy?"

Allen looked at her calmly. "It is so hot you know that."

Kat shot him a smile. "So, what do you do at Bolton?"

"Nothing," he admitted, taking a swig of his Guinness. He and Jake had opted for life-giving liquid bread, over the carbonated camel piss flavor of most domestic beer. He wiped the foam mustache off his upper lip. "I just feel the need to fling myself out of something really high off the ground every so often."

"He means two or three times a month," Jake said helpfully. "Four if the month has an 'A' anywhere in it."

Kat's eyes sparkled. "Ever done the Motley Crue thing?"

"Not *yet*," Allen admitted.

"We'll talk."

"I look forward to it," he said with a wink. "But! Let's hear about your day. Jake told me about the oh-so-personable Mizz Bessendorfer, but that couldn't be the highlight."

Kat rolled her eyes. "No. Most definitely not. I went to the dojo, worked the heavy bag until I had a good sweat going..."

"Sounds fun," Allen said, "the sweating part I mean."

"Be good." Kat grinned mischievously over her Brain.

"Aawww. That's no fun."

The comical expression on Allen's face made it necessary for Jake to hide a smile behind a sip of Guinness.

"As I was saying," she continued, "after I abused my poor body for an hour or so, I went by my roommate's store, met up with her, went home, got ready, and headed up here."

"At least you got to vent," Jake said.

"Oh, yeah. Every one of the spinning back kicks was aimed at Mizz Bessendorfer's mouth." She gave Jake an apologetic look. "I'm sorry about the roomie. She's kinda flaky and repressed, so..."

The writer held up his hand in a halting motion. "Don't worry about it. If being the fifth wheel for the night is the worst thing that happens I'm in good shape."

She shook her head and held her glass up. "To interesting times."

"To friends," Allen added, holding up his own.

Jake smiled and clinked glasses. "The girl at the door said we missed the first set," he said, looking over at the small, three foot, table-top sized stage. "When's the next one?"

Kat checked her watch. "Should be any minute now."

"I'm going to grab another," Jake said, wagging his empty pint, "Anyone need?"

"Please, sir, can I have some more?" Allen said in a high voice, hunching his shoulders and sticking out his lower lip. Kat laughed, drained her Brain, and reached for her jacket. Allen stopped her with a light touch on her knee.

"You can get the next round," Allen said, giving his friend a hopeful look.

Jake shot him a thumbs up and headed for the bar, noticing that Kat had turned her seat towards Al while leaning against the table. Classic body language that translated to, *I'm interested.*

Sighing at his luck, Jake motioned for the bartender and ordered their drinks. He reached in his pocket for his smokes because—wonder of wonders!—Bueno Dave's pretty much ignored the statewide smoking ban Ohio had imposed a few years back and continued to stick their tongues out at the establishment.

He looked around, watching the tables of gamers. They were mostly male, college age or older, with a scattering of the fairer sex here and there. Nearly everyone was playing elaborate card games or games with large maps and little painted figurines. Overall, the mood of the place suited him. It wasn't a noisy, bass-thumping meat market. He could hear some of the patrons talking about the cultural relevancy of Tolkien compared to Lucas, and no one seemed to be out for anything but a good time.

Why don't I hang out in places like this? he thought, stubbing out his smoke in one of the ready ash trays and tipping generously, as he paid for their drinks—you always tip the bartender. They can spit in your beer.

Because, fortunately along with all your stupid, noble sensibilities, you still possess a sex drive, his back-brain replied, *and sitting in a roomful of guys really isn't conducive to getting laid.*

Jake told his back-brain to shut the hell up, then concentrated on getting Kat's Brain along with their Guinness to the table, sans spillage.

She and Allen were still at it when he finally wound his way back, seemingly at ease in each other's company. Jake felt a moment of jealousy at the way his friend was able to charm women so effortlessly. If he lived for a thousand years, he'd never be that smooth.

"He did what?" Kat asked wide-eyed, leaning on the table to accentuate the curve of her neck just so. The effect of which wasn't lost on either man.

"Yup. You are looking at one of the sure-and-be-God, last White Knights. I've been trying to curb his self-sacrificing tendencies, but it's a struggle," Allen said. "Hang around him a while. You'll see."

Jake gave him a hard look. "Whatever he's been telling you, it's all lies."

Kat pressed the back of her hand to her forehead and fanned herself with her drink napkin.

"You mean you don't help out old ladies, rescue damsels in distress, and slay dragons with the strength of ten men because your heart is pure?" She batted her eyes at him in mock distress. "I do declare, that kind of news could give me the vapors."

"You're mixing your literary references," he said, then pointed at Allen, "and you're ruining my reputation."

His friend gave him a quizzical look.

"Journalists are supposed to be scum-bags. It's in our contracts. You start spreading it around I'm not and I'll never work in this town again," he said and took a swig of his Guinness. "Hell, they could take away my secret decoder ring."

They were all laughing so hard Jake didn't see the red-haired woman walk out of the back, guitar in hand. He didn't see the speculative look she gave him, and he missed the wink Kat shot over his shoulder at her. He even missed the smattering of applause the gamers gave her as she took the tiny stage, limbered up her fingers and began her set.

But he didn't miss it when she started singing.

Kat saw his eyes light up as Laurel moved into "*Suil a Ruin*." He glanced around to see who was singing and just like that, for Jake the world went away for a while. Time seemed to slow down. He was sure that he'd be able to remember every detail about that moment for the rest of his life. The set of her shoulders as she performed, the lilt of her voice as she sang, the way she strove to push that stray lock of hair out of her face time and again. His attempts to look away, briefly focusing on his beer, didn't work at all. Her voice was like a smoky feather-wrapped magnet that forced his eyes back to the stage.

What's the word? he thought. *Beautiful? Doesn't cut it. Not even close. Divine? No, she doesn't make me feel pious at all. Sexy? Oh, yeah. But not enough. Inspiring? Not quite. Shit! What's the word for her?*

* * *

As Jake scoured his vocabulary, Laurel was lost in the music. To her it was expression in the purest form possible, at least for those still locked in the mortal coil. She could bring pain, nurture joy, quell rage, and insight memories with tone and chord. She did, however, make it a point to keep her eyes closed, so she wouldn't become distracted by Jake.

Kat had been right. She hated to admit, even though her roommate hadn't really given her a detailed description, he looked just as Laurel thought he would. If she didn't keep her eyes shut she was sure she'd flub a changeover. There's really no way to hide things like that when you're playing solo, and she didn't think giving a crap performance would be a good way to pique his interest.

The next hour passed quickly. Laurel ended her set to a much larger round of applause—in which Kat, Allen, and Jake joined enthusiastically—hopped off the stage, and took her guitar to the back.

* * *

Kat was playing touchy-feely with one hand on Allen's while leaning her chin in the palm of her other. Her eyes sparked with mischief. "Liked the music, did we?"

Jake tried to answer, but his mouth was so dry that his words didn't' resemble speech. He drained his Guinness and tried again. "Absolutely," he finally croaked. "Her rendition of Lorena McKinnet's *Bonny Portmore* was wonderful."

"She's impressive. Definitely has amazing control over her voice." Allen shot a sidelong look at Jake. "Healthy set of lungs too, right?"

"Yeah..." Jake was still trying to focus. "She was... wow."

Kat gave him a knowing look and rose to her feet. "I'm going to hit the little girl's room and get another round. What did you guys want?"

"Do they have Jameson's here?" Jake tried to shake off the numbness between his ears. "I think I need something harder after that."

Kat nodded sympathetically and grinned. "I'd be surprised if you didn't already have something hard, but Jameson's it is. What about you, Allen?"

"Guinness, but I've got these." He moved for his wallet.

She calmly reached out with one hand, grabbed the front of his shirt, and brought his nose within about an inch of hers. As she pulled him nearly off his seat, Kat insinuated herself between Allen's legs so their lower bodies were pressed firmly together

"It's my turn to get the round. I said, 'what about you,' Allen?"

She artfully lowered her eyelashes.

Allen grinned and took his hand off his back pocket. He kept his gaze on her eyes and his voice steady through an exhausting act of will. "I'm good. For now. Though I might need some stimulation later in the evening. You'll be the first to know."

Kat smiled back and pressed herself more firmly against him. "I better be."

She released her grip on his shirt and strode for the bar, knowing full well their eyes followed her. Jake's displayed surprise mixed with apprehension, and Allen's were full of almost naked lust.

"That is a dangerous woman," Jake admitted to his friend, watching Kat sway her way through the tables. Not a small number of heads turned to follow her hips. "I don't know whether to be jealous or relieved."

Allen's face went to full-on smile mode. "She's awesome. Might even be able to keep up with me. She wants to go skydiving."

"So, she's crazy. Good to know," he said wryly and sipped his Guinness. "The fact that she looks like an indigo-haired, chestier Grace Park would almost make up for it though."

"Yeah, that does add quite a bit to the 'I want to screw her senseless' rating," Allen said brightly.

He gave Jake a raised eyebrow. "What about that singer though? She was hot. And I don't mean in the causal, see her on the street and think she's cute, way. I mean in a kick some ass 'in black leather' Tara Perry way."

"Yeah," Jake replied, frowning into his empty glass. Allen took it, poured about a third of his pint in before Jake could object, then slid it back.

"Thanks," he said and shook his head. "I gotta tell you that's depressing."

That earned him a confused look. "Why?"

"Well, a variety of reasons," Jake began, ticking them off on his fingers. "Beautiful? That doesn't *begin* to describe her. Smart? Seeing that she didn't have any lyrics or sheet music with her, she performed all of that from *memory*. Well read? Her selections weren't easy or commonplace by any means, which means she actually took the time to *research* the music."

He gave Allen a resigned look. "Now. All that said, what would a woman with all that going for her want with a hack like me?"

Al was suddenly and visibly pissed off. "You need to stop that shit. Seriously, man. You've got a pretty cool job you enjoy, a nice place, the Beast," he pointed at himself, "and not least of all, me! The Casanova of Freefall to advise you."

"I dunno... I mean, you saw her right? Besides I'm a writer, not a motivational speaker. I get kind of... tongue tied."

Allen folded his arms and leaned back in his chair.

"That doesn't mean shit and you know it. Look at me. I look like a geek. Hell, I am one. But I'm honest and I have a good line of patter." Allen leaned forward conspiratorially. "If I can do it, sans the benefit of a literary education, you, who actually *possess* one, sure as hell can!"

Jake searched for a reply but was, for once, at a complete loss.

* * *

The ladies were pow-wowing in the bathroom.

Even though Laurel thought she still looked great, Kat insisted on touching up her friend's makeup. Since she had been sitting with Jake and his admittedly geeky-looking friend for the last hour as Laurel performed, it had been the only way she'd be able to give her friend any info on the mystery man. So Laurel submitted to the primping and grilled Kat mercilessly.

"So?"

"Oh, this guy is *so* fine!" Kat confirmed, as she reapplied eye shadow to her roommate. "That lady he was with today? His next-door neighbor. He takes out her *trash*! He really does ghostwrite novels and edit cookbooks! He knew over half of the songs you sang by *name* for God's sake! I swear if you screw this up I'll heckle you for the next forty years."

"He knew the songs?" Laurel was stunned.

"Uh-huh," she said, making an X over her breast. "And you should have *seen* his face when he turned around and saw you singing. It was like someone had hit him between the eyes with a sledgehammer! I'm telling you. All you have to do is be yourself and reel him in."

"I couldn't look at him. I thought I'd forget what song I was playing," Laurel admitted, as she brushed that damn stray lock of hair out of her face again. "He's... well, he's *really* cute."

Kat smiled and applied some lipstick of her own. "Glad to hear it. Hate to build him up too much then have you think he looks like Quasimodo. His friend, Al, is great by the way. Adventurous, funny, a little bit of a geek. I like him. His dad owns Ryker's Auto Body on 12th and he's been tight with Jake for years. I think some serious nocturnal gymnastics may be on the menu tonight."

"Oh gods," Laurel said. "You'll go to his place right? It would just be too weird if my best friend was in the other room, doing the best friend of—"

Laurel stopped talking at that point, actually shocked as she realized that she'd been considering taking Jake to bed before they'd even met. Had it really been that long? Or was Kat just rubbing off on her?

"Hey, can we focus for a minute? You need to concentrate on your own nighttime amusements, here." Kat took her by the arm and herded her towards the door. "There's an educated, honest man, with a great ass out there, and he doesn't have a clue what's coming to get him."

Laurel stared at her with a horrible suspicion rising in the back of her mind, only because she knew her roommate had a weakness for the dramatic. "What did you tell him about me?"

"Zip. He thinks you bailed on the evening."

Laurel's jaw dropped. "Are you out of your mind?"

Kat smirked, "I wanted to be sure the whole nice guy thing was for real. You know, see if he'd try to beat out his friend for a girl, or act like an ass, or leave when he realized I wasn't interested? It was a chance to grill him and get honest answers while you performed, too. I'm sure he noticed Al and I were connecting, so he had nothing to gain by not being completely truthful. Hell, I probably could've asked when the last time he'd had some *me time* was and he would've told me without even realizing it."

That one hit a little too close to home for Laurel.

Shit, she thought, *I am repressed.*

"How much did you get?"

"You won't *believe* what Allen told me while Jake... Oh, no!" Kat said, crossing her arms and shaking her head emphatically. "You want to know you just get your tush out there and ask! I learned enough after an hour to trust him with my best friend. That's all you're gonna get."

"Alright," Laurel squared her shoulders and opened the door, "but you've got to give me *something* to work with."

"He's got a tattoo on his right shoulder." Kat followed her out into the hall, grinning wickedly. "Allen has one of a skydiver somewhere, but he said he'd get arrested if he showed it to me in public."

"He sounds strange," Laurel said. They headed for the bar to grab drinks Kat had ordered prior to their head-shed in the ladies room. "What else can you give me?"

Kat rolled her eyes. "He's only had a couple of Guinness and now asked for a Jameson's."

Laurel smiled. "Really? An educated pallet and not just looking to quaff down tons of camel piss then. That means he's not a big drinker. Which also means he's got good self-control and some restraint." Maybe Jake wasn't your run-of-the-mill guy after all. "What else?"

"Well," Kat mused thoughtfully. "He's not into threesomes..."

* * *

"Have you heard anything today about an explosion, maybe a chemical spill or something locally?"

Allen gave Jake a raised eyebrow. "That's an odd question. Why?"

Jake scratched his chin. "I've been seeing a lot of emergency vehicles racing around. Didn't you notice on the way here we stopped twice to let ambulances pass?"

"Not until you just mentioned it," Al admitted. "No, haven't heard a thing. Then again, I was either in the riggers loft or jumping out of a plane for most of the day. I haven't really been monitoring the media."

The writer shrugged. "Maybe it's just me being paranoid, but I have this weird feeling. Like I'm overlooking something."

He was staring at his glass when Allen looked past him, so he missed the look of realization, and the following smile, which vanished as soon as it appeared.

"I wouldn't be at all surprised if you were," Allen said casually.

"Thanks. I needed that."

"Hey, guys. Miss me?" Kat slid Allen his Guinness and plunked down beside him.

"Not at all," he said. That earned him a smile and a playful poke in the stomach. "Ouch. We're talking about the number of emergency vehicles Jake's been seeing today. Seems the crazies are all out and about. And here it's not even a full moon yet."

"We were almost run off the road this afternoon by a cop car," Kat said, with a frown that dissipated when Allen put his arm across the back of her chair. "You're right. Seems like there have been a lot around today."

Kat shook the feeling off and pointed at Jake. "Anyway! I didn't forget your drink. I just didn't have enough hands."

"Okay," Jake said, clearly confused by the sudden change of topic.

Why does Allen look like he's laughing at me? he thought.

"So I brought some help," Kat said, smiling widely.

"Did someone here order a Jameson's?"

Jake turned in his chair to find the stunning redhead who'd been singing earlier standing there, hip cocked, displaying a lop-sided, half-smile, holding a glass of Irish whiskey in each hand.

He knew he was totally out of his depth just then, because the first thing that came to mind was *Kreeeee-ga! Tarzan want!*, instead of just, *Hi* or *Thanks for the drink.*

Across the room this woman had been enough to not only hold his attention, but to grab it, shake it, and make it sit up saying, *Hell-o, nurse!* Up close, freckles jumping, green eyes dancing, she was a knockout. It was all he could do to raise a finger in acknowledgment. Her half-smile turned into the real thing as she placed one of the drinks on the table, eyes holding his, for which he was extremely grateful. It kept him from committing the ultimate social *faux pas*—looking down the V-neck of her tight shirt as she leaned across to place the glass before him.

Then it hit him. He looked across the table at Kat. She was grinning like a mischievous pixy. "Your roommate?" he asked.

She nodded and leaned against Allen with an unapologetic smile. "Jacob O'Connor, let me introduce you to my roomie and best friend in the whole world, Laurel St. Clair. Laurel, this is Jake. Writer, lover of Celtic ballads, Knight of the Realm, et cetera."

Jake glared at Allen because his friend couldn't pull off looking innocent if his life depended on it. He was currently trying to not look guilty. "You *didn't*."

"She clouded my mind with her ninja tricks and forced it out of me." Al said, spreading his arms. "You were sitting right there when I told her, away with the fairies."

Jake stood up and took Laurel's hand in his own. She kept her nails short and paint free, which he liked. He'd never been one for women who resembled Freddy Kruger. Her handshake was firm and her palm callused. For some reason her touch set off an explosion of pins-and-needles all the way to his shoulder.

"Pleasure. I've heard absolutely nothing about you," he said, giving her a smile and Kat a wry look, "but your performance spoke volumes."

Laurel willed her stomach to stop trembling.

Kat hadn't done him justice at all. Truth be told, Jake wasn't cover-model handsome, but he was definitely easy on the eyes. His own were the color of skies Laurel only saw in memories of her childhood. His chin was firm, almost pointed, but not blocky. His nose, which had been broken at some point, gave him the predatory look of a bird of prey. He kept his hair short. It did seem to stick out at odd angles but looked naturally haphazard, as opposed to styled within an inch of its life. Her palms itched with the urge to run her fingers through it. His chest didn't have the bulging 'roid-rage size common to bodybuilders, but he looked as if he did a lot of strength training. Lean, corded muscle rippled down his arm as he released her hand.

"It's nice to meet you, Jake," Laurel said. Forcing down her growing nervousness was no easy task, but over the last couple of years she and stage fright had become old friends. "What would you like to know?"

He looked at her thoughtfully for a few moments, and then smiled widely. "Tell me *everything*."

He held the chair for her as she sat, which earned him points. It had been a quite a while since Laurel had seen a man do that. Feminism aside, it was nice to have someone treat her like a woman and not a piece of meat. She'd always been jealous of older ladies whose husbands took their coats and pushed in their chairs for them. The way those couples looked at each other across a table or just on a bench in the park... She wanted that.

"Tell me everything," Jake repeated.

"That could take a while." Laurel brushed the stray lock out of her eyes yet again. She leaned on the table, clasping her left elbow with her opposite hand while arching her back for a moment before resting her chin on her palm and giving him a raised eyebrow.

Jake watched her in silence. He didn't so much as glance at her cleavage, because he couldn't move. Habitual movements on her part made it really difficult for him to breathe for a minute.

Damn it, you moron! His back-brain screamed at him, like the old sergeant in charge of the brick during his time with the SAS had on occasion. *Pull yourself together! Do not let this woman slip away! You. Will. Fucking. Regret it!*

He took a sip of his drink and looked Laurel squarely in the eyes. "I've got lots of time."

Allen leaned closer to Kat and she turned an ear, allowing him to speak softly, so as not to interrupt Jake and Laurel.

"You're evil. I like that."

Kat looked at their friends.

"Nah," she turned to face Allen, "I'm just really, *really* good."

* * *

Tracy Dixon had lots of company now.

Her pervy neighbor, in typical Alpha male fashion, had talked himself into believing that he would be able to live out the fantasy of two hot girls doing a guy who just showed up randomly at the door.

He'd knocked and, since Carly had left the door ajar when she'd arrived, it swung open. Taking that as an invitation, he'd moved through the flat to the bedroom door where he heard moaning.

Twenty minutes later, Nathan arrived after becoming bored waiting for Carly in his BMW.

Over the next hour, two more of the building tenants noticed the open door and decided to see if someone needed help.

Next was the owner of Darryl's Pawn and Pay. He thought he heard crying.

Then a coed from OSU on a tennis scholarship. She heard moaning and was sure someone was injured.

* * *

The powers-that-be were taking notice as well.

The numbers of attacks locally were rising. Authorities couldn't explain where the raving loons were coming from.

News stations were calling it civil unrest in the face of an increasingly uncaring and disconnected bureaucracy.

The higher-ups longed for stiffer censorship legislation...

CHAPTER FOUR

Jake was keyed up.

He sat in the Witch's Brew Coffee Shop, energized beyond all hope of sleep after dropping Laurel back at the apartment she shared with Kat. It had been obvious that Allen and the lovely Asian had no intentions of heading home when the four left Bueno Dave's, somewhere around midnight. So Laurel had tossed her truck's keys to Kat—as her roommate all but threw Allen on its hood and kissed him hard enough to curl his hair—then Jake had given her a lift home.

There hadn't been any uncomfortable silences between the two of them. With their mutual love for Celtic music and classic punk rock, appreciation for Anime, and the fact both tended to curl up with a book before going to sleep, Jake and the redhead were finding each other more and more attractive.

He was a bit surprised when Laurel invited him up to her place for a drink when he dropped her off. He hadn't wanted to come across as pushy or over-eager, so he held the door for her as she climbed out of his Jeep and was about to say goodnight. He was in the midst of hoping she'd be willing to see him again when Laurel asked if he'd like to come in.

They were walking upstairs to the third floor when Laurel's bravado broke and she stopped. He took another step before her gentle hand on his arm brought him to a halt. Jake moved back down to stand beside her, face carefully blank.

Her expression was one of anxiety, mixed with a healthy amount of fear.

"I can't do this." She hugged her arms around her torso, as if trying to keep herself from flying apart and at him. "It's just that..."

Jake leaned against the wall and put his hands behind his back. "It's okay. Really."

Laurel couldn't meet his eyes. "It's... been a while for me. As much as I love Kat, she's *way* more casual about...being intimate...than I am."

"It's a 'will you respect me in the morning' thing."

"Yeah. It's not that I don't *want* to." She looked at him then and Jake saw the heat in her gaze. It made his pants suddenly feel three sizes too small. "God, do I ever want to! I want to shove you to the floor, rip your clothes off, and find out what your *skin* tastes like."

He swallowed and tried to control his breathing.

She turned her head away. "But..."

He pushed off the wall, stepped close, and put his hand against her cheek. He could see she was afraid. Afraid of what he might do and what he might *cause* her to do. He moved his hand away reluctantly, took a long slow breath and brought his thoughts back under control.

"Look," he said with a grin, "I'll give you a call. I talked with Kat earlier to confirm, so I've got the number."

"Really? You're not... angry?"

"Angry about you wanting to see me again, *before* we may or may not end up sleeping together? No!" He gave her a worried frown. "You *do* want to see me again, don't you?"

Jake's back slammed against the wall as she kissed him. He put his hands on her hips, palms resting feather soft on her waist. Laurel however, pushed both her hands up under his shirt and began moving them across his chest, finally scraping what little fingernails she had down his stomach. He hissed in pleasure and pushed her back gently.

"That's not conducive to me leaving."

"Oops." She didn't look in the least bit sorry. Laurel snuggled against his chest and put her face into his neck. She found his pulse with her lips, felt it race as she gently bit the skin above. He exhaled forcefully, gripped her shoulders, and gritted his teeth against the urge to let his hands go roaming.

"Alright, I'll be good and let you go," she said, drawing her hands out of his shirt. Then she moved her face so close to his that he could feel their lips brush when she spoke. "But you do have to promise to come back."

She kissed him quickly and trotted up the last few steps, keys in hand.

Jake waited until she shut her apartment door before turning down the stairs. As much as he'd come to like Kat over the course of the night, she was only a pretender to the throne. Laurel was the real thing.

Sucker, his back-brain said, disgusted. *You just got brushed off at the door. That's pathetic.*

"Jake?"

He turned back to see her half-hanging out the door into the landing. One long leg, one firm breast taunt against her shirt from leaning against the frame, one hand that just sent shivers through him, all topped by a lopsided smile.

"I'm closing my shop early tomorrow," she said. "Do you have any plans, say from about noon on?"

He thought about that for roughly a third of a second. "Well I *was* planning on saving civilization as we know it, then working on a western I need to ghostwrite before too much longer. A picnic lunch with you sounds a lot better though. We can go to the woods, hike the trails. I'll even bring the basket."

Laurel's face lit up. "You're on. And dinner's on me. Italian?"

"Sure. Sounds great."

"Bring something to change into. You can use my bathroom." She smiled. "I'll wear a little black dress."

"I'll buy a tie," Jake said, solemnly.

"Go!"

"Going!" He jogged down the stairs and out the door.

The Beast came to life on the first try, as usual. Jake checked for traffic and saw Laurel watching him. Her backlit silhouette pressed one hand against the third-story window as he pulled away.

You were saying? He thought smugly towards the vaults of his mind.

Oh, shut up, was the reply.

Hours later, images of the long line of Laurels body framed by her doorway taunted him, making sleep impossible. That's why he was so very awake, sitting in a twenty-four hour coffee shop at four-thirty in the morning. He knew he wouldn't be able to sleep, so he'd headed for blessed caffeine. The battered hard-back composition book he kept under his driver's seat accompanied Jake into Witch's Brew, where he ordered a mug of smoky liquid goodness and took a seat at the counter.

About an hour later, a pair of cops strode in. Not a strange occurrence for a coffee/doughnut shop, but Jake noticed the younger of the two had the shakes.

The older one ordered a triple and sat down one stool away. The man's thinning hair convinced Jake to add another decade to his age as the younger asked for a double half-caff espresso. That caused his partner to look at Jake with a long-suffering expression.

Jake grinned and took another sip of caffeine. "Rough night, officers?"

"You don't know the half of it, the older one said, bringing his cup to his lips. He, like Jake, didn't mess around with foam or whipped cream; he just stirred in a pack of sugar and called it good.

The younger one nodded, eyes on his drink.

"What happened?" Jake said, suddenly interested. It took a lot to rattle a cop in a city full of everything from blow-snorting lawyers to gangbanging.

"Police business," the younger said.

The veteran gave him a thoughtful look. "I know you?"

"Maybe," Jake admitted. "I wrote a piece on the Party Boy Rapist a year back."

"Wrote my ass; I remember you. I'm Parker. That's Goodman." The younger cop tipped his cup as the older offered his hand to Jake. "*Lots* of people been wanting to thank you. We still get the calls."

Jake gripped his hand, shrugging. "Right place, wrong time. Besides, I just write the story."

"Before you started, Goodman," Parker told him. "Probably heard about him though. The bastard killed seven girls before he was caught. Got the needle this past April."

Goodman frowned. "So?"

"*So*," Parker mimicked. "Mr. Bashful here caught the guy. Came in. Tried to tell one of the detectives there was a pattern after we found the sixth."

The cop's eyes were far away for a moment.

"That was a bad one... said the guy was targeting girls by their horoscopes. Lead detective on the case had him thrown off the precinct floor. Ended up hanging around dark alleys for... almost a month?"

Jake nodded.

"After another victim, we hit pay-dirt. The little bastard had just grabbed number eight off Hudson. Was all set to drag her off somewhere, do her, and then kill her too. *This* genius," he jerked a thumb at Jake, "went at him. Beat the living hell outta him. Got stabbed good for his trouble, but Mr. Party Boy ended up getting the stick with a mouthful of dentures and a permanent limp."

Parker gave him a speculative look. "You heal up alright?"

"Yeah. Nothing Dr. Jameson's and about two dozen stitches couldn't take care of."

The veteran chuckled, sipping at his coffee.

Jake pursed his lips. "Sorry about the trouble I caused. I couldn't get anyone to *listen* to me. Thanks for not pressing charges, by the way."

Parker displayed a vicious grin. "Why would we? Anonymous Samaritan is kinda a tough name to get on a warrant."

Goodman looked a little less standoffish now.

"Wish tonight was only as bad as that."

His partner bristled. "Damn it, Parker, you could..."

"What? Get arrested? Lose my *pension*? Christ, be better than what's coming." Parker turned to Jake. "You got anybody you care about, kid?"

Jake was a little nervous after a question like that. "A couple people."

"Get them away from the city. Tonight."

Goodman looked beaten; he was resting his face in his hands leaning on the counter.

"Get them out," Parker told him. "Get them... shit, I don't know. Head for the middle of nowhere. Canada or the Rockies. Hell, head for fuckin' *Mars* if you can get there."

That's done it. Jake thought. *I am officially freaked the fuck out now.*

Goodman gazed at his partner, then looked at Jake in defeat. "It's the truth. God help us, he's telling you the truth."

"What's so—"

The radio on Parker's shoulder, squawked and he thumbed the transmit button. "Unit thirty-eight, Parker here."

Goodman had gone white. He sat, hands clenching the countertop, eyes closed, mouthing something that, at least to Jake, looked a lot like *No*, over and over.

"We're already there, over!" Parker ran for the door with Goodman trailing. "Come on, kid. After Party Boy, you *deserve* to know."

Jake sprinted after them, composition book forgotten. The two flew around the corner outside with him right on their heels and skidded to a stop before the third store front down the block. Jake looked up to read the sign, but it was written in some form of Middle Eastern dialect which to him resembled a bunch of bugs having an orgy.

Well that's politically correct, he thought ruefully.

Both cops had drawn their weapons and were circling wide past the first window towards the door. Jake followed, falling back on training from his time with the SAS as he moved to their left and slightly to the rear. Parker reached for the door.

"Stay behind me," he murmured. "I mean *right* fucking behind me."

Jake nodded and Parker yanked open the door, allowing

Goodman to make entry to the left. Jake screwed up his courage and followed Parker soundlessly across the convenience store threshold. They crossed the store to put their shoulders against the firewall before slowly gliding towards the rear, heading for the cold cases and beer cave. Goodman was the first in line as they came to the end of the aisle. His eyes went wide and his weapon came up to cover something along the back wall. Parker's came up too, and Jake could see the veteran's eyes playing range finder as he looked for the nearest threat.

What the hell is that noise? Jake thought. *Did someone bring a couple of pigs in here and let them into the ice cream?*

Then he smelled it. The unmistakable sickly-sweet, copper-tinged reek of blood. He'd smelled it in a little corner of Hell with the SAS. He'd smelled it after the Party Boy rapist stuck four inches of hot pain into his back. Now he smelled it again in the rear of the store, with two scared cops who looked like they'd just seen a ghost.

Jake spun out behind Parker's shoulder and thought he'd gone mad.

Three people were crowded around the body of a fourth, their clothes soiled, but not tattered. They were...

Jake felt his gorge rise.

They were *eating*.

Usually there's an enormous amount of blood in a human body, but not this one. Instead, it was everywhere else. The floor, the three people kneeling in it, the walls, the glass freezer doors, even the display of jerked beef that looked like...

Don't think! His back-brain screamed at him. Look! Deal with it later!

He watched as the three stuffed globs of flesh into their mouths. He realized all of them had a slight gray tone to their skin and were horribly disfigured. One man was missing half of his face. Jake saw the orb of his eye rolling around in the pulpy mass of damage that had once been a socket. The other man's throat was virtually non-existent. His spine showed through the mess of his neck and the flesh he swallowed simply fell through the bloody hole under his jaw. The woman was missing one eye, her nose, and her lips. All three had gore up to their elbows and smeared down the front of their clothes.

Parker and Goodman cocked their weapons almost in unison and three ruined faces came around to stare at them unblinkingly. Then the horrors abandoned their meal to slowly shuffle towards Jake and the two cops. As they did, a low moan rose from their throats.

"Remember, pick your shots," Parker said calmly. "Far right."

His gun roared and the female was blown backwards, preceded by a plume of grey matter that used to be her brain.

"Far left." Goodman put a round through the mouth of the man with no throat. It went on to shatter the glass of the freezer behind him. He dropped and didn't move again.

"Last one." Parker blew the top of the last man's head off from eight feet away. He fell over backwards and hit what was left of his skull on the floor with a sickening wet smack.

Jake was standing there mouth open, trying to decide whether or not to puke, when the body they'd been eating moved. It jerked and convulsed erratically. After about a minute, it sat up. The man wore a turban and had a kindly visage. At least he would've, if he'd had anything left of it. Along with a gaping chest wound, most of his left forearm had been eaten away and they'd chewed flesh from his face.

"Watch." Parker leveled his weapon and shot the man in the chest. Jake saw bits of lung fly out from his back and splatter over the shelf full of Combos behind him. The man just looked at them.

Parker shot him again. This time he blew a chunk of one shoulder away.

The man began to stand up.

Parker took aim a final time, fired, and the man's skull all but exploded. He sat back down heavily and, with the hole between his eyes just beginning to seep a trickle of blood, fell over dead.

That was when Jake saw movement out of the corner of his right eye.

Utter terror pumped adrenaline into his bloodstream, lending him speed. Threat-activated reflexes honed during his time with the shooters of the SAS went into overdrive and Jake sent a high, powerful side-kick whipping out at head level. The reaction saved his life.

The fourth assailant had been lying behind an overturned Hostess display. It had been a twenty-something Caucasian man, wearing a hippie tie-dyed shirt, cut-off jeans, and flip-flops. The whole bottom half of his face and most of his throat had been torn... no, *chewed* away, allowing parts of his trachea and esophagus to dangle beneath his jaw line. It's was also missing its left hand. Which was all that kept it from grabbing the edge of the soda cooler to stay vertical after catching Jake's kick square in the yellow teeth. He slid a good ten yards down the aisle, finally coming to rest under the Slushy machine.

"*Holy shit!*" Jake yelled, jumping away from the putrid horror towards the beer cooler. Goodman and Parker moved up beside him as the thing began to gather itself, slowly rising to its feet. They looked at one another, nodded, and each blew out one of its kneecaps. What had once been a *righteous dude* hit the floor face first with the full weight of its rotting body. Parker moved quickly forward and firmly put his foot down on the back of its neck.

"Watch." he said, and quickly put two rounds through the struggling things back. It kept moving, trying to push up from the scuffed linoleum with its one remaining hand. Jake had seen enough entry wounds to know that Parker had put both rounds through the man's heart. They didn't have any effect.

The cop shifted his aim, squeezed the trigger on his Beretta again, and the thing's head bounced off the floor with the impact of the round. The hippie went limp and didn't move again.

The three of them stood there for a few minutes, staring at the puddle of foul-smelling liquid spreading from the head of the now-still corpse. Jake reached for his smokes, took one for himself, and gave one to each of the cops. He grabbed a disposable lighter from the rack on the register counter, lit them all, and took in the carnage.

"You understand now?" Parker demanded. "You understand what's coming?"

Jake looked back at the dead man with the now blood-soaked turban. His nametag read Abdul. He was happy to help you.

Jake turned back to Goodman, who seemed close to having a breakdown, then to Parker. The older man's gaze was strong, but his voice broke as he asked, "You know what they were, right?"

Jake drew smoke into his lungs, exhaled, and tasted copper again.

"Zombies."

* * *

Laurel was sleeping soundly.

After Jake left, the day's long work hours had taken their toll, making her feel like her head was full of wet cotton. She'd crawled into bed after removing her clothes and slipping on a slightly oversized baseball jersey, leaving her underwear on out of habit. She was never quite comfortable sleeping in the buff.

The dreams began soon after her head touched the pillow. Laurel dreamt of pale blue eyes, the smell of smoke and cedar, and unruly hair.

As dreams often are, they were reinforced and made even more real through her movements, as she slept. *External stimuli... influencing of the subconscious*, a shrink would say. The collar of her shirt moving as she rolled to one side became the brush of lips against her throat. Her hair against her face became the gentle touch of a hand on her cheek, causing her to sigh with pleasure. The sounds of her own breathing became a soft voice in her ear. Her mind cycled through the events of the day and brought her the image of Jake's face.

The dream sped up. She and Jake ran through the woods together, bare feet speeding over the turf. They shot down forest paths, wind moving across their naked bodies, cooling them in the shadows of the trees. They coupled wildly in the moonlight, moving with the mad desperation of animals who knew nothing of death.

Her slumbering moans melded with sounds from outside. Revving engines and the sounds of panic, punctuated by the stray gunshot. The occasional scream or cry brought more images of moon-slick skin and heat to her floating psyche.

She knew nothing of the nightmare just beyond the walls and passed the night in dreams.

* * *

Tracy Dixon's building had become a slaughterhouse.

It was only a matter of time before someone noticed.

Not that it would make a bit of difference.

In every city, in every country, it was happening.

Thousands had been turned in the last hours. In remote places like the Northern Ukraine and isolated areas of South America everything human had already been consumed, leaving only empty buildings and bloody streets. Here and there the occasional ghoul dragged itself along with its arms, because someone had got in a lucky shot with an ax or a small caliber gun, but those were few. Most members of the military, and even law enforcement, had been trained to go for the center mass, the primary organs.

The dead didn't need them.

They never felt the bullets entering their bodies. By the time Jake and Laurel were beginning to feel each other out with words, the number of dead worldwide was creeping towards the million member mark.

And their numbers continued to grow.

The riots were beginning. Real ones this time. People were starting to panic. Some locked themselves in their homes. Some began the exodus out of the cities. Some decided it was hopeless and went to their places of worship, or chose to end it all in a variety of methods.

Military force was coming into play, but far, far too slowly. Besides which, the military had a finite number to work with, while the opposition's numbers rose sharply.

The media didn't help matters. What with all the live reports and minute by minute coverage, they were whipping people into a frenzy. Pictures of Baghdad, London, Hong Kong, Moscow, Washington, all in living color. All showing an ever increasing number of atrocities.

The world took a breath to scream...

CHAPTER FIVE

Jake brought the Beast skidding to a halt on the sidewalk in front of his building. He'd been a man possessed, broken every traffic law he knew, racing for his apartment.

It had taken almost an hour, due to one stop—a hardware store with a smashed front window where someone had tried to steal a snow blower of all things.

He'd jumped through the broken glass, remembering what Master Sergeant Molly Sloan drilled into the newbies during their first few weeks with the SAS.

First thing ta do in a hand-to-hand fight is t' arm yerself, she growled. A knife, a pencil, a brick...hell, even tha' top of your 'ead is a handy four kilogram weight tha' can crush a bugger's nose.

Jake tried very hard not to think about Molly in the seconds it took him to dash down the small center aisle and pull a large crowbar out of the discount tool bin. Then he quickly jogged back out through the display window, thrown the tool in his passenger seat and roared towards home.

People started to flee the city. He had to swerve around countless cars that had collided and just been left. Their drivers, opting to flee on Shank's Mare, sometimes only made it a dozen yards due to their injuries. Many still roamed the streets, but they would never drive again. All they'd do, forever, was shuffle about, looking for someone to eat. There were occasional groups of the living running blindly, yelling for him to stop. Some waved handfuls of money as they screamed frantically, offering thousands of dollars if he'd only let them ride along.

Jake avoided them to keep them from leaping in front of the Beast's tires in their desperation. It killed something inside him, but he did it.

George Foster was at the front door armed with a SPAZ riot shotgun as Jake leapt from his vehicle, crowbar in hand. The crusty old warrior pulled the security gate and opened the door as he took in the younger man's frantic expression.

"Hell of a night eh, kid?" George exhaled fragrant Cuban and secured the door again. "I never would'a expected the end to be caused by dead cannibals. Thought we'd *nuke* each other into oblivion."

Jake stared at him. "How?"

George began walking through the lobby. "I *do* know what the Internet is. Even if I didn't, the emergency channels are going nuts. The police are particularly chatty, but they're getting their asses handed to 'em. Oh, Allen's up in your place. He had the key, so I didn't bust his chops."

"Allen's here?" Jake demanded. "That's good news. I'm going to need him."

George cradled the SPAZ across his body. "You lookin' to die? Goin' back out there's a *real* bad idea."

"I don't have a choice."

Foster said nothing.

Jake looked at him like someone was holding his toes over a fire. "I *have* to go, but I need backup. Al's good in a fight. He's tougher than he looks."

Foster sniffed. "See me on the way out."

* * *

The graying man watched Jake race for the stairs and, with a leery expression, headed for his office. Fool kid was gonna get himself snuffed. George thought for a second and moved to his industrial filing cabinet in the corner, thanking his younger self for choosing a career that allowed him to prepare for situations like this.

* * *

Jake raced up to his fourth floor apartment, unlocked the door, and burst into his living room. The run up had only taken him about thirty seconds, but it was time that he wasn't on the way to Laurel.

"Al!" He yelled, kicking the door shut and dropping his coat behind him on the fly.

The mechanic's head came up from beside the couch, looking frazzled. Jake shot towards his spare room. "Al, I need you to..."

He came to an abrupt halt as he rounded his couch. Kat lay twined beneath his friend, hair splayed out like a dark blue puddle, wearing nothing but a pair of panties with a banzai symbol emblazoned on the front. Jake had an unobstructed view down the length of her body and silently admitted to himself that her great abs were the *least* of her attributes. Not a tan line in sight.

She had a Hello Kitty tattoo on the inside of her right hip, half covered by the panties.

Allen wore only a pair of tighty-whities. Badly.

Kat's upside-down face considered Jake calmly with mild surprise. "I thought you weren't into threesomes?"

"What?" Jake asked, numb from the unanticipated image of Allen in his underwear. He was doubtless going to need therapy after today.

"Hey..." Allen stood and helped Kat to her feet. "I, uh, didn't think you'd be back tonight. We would've gone to my apartment, but its way up on the north end and since you were busy...well..."

"What? "Jake echoed again.

"We can go to my place if you want." Kat bent at the waist to pick up her shirt, causing two sets of eyes to bug-out, as she pulled it over her head. She pretended not to notice.

"What the hell are you talking about?" Jake exclaimed, arms flailing out in exasperation. "Don't you know what's going on?"

The pair gave him a look reserved for people who hold conversations with themselves in public. Out loud.

"Shit!" Jake clenched his head between his hands, like he was trying to keep his brain from exploding. "There's no *time* for this! Get dressed, the both of you! I'm leaving in three minutes. Kat, turn on any TV station. Make sure you're *sitting down* beforehand and be prepared for a shock. Al, call your dad. Tell him to take your mom and your sisters and get the hell out of town. *Don't think*! Do it! I need to gather some things!"

Jake bolted down his short hallway and disappeared. The sound of objects being tossed around came from his spare room as the two of them pulled on their clothes.

* * *

"It's been a rough night for him," Allen said helpfully, tugging on his socks.

"I understand." Kat plunked down on Jake's couch and reached for the remote. "It's not every day you meet someone who you want to jump 'til their bones rattle. They'll both be a *lot* calmer once they get it over with."

* * *

Jake was in his bedroom, tossing everything in his closet across the floor. He pulled on his SAS tactical harness and donned it, making sure nothing was loose. He pulled on a pair of Nomex gloves, a set of action pads—really just high-grade elbow protectors—still used by military personnel around the world and grabbed his bug-out bag. It was a habit common in the Special Forces to keep a pack stocked for emergencies. Spare clothes, matches, compass, a good knife, things like that. Jake had maintained one after he came back from England, because it seemed like a good idea in this age of everything from terrorist attacks to killer hurricanes. He hefted the pack, gauging its weight. It would slow his movements and would add to his mass, so he'd leave it in the Beast when the time came. He'd seen some of those things in action, and he didn't want to give them a bigger target to latch onto if it came to close quarters fighting. Jake hurried back to the living room to find—thankfully, for two very different reasons—the others were fully clothed again.

Allen and Kat were in mild shock, eyes glued to the horrors playing out on his flat-screen, narrated by the local perfectly-groomed talking head. Jake bought the television as a birthday present to himself last year. Al had shown up later that day with a new game system he'd sprung on Jake as well. That, along with enough Guinness to fill a bathtub, allowed them to spend the next fifteen hours blowing away alien scum in high-def. The writer turned his TV off and faced the stunned pair.

"That's what's going on," he said. "Al? You get in touch with your dad?"

"He tried to reach me earlier. I had my phone off. They're already on my dad's plane, headed for Alaska. He waited as long as he could, but the...*things*...were making their way through the airport. He almost clipped one with his right wing taking off. We have a cabin on the southeastern tip up there. Food, water, short wave. They'll be okay." Allen shut his eyes, took a deep breath, and stood up. He looked at Jake and gave him a halfhearted grin. "Wouldn't leave you on your own anyway. You wouldn't last a day without me."

"Your dad's smart. He'll keep them safe." He looked at Kat who was leaning back on the couch, staring at the ceiling. "You alright?"

"Oh, sure." She blinked a few times and stood up, massaging her temple. "Just trying to wrap my brain around...I'm dealing with it."

"Allen," Jake said, "I won't ask you to come with me, but

regardless I'm going for Laurel. I don't know if I can get there by myself, let alone *back* again, but I won't leave her."

Allen nearly flipped. "You *prick*. You know you don't have to ask. About time you finally did something crazy. Don't know about your *timing*, but I'm in."

Kat moved forward and hugged Jake tightly. He looked questioningly at his friend who motioned for Jake to wait. He put his arms around Kat and awkwardly patted her on the back as she stood pressed against him. Her eyes were full when she took his face in her hands and kissed him.

"Thank you. You hardly know either one of us." She smiled.
"Yep. White Knight for sure."

"Alright, come on." Jake grabbed his battered leather jacket and tossed it to Kat. "Put it on. It's not Kevlar, but it should give you some protection if one of them gets too close. Leather that thick is tough enough to keep you from getting road-rash, so it should be too tough for them to bite through."

"What about you?" Kat shoved her arms through the sleeves.

"I'll fight better without it," he said. "It'd just slow me down."

They ran into the hall and down the stairwell to find George waiting by the lobby security desk.

"All three of ya goin'?" He puffed at his Cuban.

"Al and I are," Jake said. "Kat's..."

"Fucking going with you too!" She gave him a hard look. "Laurel's my best friend and I can take care of myself! Probably kicked more people's butts than *you* have. I hit the clubs on the weekend, you know. That's survival of the fittest."

Jake gave her a long look then glanced at Allen, who in turn shrugged. "All right, come on." Jake sighed.

George cocked his SPAZ. "Can't let you do it."

Jake stopped dead and the others froze behind him. He'd *seen* riot guns used before. They could fire as fast as you could pull the trigger. Foster had been a lifer in the Navy. George could turn him into a Jackson Pollock without much difficulty with that weapon.

"Chief," Jake carefully put his hands up, "I'm going. It may not be safe, but I have to reach her. So if you want to stop me...you'll have to shoot me."

Foster looked at Jake for a moment before lowering his riot gun.

"Had ta be sure you were serious." George reached down, pulled a Halliburton case from behind the reception desk, then popped the locks, "But if yer nuts enough to go, take along some firepower."

Inside were a police issue Remington 870 shotgun and a blue

steel Desert Eagle. He tossed Allen the pistol. "You know how to shoot?"

"Hey, I play a lot of video games." Allen sighted the weapon away from the others, ejected the magazine, cleared the chamber, and caught the bullet on the fly. After checking the action, he put the round back in the magazine, reinserted it, and dropped the slide. "Modified. Ten in the mag, one in the pipe. Nice."

George grunted. "How about you there, China doll?" he asked holding out the Remington.

Kat smiled, took the shotgun, and gave it a once over. Then she *side cocked* the damn thing. "My dad was in the service. Kat knows guns."

George grinned at her and turned back to Jake. "Only had a few handy, but I got something *real* nice for *you*."

He opened the bottom desk drawer, pulled out a big thigh holster, complete with gun belt and quick release, then passed it to Jake.

Jake thumbed open the locking strap and drew out the most vicious looking handgun he'd ever seen. It weighed a good five pounds, and its massive barrel had what looked like air holes all along the slide.

"What..." He was stunned.

George smiled. "That there's a high impact, multi-caliber repeater. Hammer fer short. Fires forty-five slugs or any twelve-gauge ammo. The top barrel can take a silencer. You don't want to try to use any shot with it on though, or you'll get hit by some blow-back. Only accurate to fifty yards, but you don't wanna be shootin' any farther than that without a rifle anyway."

Jake checked the slide, put the gun back in the holster, then made sure it was tight to his hip as Foster continued.

"The vents on the slides direct the combustion force of the round up at a forty-five, so the barrel doesn't jump. Double action too, so recoil is almost zero. If it bleeds, the Hammer can kill it. Either that or make it hurt so bad, it'll wish it was dead." George helped Kat don bandoleers full of loads for the shotgun, gave Allen an ammo bag full of magazines for the Eagle, and secured two pouches to Jake's Tac harness. "Ten more mags to go with the one in the gun. Holds nine. Aim for the head, not the center mass, and *count your damn shots*. Get your girl, then get your butts back here, double-time. We'll figure out what ta do then."

Jake tried to thank him, but Foster waved him off. "You wanna thank me, O'Connor? Fine. Don't get dead. Head for the rear gate when you come back. I'm gonna seal the front up tight."

The writer nodded and they made for the door. Foster checked the left, Jake the right as the small group headed out for the Beast.

"Hey."

Jake turned as Foster came just outside the door and looked towards the center of the city.

"You can't save everyone out there. You know that, right? I've got some stuff that can keep us alive. Hell, even kinda comfortable for a short time. Hopefully it won't come to that. The military could get this thing under control if the politicians keep outta it, but *that's* pretty unlikely. We could be on our own for a while."

Jake knew where he was going. "Every mouth we have to feed is less time we'll be able to hold on."

Foster nodded and puffed his cigar. "Figure we can have...ten or so total. You three, your girl, and Gertie's still here. Wouldn't leave. So we should be in good shape, but don't try to save anybody you don't want in the door. I'm not saying don't help if you can, just remember: your girl's the important thing

Jake knew, right then, that he was going to burn. George was right and he hated the man for it. But he was going to do everything he could to get Laurel to safety. If that meant damning himself then that was a price he'd gladly pay.

Listen to Foster, his back-brain told him. *You need to worry about a certain redhead. How would you feel if she ended up dead because you got soft-hearted at the wrong moment and fucked up?*

At that moment, Jake hated himself.

Simply nodding to George, he watched as the man went back inside and secured the entrance. Jake turned to find Kat already in the passenger seat, shotgun ready, and Allen behind the wheel of the Beast.

"What are you doing?" Jake asked.

"I'm a *way* better driver than you are. We're going to have to take the residential streets. I know them like the back of my hand and you don't," Allen explained. "Besides, and if you ever tell anyone I said this I *will* deny it, you're a much better shot than I am. It's a sure bet we're gonna run into trouble, and you've had combat training."

Jake tossed Allen the keys and hopped into the bed behind Kat as the Beast roared to life. Allen accelerated off the curb, took a sharp right, then started west towards Kat and Laurel's apartment. Jake prayed fervently she was still there, alive and waiting.

* * *

"Looks like a war zone..." Allen peered cautiously from the

alley.

Jake shook his head. "Trust me, this is worse."

Allen was staring at the carnage, so he missed the chill in his friend's voice. There were bodies. A lot of them. Many in pieces. All of them unmoving. From where they huddled it was hard to tell the zombie corpses from those of their victims. There was blood everywhere. Splashed on walls, pooled in the gutters, smeared on nearly every surface.

And the smell.

Most people didn't know the first thing you did after you died was shit yourself. The human sphincter muscles relaxed almost immediately, and you dropped a load in your drawers. Which to Allen, made the question, *are you wearing clean underwear?* that his mother always posed to him before he went skydiving for the day almost comical.

He pushed thoughts about his family out of his mind. Allen's father was an excellent pilot, and by now they were over the Canadian Rockies headed for Alaska.

Over the last two hours, the unlikely trio had skirted the heart of the city and come in from the north, avoiding the main roads along with any on ramps leading to the I-71 freeway. There had been traffic jams miles long of people fleeing the urban graveyard, which Allen had bypassed using the Beast's crash bumper and a healthy amount of guts.

"The operative word here is *empty*," Kat offered in a strained voice. Her butt and legs were just beginning to loosen up from repeatedly clenching to hold herself in place. Allen had blown through yards, intersections, and done a superb job of getting them within about a hundred yards of the apartment she and Laurel shared. But damn, her ass was killing her.

The drive had been bad enough, but the dead had become more numerous the farther they traveled. There had been some close calls. The worst had been when they'd crossed through northern Bexley. Its one way streets were glutted with abandoned BMWs and wrecked Lexus coups. At one point Allen had to put the Jeep into a bootlegger's turn to avoid ramming a crowd of about three dozen zombies when they rounded a blind corner. Some of them had latched onto the Beast's bumper as Allen fought to keep the vehicle under control. Then the things began to pull themselves up into the bed.

It had been a tense few minutes as Jake, cursing like a sailor, used the crowbar he'd taken to knock them off. The creatures tended to skid messily along the asphalt as the Jeep gained speed, which Allen found satisfying to the extreme.

He'd always been a Grand Theft Auto fan.

Kat hadn't been able to use the shotgun for fear of hitting him, so Jake had stood in the bed gripping the roll cage, crowbar ready, waiting for a hungry face to come over the side. When one appeared, he'd smash it.

Just like that old arcade game Whack-a-Mole, she thought, but a terrifying and gory version.

"Yeah," Jake said, "if any of these were coming back, they would've done it by now. It's been almost ten minutes. The one the cops shot in the Quicky-Mart sat his ass back up long before that."

They watched the street for another minute before any of them tested that theory, however.

"Allen, I want you to stay here." Jake cut off his friend's protest before it got past his lips. "We need a safety net. That's you. You see anything moving...I mean *anything*, dead or not, bring the Jeep up in front. Blast the horn on your way. If we're not at the door when you get there, circle the block once, then pick us up. You don't see us after your first lap we won't be coming out. If that happens, head back and link up with George."

"Fuck that," Allen said. "You're coming out or I'm coming *in*. I'd miss it if you weren't around to pester."

Jake grinned and scanned the street.

"Be careful." Allen put his back against the wall, weapon in hand.

Kat followed the writer as he moved from the alley towards her building. He held the crowbar across his body, hands white-knuckled with eagerness to go! Only the training he'd received during time spent with Britain's finest kept him from darting across the road. Jake knew if he screwed up now, he'd be dead. Allen and Kat would be too, with Laurel shortly thereafter. If she wasn't already. So he walked slowly, eyes scanning back and forth 180 degrees, watching for movement. With Kat in tow, he made his way to the building's entryway, checking under all the cars they passed in case a stray creature happened to be lurking beneath waiting for a meal. He scanned the street again as Kat moved nimbly past him to the door.

"I've got the key." She grasped the handle firmly. "Once we get upstairs, we can..."

"Wait!" Jake hissed.

A zombie fell through door as she pulled it open and landed face up on the landing. Kat jumped back against the railing with a small cry, doing her best to bring the shotgun to bear, as Jake's foot came down on the things chest. The thing had been a fair-haired man in his mid-thirties with an average build and good looks. It was dressed in loose jeans and a Blue Jackets hockey jersey. Its eyes bulged from sunken sockets; it was missing one ear, and a sizable amount of its left shoulder was gone. Its broken nails clawed at Jake's pants as it bit at the air, trying to move his boot that held it to the concrete.

"Shit, that's Paul!" Kat choked out, while Jake used his heel to keep the struggling corpse prone. "He works at Sounds and Suds Bar and Laundry!"

Jake's face was pale with fear. He swung the crowbar two-handed, bringing it down again and again, smashing the things skull like a cheap vase. Half-congealed blood and brain matter splattered across the steps as he pounded the zombie into oblivion. He knew he was losing it, but he couldn't stop. Kat finally had to pull him away from the body after he'd turned its head into a pasty mess. Jake came to his senses with her shaking him by one arm and begging him to stop.

"You need to keep it together!" She urged.

When he finally answered, his voice was raw. "It was inside...Kat, *it was inside!*"

Her eyes widened in understanding as Jake switched the crowbar to his left hand. Holding it chisel point out like a rapier, he drew the enormous handgun Foster had given him. Mouth drawn up in a snarl, he motioned for her to get the door. Kat readied her shotgun, and when he nodded she quickly jerked the door open.

The hallway smelled like an abattoir. Blood was still tacky on the walls. The floor was slick with it. Three of the dead were strewn along the stairs, all in various stages of dismemberment. Each showed gaping cuts, along with whatever damage had caused them to turn. Nothing moved, nothing breathed.

With the cry of a wounded animal, Jake bounded up the stairs, taking them four at a time. His vision had gone red, like the wasted life smeared across the hardwood boards beneath his boots. He didn't feel his feet as he flew up the steps. He didn't see the walls around him. There was a roaring in his ears and then the door was right there, only a few yards away.

Jake sprang forward, body going horizontal five feet above the floor, and with every bit of force he could muster, he threw his shoulder into the door. Kat's eyes widened in shock at the slightly mad view he presented as she topped the landing.

He turned her door into kindling. It flew off its hinges after splitting in half. From Kat's vantage point, it all but exploded. Jake went *through* the door, changing it into a cloud of oaken debris on the fly. He flew on, impacting against the wall inside hard enough to leave the imprint of his shoulder in the plasterboard. Then he dropped, half stunned, to the floor followed by most of the doorjamb. Kat had the Remington slung over her shoulder, and was helping Jake out of the wreckage when he saw Laurel.

She stood wide-eyed with surprise in the living room, gripping a Roman gladius that looked extremely sharp; it was still soaked with blood. The weight of the weapon caused the slim, hard muscles in her arms to stand out in gloriously feminine definition and, judging by the ease with which she held the blade, she could clearly use it. She'd pulled her wavy, red hair back into a single braid that hung down her back, keeping all but one rogue lock out of her eyes. She wore white leather pants with reinforced knees and hips. They hugged her legs, just covering the tops of well-used hiking boots. A large backpack also sat on the couch.

"Jake? Kat?" She lowered her sword as she took in the shotgun and bandoleers crisscrossing her friend's bosom. "You look like Pancho Villa."

"Laurel, I'm so glad you're okay!" Her roommate dashed forward to give her a quick hug, then back again to help the still groggy Jake to his feet. Once he was able to stand on his own, leaning heavily against the wall, Kat was all business. "I'll never harass you about going to all those Ren Fairs again! Alright. Gimme five minutes and we're outta here!"

She dashed to her bedroom.

Once inside, Kat grabbed her own hiking pack, the one Laurel had insisted she have before they went camping one weekend. She stuffed in most of her underwear, including her sports bras, socks, jeans, and few pairs of workout tights. She jammed in some tee shirts, a sweatshirt and a short silken Kimono style robe that she'd never had the chance to wear. Granted, there probably wasn't going to be much time for nookie in the foreseeable future—zombie apocalypse and all that—but it never hurt to plan ahead.

Thinking of which, she grabbed her handcuffs and her *massager* with variable speed action, considered it for a moment, shrugged, then dropped it back in the drawer and took all six boxes of condoms instead.

She also took her grandfather's sword.

* * *

Out in the living room, Laurel was staring open-mouthed at Jake as he attempted to shake the last few spots from his vision. Her expression was carefully neutral as his eyes cleared and he pushed off the wall towards her. He stopped a couple of feet away, face showing obvious relief.

"Hi."

"How did...Jake, what the hell are you *doing* here?" She cocked her hip, truly angry at him for risking his life. "Do you know what kind of danger we're in?"

He stood there calmly, looking at her with unreadable eyes. "Well, we had a date."

"You came all this way for a date??" Laurel demanded, incredulously.

"Of course not."

"Then what are you..."

"I came here for *you*, Laurel. It didn't matter if I was scared, and God, I'd be crazy if I weren't right now. I didn't care how many of those things where in my way. Didn't care if I had to walk through Hell, naked, yelling the Devil is a sewage-gulping *fag* at the top of my lungs." His gaze made her believe it, right down to her boots.

"I don't need you to protect me." She felt she should say something confident just then, because those eyes were making her knees feel like Jell-O. Laurel had never been much of a "damsel in distress" kind of girl. She'd taken up things like aikido, dancing, and she ran in the mornings. She made a point of becoming a capable person in her own right, a woman who didn't need someone else to define who she was.

She *could* admit to being frightened though. And she was. Right down to the marrow of her bones. If there was ever a reason for fear, dead people getting back up and consuming the living was *surely* in the top five. She didn't want to die. She especially didn't want to be eaten, or worse, turned into one of the mindless *things*, but she would be crushed if Jake got himself killed attempting to rescue her. That was something Laurel didn't think she could handle.

He looked at the sword she held. "I know that. But it doesn't change things one bit. You could be catching bullets, swinging a magic lasso, and I'd have still come for you."

He stepped back, looking around. "I like your place. It's homey."

His sudden change in topic didn't succeed in throwing her. "No! No, no! Back up for a minute. So, you were saying what?"

Jake sighed. "That I'm a sucker when it comes to musically inclined redheads that belong on the cover of Playboy, who can kick the crap out of monsters with ancient weaponry."

Laurel twined her arm—the one not holding the sharp, pointy object—around his neck with a lopsided smile. "The cover, huh?"

Kat returned seconds later lugging her pack, to find Jake and Laurel a little distracted. She coughed loudly, causing them to break their embrace with a guilty look on his part.

"If we're all ready now, I think we should get going." She cradled her shotgun. "Allen's waiting outside. It'd be a shame if a zombie or ten came along and bit off his..."

"Alright! Swiftly approaching the point of too much information. Time to head out," Jake said quickly, gesturing behind him with his crowbar. That earned a knowing look from both women, which he firmly ignored. It was a guy thing. You *didn't* talk about another guy's junk with girls. You didn't talk with other guys about *your* junk.

Basically, you just didn't talk about it.

"Let's." Laurel shouldered her pack and readied her gladius.

"You realize we're about to head back through a mess, right?" He glanced at Laurel. "It's *really* bad. Worse than anything I saw with the SAS. Even Bosnia. The dead are moving farther and farther from the center of the city, hunting. And we know what they eat."

"Are they actually, you know, *eating*?" She frowned. "Or just biting people?"

Kat's face paled. "A little of both. Some of the ones we've seen didn't even have anything left on their insides. What they fed on was just falling through holes where their guts used to be. It's like they keep chomping until you...well, die. Then, once you start moving again, they stop and start looking for another meal."

Jake nodded and checked the hall. "There are a lot of them scattered around. We ran across a pretty large group and it was big enough to make me leery of going anywhere people might congregate. A pair of cops I talked to last night recommended I take anyone I cared about and head for the boondocks. But that's where everyone will be going, so that's where the *zombies* will head. When the cities empty out, they'll go for where the food is."

Laurel gave him a suspicious look. "You had a run in with the police tonight? What happened?"

"Couldn't sleep, so I stopped at a doughnut shop. Go figure, a couple cops came through."

"Why couldn't you sleep?" Laurel asked.

"Uh." He couldn't actually make the words come out. The side of her mouth quirked skyward in the beginnings of a smile as she gave him an appraising and somewhat frank look.

Jake tried to keep his face from going crimson.

"You're really cute when you blush." Kat stepped over the remains of their door. "Makes your face go all innocent and boyish. It's adorable."

Laurel tried not to laugh. Really, she did.

* * *

The world was at the brink. Rioting was petering out as more and more people fled the cities, running from the ever growing plague of the shambling dead. Or were recruited forcibly into their ranks.

Churches and places of worship became slaughter-houses. The by-God Bible thumpers, the faithful of Allah, the children of David. They all clustered around their various symbols, sang their praises to the Almighty in loud voices, and waited to be taken to paradise. They were the faithful after all.

No gods showed up.

But the dead sure did...

CHAPTER SIX

Things began to go pear shaped about then.

Allen was only a minute from going in guns blazing when he saw the others file carefully out of the building. The girls moved slowly down the street, packs full of what he assumed were their possessions. Jake followed, eyes never still, crowbar in one hand, Hammer pistol in the other.

Wow. That'd actually make a really cool comic book, Allen thought. Apocalyptic Adventures or something. Big guns, bad guys, super-hot scantily-clad babes, lots of gratuitous violence... Nah. Too much like real life at this point.

They were halfway to the Jeep when a crowd of forty corpses began trickling around the corner, two buildings to their rear. A dozen saw the three almost immediately, and a simultaneous chorus of blood-chilling moans rose in a bubbling cry that said *Dinner!*

Kat and Laurel froze, staring at the choir of nightmares stumping down the middle of the asphalt. Jake, however, took one look at the rotting mob, shoved both women towards Allen, and shouted, "*Move!*"

The mechanic didn't wait for them to come to him. He set the vehicle heading down the street towards his friends, at speed. Screeching to a halt a car length away, he got a good look at the crowd as the others piled in. Allen was sure he wouldn't suffer from constipation for the rest of his life after coming face-to-face with *that* bunch.

Kat all but dove into the passenger seat after tossing her bag in the bed. Laurel jumped into the rear and Jake clambered in after her. He dropped to one knee howling, "*Go-go-go-go-GO!*" He brought the Hammer up, sighted on the nearest corpse, and squeezed the trigger. The gun roared. Half a second later, the thing's head blew apart like a rotten pumpkin. The body dropped bonelessly to the pavement to be ignored by the rest of the dead as they stumbled forward, eyes fixed on the still living quartet.

"*Jesus Christ!*" Allen threw the Beast into reverse. The off-road tires threw debris virtually into the faces of the oncoming corpses as it shot backwards, with Allen driving via rearview. The others hung on for dear life as he swerved the Jeep deftly around an old VW Bug, built up speed, pulled a sliding one-eighty, popped the clutch, floored the accelerator, and roared onto Broad Street, leaving the stinking horrors in their wake.

They were two blocks away before Jake's heart rate returned to normal. Laurel sat in the bed beside him, clutching the roll bar support strut so hard her hands had gone white-knuckled.

"Are you alright?" he asked gently.

She was unable to speak, but nodded in reply and gave him a nervous grin. Jake turned and knelt behind the seats. "How about you, Kat?"

"As soon as I decide whether or not to puke, I'll be good."

Jake put a hand on Allen's shoulder. "You are one *great* fucking wheelman, my friend."

Allen nodded and swallowed audibly.

Following the route Jake suggested that zigzagged north and south of Broad, Al kept them well away from the main body of the dead. There were zombies scattered everywhere, which in a show of great self-restraint, he refrained from running over. Even if only because that he didn't want to launch Laurel and his friend from the bed of the Jeep as the rear bucked over the putrid speed-bumps.

They continued east, doing only thirty miles per hour, hampered by abandoned vehicles, scattered bodies, and the odd vertical corpse. Jake remained standing in the bed, arm wrapped around the roll bar, crowbar in hand. At this speed there was a good chance he wouldn't be able to hit whatever he shot at, so why waste rounds. If anything got too close, he planned to deter it with nine pounds of steel to the temple.

"Oh, crap." Allen pointed to the road ahead.

Jake's eyes flicked forward. A quarter mile distant, the corner of Broad and James was literally piled six deep with automobiles. Dozens of them were abandoned. Many had become disabled or stuck after ramming other vehicles, adding to the mess.

"We'll never make it past that." Allen slowed the Beast and glanced over his shoulder. "Should I head north? Try to take the back streets?"

Jake considered it for a moment. DCSC (Defense Central Supply and Control) was only a few miles down the road on the north side. The sprawling square mile of government offices and warehouses would have been where those fleeing the zombies, perhaps thousands of them, would have fled looking for guns and refuge. Personally, he thought that would be the stupidest thing anyone could do. Short of stripping themselves naked, bathing in BBQ sauce, and running down the street yelling, *Come and get it!* Any government facility would be glutted with people trying to enter, and the infected would be right behind them. The creatures would gravitate wherever they found prey, anywhere people gathered in numbers. Police stations, emergency shelters, churches. Avoiding any and all of them would be paramount for the foreseeable future.

"Cut down towards Main," Jake said. "We'll have more options to the south. Should be fewer of *them*, too."

Allen turned right on James Road using the sidewalk to get through a narrow gap between cars. He scraped the Jeep's side against an old Buick, but Jake didn't bat an eye at the damage.

They traveled on, cutting west on Elbern, then north on Hampton to bypass the mass of now useless steel. They rode through streets full of empty houses, escaped pets, wrecked minivans, and blood stained open doors, avoiding anything that moved.

As they turned onto Hampton, a group of a dozen survivors came down a driveway at the sound of the Beast's engine. They were yelling *Stop!* and *Hold up a second!* They looked haggard and a few of them wore makeshift bandages that looked suspiciously like bed sheets. Four of the people in the group were women, which caused Kat to point across the hood while nudging Allen.

"We should check and see if..." she began.

Jake had drawn the Hammer, acquiring a sight picture on the closest survivor before Allen or the girls registered he'd moved. He'd seen the guns some of the party carried pointed vaguely in their direction. Bracing his arms on the roll bar, he stroked the trigger twice, sending both shots though the chest of the lead man. The one who was stepping out into the street to block their way.

"Keep down!" he yelled, causing both girls to duck. Allen watched as he double-tapped another who'd been taking aim through the sights of a rifle. The weapon clattered as it impacted against the pavement just before its previous owner fell on top of it, bouncing off the side of an SUV with a pair of Hammer slugs through his belly.

"Damn it, Allen, keep us *moving!*"

Al had taken his foot off the accelerator, and he stomped again now in earnest. He heard barks from various caliber weapons, then Jake's answering double taps, as they raced away from the group. A stray round hit the driver's side mirror, shattering the glass and tearing away the holder arm. Allen Nascar'd it down the block, fishtailed around the corner, and headed east again on Broad.

He slowed the Beast a bit and attempted to bring his shaking hands under control. Jake knelt in the bed, inserting a fresh magazine into the Hammer and glaring behind them with cold, angry eyes.

"I can't believe you did that!" Laurel said. "You didn't even give them a *chance*...You killed those two! They were trying to get away, like us! What the hell is *wrong* with you?"

Jake said nothing. He stared down at the gun like it was a viper in his palm.

I just killed someone, he thought numbly. *Again.*

His eyes were haunted as they rose to meet Laurel's.

Allen glanced in the rearview mirror and realized he'd seen that look on his friend's face before, after O'Connor had come back from his stint overseas. He'd seen it when Jake had been released from the hospital, after being stabbed by the shit-eating rapist he'd helped catch.

"What did you see?" Allen demanded.

Jake stared out the windshield. "Police issue firearms, matching jailhouse tattoos, the quartet of bruised faces on the women, the fact they were all handcuffed together..."

Kat turned around, her face a mix of horror and rage. "You're shitting me!"

Jake shook his head, then pulled a smoke out of the pocket of his Tac harness. He sheltered his Zippo against the breeze, lit up, exhaled explosively, and checked the road ahead.

"Could we..." Kat began.

"What?" he asked. "Go back? Sure. There are four of us, three of whom have guns, versus six or seven of them. Half of *them* have guns now, if they scavenged the ones I...shot. The odds aren't bad. We *might* be able to free those women. But some of us would probably get hurt, or killed in the process or..."

Allen was silent. He understood. No *real* man turned his back on a woman who needed help. He suppressed the urge to swing the Jeep around, go back, and turn those sacks of garbage into zombie kibble. Like Jake, Al was going to wonder for a long time if maybe they could've freed those women. Neither of them was willing to risk their girls on a maybe, however.

Laurel hadn't realized what prompted Jake's choice until then.

He had wanted to help those people. Everything in him was screaming to go back, but if he did, they might all be killed or worse. All sorts of scenarios played through her mind. She knew he must have considered them over the space of a second or two. He and Allen would have been shot, or maybe beaten and left for the hungry dead. She and Kat would've been cuffed, then made into slaves. The word *rape* was prominent in her mind and she knew her roommate was thinking the same. Now that Laurel had time to look back on what she'd seen, not one of the women in that group had seemed the least bit happy about their company. One looked absolutely homicidal. She laughed as the first man Jake shot hit the ground. At the time, Laurel believed the woman's mind had cracked, but now she wasn't so sure.

She put her hand on Jake's arm, since he held a smoke in one hand and his other was still wrapped tightly around his enormous pistol. She felt his body vibrating with impotent rage as he thought about the fate of the handcuffed women. "I'm sorry," she said.

He gazed at her woodenly and finished his cigarette in silence.

* * *

The next group that needed help they *didn't* leave.

They were cutting through a high school parking lot when Jake spotted them. A trio of survivors half-stumbling across the soccer field next to the parking lot, pursued by a baker's dozen of hungry corpses. He bellowed for Allen to stop and jumped from the bed, almost before his friend brought the Jeep to a screeching halt. There were three figures out in front, two of which held up the third, trying to get to the gate. A cluster of dead followed slowly, just beyond the five-foot chain-link fence.

Jake pointed at the field. "Kat, come with me! Al, make for the gate. They're almost there anyway. When you reach it, *don't* ram it! Just push it open with the bumper. And give Laurel your gun!" He started for the fence.

Allen passed the redhead his Desert Eagle and put the Beast in gear again. Laurel took the weapon and called out, "Jake! Wait! I'll come with you!"

"Laurel, please!" he begged, running for the fence with Kat close behind. "Allen needs someone to watch his back. He can't do that *and* drive, and I need Kat to cover me with the shotgun!"

Laurel cursed, frightened for them, and jumped into the passenger seat as the vehicle roared for the far side of the field.

Jake grabbed the fence rail and leapt over, only touching the top with one foot briefly as he cleared it on the fly. He was about to grab the bottom and pull it up for Kat to roll under when she tossed the shotgun at him. He caught it reflexively as she took three running strides, jumped, planted both hands on the top rail, and flipped over the fence like a gymnast off a vaulting horse. She landed in a crouch and took the weapon back as he stood, jaw hanging open.

"Allen was right." He drew his pistol and headed after the group of zombies.

"What?" Kat pulled abreast as they closed on the dead.

"You are *so* hot," he said, coming to a halt and dropping into a shooting stance. "Can you really use that weapon?"

"Watch me!" She exclaimed beside him and brought the Remington to her shoulder. "And I promise I won't mention you said that to Laurel."

"I'd appreciate that. I need you to take the left. Don't just start blasting; wait until those three are clear. Work from the outermost in." Then Jake opened fire.

He managed to kill five of them before the rest turned to see where all the noise was coming from. Kat waited with her shotgun while he dropped two more, then paused to reload as the pack began to shuffle towards them. The fleeing trio saw Allen take out the gate and made for the Jeep as she blew the head completely off one corpse, then shot another through the left eye. Jake yelled for her to hold fire unless any of them got close, slapped in a new mag, dropped the slide on the Hammer, and began dealing with the remaining five. He killed three of them before they got within forty feet, and Kat felt she needed to get involved again. She pulled the trigger, vaporizing one zombie's face. The writer fired on the last one, killing it not ten yards from where they stood, just as Allen brought the Jeep onto the field and coasted to a halt in the grass.

Jake and Kat reloaded and circled around the bodies, fearful that some might just be too crippled to rise. As they neared the others, he saw one dragging itself slowly forward. The thing's right arm and spine had been shattered thanks to Kat's work with her shotgun. The corpse had caught some of the blast which finished the third she'd killed. It would be doomed to drag itself along for the rest of its miserable existence, half its face in ruins, one arm dangling useless by a few scraps of skin. Jake holstered the gun and took his crowbar in a two-handed grip. The zombie wore only a pair of flannel pajama pants and was horribly swollen. To be fair, that was more due to lying dead in the sun for half a day, than it was to obesity.

He fully intended to smash its brains in, but a female voice said, "Stand back, will you? This last bastard's mine."

A woman dressed in dark blue, wielding a fire ax, strode past him towards the creature. She stopped, set herself, drew back and once it moved within six feet, buried the ax in its head. The corpse sagged into the grass, brains leaking from its ruined skull, and lay still. The woman put her boot against the back of its neck, pulled the ax free, and gave the body a vicious kick.

As she turned, Jake saw she would never be what people considered beautiful. She looked pleasant enough, but her face was just a little too harsh for beauty. Her hair was short and so blonde it was almost white. Her arms and shoulders were heavy with muscle, but she had high breasts tapering into a slim waist, and she matched Jake in height. That put her a couple inches taller than Allen. The woman was staring at him as she put a fist on her hip, leaned the ax across the back of her neck, and looked each of them over.

"Well, it doesn't look like any of you've been bitten and I doubt you'd have given us a hand if you were looters," she said. "So I'm guessing you're the cavalry."

"More like the Indians picking up stragglers on the way back to the reservation." Jake offered his hand. "Saw the smoke signals and came running. Jake O'Connor."

"Maggie Reed," the blonde smiled, which softened her face a bit, as she gripped his hand. "Good to meet you, Jake."

He turned and introduced the others, then started checking their surroundings for more zombies. As they gave Maggie and her companions time to catch their breath, Jake was able to take a closer look at each of them. One was a pretty brunette girl who looked about seventeen named Karen Parker. Her eyes were haunted, and she spoke with a quiet voice when Maggie introduced her.

"Thank you for saving us," she said, unwilling to look up from her shoes.

The other was a dark-haired, wild looking girl, who possessed a body that would make teenage bad-boys turn in to slobbering morons. She told Jake her name was Heather Bell, and that she'd be happy to express her gratitude later. That earned her a cold gaze from Laurel, in what Jake hoped was a moment of unbridled jealousy, and a look of tolerance on the part of Kat. Jake had encountered the type before. Hell, about six months ago, he'd *dated* an older version of the same model.

Maggie told them she'd been running last minute certifications for summer lifeguards at the YMCA eight blocks away when everything went to shit. Out of the sixty people there, only she and the two girls had been able to escape when a crowd of zombies came moaning through the doors. They'd made it this far by keeping quiet and out of sight, moving from building to building, mostly hiding. When the odd zombie got too close, well that's why Maggie had taken the ax from an abandoned fire truck.

"We were looking for a way into the high school when we came nose-to-nose with this group. Thought we might be able to wait it out in there. Cafeteria will have food, water, and the windows on the ground floor are too small for anything to get through. I spotted the fire escape on the second floor, so we were gonna boost Heather up. She could drop it down to us, but these foul fucks were between us and the ladder when we came around the corner." She kicked the body of the one she'd killed. It was a woman missing most of the flesh on her back, who in life had worn a ridiculous amount of make-up—branding her a member of the Pink Caddy Club. She continued, "Heather landed wrong as we jumped the wall near the employee lot, so we put her between us and took off. Not the best plan, really. Another five minutes and we would've had to either leave her or stand and fight."

Maggie frowned into the distance, wearing what people called the thousand-yard stare. "I'm no coward, but I've seen way too many people die already today. What if I'd gone down or been bitten? Both the girls would likely be dead the hard way by now." She motioned Jake to the side as Kat wrapped Heather's ballooned ankle with an ACE bandage from the med-kit Laurel pulled from her bag, and Allen managed to get a timid smile out of Karen with an impression of Invader Zim's robot singing the "Doom" song.

"Karen's family is gone," Maggie said in a low voice. "No one at her house, no car in the garage, just some bloodstains. Don't know if they were turned or killed or what. Heather's a student at OSU with no family after 9/11. Karen's the one I'm worried about though. She hasn't said ten words since this morning. I figured I could keep her with me, at least until we reach the army or someone in charge."

Jake felt cold and shot a glance at the girl. "Parker? Was Karen's father a cop?"

Maggie looked at him quizzically. "How did you know?"

Damn it, he thought.

She was a kid. Young, scared, no clue what to do next, not made to survive in a world of monsters and escaped cons. Besides, he owed her father for last night. Jake made his decision right then.

"There's no military presence that we've seen. No army, no National Guard, no police. Shit, I haven't seen so much as a meter-maid. Whatever this is, it's everywhere." He pointed at the body she'd just booted. "There are so many of those things, I'd be surprised if the people left in charge will be able to even *think* about sending help to anyone for a while. Days, weeks...who the hell knows."

He took out his smokes and, seeing the look on Maggie's face, passed her one. As he lit them both, Jake considered what Foster had said to him before they'd left. While it was true the two teenage girls wouldn't contribute much at first, they both seemed bright enough, and Maggie was an EMT. That gave her more medical training than anyone in their tiny group.

Jake exhaled. "The three of you need to come with us. It'll be tight, but the Jeep can handle three more. We're headed somewhere that should be safe."

She took a long drag from her smoke. He could see her mind weighing the options. "We've got good reason to trust you people after pulling us out of that mess. Not many would've risked it. We'll come along."

Jake and Allen helped get the limping Heather into the Beast while the others piled in. Kat took position riding shotgun, while Karen and Maggie backed up against the seats. They had to sit on the bags the girls had brought from their apartment, but at least it was better than the metal floor of the bed.

He heard another wounded zombie pulling itself over the turf as Laurel jumped up into the vehicle. Jake had been marveling at the way her legs propelled her, dancer graceful, over the raised tailgate when the unmistakable sound of moaning brought him back to earth. He pulled his crowbar from the bed, strolled over and calmly smashed it into oblivion. He turned its snapping teeth into flying Chiclets. Shattered its arms as it reached out, hungry for his flesh. Finally, Jake stood over the helpless zombie and, with a swing that started at the soles of his feet, crushed its skull, sending pieces of its brain flying across the field.

He walked back numbly and squeezed into the rear, pressing himself against the tailgate as Allen brought the Jeep to life. Jake gazed behind them as the soccer field shrank into the distance. Three saved. Three that might live another hour in a world where even death offered no escape.

"I saw that, by the way."

Jake looked at Laurel, baffled.

"Your *appreciation* as I was getting in?" She tried to sound offended and failed. "I guess even nice guys stare at your ass once in a while."

He gave her a half-hearted smile. "Guilty."

"I won't make you feel too bad about it." Laurel took his free hand. "I was staring at yours so hard while you were lifting Heather in I'm surprised you didn't feel it."

"She was. I saw." Maggie grinned widely.

"My roommate. The Butt Whisperer," Kat said, causing them all to laugh uproariously and Allen swerved a bit. "You watch the road!"

Jake chuckled and squeezed Laurel's hand.

Heather rolled her eyes and wondered if these gimps could get any mushier. Alright, zombies bit the big one, but these guys were acting like it was the end of the world. Even if everything was going down the tubes, bitching and moaning about it wasn't going to change the fact. That guy driving was a hottie though. Brown eyes, thin, funny. Cute, in a goofy sort of way.

Karen sat quietly next to Maggie, listening to the way Kat joked with Jake. Seeing the way Laurel's eyes watched his face as he sat there, head down; he was obviously upset but was trying to keep himself together. Her teenage mind decided that she would watch Kat and Laurel very closely.

The teen had already come to terms with the fact that her parents were dead. She knew they never would've left without her, no matter what. They'd always talked about what to do in case of an emergency. *Come home*, her father always said. *We'll all meet at home.* When she'd seen the blood trailing from their room towards the door, she knew they were gone. So she followed Maggie back out into the horror, empty inside, but not ready to sit on the curb and wait for the monsters to find her.

They drove on, avoiding occasional packs of zombies, shooting a few others that got too close, moving east as parts of the city burned behind them.

Jake looked back at the city of the dead and dying. As he watched the smoke rising, he thought of a bit of poetry that before last night he'd enjoyed. Now it sent a shiver of fear through him, like a chill December wind.

This is how the world ends.
Not with a bang, but a whimper...

* * *

The dead were legion now.

Between shootings, riots, people stealing anything still drivable, and those dropping from exhaustion, the creatures' numbers swelled like the flood waters of the Mississippi after a weeklong downpour.

Police units that hadn't retreated to secure locations had been overrun. The dead were teaming south, heading for the freeway interchange just below the heart of downtown. People were leaving their cars and taking to their heels. The more forward thinking had mounted bicycles and were weaving in and out of traffic, carrying themselves over roadblocks, and dying by the dozens as those on foot assaulted them for the fragile machines in hopes of escape.

Desperate people began striking out across country. Fields were trampled as more and more fled the highways.

The dead followed...

CHAPTER SEVEN

The corner of Hamilton and Broad was a mess.

A couple hundred corpses were milling around between the Check-4-Cash, Floweropia, and the two gas stations on the corners. Bodies were everywhere, some mobile, others not so much. Many hadn't had the chance to reanimate after being torn limb from limb by the hungry masses, and flies were having the feast of their short little lives. A tricked out Caddy had tried to blow through the Circle K on the northeast, only to take out a gas pump which still spewed premium across the lot.

It had been the unmistakable aroma of highly-refined dead dinosaurs that alerted the survivors. Allen noticed it a few blocks prior as they were cutting through a now vacant apartment complex. The group had moved farther south to avoid a crowd of creatures, thousands-strong, that had almost gained entry to DCSC. From half a mile away, Jake viewed them through the mini-binoculars he kept in his Tac vest and pronounced the military supply base well and truly fucked. The fence buckled in half a dozen places on the south side alone, and the dead had already torn the razor wire down in many places. The main entrance was being held by a trio of Bradley assault vehicles with M240C machine guns. Even though they expended hundreds of rounds per minute, it barely held back the flood of hungry dead.

They turned south on Watson, cutting wide around the southern edge of the horde, and came back to Broad by going off-road through a golf course. Allen had always dreamed of tearing the living crap out of those perfectly manicured greens and, after all the damage he did roaring over the sixteenth hole, even if the zombies were eradicated no one would *ever* offer him membership to the country club.

They came to a halt a block later, allowing Jake to get a closer look at the intersection through his binoculars. The creatures were clustered tight, and he knew if they attempted to break through his group would swiftly become tartar. Even the Beast couldn't make it through that many walking pus sacks. There was a SWAT van in the middle of the mess, flipped over on its side. Many of the creatures were pounding on the undercarriage, roof, and rear door. The front windows, even though bullet-proof, hadn't been able to withstand the ever-increasing pressure of the crowd and had buckled inwards. Jake didn't have high hopes for the vehicle's occupants.

They needed a distraction.

"I could take a jog," Allen suggested. "Those things are pretty slow. Hell, I could probably outdistance them at a fast *walk.*"

Jake shook his head. "No. All you'd need to do is twist an ankle and it would turn into a rescue mission. Or a funeral." He gazed towards the apartment carports with a thoughtful expression.

The body of a man in his late forties lay next to an overturned Kawasaki 450 motorcycle. He had been virtually torn apart. The only reason Jake was able to tell it had been a male was the beard. The corpse was missing everything from the navel down, and the top of its head from the nose up.

Striding quickly across the gore-splattered asphalt, he righted the bike and began to check it over. Its previous owner had managed to get to it— he'd even inserted the key in the ignition— but had been pulled off and consumed before he could make good his escape. Checking the gas tank, the writer found it to be almost full, and when he turned the key the idiot lights came on, so the battery still had a charge. Considering it worth the risk, he kicked the starter over and the bike sputtered slightly, then came to life.

Jake pulled it over to the others, killed the engine so as not to attract the attention of the dead just yet, and told them his plan. The women would stay with Allen in one of the carports while Jake drew the dead off towards the airport. After he led them away, he'd circle back, join up with them again at the apartments, ditch the Kawasaki, and they'd head for Foster's.

Neither Laurel nor Kat liked his plan at all.

"You shouldn't go alone!" Laurel insisted. "What if you wreck or get surrounded or..."

"Then taking another person would get us *both* killed." Jake checked that he had the extra magazines for the Hammer, then secured his crowbar to the handlebars with a couple of strips of duct tape. He made sure to leave a four inch pull tab on both ends so he could release the weapon quickly if need be.

"Not necessarily. A passenger could keep them at bay if you get cut off and need to look for an escape route." Kat watched their surroundings from beside the Jeep.

"*No.* I'm risking my own ass here, no one else's," he insisted. "Al, move into one of these carports. If any of those bastards find you, take off. Otherwise, I should only be about thirty minutes. Stay hidden, stay quiet and stay alert. Be back soon. I hope."

Then he kicked the bike to life again, dropped it into gear, and headed for the street.

Jake disappeared around the building as Maggie and Kat took positions in opposite carports. That way they could see both sides of the complex and watch each other's backs from their hiding places. Laurel and Allen stayed in the Jeep with the girls, just in case they all had to make a hasty getaway.

Laurel looked worriedly north, checking for zombies. "He'll be fine. Right?"

"He's careful, and these things are damn stupid. At least from what we've seen," Allen said.

They sat in the Jeep, sweating quietly for a minute or two, before she spoke again.

"You didn't answer my question."

Allen remained silent.

* * *

Jake's plan worked flawlessly up to a point.

He shot through the wrecked gas station, avoiding the spilled petrol, hoping all the while this little side trip wasn't going to end up with him splattered across the hood of an abandoned Ford.

Or eaten. He'd *really* rather not be eaten.

As he jumped the curb, the bike's engine drew every set of piss-yellow dead eyes in the intersection. Almost in unison, two hundred rotting jaws dropped open and began howling out their only desire: to find out what his flesh tasted like. Their gurgling moans chilled him. The thick, guttural cries sent awful thrills of fear from the base of his spine to the primitive portion of his brain, which made bringing the motorcycle to a halt one of the hardest things he'd ever done.

The dead were seventy yards distant. He didn't want to waste any time getting on and off the bike, so Jake parked it on the double yellow lines, front wheel pointed away from the dead at a ninety degree angle. He pulled the Hammer, sighted on the nearest ones, and started firing. He dropped nine out of the first eleven he targeted, holstered the enormous pistol, turned the motorcycle, and sped another hundred yards north. Then he stopped again and repeated the process.

The ghouls that were mobile followed. A few had broken or even missing legs, so they merely continued banging impotently on the sides of the SWAT truck.

He drew them for a mile, leading the dead beneath the railroad overpass and up the hill, before bagging it. Turning west down the access road bordering the south side of the airport, Jake fled. The creatures continued following his shrinking form, hopelessly outdistanced, but lacking the mental capacity to realize said fact.

Just before turning south to Broad, he noticed chunks of pavement kicking up in front of the bike's front wheel.

What the hell? Jake thought. *Those look like...*

The driver's window of a Prelude, a dozen yards ahead and to his left, exploded inward.

He couldn't hear the weapon discharge over the sound of the wind and the 450's engine, but it was pretty clear someone was trying to put a bullet in him. The road was free of obstructions, so Jake opened the throttle wide. The shots had to be coming from one of the hangars to his right, behind the airport fence, so he didn't waste any time zigzagging and concentrated on speed. More rounds peppered the street behind him as he cornered the bike at the first intersection and flew out of sight behind an equipment supply warehouse.

A minute later, still shaking, he slowed the bike and turned onto Broad. He knew with everything that had happened over the last day, crazies were a real possibility. Having it confirmed though scared the shit out of him. In less than twenty-four hours, people had begun to revert to barbarism. Frightened and desperate, many would be equally, if not *more* dangerous than the repulsive creatures now hunting them. They would have to be very careful of both from now on.

Jake paused to scan the intersection half a mile distant before moving to retrieve his people. Other than the odd crippled ghoul, there were only two that hadn't followed him north. He moved cautiously into the complex, using the buildings as cover when he killed the motorcycle's engine and coasted forward. If the others had to bug out, there was no need to advertise his presence to every creature within earshot. He removed his crowbar from the bikes steering column and began walking quietly toward the lot's far end. Halfway down the row, Kat and Maggie stepped out from opposite carports and began waving at him, both wearing expressions of relief. Kat beamed at him, shotgun in one hand with the other on her hip, showing off her flat stomach under her belly shirt.

"We were getting worried there, hero," she said. "You were

gone almost forty-five minutes. A little longer and we'd have come looking for you."

"That would've been a bad idea." He pulled a smoke out of his Tac vest and put it between his lips, but when he tried to light it he couldn't keep his hands steady. He was getting dizzy too.

What's wrong with me? He thought. *I shouldn't...*

The next thing Jake knew he was sitting under the carport, his back resting against the Beast's front passenger wheel. Laurel was against his one side, Kat the other, and Maggie was kneeling before him, holding his chin as she shone a pen light in his eyes.

"Follow my finger." She released his chin and moved her index finger from side to side in front of his face.

Jake did as he was told, groggily.

"Drink some of this." Laurel pressed a bottle of water she'd retrieved from the Jeep to his lips. "Not too fast."

It was warm, but the liquid felt good going down his scratchy throat. After a few sips, Laurel took the bottle away and recapped it. Maggie pressed two fingers to the side of his neck while she looked at her watch.

"Pulse is normal again. Give it a minute and we'll help you into the bed."

"I'm alright." Jake said. "I was just dizzy."

"You were going into shock," Maggie told him. "Not surprising, considering all that's happened today. Where's your ride?"

"Later." He levered himself unsteadily to his feet. "We need to move before any more of those things come calling."

As if on cue, a chorus of low moans emanated from just around the apartments to the west. A haggard looking man stumbled into view, pursued by five zombies. He bled from several wounds at the creatures' hands and a large chunk was missing from the meat of his upper bicep. He was concentrating on looking over his shoulder, so he didn't notice the dumpster in his path, literally running headlong into it. The impact against the steel knocked him from his feet, then the infected were on him.

Jake pulled his pistol and motioned the others into the Jeep.

"We're not going to help him?" Maggie demanded.

"There's nothing we can do."

"We don't know that!"

He looked at her calmly. "*Zombies.*"

The blonde EMT had no illusions about what happened if one of the things sank its teeth into you.

Jake put a hand on her arm. "Even if we managed to save him now, soon one of us would have to take care of him or he'd *turn.*"

Maggie looked at the struggling dog-pile again, then

reluctantly allowed him to pull her to the vehicle.

The creatures looked up as Allen brought the Beast to life, but disregarded the survivors as they sped away and returned to their meal.

Laurel checked the intersection with Jake's binoculars, ignoring his protests that he really was fine. His shaking hands told her otherwise. After she deemed it clear, Allen pulled out onto the street. He ran over the crippled ghouls and Laurel dropped the remaining two with impressively placed shots to their frontal lobes. The redhead hopped out quickly, peered through the window on the top-most door of the SWAT van, and her face paled. She hurried back to her seat next to Jake in the bed.

"Two inside. They've turned," she said, shortly.

Allen said nothing and put the Beast in gear.

They continued east.

* * *

The end of their return trip was uneventful, with the exception of Kat shooting a zombie who reminded her of her boss.

That prompted Maggie to request she shoot one that looked like *her* boss.

Jake finally had to switch places with Laurel's friend, just to be safe. In retaliation, Kat made sure she fell against him while they changed places, as Allen swerved to avoid an abandoned bus. Jake tipped backwards over Maggie and Karen's legs, finally coming to rest against the tailgate, one hand pinned behind his spine. His other had reached out as he fell and ended very high up on Laurel's inner thigh. He would've been sufficiently embarrassed with that alone but Kat, who'd fallen with him, was straddling his hips, pressing her rack in his face. Literally.

"Oops. How clumsy of me." She scooted back along his legs and pulled away.

Jake was about to tell her to stop screwing around when Laurel coughed mildly. He looked at her and she flicked her eyes at his hand, which was only a couple of inches from the crotch of her leather pants.

"Sorry!" Face flaming, he snatched his hand away.

There were giggle fits from the girls, which he pointedly ignored, as he assumed the co-pilot seat.

They entered the alley leading to the enclosed lot at the rear of Jake's building and were stunned by the number of dead that lay scattered at its mouth.

"What the *hell*..." Allen stared at the two dozen corpses, all

KEEP YOUR CROWBAR HANDY

missing large portions of their heads. There was blood and brain matter smeared across the walls of the buildings for a good twenty-five yards, beginning about ten feet down the grungy pavement. "Someone blew the living *crap* out of these things."

Karen kept her face averted, eyes locked on the backpacks. Kat hefted the shotgun (Jake had given it back to her because she pouted), looking back the way they'd come along with Laurel, Desert Eagle ready, and Maggie who held her trusty ax.

Jake stood and looked up at the roof of the carports. "I'll be damned. That sneaky old bastard."

Allen followed his gaze and saw George Foster rise from the garage roof. He walked to the edge, slid down the ladder attached to its center support and unlocked the gate. Al revved the engine, four-wheeled over the bodies in the alley, and the Beast growled into the resident lot. They all breathed sighs of relief when George cranked the steel gate closed and threw its locking bars shut. Jake hadn't understood why Foster previously insisted on a twelve foot wall with a solid steel gate when the contractor told him it would double the cost, but right now he was thankful for it.

Foster was lugging a silenced Heckler and Koch Long-Arm sniper rifle, complete with a large capacity magazine. The writer had seen them used with great success by three snipers in the SAS brick he'd shadowed. The Long-Arm was dead accurate at distances up to eleven hundred yards, and could deliver enough punch to send a Teflon-tipped round through the engine block of a truck.

"Made better time than I thought ya would," the grizzled chief said.

"I thought you only had the three guns?" Jake helped the girls out of the bed and lowered the tailgate so they could grab their bags, after Maggie half-carried the limping Heather down.

"I said I only had the three *handy*. 'Sides, looks like ya did alright. I can smell the cordite on yer clothes." George pulled out a Cuban and used a wooden match that he scraped down his *cheek* to light it. He looked at Maggie and the girls, grinning around his stogie. "Startin' a harem? Thought you were only goin' after *one* girl."

"We saw them running from a group of those things a few miles back," Jake replied, as Foster led them into the lobby.

George nodded. "Good work, kid."

"Not to break up the male bonding," Maggie said—she still had Heather in one arm and her ax in the other—"but we need somewhere to take five, check the girl's ankle, hide from the zombies. That kind of thing. What floor are we staying on?"

"Don't bother with that." Foster waved towards the elevator. "Shut it down. If there's anything you need at your place, O'Connor, grab it and get your butt back down here. Meet us in my office."

Jake gave him a wry look. "I think we need somewhere a little more secure than that, Chief. We should..."

George exhaled a cloud of smoke. "I got a panic room."

"I should've *known*." The writer wasn't surprised. "Is it big enough for all of us? I still have to get Gertrude."

"Already there, boyo," Foster said. "While you were out doin' the hero thing, I packed her up and got her in. I don't *think* those things can get through the front doors, but I'd feel a whole lot better with us nice an' safe in my little bolt hole. Take the stairs and don't lolly-gag. Cept for us, there's nobody left in the building."

"Alright," Jake sighed, "follow the Chief here and nobody wander off. I'll just be a minute, then we'll head into his bomb shelter."

He made for the stairwell. The stress was beginning to catch up with him. Jake was running on adrenalin, and the crash was sure to come at any time, so he had to be quick. As he started up the stairs, Laurel caught the door before it shut and fell in step beside him.

"I don't mind the company, but you can stay with the others if you'd like. I'm just going to grab a couple things."

"Hey, this could be the only chance I get to evaluate *your* place," she said, with a smile. "You got to see mine. It's only fair."

He chuckled and started up again. "Just so you know, I don't have any battle axes on my walls. It might be a little disappointing."

They climbed to the fourth floor and Jake unlocked his apartment, sticking his head in for a quick look around before holding the door for her. Even though George said everyone had left, you just never knew.

"If you want something from the kitchen, go for it. I'll be quick." He hurried into the bedroom, grabbed his extra pack, then shoved some clothes and sundries inside. He also added three thick blank journals and a pack of ballpoints. If they managed to survive, it might be important to have a record of their actions—to keep them out of prison if for no other reason. Jake took the photo of himself, his brother, and parents out of its frame and stuck it in his the bag as well, then gazed about.

There was nothing else, really. The unfinished cookbook he was reviewing, a few awards, a bed, the SAS foot locker they'd issued him on his first day. Things that were important in everyday life, now useless junk. Not much to show for twenty-eight years of life, but then Jake had never been one to accumulate possessions. He only kept or bought what was useful and left the bric-a-brac. He occasionally wondered if that was thriftiness, or if he just couldn't decide what he wanted.

Laurel looked through his CD collection as he packed. Jake had many of the artists she enjoyed herself. The Young Dubliners, U2, The Chieftains, Loreena McKennitt, The Ramones, The Clash, The Sex Pistols, Butch Walker, and several collections from various bagpipe and pipe artists.

She began to wander about the room, taking in the things with which he surrounded himself. There was a distinct absence of the normal guy toys. Jake's furniture was older, but well maintained. There was a comfortable couch facing the bay window, not the TV, which told her he didn't like to sit in front of it mindlessly for hours watching sports. There was a serviceable PC and writing desk against the wall, which also held a plaque mounted photo of Jake with a military unit. She read the inscription. *To Jake O'Connor, one bloody brave wanker. From: the Boys. Cheers, mate!*

There was no glitz or glam. With the exception of the TV and a game system, Jake's home was steeped in culture. One whole wall was lined with bookshelves and she read the spines. *The Art of War, The Celtic World, Cuculian, The Hound's Tale, The Tempest, Containing the Beast: Way of the Open Palm and the Closed Fist, The Tao of Jeet Kun Do.* Sir Thomas Malory's *Le Morte d'Arthur* was on the first shelf. There were more. Authors like Plato, Yeats, Keats, Frost, Green, Cook, Tolkien, Brooks, Bourne, Monchinski... the list went on and on.

There were also photos of what people called fairy rings in both England and Ireland. Charcoal rubbings of stones with knot-work twining in hypnotic shapes, and a small rock from the slopes of Mt. Tara. Jake had made a real effort to know his heritage. He tried to connect with the past, just as she did with the songs she loved and the music she played. Laurel smiled.

Then she looked outside. She was still gazing out the window when he returned.

"Hey." Jake strode from the back room, bags in hand. "I'm all set here."

He looks wiped. She thought. *No sleep for almost two days, fighting those things to make sure I was alright. Doing it again to get us all to safety...*

"What's wrong?" He dropped his bags by the door and strode

to the window where she stood.

"What could be wrong? People killing each other, zombies everywhere, running for our lives. Oh gods." Laurel put her face in her hands. He'd seen through a lot in the last thirty-six hours, and she didn't want to add watching her cry to the list.

Jake put his arms around her shoulders and held her.

She drew back so she could see his face. "I never thanked you."

"For what?"

"Coming for me. Trying to protect me. My hero."

Jake knew differently. He was just a hack-writer who knew a little bit about survival. He was a fraud. A fake. Otherwise he'd be able to keep her alive and, right now, he didn't have the first fucking clue how to do that.

"Laurel, I don't know what the hell I'm doing. Everything so far has just been dumb luck. I was ready to try to reach you alone if Kat and Allen hadn't come with me. I'd never have made it. I wouldn't have been able to help Maggie and Karen and Heather and..." He looked away from her. "I thought you might be dead. It scared the hell out of me. More than those fucking *things* outside do."

Laurel took him by the chin and turned him back to face her.

"You came. It doesn't matter that you were scared." She held his face in her hands, much as Kat had when he told them his lunatic plan to cross a city full of walking corpses. "Do you *really* think heroes don't get scared? They're no braver than any other person, Jake. They're just brave for one second longer."

"I'm not a hero."

She gave him a lop-sided smile, kissed him lightly, and picked up his half empty duffel bag while he shouldered his pack. As they walked into the hall, Jake started to pull the door shut, then reconsidered. He tossed the key on the floor inside the doorjamb then turned away. If someone wanted the few items he'd left, they could have them.

Besides, he thought, *it's not like I'll get my security deposit back.*

Down in the lobby Foster waited, leaning against a column, enjoying his Cuban, and whistling tunelessly. When they exited the stairwell, he pushed off and waved them towards his office.

"The others are settled." He locked the door to the small, no-frills room. It held only a desk, two uncomfortable looking chairs, and four industrial filing cabinets that lined the entire right wall. "Got everything?"

Jake nodded.

George opened the bottom drawer on the nearest cabinet,

reached inside, and pulled on something in the space behind. There was an audible click and the center cabinet swung away from the wall smoothly, revealing an entrance to the warehouse next door.

"Watch yer heads," he told them.

The ugly warehouse had been vacant for almost thirty years. It was a cinder block job with sheets of plywood over the windows on the first and second floor. There was a gap about four inches wide between it and the other building that Foster owned, and Jake could barely make out the deli across the street as the three of them hunched down to shuffle quickly through. A thick steel plate, recessed a good four feet on each side (as far as he could tell,) sat between the double rows of blocks that made up its four-foot thick walls. He also noticed a deep groove in the floor that would allow the plate to fall into the foundation, effectively sealing the wall against anything short of a wrecking ball.

He followed Laurel's shapely posterior through, feeling a little better as she threw a knowing glance at him over her shoulder and stood up slowly, exaggerating the sway of her hips. Foster came through with a grunt as his knees twinged from stooping, pulled a lever on the wall, and the plate came down causing vibrations to roll up through their feet.

"Welcome to *Casa de* Foster." George reached into the full-size fridge next to the door, tossed them each a Guinness, and pulled one out for himself. "Make yourselves at home."

The first thing Jake noticed was that the ground and second floor windows were fakes. The reinforced inner walls covered them completely. Iron girders above had been coated against corrosion and the ceiling, which was free of rot, was broken only by stairs running up the back wall. The lower level was split into two parts. One was a machine shop complete with power tools, workbenches, and supplies for making reloads for various weapons, the other was a storage space and workout room.

The second (really the third) floor, Foster told them, was a large common room with a couple of weight benches, a nautilus gym, three treadmills, am actual pinball machine, some couches, a huge flat-screen hooked to a Bose sound system, about a thousand DVDs, a full kitchen with propane stoves fed from tanks in the garage, four refrigerators, and an office/security room complete with a short-wave set up, satellite Internet connection, and a large map of North America on the wall. There were short hallways leading to the stairs up to the third floor, which Jake recognized as choke points since they turned sharply with the outer walls.

"The top is a block of a dozen suites," George said, causing them both to stare at him wide eyed. Taking the building's size into consideration, that made them roughly three times the size of an average hotel room. "The bathrooms and showers are both at the end of the hall. Each can hold six at a time, and the roof access is through the back hallway around the far showers."

Jake was impressed. And stunned. "What the *hell*, Chief? When did you do all of this?"

"Started during the cold war. Used it as a jump off point for a few domestic operations, if ya get my meaning. Not that national security matters a pinch of now... The teams helped me fix it up 'bout ten years ago." He gave Jake a raised eyebrow. "What? You didn't *really* think I slept in the basement, did you?"

"Yeah! Everyone did."

Foster gave him a pitying look. "You think that bozo in Dallas shot Kennedy too? I thought ya were a journalist, kid. Jeez. Come on; let's go upstairs."

They went up the iron steps to the second floor, Jake and Laurel carrying their bags and still unopened lagers. He was so distracted by Foster's revelation that he didn't notice Laurel behind him, looking at the way *his* butt moved as he walked. She wouldn't admit it out loud, but Kat had been right. Jake had a cute butt.

The trio came up into the large common room to see the others scattered around the TV. CNN was showing images the FCC would pitch a hissy fit over if any of them were actually still in their offices and not running for their lives.

Maggie was rooting in one of the refrigerators with Kat, while Karen sat quietly on one of the stools next to the lunch-counter-sized, bar-topped, half-wall that separated the kitchen from the common area. Heather was lying on one of the couches with a bag of ice on her swollen ankle. Opposite her, Gertrude Jennings sat sipping tea from a large mug, chatting with Allen.

Jake went down on one knee beside the couch and took her hand. "How are you holding up?"

"Much better than you, it seems." She patted his arm and gave him a worried gaze. "You look done in. When did you last eat? Or sleep for that matter?"

He rubbed his eyes. "Seems like forever. I haven't had the chance for either since my oh-so-brilliant plan to see what the zombies on Broad Street were up too."

"Allen's been telling me about that," Gertrude said. "Who's this?"

Laurel had come to stand behind Jake as he knelt. "I'm the girl *this* one almost got himself killed over. I haven't decided whether or not to forgive him for that just yet. Laurel St. Clair, ma'am."

Gertrude took her hand and smiled enthusiastically. "I am *so* happy to meet you, Laurel. And call me Gertie. What happened to bring you here?"

She shrugged. "Well, I was all set to make a run for it, then this knight showed up in creaky white armor and started slaying dragons left and right, poor things. I had to promise to go back to his castle with him, just so he'd leave a few of them alive."

Gertie smiled fondly at Jake and patted his cheek with her tiny hand. "Yes, I think I might have run into that fellow a time or two myself. Brave as anything, but not very bright."

"I've noticed that." Laurel said.

"Oh I *like* her." Gertrude motioned Laurel to sit beside her. "Come, dear, you have to tell me how the two of you met. Jake, go get yourself something to eat and sit down. You're as pale as a sheet, and if you pass out you'll make an *awful* racket as you hit the floor."

He knew better than to argue, so as the women destroyed his reputation, he made for the kitchen. Jake was almost drooling with hunger as he pulled some lunch-meat and bread for a sandwich from the fridge. Kat and Maggie were occupied in a hot pepper eating contest, both of their faces beet red, laughing at each other as they consumed little agony bombs straight from the jar.

Jake smeared some horseradish mustard on his pastrami sandwich, then started feeding his face. Maybe it was the fact he hadn't eaten since the afternoon prior, but it tasted like heaven.

Allen sidled over as he finished, wearing a strange expression. "Jake, we should talk." All traces of humor absent from Al's normally light tone.

"Give me a minute here." Jake washed the remnants of the sandwich down with a swallow of Guinness. He drank about a third of it and then pressed the chilly bottle to his aching head. "I can't believe we made it."

Allen looked at the stairs leading up to the fourth floor apprehensively. "Yeah, that's one for the record books. Look there's something..."

"Can you *believe* this, Al? Zombies. Who would've thought? And George! This place! I should've *known*..." Jake couldn't register anything except how good the frost covered beer felt against his forehead. "I have to say, pal-o-mine, I never saw zombies coming. Personally, I would've picked global warming or ozone depletion..."

"Jake, really, I've got to tell you..."

"Or a super-virus. Or aliens!" Jake shook his head. "Giant, super-intelligent, highly-evolved, space badgers or something."

"That's great, but seriously, you..."

"I'm telling you, I don't know how things could get *any* worse."

"Jake!"

They both turned to see a blonde bombshell straight out of a lonely man's wet dream. She'd followed George and a couple other new faces down from the fourth floor. In another setting, she'd be enough to arouse a dead stick. The right shaped parts crammed inside a painted on pair of jeans, a strapless push-up style bra showing under a pitiful excuse for a baby-doll tank, all topped by a wreath of wild honey-blonde hair. Even looking frazzled and half out of her mind with fear, she projected an aura of raw sex.

"They're worse." Allen closed his eyes.

The blonde ran towards Jake and tried to throw herself into his arms. Instead, he caught her by the shoulders and held her back, wearing an expression of utter horror.

I don't know how things could get any worse, his back-brain mocked. *What are you? Retarded? Did you really think you could say something like that, out loud, and the fates wouldn't take it as a challenge? You dumb-ass.*

"Who is that?" Laurel asked Mrs. Jennings in a whisper.

"That *awful* creature is Jake's ex-girlfriend," Gertie said, with a sniff of disdain. "He ended it with her over six months ago and was *very* glad for it. He wouldn't want anything to do with her again if the alternative was a monastery."

The blonde finally stopped trying to wrap herself around him and Jake stepped away a couple of paces.

When he spoke, even Maggie and the hard-headed George Foster caught the chill in his voice.

"Hello, Nichole. What are you doing here?"

* * *

The city was done screaming. Now, it burned.

Stoves left on when the wealthy elite left their homes—because their servants had abandoned them—started house fires. Thick columns of black smoke plumed into the clear May sky. Flames, fanned by the winds, raced towards the now blood-drenched campus and empty dormitories. In a matter of minutes, the stadium where enthusiastic cries of 'Oh! Aich! Eye! Oh!' had been chanted on game days became a roaring furnace of hot, glowing steel.

The dead didn't pay it any notice.

They shuffled through the flames, hundreds burning down and finally falling to the concrete, truly dead this time. Others exited the fires resembling used up matchsticks, charred and crisped like burnt paper. These were little more than blackened skeletons bereft of even sexual characteristics and, in many cases, with their clothes fused to their blackened bones.

It didn't matter how many were cremated by the awful heat, there were more. So many more. The dead were coming close to outnumbering the living across the globe and millions fled cities from Plano to Paris. The ones that couldn't, or wouldn't flee, began to barricade themselves within their homes. Some tried to get to government buildings. People fled to havens like police stations or courthouses, seeking shelter from the moaning horrors. The few, who survived their harrowing journey, huddled together behind oaken doors and barred windows, hoping for the authorities to save their collective asses.

Not realizing the authorities couldn't even save their own...

CHAPTER EIGHT

Three weeks later Jake was ready to commit suicide. Or homicide.

He worked the heavy-bag near the common room's north corner, wearing nothing but a pair of sweat pants and hand wraps, trying his best to make the leather-sleeved sack of sawdust and sand say uncle. Maggie lay on the weight bench close by, pressing about two hundred and fifty pounds for the eighth time, while Allen exercised his eyes spotting her. Kat stretched on her yoga pad not far from Laurel and the soft-spoken Karen, both on the treadmills working out the kinks. Unlike Maggie, who wore a tank top, boots, and a pair of army-issue pants, they were in the tights and sports bras Kat had stuffed in her pack on the day of the outbreak.

The sight of Laurel, skin glistening, her breasts pushed high and breathing heavily, did little but feed his aggravation. They'd had precious little time together since the steel plate had come down and sealed them all inside Foster's bolt hole.

As a group, they decided to split watching the monitors George had connected to the warehouse's exterior security cameras into four-hour shifts. That meant *everyone* had to take a turn, which pleased the ever-more abrasive Nichole to no end. They divided their time between monitor watching, checking their supplies, inventorying Foster's *more* than impressive armory and desperately trying to glean some small bit of information from the outside world.

However, the only things broadcast on TV anymore were the occasional talking heads with bad scripts and automated public service announcements. The Internet slowed further every day as servers went down and the people manning the infrastructure died by the thousands. But they kept trying, hoping for some tidbit of information on possible aid or rescue. They spent fruitless hours trying to contact other survivors via shortwave radio. Those who had families rarely spoke of them, but they did try to search for them via the web. All of these things left their days rather full, if not terribly stimulating. But none of these issues were bothering Jake very much.

What did piss him off was that every time it seemed he and Laurel were beginning to get close, Nichole would appear and make unwanted advances. That always caused the redhead to cool off quickly. He was losing patience with his blonde ex at an *accelerated* rate.

"So what's the word on Chicago?" Maggie dropped the bar she'd been pressing into the cradles and sat up. Allen found her quite attractive. In a barbarian sort of way. Muscles rippled as she worked the stress out of her shoulders, causing him to have a flash of said shoulders holding her up as the two of them lay on fur sheets. Like Mrs. Schwarzenegger.

"George's friend on the short wave said the military is continuing to pull west. They're retreating, trying to build up a rally point, but the zombies aren't giving them time. The things don't sleep, so they just keep stumbling on and on after them." Allen shook his head. "They're trying to fight them like they would another army and that just won't work."

"Why not?" Kat folded herself in half at the waist, one leg straight on the ground in front, and the other stretched out behind, as she grasped her lead heel with both hands and sank horizontally to the floor.

"No command structure." He shrugged. "They don't have any organization. They don't feel fear or pain. *Shock and Awe* be damned... might as well be throwing spitballs at a bulldozer. It doesn't matter how many of them you kill, the others will just keep coming. Makes it tough for the living to stop and rest, let alone win a fight."

I hate this, Jake thought. His wrapped fists beat a staccato on the bag and it started to indent with the force of his blows.

"Are they planning to send any help?" Maggie asked.

Allen shook his head. "Nothing yet. Mostly people have headed away from the cities, trying to find safety. There's one group in Montana that's doing pretty good, another in the Black Hills and some in Texas...a few in Canada. Other than that, it's just a bunch of isolated people, trying to hold out."

I hate this. I fucking hate this. Jake's blows were coming faster now and the bottom of the bag was beginning to lean away. He ignored the first twinges from his hands and really started to lay into his strikes.

Laurel and Karen slowed their treadmills and started to cool down, but Kat kept at it on the mat. She was able to run for over eight miles now anyway, so she concentrated on stretching. Lots of people built their bodies, spent thousands of hours making themselves look good, but they didn't possess the ability to scratch their own backs because they were so inflexible. Besides, with Maggie around, she was going to stay in top shape.

That wasn't fair really, she thought. The blonde woman was honest, open, and extremely nice. But that didn't change the fact that the girl was *stacked* in front.

"So we're stuck for a while," Laurel huffed, still walking, hands behind her head, bringing some guns of her own into play.

"Looks like, and who... knows..." Allen trailed off, looking from face to face. The others were staring at something behind him. He realized he was hearing the sounds of meaty impacts and turned.

Hatethis!Hatethis!Hatethis!Hatethis!Hatethist!Hate...The bag was tilting up at an angle. Jake's hands were a blur as he landed blow after blow, sending little puffs of sawdust into the air. His face was drawn up into a snarl of animal fury. His eyes were wild, as he tried to shove his fists through the bag and into the wall beyond.

"Jake... *Jake*!" Kat yelled.

"What?" he exclaimed, turning.

"Are you alright?" she asked.

He blinked a few times as reality imposed itself into his eyes again and he straightened up from his predatory crouch. "Yeah, I'm good...why?" He turned his head, giving each of them questioning looks.

"You went a little... odd... there for a minute," Maggie said.

Jake looked around the group. "Don't know what you're talking about."

Kat rose from the mat. "Alright. Enough pulping that helpless bag, killer. Time for your daily beating."

"You want to skip it today, Kat? I was thinking..."

"You need to practice *every day* or you lose your edge," she said peevishly. "*You're* the one who wanted to have these sessions. *You're* the one who said you were getting rusty. *You're*..."

"Okay, okay!" Jake said in defeat. "You win."

"Good," Kat said brightly, "I like to win. Karen? Can you come get us in an hour if we're still at it?"

The girl nodded sheepishly and gave her a thumbs-up.

"You'll realize that trying to talk her out of something is pointless. Eventually," Laurel sipped her water, "I'm going to have a shower and go roof side for a while. I'm starting to feel like a mushroom cooped up in here. Want to come with, Mags?"

The blonde EMT did another ten reps and set the weights down again with a clang. "Sure. I'm done. I'm not due to relieve Foster for another two hours for camera watch. Let me grab a pair of scissors and cut myself a top."

Laurel's brow furrowed in confusion. "Why?"

Maggie looked at her, stunned. "You're going to go nude?"

"Sure. Rooftop, four stories up, abandoned city...who's going to see us?"

The blonde thought about that for a moment. "Good point."

Jake's eyebrows rose and Allen waggled his own.

"Don't even think about it," Maggie told them.

Jake toweled the sweat from his face just as Mike Barron came down to get himself a beer. The writer kept his eyes averted, hoping Mike would just go away, so of course he made a beeline for their group.

The too-pretty clubber had climbed a rear gate to get away from zombies, who'd followed him from the overdone and now useless Mitsubishi street racer he'd totaled. After swerving around an ambulance, Mike had wrapped the front end around a light pole. He almost matched Jake in size, but lacked anything resembling grit, had a face like an evil cherub, and the standard line of memorized catch phrases to go with it. His frame was a little skinny, but like Allen he was fit in an understated way. He wore his shirts either half open or with only the bottom button done up to show off his great tan and Egyptian hieroglyph tattoo, just under his navel.

Jake couldn't stand him. His dislike for the man stemmed from the fact that Mike was an unscrupulous, pussy-hound. He hit on everything with a heartbeat, including Laurel, and he didn't like the way the guy looked at eighteen-year-old, Karen one bit. If it hadn't been for the fact that Mike did the same thing to Maggie, and even tried to flirt jokingly with Gertrude, Jake would've politely asked him to turn down the charm ray a few notches.

With something heavy and blunt.

"How ya doing, O'Connor?" Mike took a sip of his beer after pulling it from the fridge, looking curiously at Jake's hands.

"I got bored with my current career and took a job as a meat tenderizer."

Mike thought about that for a moment. "Going well, I take it?"

"It has its moments." He glowered.

"I heard something about gettin' a little sun before it goes down?" He gave Laurel what he thought was a compelling look and a winning smile. It would've worked better if his eyes hadn't been glued to her breasts. "How about it, Red? Want some company?"

Jake seethed inside and put another black mark next to the man's name on the list he carried in his head.

Laurel managed to keep the revulsion out of her voice when she answered. "No thanks."

Mike knew better than to ask Kat. Especially with her smiling at him in a truly evil way.

"Ah well, another time then."

Jake had visions of murder.

"How about you She-Ra?"

"I've asked you *not* to call me that." Maggie cracked every one of her knuckles twice for effect, which was lost completely against the side of Barron's thick skull. "Next time you do? I'll tie your package in a knot."

Mike smiled and made his way upstairs again, for which Jake was very grateful. He'd been fighting the urge to strangle the son of a bitch.

"You know, that guy has to be why some animals eat their young," Kat said. "They're trying to keep the *asshole* chromosome out of the gene pool."

She and Jake headed down to the Rumble Room. They passed through the machine shop Foster had turned the first level into and entered the thirty-by-thirty expanse. Two-inch thick Olympic mats covered the floor and the far wall was lined with mirrors. A variety of weapons, from kendo swords to knives to billy clubs hung on racks, but they weren't using any of those today. Today was all hand-to-hand.

"Don't worry. I promise I won't hurt you. Much." Kat gave him her crazy raised eyebrow, after tossing her towel and water bottle to the floor.

Jake chuckled and pulled his shirt off over his head.

They stretched briefly, centering themselves, then bowed to one another and took up fighting stances. Kat enjoyed fluid movements, techniques that combined redirection of force, along with swift, knife-sharp strikes, gymnast-level vaults, and kicks that seemed to defy natural laws. Like gravity. A lifetime of practicing both aikido and kung fu had provided her a natural grace, along with a sense of balance second to none.

While Kat was a stinging whip, Jake was the razor fist. He'd taken half a dozen different martial arts, at one time or another, since the age of thirteen. Most recently, he'd studied Krav Maga for two years, during his time with the SAS. He'd learned to do brutal, painful things to people. How to break bones almost effortlessly. How to internally rip flesh, crush throats, and drive someone's nose into their brain with his bare hands.

They squared off moving slowly, circling, looking for holes in the other's defenses. Feet gliding over the mat, hands never still, weaving patterns, changing in preparation of deadly games.

"So how are you and Allen doing?" Jake asked.

"We decided to cool it."

He blinked. "What?"

She shot forward with a series of blurring open-handed strikes, aiming for his throat and eyes. He blocked each one and answered with back-hands and elbows, which she avoided by dancing out of the way. As she did, Kat dropped low and swept his legs. Jake rolled across the mat and came to his feet, guard up.

"That's my point," She said, sweetly.

He nodded. "I can't believe it. What happened?"

"We just didn't have much to talk about," Kat admitted. "Sex is nice, but we really had nothing else in common."

She advanced again and he ducked her flying hatchet kick, moving to the outside.

"Damn, Kat. I'm sorry." A wry expression moved over his face. "You know, I realized Al could be a little flaky, but I didn't know he was an idiot."

"How so?" Kat asked.

"Personally? I'd have *found* something to talk about."

He was a little distracted as he moved left and switched his guard, so he didn't catch what his subconscious caused his mouth to say.

She smiled dazzlingly. "I'll keep that in mind." Then he had to block her knife-edged chop that would've broken his collarbone. Jake caught Kat's arm as she followed through (just an inch or two more than she should have,) spun to the outside, extended his inner leg, and tossed her from her feet, using a classic hip throw.

Instead of tumbling over the padded floor, she hit the ground palm first and in a display of great agility, cartwheeled twice before coming back to her feet, half-way across the room.

"That one's mine," he said, gliding to the right.

"Not bad," she admitted, mirroring his move. "You've improved. It's become really hard to read your body language since we've started these sessions. And why do you say that, by the way?"

"I *was* a little disappointed when we met up at Bueno Dave's, when you and Al hit it off. Luckily, your evil plan was to have Laurel lurking in the wings."

Kat grinned mischievously. "That *was* fun. How are the two of you getting along? Any nocturnal gymnastics?"

Jake avoided her roundhouse kick and circled again. "Um. No."

"Why the hell not?"

"It just... well, it never seems like the right time," he answered.

Then she was coming at him. Jake sent a jab her way, trying to slow her charge, but she passed under it. He managed to avoid the vertical punch she threw at his chin, but never saw the choke hold that followed, as Kat wrapped her arm across and over the back of his neck to come up under his Adam's apple. She jumped, locked her legs around his ribcage, and leaned backwards, taking them to the floor. He was able to break the hold before they hit so he ended up on top, but she managed to immobilize one of his arms with a joint lock. Then Kat's legs began squeezing his ribs. No matter what he tried, he couldn't get a good breath, and he sure as hell wasn't having any luck getting free.

He quickly approached the point of passing out, so he used a trick he'd learned from a brown haired, sexy, crass, and outspoken Major named Molly Beck. At twenty-nine, Molly was in charge of most of the hand-to-hand training courses for her unit, and she'd made his life in Merry Old England a living hell for the first two months. Everything the brick did that required guns, knives, dirt, pain, sweat, sleep deprivation, or any smelly combination thereof, he was required to do right along with them, per her request. After two months of abuse under Molly's watchful eye, he met the physical requirements for a special op journalist consultant and obtained the government's certification to document live action operations.

That night she'd taken his bruised, aching body into account, so they'd only spent most of the night 'Screwing *like lemmings'* as she put it. Earlier that evening, somewhere between the eighth and ninth shot of Bushmills, things got a little jumbled. What had started with her betting him the next round against the number of push-ups they could each do, ended with them tearing at each other like animals in the shower of her loft.

When he'd posed the question of why the next morning, as they lay tangled in the sheets and each other, Molly simply said, "Wot? The girls din't like you back 'ome, then? Their bloody loss mate..."

She also taught him a little trick when it came to fighting opponents of the fairer sex. He resisted, right up to the point where Molly asked if he were stupid enough to believe that all terrorists were men. It didn't sound like such a bad idea when she put it like that.

The secret was, just like a man's testicles, a woman's breasts were *sensitive*. So, just as men instinctively protected their dangly bits...

With unconsciousness looming, Jake used his free hand to grasp Kat's breast and roughly pinched her nipple through her cut-off tee.

The problem was she didn't react quite the way he'd expected. Yes, she gasped in surprise. Yes, she loosened her lock on his arm. Yes, her legs did release their suffocating grip on Jake's torso which allowed him to breathe again.

What he *didn't* expect was for Kat to throw her head back, her eyes to flutter shut, and a lusty moan to force its way from her throat. Jake froze in place as she writhed beneath him, mouth wide in a soundless cry. When her eyes opened, she grabbed him by the back of his neck with one hand and pulled him down into a kiss.

At one time, he thought her to be a runner up when it came to passion, that Laurel had a lock on the throne. The truth was, beneath all the witty quips and one-liners, Kat was a whole new level of heat that rivaled the surface of the sun.

She wrapped her arms around his neck as her thighs slid over his hips, drawing him closer, and she began to make small animal noises under her breath. Her lips were wild, devouring. He was already getting lost in the kiss, so he tried to focus on getting his hand off her boob. She had them locked together so tightly, however, that all he really managed to do was, well... feel her up. Kat shivered and her hips pressed against his groin confirming that: A-he was male and B-he was getting pretty damn aroused despite his convictions.

Jake was running pretty low in the resistance department by now, but even so he realized toying with her feelings would be a *bad* idea. They were all trapped together and emotions were running a little higher than normal. The end of the world would *definitely* be an acceptable argument to have as much wild sex as was humanly possible if you wanted to be honest about it...

The problem was that the two of them were friends. You can't put your back up against someone, fight beside them, trust them with your life, and not develop some kind of bond. He was unsure as to what he thought of Kat. She had a great—if somewhat sarcastic—sense of humor and a quick, analytical mind when the situation called for it. Thanks to her martial arts training, she had proven *more* than capable of being able to take care of herself. She was gorgeous, that went without saying, even after nearly a month without salon-level maintenance, and her hair was growing out into its natural black, which made her look like one of those butt-kicking Anime girls. While that made her extremely appealing, it also told him he'd spent too much of his life watching Anime.

Then there was Laurel. He thought her attraction was based on his genetic predisposition for redheads, being an Irishman and all. He enjoyed her company and was *beyond* frustrated at the lack of time alone with her. Whenever Nichole entered the room, all her walls went up, and Laurel found some reason to be elsewhere. Granted, his ex caused him to want to be somewhere else too. *Anywhere* else. He didn't want Nichole to come between them, but Laurel didn't seem willing to confront the bubble-headed stripper. If she would just take some *initiative*. It was probably the end of the world. If there was ever a time to put the pedal down and toss your hang-ups to the wind this was *definitely* it, but she kept idling in neutral.

Kat didn't seem to have that particular problem.

She rolled them towards the wall and ended up astride him in the classic position. Jake slid his hands up over her lower back, then traced the lines of her ribs below the edge of the cut off shirt. She took his wrists, attempting to pull them upwards under her shirt, but he clasped them against her sides and gently pushed her back until she knelt over him.

"Kat," he managed to croak out through a desert dry throat, "I, uh...I think we should stop."

"I thought you said the two of you hadn't slept together?" She ran her hands over his chest, but he had his second wind now and his conscience was screaming at him. Loudly.

"We haven't. But that doesn't mean I'm going to with anyone *else* because of that fact." Jake attempted to put his thoughts in order. "If I were that kind of guy, we'd both be naked already. If things had gone differently, and I'd never met Laurel, well... I wouldn't hesitate for a second. But she and I are involved. I think. And you're my friend. I trust you the same way I trust Al."

She raised an eyebrow. "Well, that's an image I didn't need."

He blushed. "You know what I mean. If we had sex, I'd call it quits with Laurel, and your friendship would definitely be crippled if not destroyed altogether. Would you really want that?"

Kat remained poised over him silently. She was saved from answering by Foster's voice crackling out of the intercom on the wall. George had installed one in his office, one in the common area, and another in the Rumble Room when the safe house was first used by Black Ops teams in the 1980s. He said it saved a lot of time, not having to trot up and down all those stairs.

"O'Connor? You and that girl, who's probably kickin' yer ass right now, should get up here. There's somethin' you're gonna wanna see out front."

After hesitating for a moment, Kat reached up and hit the button on the squawk box. "Hey, George. We're on the way."

She released the button and sat back on his thighs as he sat up, then put her arms over his shoulders.

"Damn it." She leaned her forehead to his.

"If I were a lesser man..." Jake shrugged.

She kissed him again briefly, then they helped each other to their feet and headed back upstairs. Kat took consolation in the fact that he'd regret not taking advantage of the situation.

* * *

Maggie, Kat, Laurel, and Jake were all gathered in George's office, watching the CCTV monitor. The camera on the front of the building showed a horde of infected, slowly shuffling past their haven, moving east.

There were hundreds of them. Maybe thousands. Jake had a flash of The Who concert he'd attended in Glasgow with Molly. The walking horrors on the screen reminded him of the British crowd, eighty thousand strong, that had cheered their hearts out as Roger and the boys brought the house down with every song. The dead were packed almost shoulder-to-shoulder, surging and flowing between the buildings, as they left gory evidence of their passing. Bloody scraps of cloth from shirts torn on the jagged glass in the shattered display windows of storefronts. Streaks of congealed blood, pus, and other bodily fluids on vehicles and lampposts. Smears of skin and tissue on brickwork where shoulders, arms, and even skulls scraped along their surfaces. They showed wounds of every kind. Cuts, stabbings, bullet holes. Quite a few even wore the blades of their victims still protruding from their unfeeling flesh. Some of them had no eyes. Others had no face. They were missing jaws and throats, missing hands, sometimes entire limbs. Many looked like hollowed out puppets where all but ribs, pelvis, and spine had been consumed, leaving only primitive, anonymous stick-figures.

Their group had been insulated as they'd sheltered in George's safe house, even though they all experienced moments of cabin fever. Every single person currently within their haven had seen the death and horror, but shy of the initial day of the outbreak, only Jake, Foster, and Allen had come into contact with the creatures.

They'd gone to retrieve a few items from the top of George's now abandoned tenement and come face-to-face with five dead, hungry, hungry hippies.

Seeing that Foster had secured the entrances and the lot gate, there was really no way for any of the creatures to gain entry to the building. The three had been relaxed and fairly nonchalant as they trooped up to the eighth floor. Their attitudes had changed abruptly however, when George opened the stairwell door and five pairs of milky yellow eyes turned to focus on them from halfway down the hall.

Four double taps and one swing of a crowbar turned the five fans of cannabis into true *deadheads*. After retrieving a sack full of old spark plugs, a small camp shower, and an old calvary saber (all of which Jake found pretty useless at the time), the three men hurried back down to the hidden entrance and sealed the immense plate behind them again.

Even so, nothing could have prepared them for the exodus of rotting hunger, slowly making its way past their refuge.

Laurel and Maggie had been on the roof when the gristly procession approached, so the sounds of uncountable feet and falling objects had alerted them during their sunbathing. When the two peeked over the roof's rim, they experienced a moment of soul-chilling fear, before quickly grabbing their clothing and silently creeping through the roof's access door together. Evidently Foster had received an eyeful when they rushed into his office, because he kept glancing at the two and chuckling every so often.

"We need to stay out of sight until those things move on. We'll need to keep everyone off the roof for now too. If one of us got spotted..." Jake said, quietly.

George nodded. "Not ta worry. Already secured the door. Got the key in my pocket. Unless some idiot takes some C4 to it, no one's getting up there fer a while."

Over the course of the next hour, the girls found reasons to excuse themselves from the room, and Jake couldn't blame them. What was passing in front of the camera was awful beyond description. Laurel went to help with the group dinner and Maggie headed to check on the solitary Karen. Only Kat remained and when Jake called for Leo to bring Allen into the office, she went upstairs for a shower.

Leo Santos was a seventeen-year-old wiry boy with an affinity for old horror films, books, and anything involving swords. He lived with his stepfather after his mother left them both for a lawyer in Ashville last year, but the two hadn't been close. George had seen him on the street, hacking his way east with a machete, killing the odd zombie here and there, and George bellowed at him from the door of the empty apartment building to get his scrawny ass inside, before it was bitten off.

Jake liked the kid. Leo reminded him of how he and Allen were in high school. Kind of geeky, more interested in girls than football—though Allen was the only one who had any success with them at the time—and generally a nice guy. He was built like a fencer, with muscled wrists and knowledge of edged weaponry that rivaled Kat's.

Jake's friend paled visibly when he saw what was on the screen and sat down in the only other office chair Foster had. The procession continued for another fifteen minutes before finally petering out. Here and there, stray creatures continued to pass on the street. Some of them lost interest in the journey altogether and began to scatter through the neighborhood, into buildings or down alleyways. Many even turned and started back the way they came, eventually moving again into the city center to mill endlessly among the empty skyscrapers.

Foster cracked his neck both ways, then took a healthy swig of his coffee. They sat around the table full of maps and printed satellite images, watching the monitors for a while.

"What do you know Chief?" Jake leaned against the table and crossed his arms.

His stomach fell at George's expression. It reminded him of the one his first martial arts instructor, Frank O'Brian, displayed when he hadn't been practicing his katas enough.

Frank had been an excellent teacher, even though Jake hadn't seen him for almost ten years. Some idiot had crossed the line in a minivan and hit him head on when he was out one day on his Harley. Jake was overseas when it happened and hadn't been able to go to the funeral. He'd gone to Frank's grave sometimes. Before the dead rose that was.

Foster pulled a bottle of Jameson's from his desk drawer, poured some into his mug, then tossed the bottle to Jake. Allen declined with a headshake when his friend offered him a drink, so Jake uncorked it for a big pull himself. If George's expression was any indication, the news was bad.

"The news is bad." Foster settled back in his chair.

Sometimes, things wouldn't go right if you paid them, Jake thought.

"Tell us."

It *was* bad.

After George finished they were all silent for a while.

"Can I have that for a minute?" Allen motioned for the bottle.

His friend gave it over and the mechanic took a drink, then

another, before handing it back to him.

Jake swallowed another mouthful himself and corked it. "What you're saying is that we're on our own."

Allen hung his head, looked at the floor, and then smiled at Jake ruefully. "Figures. You finally meet a really cool girl, then Armageddon comes down the pipe. Man, that *blows*..."

Jake was frowning, his eyes far away. He looked at George and asked, "How long?"

Foster rubbed his chin and considered it. "Water's no problem. The gravity system's good for at least four or five years. The battery bank and solar panels for eight. I've got lots of spare long-life bulb replacements. Plenty of cleaning solutions, most of which can be used as soap and disinfectants in a pinch. Medical kit's in good shape even with the eleven of us. The problem is..."

"Food," Jake said. "We've only got enough for...three more months?"

"Four. If were careful," George confirmed.

"We'd all starve to death long before anyone got to us," Allen said, bitterly. "If they *ever* did."

Jake stared at the materials on the table. The look on his face went thoughtful as he traced the lines from Ohio to the Rockies. Roughly two-thousand miles. Four months of food. A massive assortment of automatic weapons, rifles and ammo. Tools and supplies versus time and numbers.

"We've going to have to save ourselves."

The other two men gaped at him.

"We can make it to the Rockies," he said. "We just need transportation. We avoid population centers, stick to small towns and back roads. With people running for their lives during the outbreak, there's going to be a lot of food still in farmhouses, small town general stores, even gas stations. We could make it."

Allen was looking at him like he'd lost his mind. "Oh, sure!" he said, brimming with false enthusiasm. "We just need an RV to carry us all, a dump truck for the supplies, an armored car for when we have to push our way through the dead with a damn *snowplow* on the front, and oh yeah! A wrecker to move any stalled cars out of the way! Other than that we're fine..."

"Allen we're going to have to find a way," he insisted. "You like Heather, right?"

"Of course I do!" he bristled. "I like everyone here! Well, except for Nichole. And maybe Mike."

"Could you watch her starve to death?"

Allen looked scared for the first time Jake could remember since high school. "No. No, I couldn't do that."

"I won't let that happen to Laurel," Jake said, resolution burning in his eyes. "Or you. Or Kat. Or Gertie."

"So how are we going to get the vehicles? The fuel?" Allen demanded. Jake was right. If they stayed, they'd die. But they could only handle the smallest fraction of the huge numbers of dead that were sure to be still roaming about hungry. Sneaking around, looking for working transportation would take time, and who knew if they'd be found by a group of ghouls, then end up drawing more by fighting them? Granted they were slow and dumb as turnips, but there were so *many.*

Jake pulled out a smoke, lit up, shook his head, and stared into space. Foster fired up one of his stogies and blew some truly impressive smoke rings.

"You know what you're talking about?" Foster laid it out for them. The distance, the probable conditions of the roads, bands of raiders, psychotics, maybe even people that have turned *cannibal* from lack of food and, of course, the ever present threat of the infected. "The two of ya ready to kill, not just zombies, but maybe *living* people who wanna take what you got? Food, weapons, hell... the women? You boys ready ta do that?"

Jake's face was harsh and unforgiving. "I'd do worse. And it wouldn't be the first time I've had to kill. I'll slaughter a path through those shit-bags all the way to the Pacific if it means keeping everyone alive."

Foster turned to Allen. "What about you, son?"

Al picked up the bottle again and took another drink. He sat for a minute, letting the whiskey burn its way down to his stomach.

"Anything," he said, thinking about his family. "I'll do anything."

George nodded slowly then stubbed out his cigar. "Alright. Follow me."

Foster led them down to the ground floor, through the machine shop, and into the storage space beyond. He cranked open an eight by eight, three inch thick, steel door that Jake had thought led outside, to reveal another stairway leading down into a basement level. They followed him down into an echoing, vaulted chamber that seemed to run on forever into the darkness.

Allen looked around nervously. The only dim light came down the stairway from above and his eyes were flicking about the expanse, looking for movement. "Are you sure we're safe down here?"

Foster nodded. "The only way in except for the stairs is covered by a twelve ton steel door. We're good."

Jake was looking off to his left. There was something large there, outside the dim rectangle of light. Try as he might, his mind couldn't make sense of the shape.

"Have you got a couple of tour buses down here?" He asked.

George reached for the wall and flipped on the overheads.

The younger men stood there, jaws slack, shock plain on their faces. Allen's mouth began moving in a fair impression of a goldfish, but no sound came out. Jake recovered more quickly and at that point, little things about the building's sup that had never quite added up before, started making a *lot* more sense.

Foster had fooled them all.

Jake started to smile. "Why you sneaky, lying, *brilliant* old bastard."

Now it was George's turn to smile.

* * *

Tracy Dickson walked along the riverfront.

She would never know that the corpse that had bitten Carl Davis, who had in turn bitten her, was still stuck in the drainage culvert eighty yards to the north. It would remain there until the enormous catfish living in the murky waters of the Scioto eventually picked it clean.

Tracy had been shuffling round and round the Riverfront Mile Fountain all day. Endlessly following the wall...

CHAPTER NINE

Dinner was outstanding.

Maggie let it drop the fact that Karen turned eighteen that day, so they'd planned a celebration. Kat and Laurel had kept her occupied with girl talk in the office, along with ogling some teenage idols on the ever-slowing Internet. They'd taken a case of Coke, a box of chocolate chip cookies, two bags of crackers, some salsa Laurel had made two days prior, and locked themselves in Foster's office with a few chick flicks. Leo baked Karen a cake while Gertrude altered some of Foster's army-issue clothing into a few new outfits for the girl.

Young Salazar had surprised them all by being a damn good cook. He'd considered going to culinary school after graduation that year and had done wonders with the bags and bags of George's dehydrated foodstuffs. He'd even discovered a way to make great eggs out of the normally tasteless powdered egg mix, which previously always reminded Jake of flavorless globs of shower caulk.

"Why chocolate with white frosting?" he asked.

"Karen said she liked it when they served it last year at homecoming." Leo replied, then blushed furiously when Karen gave him one of her rare smiles. He and the pretty brunette had gone to the same high school and knew each other only in passing, but he seemed to remember a great deal about her likes and dislikes. He obviously had a crush on her from the way he went quiet every time she walked into a room. He talked about her endlessly when he, Jake, and Allen repaired their leaking water tank. Even after they asked him emphatically not to.

After the meal, and the truly horrible rendition of 'Happy Birthday" that followed, Kat and Heather went upstairs with the birthday girl to help her try on the newly altered fatigues. Foster retreated to his office again to talk on the shortwave and search the dying Internet for satellite photos of the areas southwest of the city. Leo vanished downstairs to the machine shop, excitedly working on a way to make swords for each of them, just in case. Allen was playing George's game system on the flat screen, having a grand old time blasting unsuspecting aliens into little bits. Nichole sat on the other couch leafing through a Cosmo, making disgusted noises at the models. Jake had convinced Gertrude to sit at the counter with a cup of tea next to Maggie, while he and Laurel did the dishes. The aging woman only took her pain medication every few days since she was trying to conserve her supply, and her hands were bothering her that evening. She only had enough for two months.

Laurel flat-out told Jake she'd deck him if he tried to stick his raw-knuckled hands in dishwater, so he settled for the task of drying them by hand and stacking them in the cupboards. She drained the sink, wiped it down as he put away the last of the forks, then she grabbed two Guinness out of the far fridge. She popped the tops and emptied them into a pair of large mugs.

"I've been meaning to ask you about something." Maggie leaned her chin on her palm and sipped her drink.

"Shoot." He took a swig of the god's own brew

"Allen mentioned you were the *Last of the White Knights*. What did he mean by that?"

"Ah..." He looked uncomfortable. "He was just messing around. You know how Al is."

"Bull feathers," Gertrude mumbled.

The muscular EMT gave him a narrow look and turned to Gertie. "Do you know what he meant?"

"I do. And *shame* on you, Jacob, for being embarrassed over something like that." She put down her tea and ignored him while he cringed. "He was knighted during his time with the SAS."

Maggie's jaw dropped. She rubbernecked back and forth between them. "Really?"

Jake kept his eyes on his beer.

"They were in... where was it again?" Gertrude began.

"Bosnia," he replied, softly.

"Thank you, dear. Bosnia," she continued. "His brick as they called it, we call it a squad, was ambushed by a much larger group and virtually wiped out. Jake helped get the survivors to safety, when the helicopters finally came to pick them up. The Queen Mother herself knighted him, along with two others, for their actions that day."

Laurel smiled covertly as Maggie tried to wrap her head around it. She looked at Jake to find him frowning into his

Guinness. "I'm impressed," she admitted.

"*Now* you're impressed?" He had to laugh.

"You forgot the *good* part," Nichole rose from the couch, half-full glass of vodka in hand. She sauntered over to lean on the bar under Gertie's openly hostile gaze. Laurel was sure that if Gertrude Jennings were ten years younger, she'd have kicked the mouthy Miss Young's ass up one wall and down the other.

The dancer's eyes twinkled with malice, and she took a sip of her vodka. "You forgot how he took off when the choppers set down and got shot in the back as he ran. It's alright though. You always did have that poor, helpless, widdle puppy look. It's no surprise you scampered off like a frightened dog when things got intense."

Jake went still. "Nichole, you don't know what you're talking about. You're drunk."

"So?" She glared at him defiantly.

Jake put his empty mug in the sink and headed for the stairs up to the top floor. "Okay. That's all of *this* conversation I can stomach. See you all in the morning."

"Sweet dreams!" Nichole called after him, rocking on her stool with laughter. Jake trooped up the stairs without looking back.

"You lying *bitch*." Allen looked over the couch at Nichole, game forgotten. The expression on his face could only be described as utterly fucking pissed.

"You know damn good and well Jake didn't run. He wasn't even one of the *unit* for God's sake. All he had to do is flash his press pass and the insurgents would've taken him to the nearest embassy, so he could tell the world about their victory. But he didn't," Allen continued coldly. "He picked up a gun and killed *eleven* of them. He helped hold them off until the choppers got there. Christ, he carried a friend to one after being shot *himself*, then had to hold her while she died."

"Oh boo hoo," Nichole said. "My heart bleeds. That doesn't change the fact he's nothing but a wishy-washy coward."

Maggie considered putting the offensive stripper in a chokehold but wasn't sure she'd be able to let her go before killing her. Nichole was definitely one of the reasons blonde women were thought to be vapid-eyed idiots.

"You think?" Lauren asked.

Nichole turned back to the redhead and snorted. "Yeah, I do."

"He isn't wishy-washy in the least," Laurel said. "Jake led Allen and Kat across the city *during* the outbreak. You know, when everybody else was running for the hills? He fought his way through those things to reach me, *then* got us all back here safely.

He even had us stop to rescue Maggie and the girls along the way. That doesn't sound cowardly to me at all."

Gertrude's was smiling from ear to ear.

"I'm just saying this for your own good, honey." Nichole gave her a compassionate look. "You need to realize Jake's nothing special. He's got a *little* more intelligence than most, but that's all. He'll figure out who's holding the strings soon enough. I'll work on him till he's too tired to fight anymore. Then *maybe* I'll give him a pity fuck."

Nichole completely missed Gertrude's look of revulsion.

Laurel put her hands on her waist and cocked her hip. She realized that while Nichole was good at being sneaky, she was lost inside her own head. The woman believed she was entitled to whatever she wanted, which evidently included a certain writer. Thankfully, so far he'd firmly squashed her attempts to pull him into bed. Nichole had tried everything from pressing her ass against his groin as he squeezed by her in the stairwell, to, most recently, trying to join him for a morning shower. The thought of her touching Jake was enough to make Kat's friend just short of violently ill. The fact that he'd thrown the blonde out of said shower buck naked gave her a shiny, happy feeling when she thought about it. That, in turn, caused Nichole to become the haughty, unpleasant bitch she'd been for days now.

No, Laurel was determined not to let this bleach-blonde bimbo anywhere *near* Jake.

"Thanks for the tip." She looked at Gertrude. "Are you turning in?"

"No," Gertie said, pointing at Allen. "This one says he found a classic movie in George's collection he wants me to watch that never got the recognition it deserved. What was it, dear?"

"*Hobo with a Shotgun*," he said with a straight face.

"Seriously?" Maggie's eyebrows shot up. "That's almost as good as *Blind Fury*! Hauer was always one of my favorites, ever since *Blade Runner*! Can I join you guys?"

Allen smiled. "The more the merrier." He was sure he'd be able to get in a little discrete ogling time while she was focused on Rutger's gritty visage, and he silently thanked the powers- that-be for impressively buxom, Nordic women who wore shirts three sizes too small.

"I'll see you all in the morning then." Laurel strode from the kitchen.

She stopped by her room upstairs, got rid of her shoes, and took a quick look in the mirror. She frowned at her reflection, then took her hair out of the braid she'd begun to wear out of habit.

That helped a little, and just this once she left that damn stray lock alone. Laurel considered the results and after a minute of indecision thought, *To hell with it.*

She rid herself of her sports bra, workout sweats, and finally her underwear. After some thought she pulled on the tight, light green, spaghetti-strap t-shirt she was so fond of, along with a black pair of short silk boxers she'd kept in her backpack with the rest of her under things.

Padding barefoot down the hall to the bathrooms, she turned into what had been deemed the *men's side.* It didn't really matter which was which, considering the fact George had installed urinals and stalls in both. It was simply a matter of propriety. Most women (and all men) were touchy about members of the opposite sex, or even the same sex, watching them take a dump. The door's oiled hinges opened without a sound, and she moved past the line of sinks, through the modest-sized dressing room with its rack of towels and took a look into the shower.

The writer was leaning against the far wall, back to her, head down, hands against the tiles. Everything Laurel could see was *very* easy on the eyes and looked like it had been chiseled out of stone. The muscles in his shoulders and back stood out as he leaned there, palms pressed flat to the wall. His calves and thighs were firm, not bulging, telling her he was more interested in using them as opposed to shaping them. And she could *now* confirm without a doubt that, yes, he had a cute butt. Even though the air was sauna-thick with moisture from vapor swirling about in the eight-spigot shower, she shivered.

* * *

Jake was oblivious. The hot water was beginning to loosen his sore muscles. It ran over his head, down his face and chin that was finally getting to the point where he'd have to shave again. He never did get a five o'clock shadow. He had something more along the lines of a *you'll only have to shave every three days or so* scruff.

He didn't think he could stay cooped up here much longer. Nichole was making his life as miserable as possible. Laurel was utterly disinterested in him because of said blonde, despite his efforts. That ass-clown Mike Barron was hitting on her all the time and, since Jake didn't really have any right to insist he knock it off...

* * *

Laurel watched him for a few minutes. She ran her eyes over his form, thinking about everything Gertrude had said. Of everything he'd accomplished on the day of the outbreak. Killing those men, saving Maggie and the girls. His face when he realized she was alright after diving *through* her door. The way he looked at her that made the butterflies in her stomach start racing around, every, single time he turned those eyes her way.

She picked up one of the towels from the rack and cleared her throat.

Jake's head sank lower. She saw the lines of his body go sharp again as his muscles tightened and his fingers curled against the wall like claws. "Damn it, Nichole. I told you before; it's *not* going to happen. So please, leave... beat it... scram... *Just leave me the fuck alone!*"

"Well, that was plain enough," she said, wryly. "Even *she* might get the hint from that one."

Jake's head snapped around. His eyes widened for a moment, then took on a wary look. He remained facing away from her and made it a point to think pure thoughts. "Laurel? You, uh... you know you're in the wrong shower, right?"

"I thought you might need a bodyguard after a certain bimbo's tirade downstairs. Besides, we should talk." She tossed the towel intentionally to his left, causing him turn as he snagged it out of the air involuntarily. This gave her an unobstructed view while he struggled to unfold the towel and cover himself. He looked good. The sight made her mouth go dry. She swallowed and yanked her gaze back to his face while he wrapped the towel around his hips.

Here it comes, he thought, *this is where the "let's just be friends" conversation happens.*

It's your own damn fault, his back-brain told him. *If you'd listened to me, you'd have had her already. But no-o-o-o-o...*

He tried to ignore his sinking stomach and shut off the water. There were four, eight thousand gallon tanks on the roof, fed by larger ones at the top of the apartments next door, so they had plenty for months to come. He wasn't going to be able to finish washing now, however. Not with her standing there, leaning against the shower entrance, hair tossed over one shoulder, shirt sticking to her body from the steam...

Pure thoughts, pure thoughts. He chanted silently. *Don't turn your towel into a pup tent. Think pure thoughts. Puppies... flowers... baseball...*

"Alright... What about?"

Laurel was having a hard time staying composed herself.

Jake's body was still covered with water and she had an almost undeniable urge find out what the moisture on his chest tasted like. She brought her thoughts back in order and said, "Us."

Jake glanced away. "I, uh...I wasn't sure you wanted there to be an us. Not with everything that's happened. Zombies rising and all. Then Nichole..."

"I don't want to talk about her," she said shortly. "For the life of me, I can't figure out why you haven't just told her to piss off and die."

He was shocked to hear her put it that way.

Laurel went on. "That woman is a user, Jake. Everything is all about her and to hell what other people want."

He frowned slightly. "I thought you didn't want to talk about her."

"I don't!" Anger flushed her cheeks and caused Jake to chant his mantra a bit quicker. "She's not going to let up, you know. She's determined to screw up your head. Or screw *you*."

"How do you think I feel?" He put his hands on his hips, causing his pectorals to ripple. Laurel felt a rush of heat on her face and tried to remember why she'd started this line of discussion. "I *have* to take her abuse or this place is going to turn into a battlefield that would put *Housewives* of...wherever to shame! She harasses me every moment; she follows me around. I had to throw her out of *here* when she tried to reenact a scene from a bad porno!"

"Which wouldn't be an issue, if you'd just tell her you're not interested!" she quipped.

Jake stared at her in disbelief. "I threw her out of the *room*, Laurel! How much more clear could I *possibly* be? She's not right in the head! She thinks every male on earth just has to have her, no matter how twisted up she is! What the hell else can I do?"

They were close now, snapping at each other almost nose-to-nose.

She was getting upset. "Then why don't you give her what she wants and get it over with?"

He stood there, jaw hanging open. "What?"

"Sure!" she said, arms waving. "Why don't you just screw her? That way she'll leave you alone! You won't have to take her crap anymo..."

"*Because, I can't fucking stand her!*" Jake had her by the upper arms before Laurel knew it, keeping her from stepping back from his anger as he all but yelled in her face. "She's sick, self-centered, and enjoys being cruel! She wouldn't know what a moral was if you slapped her across the face with one and said, *look, this is a moral!*"

He was furious. She would've recoiled, but his grip held her in place. She'd wanted to clear the air, but this was turning into a case of *be careful what you wish for.*

"She thinks monogamy is a species of *tree*! She doesn't care about art, music, literature... *none* of it! I couldn't tell you whether or not she even has as much soul as those fucking things outside! And, oh yeah! Most importantly, *she's not you*!" he bellowed.

Jake let her go quickly and stepped back, his face a mixture of embarrassment and fear. He had an awful suspicion that he'd just said *way* too much.

"What?" Laurel asked.

He shook his head and started to walk around her from the shower. "It doesn't matter."

She put her hand out, stiff-arming him in the chest and bringing him to a halt. "What. Did you. Just say?" Laurel asked, prodding him with her index finger in the solar plexus with each word, until his back bumped against the wall of the shower.

"Well?" Laurel demanded as he turned his face away. She put her weight against him, her hand, letting Jake know he was either going to come clean right then, or there was going to be a fight.

When he looked back at her, his eyes were deep enough to drown in.

"I said, she's not *you*." He pushed off the wall despite the pressure of her palm, causing her to take a step back.

Jake's words sent a thrill through her. Laurel was suddenly short of breath as his voice started something reverberating, just over the small of her back. "Her mind doesn't make me want to know it better than I know my own. The way her body moves doesn't keep me awake at night in this human-sized hamster cage, half-crazy to have it next to me. Her voice doesn't make me *burn*..." He clenched his teeth.

She was right there, inches away...

"You should go. It's been a *really* bad day. My hands are killing me. We watched I don't even *know* how many zombies walk by this place. I'm pretty stressed out right now and I'm feeling just a *little bit* like ripping your clothes off, so... you should go."

Instead, Laurel kissed him.

Jake's hands moved to hold her against his chest. They never paused, as if he was trying to imprint the feel of her skin into his fingertips, so he'd never know the texture of anything else. He matched the passion of her kiss, crushing his lips to hers.

She sighed into his mouth as his hands moved her shirt up from behind and whipped it over her head, forcing Laurel to break the kiss. Then taking her by the waist he spun her around and ran his hands up her arms. She raised them back around his neck, pulling him towards her and rubbed her cheek against the roughness of his chin.

Face close, he nipped at her jaw, hands slowly moving down her ribs, tracing the silken waistband of her shorts and the muscles in her stomach, before moving up slowly to cup her breasts.

Laurel dropped one arm down and ran her short nails along the edge of his hip, just under the towel. He drew a quick breath as she flicked the half-knot loose, so it was held in place only by their tightly pressed bodies.

Jake turned her quickly back to face him and ran his lips under her jaw. He moved down her neck, her collarbone, finally to her breast, one hand pressing into her spine, the other cradling her head. Laurel's world spun. He moved from one to the other, applying his teeth gently. Head thrown back, she gripped his hair, all the while making soft noises in the back of her throat that brought something very much like a growl from the writer. He sought her lips again, and Laurel ran her hand down the front of his thigh. Jake managed to pull his thoughts back together briefly and pushed her gently then, when she refused to be moved, more firmly, away.

Her body was humming with tension and Laurel had to make an effort to focus her eyes. "What's wrong?"

"We, ah...we should get some protection." Jake had to force the words out.

Laurel nuzzled his chin, smiling. "You really are a gentleman at heart, aren't you? Most men wouldn't even bring it up."

He'd locked his eyes on hers to keep from watching the rise and fall of her breasts as she spoke. It required every bit of his will. His back-brain was howling at him to shut the hell up. "Yeah, but really..."

She put her hand over his lips. "Don't worry. A benefit of having a promiscuous, pharmacy tech for a roommate is you get birth control at employee prices. I had the injection eleven months ago. Just over three years left."

He still looked worried. "Laurel, are you *sure*..."

She grabbed him by his hair again and grated her next words into his face, rubbing herself against his chest. "Oh gods, Jake, will you *shut up*? We've been together every day for a month now; we're not hopping into bed on the first date. I know I'm not reacting to my hormones and you're not just looking for a quickie. This isn't going to be remotely casual for either one of us. It'll change things. Now, here I am, half naked, wanting you so badly I can't *stand* it and..."

She forgot the rest of what she was going to say when he kissed her again. He held her like a drowning man grips a life preserver. Laurel closed her eyes and felt as if gravity had lost its hold on her body for a moment.

His towel had fallen to the floor, forgotten. They were separated now only by the thin pair of silk shorts.

Without a word he gripped them by both sides of the waistband, smoothly ripped the interfering silk in half, and tossed the pieces across the shower.

Jake all but threw the two of them against the tile wall and her breath quickened. She tried to devour his mouth with hers as she pulled at him. Her legs came up and Laurel curled her calves around his waist, forcing him to draw a hissing breath. He watched her face as they finally came together. She cried out and bit her lip, then the two of them fell into a slow rhythm. They moved against each other languidly, achingly, attempting to forget the hell outside their refuge.

It wasn't long before they were both panting and frenzied. Laurel's movements became short and jerky. Her eyes screwed shut and she bit Jake's shoulder where the meat of his neck met his collarbone. Her teeth left marks there and she shook violently. He simply pulled her against his chest and hoped his ribs would hold out. He could feel them creaking as her legs squeezed him, but continued to hold her while her shudders gradually lessened. Then he realized she was crying.

"Laurel? Did I hurt you? Why didn't you say something?" He began to pull slowly back, nearly out of his mind with worry.

Her face came up, eyes out of focus as she held him stationary. "You didn't... hurt me."

"Then why are you crying?"

She panted against his lips. "Because that was *wonderful*... and I'm happy... you sweet... bumbling idiot... Did you think... the last month was only difficult for you? I've wanted this since... you showed up, on the day of the outbreak. But we didn't really know each other."

She dropped one foot to the floor, keeping her other leg wrapped firmly around his waist. The movement caused such a rush of pleasure that Laurel caught her breath. "I wanted you. *All* of you. That means more than just your body. Though I'll admit, that's a bonus." She gently bit his pectoral.

He kissed her again, sending a rush of heat up her spine. Jake's breath caught in his throat at the look on her face and his hands slid up her back.

"So?" she said, from behind low lashes.

"The night is young," he replied.

Her lop-sided smile came to life.

"Tell you what," she said, pushing him back, eyes hot. "Why don't you finish cleaning up, then come meet me in my room? We'll see if practice really *does* make perfect."

"Screw that." Jake scooped her up and strode from the shower. The hallway was empty and he opened her door by feel, because what she was doing to his neck with her lips was distracting as all hell.

* * *

Laurel woke slowly.

The first thing she noticed was that she wasn't alone, and the other person in the bed holding her was emphatically male. She could tell because her leg lay over his hip and groin.

Jake. She smiled.

She lay half-across him, cheek resting on his shoulder as he held her nestled against his side. She brushed her hand across the tightness of his chest and pressed her face to it. He smelled like cedar.

How is that? She wrapped her free arm over his ribs and snuggling closer. He never used anything but deodorant, and no cologne she knew of smelled that way.

As she lifted herself on one elbow, the second thing she noticed was how sore her body was. Her *entire* body. Every muscle was stiff and protested the smallest of movements.

Kat's right. Nocturnal gymnastics. Next time—tonight, hopefully—she'd stretch beforehand.

Laurel stroked her hand slowly around his face and Jake stirred in his sleep. She leaned down, pressing their lips together as he came awake and opened his eyes.

She smiled, "Good morning."

He brushed the stray lock of hair out of her eyes, answering with a smile of his own.

"I was afraid it was a dream." His face fell. "I'm not dreaming now, am I?"

She lowered herself to his chest and kissed him again.

"Nope," Laurel said, "definitely not a dream."

She cupped his jaw with her hand, then shivered as his own moved across the small of her back. "I don't think my aching body can take much of that this morning, O'Connor. If you don't stop,

I'm going to kick your butt."

"You'll kick my butt?" Jake fought a grin.

"Hey, I lived with Kat the Ninja, remember? I kick butt." She sat up, swiveling her legs over the edge of the bed. Laurel raised her arms over her head and stretched, working the kinks out as Jake moved up behind her. He pushed her hair to one side and ran his palm from her neck diagonally down one shoulder blade. She put her hands on the bed and leaned her head forward, eyes closed, enjoying the moment.

Jake's palm remained at her waist as he kissed her low over her spine. Laurel's back arched as she inhaled sharply, but she didn't pull away. He sat up, looking over her shoulder, watching as her lips pursed and she breathed raggedly. She turned her head towards him, with an expression that was half annoyance and half lust, and she raised one eyebrow.

"I'll get you for that, later. Right now, I need to get up, or I'm going to be as stiff as you are." She looked pointedly at the sheet, half covering him. "Meet me downstairs. I'll make coffee."

"Mmm, coffee. You're trying to bewitch me, woman. And it's working." Jake tossed the sheet off and rose. "I should finish the shower I started last night, then I'll be right down."

"Running for the shower?" she joked.

He walked around the bed and took her in his arms. "Want to come along?"

The expression on Jake's face made her knees weak. She blushed furiously as the image of him soaking wet flashed in front of her eyes. He bent slightly, moving his lips along her neck.

Oh lordy. I could turn into a nymphomaniac with this man. Laurel was ready, despite her aching muscles.

"I, uh... I don't think I have your willpower, and you're not going to get any coffee if you keep this up," she said, breathlessly. Their actions last night had left both of them more than a little sore, and the sensation of their bodies moving together walked that fine line between pain and pleasure, about which poets wrote verse. "I'd also be... Oh! Don't do that, you'll set me off again... worthless for the rest of the day. Let's make it a date for later. And you'd *better* not stand me up."

"I think we covered the standing up part last night, but I'm willing to engage in as many repeat performances as you'd like." He assured her. That earned him a stiff-fingered poke in the ribs and a thin-eyed glare, which competed with her lusty grin.

Jake followed Laurel to the door, stuck his head out into the hall, looked both ways and, still naked, walked calmly towards the shower. She watched him stride out of sight, shut the door, then leaned against it.

"Oh, *this* is going to complicate things."

* * *

The dead were patient.

They stalked the urban corridors now. Legion upon legion of rotting evil, across every country.

While many remained in the cities, some began to roam farther and farther, seeking prey. The noticeable lack of victims was something that even their deteriorated brains recognized.

It was a slow process. One here, a trio there, heading north or south along the I-71 freeway. There was no method to their egress. They were driven only by tireless hunger. The ever-greater need to feed...

CHAPTER TEN

Laurel entered the kitchen minutes later.

She'd put her hair back in a thick braid, then pulled on her loose, calf length, green pajama pants and one of Foster's supply of tank tops. When she walked into the room, Kat waved over her tea. She grinned back, watching as Maggie filled the blender with dehydrated fruit, powdered milk, and about two cups of water.

"Mornin, Red." Maggie had fallen to using pet names for Laurel and Kat, to their delight. She also didn't complain when Kat dubbed her 'The Chesty Texan.'

"A good morning to you too." Laurel saw Gertrude sitting at the table to Kat's left, sipping her ever present cup of tea, and smiled at her widely. "Morning, Mrs. Jennings. Is there any water hot?"

"A bit." Gertrude gave her a fond look. "You might want to put some more on. George and Allen have been awake for hours, and heavens can they put away the coffee. And I've told you before, dear, call me Gertie. It took me forever to break Jake of that habit too."

Laurel dropped a teabag into a mug and filled it about three-quarters full before the pot went dry. She refilled the teapot and lit the gas on the stove as her mug steeped.

"Imagine Jake acting all stuffy. Like a refugee out of a Victorian romance novel. Shocking." That was given voice by the ball of sunshine sitting at the counter, sipping a Bloody Mary. Nichole was wretched that morning, but that was no surprise. She always was.

A month of nothing but movies, the Internet, and getting blind, stinking polluted, had done nothing to improve the dancer's personality. The fact that there was no escape from her bouts of vindictive pettiness made it worse. Most of the group had taken to long workouts, something she didn't enjoy, to escape her yapping.

I get my work out on the dance pole, she insisted, which Laurel supposed was true. Nichole was shapely and would be considered very attractive if not for the fact she had the soul of a snake. Once anyone spent more than a day or two around her, they developed a strong urge to be elsewhere. Like say, China.

"If you considered what it would be like to actually care about people, you'd understand why *some* men actually treat women with respect." Gertie added honey to her tea. She thought it tasted better than sugar. She turned to Kat. "You wouldn't have remained close with Allen if that weren't the case, right dear?"

The blue-haired woman smiled widely. "Absolutely. He's a goofball, but Al's got a good heart. He wouldn't talk about it, but he's super worried about his family. He didn't sleep much while we were together, even after...well, you know." She looked uncomfortably at Gertie.

"I *was* married for many years," the older woman said, with a stoic grin. "I *do* know that a man's first instinct after making love is usually to go looking for a sandwich or to fall asleep."

Everyone but Nichole laughed, and Kat went on. "They headed for Alaska just as the outbreak started and he's been on the shortwave every day trying to get any kind of word about what it's like up north. He hasn't had much success though."

"Probably be a while before any news filters down." Maggie muscled the top from the blender and poured the tasty—if disgusting looking—concoction into a large glass. "No phones, no travel, not much of a satellite connection anymore. There's still radio traffic on the military channels, but nothing close. We don't have enough power to punch a signal through, and no relay tower to push it on, so we're limited to receiving, not transmitting."

"Wonderful." Nichole rolled her eyes and sipped her drink. "Who knows how long we'll be cooped up here."

"You could always go for a walk," Kat mumbled, causing Maggie to press her hands together and look skyward hopefully.

The blonde gave her a sour grin, then her face went thoughtful. "Well, that just means I'll have to work on Jake a bit more. Any entertainment is better than none."

That was an image Laurel didn't need. It made her want to vomit in Nichole's smirking face, but she kept her voice neutral. "I thought you said he wasn't worth the effort?"

"He not really, but it's *something* to do." That earned her a scathing look from Kat, as Maggie scratched the bridge of her nose with her middle finger. Nichole ignored them. "He can amuse me while we're stuck. Should be able to do that at *least*... It's not like we'll be here forever. Eventually, the government or someone will pull it together and get us out of this shit-hole. Then I'll find one of the higher-ups to blow in exchange for being kept in the way I deserve, and Jake can scurry off. There should be plenty of appreciative, lonely men that will be *more* than happy to treat me how I want."

Laurel was getting upset. "Why bother?"

Nichole smiled cruelly. "Like I said, it's something to do. Believe me, it's *not* due to his prowess in the sack; I'll tell you that for free. He's not adventurous. Never wanted to experiment. No games, no additional partners, not even a *little* interested in S&M. Can you believe he's never owned a single whip or paddle or *anything*?"

"Shocking," the redhead said, aping the blonde woman's previous words in a voice that dripped sarcasm. Gertrude tilted her head and gave Laurel a thoughtful look.

"I know!" Nichole missed the chilly anger in the other woman's voice. "Makes me wish he ran on batteries. At least then I'd get *some* satisfaction out of him."

Laurel knew then that Nichole was full of shit.

"That bad?" She took the tea bag out and threw it away.

Nichole sputtered. "Bad doesn't even come close. I'm telling you, I had to fake it *every* time, just to keep from laughing in his face."

Gertie was still considering Laurel. Kat on the other hand, looked around calmly for something heavy and blunt to hit Nichole with. She could've just punched her, but that meant she'd actually need to *touch* the bitchy blonde, and she didn't want whatever this woman had to rub off on her. Finding nothing suitable within reach, she settled on taking a swig of her tea.

"Really? Huh." Laurel considered that for a moment, then raised her eyebrows. "I didn't."

Kat sprayed tea across the table and fell into a fit of coughing. Maggie rushed over and repeatedly slapped her on the back. Gertie gazed at Laurel, a smile threatening to break across her weathered face.

Nichole gave her a look filled with disbelief, which quickly turned to open hostility. Laurel stood calmly gazing over her mug.

"You're lying. Jake doesn't like to hop in the sack on a whim. He wants to take time and get to know you. *Make a connection,* he insists."

"Our first date was the night before the outbreak." Laurel swirled the liquid in the mug. "We've been together in this building for the last month. Jake and I know each other very well."

"*You're lying!*" Nichole insisted hotly.

"If you say so."

The blonde sat there, drink forgotten. Laurel could almost hear the gears grinding slowly in the woman's head.

"Well, well." She gave the redhead an appraising look, like a female cat sizing up a rival that had walked across the window ledge. "It seems like Jake's learned a few tricks. Maybe I'll give him another evaluation."

"I don't *think* so," Laurel said firmly, as she set the mug on the counter and turned to face Nichole. "Unlike you, I happen to have a very high opinion of Jake, and I want him to be happy. He's kind and brave, and *you* aren't good enough to wipe a *turd* off one of his boots."

Nichole's jaw dropped open as Gertie's smile grew past large, to beatific.

Laurel moved to the counter, opposite the bimbo. "Since the moment you found out he wouldn't take you back, you've been petty, hurtful, and obnoxious, and you will... not... treat... him... that... way... any... more. Because if you do? I'll knock every *fucking* one of your perfectly capped teeth out."

Maggie's smile matched Gertrude's as she helped Kat clear the last of the tea from her throat.

"So," Laurel said coldly, leaning on the counter in front of Nichole's still-gaping mouth, "I'll make this very clear. I'll use small words, so you can understand. *Hands. Off.*"

Nichole's face cycled through shock, fear, then rage, finally settling into undisguised loathing. She spun off her stool and stalked from the room, leaving her Bloody Mary forgotten on the counter.

Gertrude rose and hugged Laurel, held her at arm's length, nodded in satisfaction, then walked to the cupboard and took down three mugs. She filled them with coffee, mixed one with milk, left the second with just a spoonful of sugar, and started towards George's office with the third.

"Jake only takes sugar in his, dear," she said. Then made her way out of the room, still smiling.

Laurel was surprised at her own reaction to Nichole's words. She hadn't planned on taking it *quite* that far, but now was glad she'd made it clear she wouldn't put up with any more of the woman's abuse being thrown in Jake's direction.

She was attempting to decide if she should be ashamed of her actions, when Kat spoke up. "Laurel!"

She looked around to find her friend staring at her in unabashed joy.

"Tell me everything! *Right now!*"

Maggie was grinning beside Kat and pushed out the opposite chair for the redhead with her foot. "That was brilliant. I wish I'd had a camera so I could've caught the expression on the bitch's face. But Kat's right. Spill."

Laurel sighed, positive the next few minutes would be extremely frank, quite naughty, and more than a little embarrassing.

After explaining her reasons, which Kat waved off insisting that she get to the good parts, she told them what happened while glossing over as many of the details as they'd allow. She finally came to the end of it, believing that the FBI wouldn't require as much information as the two across the table demanded.

"He said what?" Maggie asked.

"That he was afraid he'd hurt me," she replied. "As slow as we went, there's no way that could've happened, though."

The two women looked at each other, then back at her.

"No wild positions? No impatient rushing? No *a little lower*?" Kat got up to refill the teapot, after taking the last cupful for herself.

"Huh-uh."

Kat put the kettle on to boil again, giving her friend an excited look. "Do you know what the two of you did?"

Laurel looked at her quizzically.

"Roomie," she exclaimed, "you made love!"

"Ye-e-e-es. That was kind of the idea." She didn't understand what Kat was getting at, but Maggie was nodding in agreement.

"No, no, no." Kat insisted. "He made *love* to you! Anybody can have *sex*. What you're describing is a completely different animal!"

Laurel thought about that, her eyes focused worlds away. She remembered Jake afterwards as they lay there half-exhausted. How he'd propped himself up to watch her as she floated in the afterglow and brushed the hair out of her eyes. The expression on his face hadn't been the regular *I Got Mine* that every woman had seen at one time or another. He looked amazed and held her gently when they'd finally collapsed, still wound together.

She smiled. "Yeah."

Kat pointed at her emphatically. "You did too, didn't you?!! Holy crap! I'm an awesome matchmaker! Cupid can kiss my Squaw ass! Yay me!" She did her happy-dance, right there on the kitchen linoleum. The pretty Asian plunked down abruptly in her chair again, a conspiratorial expression on her face. "Did he make you... you know?" Kat looked up, twitching her shoulders.

"Kat!!"

"Oh, come *on*! It's me!"

"It's private!"

"Okay!" Kat played with her teacup and gave her friend a sidelong glance. "Did you though?"

"Oh, yeah..." Laurel said, eyes widening with the memory.

"More than once?" Maggie asked in a low voice.

The redhead's mouth was *really* dry. She could only nod.

Kat spread her hands over her tea impatiently.

"I... lost count. Three? No, four." She shook her head, then rubbed her arms as if chilled, and covered her mouth with an unsteady hand. "I... Wow. Just wow."

The two women were staring at her, open-mouthed.

"You're my idol," Maggie said finally. "I am *so* jealous right now."

"You're not just going to leave it there, are you?" Kat demanded.

"We made a date," Laurel admitted. "We were supposed have a picnic the day everything happened, but... I guess it's kind of a silly idea. You know. Having it in the middle of a ruined city, on a rooftop?"

Maggie gaped at her. "Oh. My. God! That's the most romantic thing I've ever *heard* of!"

Laurel smiled widely.

"This girl's got it *bad*," Maggie said. Kat gave her an emphatic nod, coupled with what could only be termed as a shit-eating grin.

They heard footsteps in the stairwell and Jake entered the kitchen, hair still a little damp from his shower. He wore his ever-present, combat boots, khakis and a light-grey fitted t-shirt half stuck to his body, due to stray moisture from the shower.

"Morning all," he said. Smiling, he picked up the cup on the counter and checked inside. He gave Laurel a surprised look before pouring in water from the kettle and stirring the sweet, java goodness into drinkable form. He took a seat at the table beside Laurel, before he noticed the other girls were giving him frank, appraising looks, along with big smiles.

"So-o-o-o... what's up, stud?" Kat dropped the pitch of her voice lower, to mimic her favorite cartoon character, Jessica Rabbit.

Jake's eyebrows went up in confusion and he glanced at Laurel. Her cheeks were flaming, and she covered her face with her hands, while hunching halfway to the tabletop. He looked from Maggie to Kat quickly, eyes flicking from face to face, and realization began to dawn in his eyes.

"I take it a certain criminally-sensuous redhead would be the reason why Nichole headed for her room in a huff?" He slowly turned back to the redhead in question.

Dropping her hands, Laurel gave him a guilty look. "Do you hate me?"

His laughter surprised her, and he put his mug on the table. It was a decidedly masculine sound that made her heart race as a thrill went up her spine. He pulled her close, one light hand behind her neck, under her thickly braided hair.

"For what?" He shook his head and gave her a look brimming not with amusement, but affection. "*You* protected *me*. My hero."

Laurel had never been the type to make out in front of an audience, but just then she didn't care. He leaned forward, turning her head slightly, and kissed her. His eyes closed as she put one hand on his chest, half to steady herself, half so she could feel his heartbeat. She would've moved over into his lap, if not for the sound of Kat's feet happily bouncing on the floor, coupled with an appreciative "Ye-ah!"

Laurel pulled back to see Jake blushing and gave Kat an arch look, which caused her to jump up from the table before exiting stage left.

"So, you guys are together?"

The three of them turned to see Karen leaning shyly around the corner. She'd been abnormally quiet during their stay in Foster's little fortress, despite attempts by both Kat and Laurel to draw her out of a self-imposed shell.

"Hey, kid. Take a load off." Maggie nodded at the chair Kat had vacated. Karen thought about it for a moment, then edged over and sat. Her eyes darted from person to person as she shifted uncomfortably in her chair.

"Are we?" Laurel asked him.

"I'd like to be. Very much." Jake took her hand resting on the tabletop. "Unless you think we made a mistake?"

She looked at him, face blank. "What would you do if I said we had?"

He considered that. "Cry a lot."

She brought his hand up to her lips and kissed it lightly. "Can't have that."

She knew Jake hadn't smiled, really smiled, since their exile began. It made the one he gave her then all the more wonderful.

"I think you really made Nichole angry," Karen said, working up the courage to meet their eyes. "She's pretty mean most of the time, but she'll be awful now."

Maggie chuckled. "I wouldn't worry about that one. I think Laurel has some ideas of her own in mind for Blondie's next explosion."

"Oh." Karen sat quietly for a few moments. "Five bucks on Laurel."

That earned a round of laughter, and Jake rose to get a refill as Allen came into the kitchen.

"Hey, guys. Nice to see you finally decided to get outta bed." Al said with a grin which Laurel tried to ignore. She could feel her cheeks lighting up again. "Jake, Foster wants to talk with you."

"Gotcha." Jake stirred some sugar into the cup. His friend walked over to lean beside him against the counter as he tossed the spoon in the sink.

"So, uh..." Allen leaned his head slightly towards the table where the others sat and raised his eyebrows.

Jake looked down, smiling. "Yeah."

"Bout time." Allen backhanded him in the shoulder and they started out of the kitchen.

"What? That's it?" Maggie said in disbelief. "That's all you're gonna say?"

The two men looked at each other, then back to her. "It's a guy thing," Allen said.

Jake nodded in agreement.

They headed back for George's office, but Jake stopped to kiss Laurel on the way. It warmed her all the way down to her toes.

* * *

Laurel learned just how much of a letch Mike Barron was later that evening. Her stomach fluttered with anticipation as she climbed the stairs to the second floor, intent on changing to meet Jake. Kat had surprised her with the LBD (little black dress) she'd never had the chance to wear. The blue-haired woman had been quite specific on what she was to do make-up wise too. Though Laurel trusted her, her friend had a habit of going overboard. She had no intention of putting on the array of pastes and substances Kat recommended. She'd brush her hair, maybe put eye-shadow on her upper lids, and call it good.

She was considering the addition of lipstick when she turned the corner and saw Karen pressed up against the wall, clutching a towel around herself firmly. Mike leaned one-armed against the wall over her. He was smiling in a way that brought a frown to Laurel's face and obviously made Karen uncomfortable.

"So really, why don't you think about it?" He ran the back of his hand down the outside of her arm. The young woman shied away, trying to get around him to her room, but he put his other arm on the wall and she shrank back again. "It's not like there's many options, you know. We're stuck here. Who else do you think..."

Laurel'd had enough at that point.

"Karen! Just the person I wanted to see." She strode down the hall and came to a halt a few feet away. She left enough room for a good spin kick between her and Mike. "Kat's busy and Maggie is hopeless, so I wanted to ask you for help."

Karen's eyes shone with relief while Mike's held annoyance at the interruption. She ducked under his arm and moved towards Laurel.

"Sure," she agreed softly, casting a nervous glance behind her.

"Why don't you go get dressed and meet me in my room?" Laurel gave Mike a sorrowful look. "Sorry. I'm a little pressed for time."

Karen scurried quickly down the hall under his gaze, which he then turned to the redhead. She saw anger there and something else that made her hackles rise. Mike leaned against the wall smiling, then looked her up and down. His blatant eyeballing repulsed her. This was the type of guy she'd spent years avoiding. One that looked at a woman as a conquest or an object, rather than a person. Almost like a male version of Nichole, when you got right down to it. Definitely the sort no sane woman would consider having a relationship with.

"So," Mike said with a greasy smile, "what's the occasion for dressing up? Big plans?"

Laurel smiled. "You might say that. Something that's long overdue."

"Never a good idea to keep a woman waiting. If you'd had plans with me, I'd have made good on them a long time ago." Mike came off the wall and half circled her, like a shark trying to decide whether or not something might taste good before it took a bite. "I make it my motto to never disappoint a lady."

"Then you must not date much." She cocked her hip.

The tanned clubber stopped, confused. His reptilian under-brain was getting signals that this might not be prey but, in typical alpha male fashion, he chose to ignore the danger signs.

"I don't know what you think," she continued, grinning coldly. "But it takes more than a lick and a promise to satisfy a woman. A *real* man knows that. I'm sure someone will eventually find the time to explain it to you. Right now, like I said, I have plans."

"You know what I think?" Barron's brow furrowed with a heavy scowl and he reached out for her when she moved by. "I think-errk!"

The last was forced from his throat as Laurel brought the point of her elbow into his solar plexus. His lungs seized up. While he struggled for breath, she grabbed the hand he'd planned on touching her with, bent the wrist back painfully and shoved him away. He stumbled a few paces, staring at her in a combination of fear and disbelief.

"Don't. Oh, and if you try that kind of thing with Karen again? Well, let's just say I've got a *r-e-e-aly* sharp sword in my room, and I'm not afraid to use it."

With that, Laurel turned her back on him, entered her room, and shut the door on an extremely bruised ego. She'd have to tell Jake and the others about this. It wasn't something she felt she should keep to herself.

"He's tried that before," Karen said, after Laurel sat in the room's only chair. The girl began twining two small braids just over her ears and went on. "He tried to get me alone on the roof last week, but Kat and Maggie came up to run the roof-line. Mike went back downstairs after."

Karen shuddered and began a smaller braid, starting at the crown of Laurel's head, leaving the rest of her hair loose. Laurel had worn the style before when she'd performed at a few renaissance fairs and it had always brought her great success, along with more than a few phone numbers.

"Just stay close to Kat or Maggie, and lock your door tonight," Laurel suggested, putting a lot of confidence into her voice in an attempt to reassure the girl. "I think I got my point across."

Karen nodded, unconvinced and pulled a brush through Laurel's hair, turning it into smooth waves. She'd hoped Mike would stop after the first time she'd said no, but he kept pressing her.

She didn't know which was worse. The monsters outside, or the one locked in with them.

* * *

That evening passed without incident. Kat went to bed early, leaving George to ride herd on the kids along with Maggie.

Jake and Laurel were absent for the rest of the night.

* * *

George was glad for a break when the others filed down into the metal shop. He'd been fighting the damn Internet for thirteen hours, pulling scraps of intel here and there. It was almost done for. The servers were going down left and right. The satellite connection was a sometimes thing, at best, now that no one was manning the control centers. He'd been up for almost twenty-four hours straight too. That wasn't as big a deal when he was younger, but seeing as he was approaching middle age—middle age as far as he was concerned—his body didn't want to obey him the way it used to.

"We have a decision to make," Jake said, once they'd settled around the room. He wore his khakis again with a CBGB tee, and stood sipping coffee next to Laurel. She was leaning against a table saw in a pair of jeans and an olive green tank top from their supplies. When Jake asked George why he had so many women's clothes on hand, Foster smiled and said, *Boy Scout motto, kid.*

The group was gathered around a large shop table full of maps and photos that George, Allen, and Jake had pored over the previous day. Maggie stood beside Karen and Leo, arms crossed over her remarkable bosom. Kat sat sipping tea on a bench beside Gertrude, Allen, and Heather. Mike and Nichole were slouching on a worktable opposite them, sporting truly impressive sets of bloodshot eyes.

Jake gave them the no-shitter. He'd learned the phrase from a SEAL who'd visited the brick he'd shadowed and had used it since, to remember the man. Though the crusty old frogman had been decades older, Jake had nothing but unbridled respect for him. Even though Jake was just a *cake-eating, civilian, good-for-nothing, dip-shit, journalist* (as the man told him the first day,) he had, in all truth, treated the writer like anyone else in the unit. If he succeeded in a section of the training, he got to rest. If he failed—and he did fail sometimes— Jake got to run. Do another twenty push-ups or pull-ups or sit-ups or crawl through assorted foul substances. Or... Well, that pretty much summed it up. He'd never thought to complain. The aged warrior had been right there, crawling through the muck with them, but doing it *faster.*

One trainee had questioned his instruction methods and earned a pitying look from the unit commander. The SEAL had stripped off his shirt to reveal a body almost untouched by age, covered in muscle and long healed wounds. He'd moved face-to-face with said Englishman and, in his friendly way, educated the poor sod.

"See these scars?" he growled. "I got those by *doing*, you stupid-ass, tea-slurping, wet-behind-the-ears, shit-eating guppy. So sit the fuck down, shut the fuck up, and pay fucking attention. You will see this material again..."

That had been the end of the discussion. Who could argue with that logic?

So, Jake took the advice that Englishman should've. (The man was washed out of the course a few weeks later.) He watched, he listened, he learned. Two months later, Jake was one of the men drinking Guinness with the rest of the brick, while Molly arm wrestled the old SEAL in a pub off Boddington Circle.

Jake pushed the memories away and laid it all out for his companions. News reports, emails, grainy satellite images, everything.

"In layman's terms, we are completely fucked," he summed up. "No help's coming."

Silence reigned.

"How long?" Maggie finally asked.

He passed a hand through his unruly hair. "Minimum? Two years."

"How long will our supplies last?" Kat set her mug of tea on the worktable.

"Just over four months," George said around his ever-present stogie.

That caused some uncomfortable shifting amongst those gathered. The prospect of starving wasn't a pleasant one. Then Jake explained The Plan that he, Foster, and Allen had worked on so laboriously. They'd mapped a route west around the cities, keeping always to the secondary roads. The carefully detailed journey bypassed any major population centers and wound a circuitous route south, past the Rockies. He covered the weapons he thought they'd need, food, and medical supplies, all of it.

"So, that's everything," he summed up. "We have to make a decision and we have to make it soon. Try for the safety of the mountains, or stay here and... die."

The others absorbed the news with varying degrees of civility.

"How do you expect us to survive out there?" Nichole demanded incredulously. "How are we going to *get* there for Christ's sake? What, we're all supposed to hop in that stupid Beast of yours, point the grill at California and say, *Westward Ho*? You're out of your fucking mind!"

Mike looked at her thoughtfully. "She's got a point, O'Connor."

"What choice do we have? Wait in here until we starve?" Allen came up off the bench. He was trying to retain his composure, so he kept his eyes locked on the offensive blonde. She didn't repulse him as much as she did Jake, but it was getting to be a near thing. "I for one want to breathe open air again."

"Oh, please. They'll send people to help us."

"*They* who?" George asked, curiously.

Nichole sputtered and flapped her hands at him. "Well... them!

The..."

"The government? What's left is holding on to Hawaii and the west by the skin of its teeth. It's in shambles." George shook his head and flipped ashes off his cigar. "The overseas troops? If they're *lucky* and not running for their lives, they're in the same boat we are. The soldiers in the Fleet? They're all headed for the west coast and Hawaii. Besides, you see an ocean around here somewhere?"

The stripper sat with her mouth hanging open, trying to think of something, but it was evident the blonde's brain wasn't supplying her mouth with much.

"It's not a question of choice. The simple fact is we just don't have enough food to last. Water, reinforced walls, solid steel doors, none of it matters a pinch of shit without food." George stuck the stogie back in his mouth.

"That's why we're going to make our way west," Jake said, looking at each of them in turn. "But first I think I should introduce you to our host. Mr. George Montgomery Foster. Navy lifer and fixer."

Everyone's eyes flicked to George, who looked more than a little shocked at Jake's introduction.

"Damn, son," he laughed. "I didn't think you'd ever put it together."

"I wouldn't have, if not for my time with the SAS," Jake admitted. "Something like that isn't covered in journalism one oh one."

George laughed.

"What's a fixer?" Kat asked.

Allen was giving George what could only be described as the stink-eye, clearly reevaluating him. "A fixer runs a safe-haven for special operations groups. They provide weapons, equipment, tactical information, large sums of untraceable cash, all supplied covertly by the government. That explains this place. It's a damn military safe house."

George rolled the cigar in his fingers, grinning. "Smarter than you look there, boy. Been doin' it for forty years now. Got started just after Vietnam."

"Oh *please*!" Nichole rolled her eyes. "You expect us to believe you're some secret agent whose cover is a building superintendent? That's the lamest thing I've ever heard!"

Foster gave her a wry look. "You probably think Oswald shot Kennedy too, don't ya'?"

Gertrude sighed.

Allen gave him a strange look, while the others tried to absorb that comment. "So... it *was* the second gunman on the grassy knoll?" he asked.

George shook his head. "Nope. It was the ninja in the tree 'bout a block away. Second guy couldn't get a clear shot."

"Third... ninja?" Allen had a noticeable tick under his left eye.

"What a load of crap," Nichole said.

"Nobody saw 'em did they?" Foster demanded. "Ninja are great at concealment. Besides, Kennedy was a murderin' pig. Had that woman offed, what's her name...Norma somethin'."

Kat's mouth hung open. "Norma *Jean*?"

Foster pointed at her. "That's the one. All because she wouldn't let 'im poke her. Dirty son-of-a-bitch. The higher-ups realized if he'd be willing to do that, he was capable of anything and took steps."

"I think we're getting a little off the point," Maggie said. "What's going on overall? I mean, maybe the situation isn't as hopeless as we think?"

Foster added to the information Jake had provided. Frighteningly, the human race had been pushed almost beyond endurance in just over a month.

It had begun when some idiot set off a nuclear bomb outside the pyramids. George told them how every country in the region had responded and now the entire Middle East would be uninhabitable for about forty-thousand years. Russia was on the brink, while China and eastern Asia had been overrun. Japan had evacuated everyone it could, but millions had been left behind to become part of the massive, moaning horde currently occupying Tokyo. The rest of Europe was pretty much fucked. Germany, France, and Italy each had a few small areas holding out, but all were largely empty now. There was a *little* hope. The Greek Isles had survived almost completely intact. Ireland, during the initial outbreak, had armed itself to the teeth. All the forgotten weapons of yesteryear, broadswords, axes, maces and shillelaghs, had been taken from museums, castles, even local pubs and had been put to use. The military, backed by every civilian who could swing a sword, cleared the entire Emerald Isle of the creatures. Then they set every ship they had afloat to England, put their shoulders up against those of Britain's finest, and were currently keeping the ancient line of Hadrian's Wall secure.

Australia was, to everyone's surprise, doing quite well. As were Hawaii, Alaska, Cuba, and the northern half of Canada.

The news closer to home wasn't good. The entire East Coast was a slaughter house and the Midwest wasn't any better. The Deep South was fighting a running battle, as were the residents of the Great Plains as they retreated to the Rockies. The west, California, Washington, and Montana, along with parts of Colorado and Nevada, were all cut off by strategically destroyed bridges. The defenders were sitting tight, letting the dead splatter against the bottom of the gorges and ravines when they attempted to cross the chasms.

"What's left a' the military's pulled back behind the mountains, and the fleet's been called around ta help guard Hawaii, Alaska, an' the West Coast," George told them. "The long and short of it is there's no help comin'. Not anytime soon. Could be a year or two, more likely three, before it's possible ta *start* reclaiming the country. It's jus' too big. There's too many dead scattered all the hell over the place and too few men. None with the training ta make a difference and not enough resources ta maintain a push. At least fer now."

"So how do we survive?" Kat asked.

"I'm glad you asked," Foster said, smiling widely.

* * *

The dead roamed the world's cities.

From Belfast to Bangkok. Bangladesh to Boston. They staggered woodenly through the hallowed halls of the Louvre, along the flagstones of China's Great Wall, and down the willow bordered streets of Williamsburg.

Survivors were being pushed to their limits. Constantly on the move, scrounging for edibles, water, weapons. They desperately sought refuge in hastily fortified disaster aid centers and abandoned houses. Some pressed on, ragged, dirty, tired, little more than zombies themselves due to lack of food and virtually no rest. The dead never stopped, so those that fled death and worse at their cold hands had to move twice as fast.

There was virtually no military presence. The odd platoon of Army Reserve members, a few Special Forces units, scattered Air National Guard recruits here and there. They all tried to save as many people as they could, while battling the ever-present hordes of corpses. While some of these brave men and women managed to lead their units and a few survivors to safety, the majority were overcome by the dead.

But they bought time, paying for their friends' survival with their lives...

CHAPTER ELEVEN

George led the others down through the plate behind the machine shop, into the subterranean motor pool. Once they were below, he hit the lights and everyone, save Allen and Jake (because they'd seen it before,) stood there with their mouths hanging agape.

"What in the blue hell is *that*?" Maggie exclaimed.

That, was a vehicle unlike anything the survivors had seen. It was segmented, like a trio of subway cars, and longer than one of those intimidating, double-trailer, eighteen-wheelers. The nose tapered back from a narrow, vertical, eight-foot tall wedge that protruded from the front, almost like a snowplow blade, and met seamlessly with the first segment just before the lead wheels. They could all imagine how easily it would push, or even just ram right through, the mangled cars that were surely littering the roadways. Its bottom hull sat a good three feet above the ground, riding heavy independent axles and gigantic off-road tires. None of the segments showed any obvious access hatches and there was a 1940s circa pin-up emblazoned on the side—a dark-haired girl riding a bomb. Below her, hand painted letters read, "The Screamin' Mimi."

It was also the most hideous shade of *Holy-Fucking-Shit,-That's-Fucking-Ugly*! pink, any of them had ever seen.

"This," Foster said proudly, "is a MATTOC, a Mobile, Armored, Troop Transport and Operation Command vehicle. Originally designed for use in case of widespread riots during the aftermath of Y2K. Her hull's covered with SEP skin. That's short for synthesized electron polymer. Impervious to damn near any impact, short of a nuke. Can't be cut, won't burn, and it's almost frictionless. Developed initially for the outside of the space shuttle, but it couldn't be produced in any other color and NASA didn't want to be known for sending big, pink peckers into space. Never mind that without all the wind drag, they could'a launched missions using only an eighth of the fuel it normally takes to achieve orbit. Pretty dumb for a bunch of eggheads if you ask me."

"Yeah, right," Mike sputtered. "Don't tell me any of you are buying this shit? Frictionless rocket skin? Gimme a fucking break."

George gave the clubber an amused look. "Go see for yourself, smartass."

Mike strolled over and leaned against the vehicle's side one-armed, wearing a smirk. His hand slipped along its surface. He stumbled and fell to the concrete floor. There was a round of unrestrained snickering from the others as Barron got back to his feet. After brushing dust from the seat of his scuffed pants and giving George a dirty look which the fixer ignored, he walked back to stand with Nichole.

"Now, we've come up with a route that could get us west. We'll have to cut south and avoid any population centers, but with a little luck we should be able to make it." Jake waved at the unbelievable machine. "We can load this up with enough food for just over a month. George can get us to other caches along the way too, so we can restock as we go, or even just scavenge for supplies if need be."

The group was silent, while each of them considered what he proposed.

"That's it. Those are our options. But if we're going to do this, I think we all need to vote on it." He pulled a cigarette from his pack and lit up.

"Yeah! Great, damn idea!" Nichole said, hotly. "You can fucking forget it! I'm not hopping into what amounts to a big, cotton-candy colored, tuna can and heading for the boonies, hoping I won't get my ass bitten off by all those zombies out there. I'm for staying right here where it's safe!"

"Well, there's one point of view. Maybe not a realistic one, but still an option. Feel free to stay here and starve, blondie," Foster said.

"Screw you!"

"Enough!" Jake exclaimed. "I vote for going. And just so you all know up front, I vote that George lead us. He has the technical knowhow and the most experience, so..."

"Not a chance," Foster replied, puffing away on his cigar.

Jake was confused. "What? Why the *hell* would we spend all night coming up with this plan if..."

"Hey, don't get me wrong. I'm damn good when it comes to shootin' things, and there's no way I'm gonna sit here while you all go hell-bent for the horizon. But I'm not leading this trip." He pointed at Jake. "That's *your* job."

"Me?"

"Ya managed to get Red there in the middle of the shit storm." Foster gestured at Laurel. "With hardly any resources, 'cept a couple a' guns and a piece of shit Jeep. Ya handled yerself pretty damn good for a civi with those five, puss-sacks next door, too. Guts *and* brains, O'Connor. That's what makes a leader." He raised his hand. "I'm with Jake. So let's vote people. Show 'a hands. All for heading west?"

To Jake's horror, almost everyone's hand went up, echoing Foster's opinion.

"Fuckin'-a, you're leading. The girls and I would be dead if not for you," Maggie said, with nods from Karen and Heather who was leaning back in the circle of Allen's arms.

"You know I'm in." His friend gave him two thumbs up.

Gertrude sighed. "Well. I suppose I can still move faster than those creatures outside. Maybe we could find one of those Segway contraptions?"

Nichole freaked out. "Are you people *crazy*? Travel two-thousand plus miles, with all those things out there? What kind of suicidal plan is that? Why don't we just stay here? Get supplies from the stores?"

"Damnit, haven't you been listening?" Jake asked. "If we try for the Rockies we've got a chance. If we stay here, we are going to *die*!"

"And we're supposed to take your word on that?" Nichole sneered. "An apartment sup and a hack journalist? What? You didn't get enough of getting people killed overseas, so you need to up the body count? Maybe..."

The blonde's voice cut off as Kat struck her sharply across the mouth with a resounding open-handed slap. The force of the blow propelled Nichole back a few steps where she stood holding her cheek, staring at the blue-haired Asian in shock.

"You know what? I think I speak for everyone here when I say, we've all had *enough* of your shit." Kat gave her a look of utter disgust. "Now, if you have anything *useful* to contribute to our situation? Feel free to do so. However, if I hear one...*just one* more snide, abusive comment come out of your mouth? I will kick your nasty twat up around your ears."

"You hit me when I wasn't looking!"

Kat squared off with her from five yards away. "Okay. Come on, then. You can watch the next one coming."

Nichole glared daggers, still holding her slowly reddening cheek. "You know what? Fuck you! Fuck *all* of you!"

"Think you might have gone a bit too far?" Mike asked and Jake could see the cogs in his slimy, little brain turning. Barron stepped closer to the stripper, putting his hand on her lower back. None of the others believed he was trying to be supportive or comforting for a moment. The blonde gave him a grateful look, however, as he steered her towards the stairs and up to the door leading to the machine shop above.

After the pair shut the door behind them, Jake smiled at Kat. "I appreciate the sentiment. Really, I do. I've never actually seen you pissed off before."

"You still haven't," she replied, voice full of bounce and energy. "I just figured a good smack from me was more preferable than my best friend shanking the stupid bitch."

All heads turned to Laurel, who calmly looked around wearing an innocent expression. "I have no idea what you're talking about."

They all broke into helpless laughter, which allowed the redhead to discreetly place the screwdriver she'd been holding against the inside of her forearm back on the worktable.

The group started planning and assigning responsibilities right there. They were going to have forty-five days to get in the best physical shape they could, so Maggie wrote up a cardio, strength training regime for them to follow. Gertrude was her only worry. No matter what, the tough, old woman's sprinting days were over.

Jake and Foster began to put them through basic weapons training with both sidearms and assault rifles. One wall of the motor pool was covered with weaponry. Silenced pistols, riot shotguns, suppressed MP5s, the works. There were enough tactical vests to equip them all twice over, so all the spares went into one of the massive vehicle's storage compartments. Because you just never knew.

Laurel and Gertrude went through their food stores, supplementing cases of MRE's with protein mixes George kept on hand (because most of the units used them as meal replacements in a pinch), and eight cans of freeze dried fruits. Even with Foster's knowledge of the whereabouts of numerous caches, again, it couldn't hurt.

They filled the storage bins in the front and the rear of the Screamin' Mimi with ammunition for their weapons. George said it would be a good idea for one reason. If the rear units were damaged—not that he believed that could happen—the front could be used as a temporary vehicle/shelter until a feasible replacement could be found.

They cleaned weapons. A *lot* of weapons. Each of them would carry a primary (suppressed MP5s, M4s or AR15s), along with silenced Beretta M9s or Glocks as backup sidearms. Both took 9mm which negated the need to evaluate what types of ammunition they might need, or how much of each to take. A few of the riot shotguns and other assorted engines of destruction were packed away in the Mimi, including various types of grenades which worried Jake to no end. George assured him they were safe. "Unless," as the fixer put it, "some dipshit pulled the pin."

Kat and, surprisingly, Leo began teaching them swordplay and the use of sharp pointy things. Young Salazar was quite good with a blade. Easily a match for Jake, he could hold his own against Laurel, but Kat still far outshone them all. She was *deadly* with her grandfather's katana in her hands, and could slice faster than most people were able to follow visually. The group began with Foster's bamboo, kendo swords, then she moved them on to the real thing. Granted, no one—except for Kat or Leo—would attempt any serious fighting with a blade, but at least none of them were utterly clueless now.

Mike and Nichole didn't take part in any of their preparations. In fact, neither of them associated with the group, even in passing, which suited most of them just fine. The pair kept to their rooms and only came around the others at meals, during which they ate quickly before sequestering themselves away again. Neither rose before noon, and were up virtually all night watching horrible B-movies from George's DVD collection, drinking heavily, and generally acting like asses.

Things came to a head when they tried to force Karen into their bed.

Jake had gone up for a post-workout shower and found Leo on hands and knees, blood dripping from a split at the corner of his mouth. The young fencer was obviously in pain as Jake helped him stand, but his eyes were full of nothing but anger and worry.

"They took her!" he slurred.

"What?" Jake wondered if Leo'd hit his head on the way down. "They who?"

"Them! Nichole and Mike!" He shook the cobwebs from his head and pushing off the wall. "I was coming up to get my dirty clothes, you know, to do laundry? Well, Karen and Mike and Nichole were up here in the hallway. They were acting all weird. They kept *touching* her. They were talking low and stuff, trying to get her go into Nichole's room. Karen started to yell and Nichole put her hand over her mouth, then they started pulling her inside!"

"*What*?" The writer demanded.

Leo looked ashamed. "I ran at them, you know? I thought

maybe they'd stop if they saw somebody up here. But Mike turned around when I got close and clocked me! It was just a minute ago! Please you gotta help!"

Jake's eyes widened and he raced for Nichole's door, Leo following more slowly on unsteady legs. He grabbed the knob and tried to force it open. "Shit! Locked. Watch out!" Jake took a step back and kicked the door hard enough to send it back against the interior wall, shattering the side of the frame that held its bolt in place.

He blew into the room with Leo still in tow, to find the three of them struggling on the bed. Nichole, clad only in a pair of cut-off shorts she'd made from her jeans, knelt ensconced firmly between Karen's frenzied legs. The blonde had already pulled the girl's shirt away and held one of her arms down as she worked the front clasp of her bra loose. Mike had her other arm pinned and held a syringe in one hand. He'd been about to inject her with its contents, but fumbled it in surprise when Jake smashed his way into the room.

Nichole seemed unaware of their presence as she bent and ran her tongue over Karen's stomach. The girl tried to yell out through the gaffer's tape the pair had used across her mouth to keep her quiet. She squirmed and bucked on the sheets attempting to free herself, but Nichole had the leverage and kept her down easily. Then the blonde ran a free hand down the length of Karen's torso until she reached her hips, flicked open the snap on the waistline of her pants, and began unzipping her fly. Karen's back arched and she screamed against the tape.

Her cry sent flames up behind Jake's shocked eyes. He dove at Barron and the two of them sailed over the opposite edge of the bed. The enraged man smashed his elbow into Mike's face as they hit the floor, dazing him, and then sent a short punch under his jaw, putting the shit-head out cold. As Barron slumped into a knuckle-induced nap, Jake turned to deal with Nichole. He found Leo already had the problem well in hand.

While Jake pummeled Mike, the teenager had taken a double handful of Nichole's bleach-blonde hair, dragged her off Karen, and was using it to yank her around the room. The stripper screeched, attempting to get her feet under her as he backed round and around, but just couldn't keep up with him. The corded muscles in the young man's wrists gave him an especially strong grip and he was *really* ticked besides, so all bets were off. He still couldn't hit a *girl*, so he settled for playing tug-o-war with her hair, keeping her busy until help arrived.

Karen, however, didn't have *any* problems hitting a girl. She jumped off the bed, waited until Leo dragged Nichole by again, cocked her fist way back and punched the other woman squarely in the face. Leo let go of Nichole's hair and she fell unconscious to the floor in a boneless heap.

Jake yelled down the hall for someone to help and tied Mike's shirtless elbows together with his own belt. If Barron had the misfortune to wake up before he finished securing him, Jake swore he'd break the bastard's arms. Then toss him off the roof. He applied duct tape around Mike's wrists and hands then, in a moment of pure vindictiveness, knotted his shoelaces together. Tightly.

As Jake worked, the two teens stared down at Nichole. Leo tried mightily not to look at Karen's bare breasts. Her shirt was in ruins beside the bed, so he stripped his own off and handed it to her. He made sure to keep his eyes averted while she pulled it on. When Karen settled the shirt, she noticed the red spots on its front and her eyes went to Leo's face. His cheek and lip was already beginning to swell darkly and blood had leaked down his chin from the split in his lip.

"Sorry." He looked down at his shoes and shifted uncomfortably from foot-to-foot.

Karen's face became confused. "About the shirt?"

Leo shook his head. "I tried to stop them, but I wasn't strong enough. I just... sorry."

The girl's eyes teared up and she started to shake. Leo looked up just in time to catch her as she threw herself forward, wrapped her arms around his skinny ribs, and began sobbing into his chest. He looked helplessly at Jake and put his hands against Karen's shoulder blades to hold her awkwardly.

"Why don't you two go downstairs?"

Leo nodded and gently steered Karen towards the door. As they left the room, Jake could hear the sounds of running footsteps coming up the hallway. Foster, Allen, and Maggie bolted into the room where he stood seething over the horizontal pair.

After a few moments, George broke the silence.

"What the *fuck*?"

* * *

The dead were hungry.

It wasn't a biological need, but a constant mental urge. One of the few they had.

The creatures were driven to seek out and consume flesh, type unimportant. Something in their makeup drove them to feed endlessly, well past the point of complete engorgement. Some had stuffed themselves, literally, to the point that the rotted meat they'd consumed was forcing its way from their anus, their navels... In some extreme cases, even their sex organs.

Luckily, however, it seemed Homo sapiens were the only animals in the food chain that would reanimate after death. Thoughts of zombie Doberman Pinschers were prominent in some survivor's minds, though (thanks to Holly-weird). Moronic animal rights activists, during the initial week of the outbreak, had continued their crusade to save those poor, helpless animals made prisoners for man's amusement. What they hadn't considered, was what would happen to said animals once they were freed. Some were eaten outright. Others died from their wounds after escaping their mindless attackers. Many more starved to death, due to lack of wild edibles or by being deprived of medication. Some of the predators made it to the safety of the suburbs, through the rural neighborhoods, and finally into the wilds beyond.

Silverback gorillas and Bengal Tigers had never been native to North America before...

CHAPTER TWELVE

"What the fuck?!?"

The comment was drawn from Mike Barron's lips by the liberal application of smelling salts and a pitcher of ice water in the face. The mechanic stepped back and set the empty pitcher on the bar while Maggie took a penlight to Mike's eyes, checking his pupil dilation. She had begun working on him five minutes prior and had not been gentle. They had seen the track marks on his arms and the stupid hieroglyph tattoo. She kept his head still by gripping a handful of his ridiculously long hair until she was satisfied he wasn't bleeding from his brain. Then she roughly released her hold and began repacking the med kit Foster had provided her.

Mike and Nichole were restrained in a pair of chairs normally used at the dining table. Fittingly enough with duct tape. Jake, with help from Allen and Maggie, had lugged the pair down from the room where they'd assaulted Karen. Foster had immediately begun searching—read: tearing apart—the room, looking for Barron's stash and he planned to do the same to the stripper's. He'd been livid when he'd seen the syringe, and Jake had found it necessary to talk pretty damn fast to keep the old warrior from capping the sleeping perverts right there. After the two were carted downstairs, Maggie suggested using handcuffs to secure them.

Jake insisted on the duct tape.

He and Allen had used so much that the seated pair resembled slightly bloody mummies. Silver ones anyway. He also had Maggie put a shirt on Nichole before they'd started applying the tape, even though the EMT had been all for leaving the unconscious woman half-naked.

"Maybe we'll get lucky and it'll rip her nipples off," she said viciously. "Does anybody here really have a problem with that?"

Jake had other plans. He didn't like it, but there was no other solution. Their group didn't have any real long-term way to keep them confined. So, as the others gathered, he steeled himself to add one more log onto the bonfire waiting for him in Hell.

"Well, they're awake." Maggie crossed her arms as she leaned against the faux-wood table. "They've both taken something. Probably cocaine, judging from the dilation of their pupils."

He nodded in acknowledgment. "Alright...do either of you have *anything* to say for yourselves?"

Nichole just glared at him, but Mike tried to play dumb.

"You've lost it, O'Connor! Tying people up? What the *hell*, man? You can't do this, man! You have any *idea* how much..."

Jake slapped him hard across the face. The sound of the blow was loud enough that Foster heard it as he tromped down the stairs into the room. He carried a MOLLE pack along with a large Ziploc bag, and his face was as harsh as Jake had ever seen it.

"Look at *this* shit!" George opened the pack, revealing a pair of 45s and a snub-nose 38. There were also a few boxes of ammo, a dozen MREs, a large kitchen knife, a flashlight, a roll of toilet paper, and a quartet of water bottles inside.

"Found all that stuff in Blondie's closet. *This* however, was in his room. Shithead there stuffed it under his *mattress* for Christ sake." He tossed the Ziploc to Maggie for her to identify its contents. It held a smaller bag the size of a softball and was full of white powder, around three hundred large, blue capsules, and three small glass vials, one of which was only half full.

"Definitely cocaine." Maggie prodded the smaller bag with her fingers. "Those pills sure as hell look like Rohypnol. It's one of the current date rape drugs and this is... *Mother fucker*!"

She pulled out the half-empty vial. "This is morphine! Is this what you were trying to shoot her up with?!?"

Barron looked away sullenly.

The writer slapped him again. "Answer her question."

"Jake..." Laurel began, but swallowed her comment as he motioned for silence.

"Hey, she's eighteen! It's not like..."

Jake slapped him harder this time, knocking Mike back in the chair. "Answer. The. Question."

"Yes!" Barron spit out some blood from where his teeth cut the inside of his cheek.

Jake passed the syringe he'd retrieved to Maggie. She checked the contents and glared at the duct-taped club hound.

"*You stupid asshole!*" Maggie moved towards him, syringe gripped point down like a dagger. "A dose this high would be *fatal*!"

Foster interposed himself between the enraged EMT and Barron. She blinked and moved back, relinquishing the syringe.

"So. Assault, attempted rape, attempted manslaughter. You're a real piece of work." Jake was boiling inside as he looked over to where Leo still held Karen protectively on the couch. She was still shaking, eyes bloodshot from crying, and had paled when Maggie confirmed her near-brush with lethal injection. "What do you think we should do with you?"

You're not going to do shit!" Nichole raged, struggling in her chair. "You don't have the right to..."

Karen came up off the couch, screaming as she ran at the blonde. Foster and Maggie intercepted her, holding the girl back as she clawed and kicked away, just short of Nichole's chair.

"The right? *The right*?" Karen yelled, causing the stripper to shy away. "What *right* did you have to do that to me, you bitch? You'd better hope for a bullet in the brain, because if these people don't kill you, *I will*!"

The girl seemed to lose strength after her outburst, and let Maggie take her back to the couch where she sat close to Leo again.

"Jesus. It was a mistake, alright?" Nichole exclaimed. "Nobody got killed! Alright the kid there caught a punch in the mouth and the girl's shaken up, but they're fine! I swear, you people are only making a big deal out of it because the little drama queen over there..."

Jake had never, in his entire life, considered hitting a woman before that moment.

Foster beat him to it.

The resounding smack almost knocked Nichole over in her chair. The sound of the blow echoed through the common room, causing Leo and Karen to wince.

"Now you listen to me, you pathetic little clam-box..." Foster began.

"Chief," Jake said. "It won't do any good. Look at them."

Foster saw he was right. Nothing had penetrated either of their self-centered, pea-sized brains. The restrained pair sat looking daggers at everyone in the room. Jake could clearly see what would happen if either of them ever caught one of their group alone.

George shook his head in disgust. "What do we do with these morons?"

The writer gazed at them and Kat saw his shoulders sag, as if suddenly burdened by some terrible weight. He slapped a magazine into one of the pistols, racked the slide, and turned to the others.

"We give them a choice," Jake said.

* * *

After cutting both free of their duct tape restraints, Jake and the others marched them down to the first floor and through the access door to the tenement next door. The pair became visibly nervous as he motioned them to the rear of the building, and then attempted to dig in their heels when they all reached the door to the secure parking lot.

"Why are we going out there?" Nichole's eye was blossoming into an enormous shiner. Jake had to admit, Karen had one *hell* of a right hook.

"Keep moving," he said.

"Hey, man, those things are out here!" Mike exclaimed. "We..."

"The goddamn security gate's shut," Foster growled, fingering the safety on his Glock. "They're *zombies*, you stupid son of a bitch. Not kangaroos. The things can't even *run*, let alone make a twelve foot vertical leap, ya dipshit."

They all filed out into the lot, and Jake called a halt forty feet from the door.

"You two have a decision to make," he said, refusing to look away from them. If he was going to commit this act of barbarism, the very least he could do was have the courage to look them in the eye. "Everyone here has had enough. You don't possess a single moral between the pair of you, and for the life of me, I can't imagine why you both weren't in prison when the outbreak occurred. Regardless of what either of you think you're *entitled* to, you don't have the right to treat others like dogs, dirt, or slaves. You don't get to use people for your amusement against their will."

The pair stood scowling at him until he pulled the keys to his Jeep from his pocket and tossed them at their feet.

"Leave."

"What?" Nichole demanded, eyes wide.

"Neither of you can be trusted. You're not welcome here. I'll keep an eye on Mike here with Kat and Maggie." He pointed at Nichole. "Foster and Laurel will take you inside and pack up whatever belongings you two have."

The pair immediately started arguing that he couldn't just toss them out, that they'd be killed by the dead roaming the streets. Jake pulled the pistol from the small of his back and thumbed the hammer. The sound of the gun cocking shut them up, mid-hissy fit.

"This is not a debate. Or a request. You were both out for a while, and we had ample time to talk about it." He motioned at the others, who each nodded in turn. "By unanimous decision, you're out of here. If you'd shown *one iota* of guilt or remorse over what you tried to do, we'd have just locked you in one of the top apartments until we're ready to leave. They're reasonably secure with the lobby and stairwell doors barred. But you've made that option unworkable."

There was a sour taste in Jake's mouth. Doing this was almost surely a death sentence for the self-centered pair, but they'd all agreed on this course of action and there was no turning back.

"Now, if either of you think I'm not serious," he firmly took hold of the remains of his conscience and raised the weapon, "then I'll save you some trouble or put a bullet in your head right now. You have one minute to decide."

"You can't!" Mike stepped forward, face darkening in anger. "You can't just..."

"Back! Up!" Foster snapped. Jake realized George and Kat had stepped up beside him, guns pointed at the wide-eyed duo.

"I'd do what he says. He'll shoot you in the head." Kat had one hand braced under the grip of her 9mm, her other index finger on the trigger. She dropped her aim. "I'll shoot you in the *balls*."

Barron scurried back to stand beside the blonde.

Nichole was trying to find a sympathetic eye somewhere in the group, but every gaze held contempt and steely resolve.

"Well?" Jake asked. "What's your decision? We have preparations to make, and quite frankly I'm sick of the sight of you."

* * *

As the Beast roared away, Jake gave it a silent goodbye.

Mike was hunched over the wheel in concentration. He couldn't drive a standard very well, which explained why he'd wrapped a sports car around a pole. Nichole was screeching at the top of her lungs, telling the world to kiss her ass as she continually flipped them the bird. The pair motored west to the freeway and out of sight down the on-ramp under Foster's watchful eye. George had one of his silenced long-arm rifles on the tenement's roof and had informed them both if they tried anything funny, after he had to climb all those steps, he'd vaporize them.

They'd taken him at his word.

After securing the gate and outer door again, Jake waited for

Foster as the rest retreated into the safe house. A certain redhead, watched from where she stood leaning against the lobby wall, as Jake paced back and forth across the dusty floor.

"*Damn* those two," Jake fumed. "I can't believe I had to throw them out with the maggot-heads everywhere, but I didn't have any choice!"

"We really didn't," Laurel agreed.

"If we'd let them stay, they'd have *killed* someone. Even if we locked them up, they'd need to be guarded every minute." He went on pacing. "We don't have enough *people* to watch them every hour of the day and still make preparations."

She nodded. "Maybe with twice as many we could've..."

"I don't understand what they were *thinking*." He was still lost in his head and missed Laurel's attempt to sooth him. "How did they expect to get away with it? Even if they'd had the brains not to OD Karen, they *had* to have known we wouldn't let that shit slide."

"They didn't *care*." She pushed off the wall and strode towards him. "No one *forced* the syringe into Barron's hand. Nobody put a gun to Nichole's head and told her to disregard any sense of human decency."

"I can't believe I tossed them out. You know the worst part? I don't feel guilty about it." He looked towards the rear of the building. "Not one damn bit. What does that say about who I'm becoming?"

Laurel just put her arms around his waist and held him. Jake sighed and wrapped his around her shoulders in turn, enjoying the rare moment of peace. She began stroking his back while her breath warmed his neck, her cheek resting under his jaw as her fingers worked their magic. When Laurel spoke, her lips brushed Jake's throat and sent a slow thrill up his spine.

"You need to stop taking all the blame on yourself," she murmured. "We all agreed with what had to be done. It wasn't just your decision."

He grunted noncommittally.

She bit him lightly along the line of his jaw. "That's not the correct reply." Laurel's hands moved to rest on his narrow hips.

"Aw jeez," Foster grumbled, as he stumped up from the stairwell. "Would you two get a room already?" His knees were bothering him, and he'd really been looking forward to blowing Mike or Nichole's head to a pulp from ten floors up. Laurel stopped nibbling at Jake's ear, but retained her grip on his hips.

"George, don't be a butt head," she said with a smile. "Did they keep going?"

"Yeah. Hopped on I-270 north. Barron was weavin' through all the cars like a moron." He laughed. "I'll be shocked if he and Blondie last more than a day. Two at the *most*."

They filed back into the safe house and the fixer sealed its immense door plate again, locking out the horror of the world for a little while longer.

"Well, *this* old man is exhausted. Gonna head into the office for a bit, keep an eye on the outside. See what info I can get out of the Internet." George cracked his neck again. "We should start gathering a few things from the immediate area tomorrow. Since we're headin' out soon, we could use some supplies from the camping store down the road. Bottled propane, water purification tablets... That kinda thing."

"We'll take a look tomorrow," Jake replied.

"Goodnight you crotchety old turd," Laurel said, grinning.

Foster beamed. "Ya got a lot better in the last week, Red. Have ya talking like a Squid in no time."

As he trudged up the metal stairs, said redhead gave Jake an inquisitive look. "Are you hungry?"

He shrugged. "Not really. I guess I could eat, but I don't have much in the way of appetite right now.

Laurel sauntered over to the stairs. She put one foot on the lowest step, cocked a hip, and looked back at him, blatantly exaggerating the curve of her spine.

"I was thinking about heading to bed. It's been a long day, and I'd like a little sack time." Her lopsided grin made a slow appearance. "Feeling energetic?"

He smiled. "Race you."

* * *

Tim's Emporium was technically a camping supply store even if half its stock items were army surplus.

Jake had visited it a few times since he'd come back from overseas, but he hadn't purchased much. Now, he wished they could take the whole fucking *place* with them. Tactical boots, thermal gear, balaclavas, canteens, can openers. Everywhere he looked, items that would be oh-so-useful on the road seemed to jump out at him. He fully intended to leave with as much gear as Forster's old, half-ton could hold.

Especially since just getting there had been an adventure.

The writer had decided that only he, Allen, and George should make the trip, but had been convinced—read: bullied—to reverse his decision by the women. Men going out and about, sans female supervision, incensed them. Laurel was livid—and as it turned out *really* sexy when she was mad—that he was trying to protect her. Kat just laughed. Maggie offered to arm-wrestle him to see who went on the outing so, when Jake lost, *he* could stay and keep the home-fires burning. None of their arguments swayed him, so they did something so sneaky, so underhanded, that it shocked him to his very core.

They went to Gertrude.

After she'd heartlessly explained to the three males the possible shortage of feminine hygiene products—in such a way that even the stubborn Foster cringed—Jake, Allen, Laurel, and Maggie headed out to begin the trek.

Kat got to stay behind, since she'd been the one who'd come up with the idea to get Gertrude involved in the first place. She took the news well. She had pouted adorably which Jake ignored her— but it was *so* cute— and had loudly sworn revenge.

The four kept to alleys and backyards, due to the scattered dead shuffling about nearby, while attempting to stay quiet and out of sight. They crept within a block of the Emporium before being noticed by the creatures. Then, over the course of about three seconds, the following happened.

As they came to the end of yet another privacy fence, a lone zombie stumbled around the corner in their direction, coming almost nose-to-nose with Jake. Everyone, including the zombie, froze. Jake dropped into a crouch. He'd opted to keep his crowbar handy, since he didn't know how loud the Hammer pistol actually *was* with its suppressor attached, for any up close encounters.

The creature looked to be in pretty good shape; if you took into consideration it was missing everything in its abdominal cavity and only had one dull eye. The other had been torn out somehow, allowing them all to get a good look at the maggots squirming about in its empty socket.

It saw prey was nearby and its arms came out to grasp anything unlucky enough to be within reach. The thing's dried lips pulled back from grey teeth, and its jaw dropped open as it prepared to let loose a moan, possibly alerting more nearby infected. Then the chiseled end of Jake's crowbar speared it under the jaw. As the creature raised its arms, he'd taken a wide, two-handed grip, stabbed the steel point up behind its chin, shattering the things palate and finally, speared its brain. The zombie slumped to the broken surface of the alley and lay still.

Nomex gloves or not, he didn't feel like touching the horrible thing. Jake grasped the weapon's hook end with both hands, put his foot on the corpse's lifeless jaw and yanked his crowbar free. After wiping blood from the steel as best he could on the overgrown strip of grass lining the fence, they continued onward.

Reaching the alley's mouth, Maggie and Jake carefully checked the street for any mobile dead, while Allen and Laurel watched their backs. There was movement a block to the south. Jake checked it through his binoculars. It turned out to be a group of eight ghouls, moving away from their party. The four used abandoned cars as cover and, keeping low, moved across the street to the opposite alley.

The rear door of Tim's was next to the loading docks. Jake bypassed this door via his universal lock-pick crowbar, cursing at it under his breath all the while. Upon entering the building, they fanned out around Allen. He proceeded to secure the door with a length of chain and a large C clamp that he'd brought in his Alice pack, wrapped in a blanket to keep it from clanking when he moved. They all wore tactical vests along with empty packs and carried suppressed firearms. Jake had his monstrous pistol; Allen and Maggie both carried MP4s, while Laurel wore a silenced Glock in each thigh holster, and gripped a third. Each of them carried five full clips, preloaded with ammunition for their weapon of choice. Granted, this was supposed to be a *sneak and peek*, not a *run and gun* excursion, so none of them planned to empty five full magazines. But just in case...

The redhead pulled out the secure radio Foster had stuffed in her pack and punched in channel 007. He'd insisted on it, claiming he'd *saved Ian Fleming's ass in '58*, so the guy owed him at least that much.

At the time, everyone believed the aging fixer was full of it.

"George? We're here. Over."

Foster's voice crackled back seconds later. "I hear ya. Forget that over crap. Ain't nobody around to get mixed up with while we talk. What'd ya all do? Stop for snacks?"

"We ran into a friend in the ally, but we're inside now. We have to check it still," she replied quietly, looking to Jake.

"Fifteen minutes, tops." He watched the short hallway that led to the showroom floor.

Laurel relayed his words to Foster, who acknowledged and signed off until their next transmission. If they didn't call him in half an hour, he'd know they were in trouble. Or dead.

They moved through the hall, making sure the small office halfway down was clear. Its only occupant was presumably the store manager, who was missing the back of his head due to eating the barrel of his Luger. Pressing on with Laurel and Jake in the lead, the four moved onto the sales floor.

If it existed and was somehow connected to survivalism, it was in Tim's Emporium. Uniforms, flight suits, gas masks, backpacks, and camping gear hung from the walls in abundance. There were bins full of water purification tablets, canteens, web belts, machetes. Seemingly, anything and everything a zombie apocalypse survivor could want, except for a safe location to keep it all.

"I think I'm in Heaven. Seriously." Allen looked around with raised eyebrows. Jake's slim friend was certain he'd heard angels sing when he caught sight of all the stockpiled gear.

Nine minutes later, once they were sure there were no creatures lurking and the front doors were secure, Laurel called George again to let him know they'd begun collecting items. He'd monitor his radio and once they gathered the needed supplies at the dock door, roll out, meet them, load up, and scram back to their safe house. As she signed off again, they split into two teams and started looting. Luckily, Tim's had actual shopping carts and not those stupid, little baskets all the oh-so-trendy stores provided.

"Boy, listen to all this," Laurel said. "Collapsible shovels, hatchets, socks, boots for everyone, balaclavas, water purification tablets one-thousand count, canteens, magnesium fire-strikers, machetes, Field Fighter knives, full spool of para-cord, car battery chargers, antibiotic cream, iodine, double A batteries, NVGs..."

"Night vision goggles," Jake said. "I doubt they'll have any here, though. We should check the control tower at Bolton Field on the way out of the city. They should have a few sets there for the air traffic controllers."

"Huh. Good idea. I never would've considered that."

"And here you thought you only kept me around for my body." He grinned and emptied the battery display.

She went back to their list. "Trench spikes, hand-crank meat or coffee grinders...Really? For what?"

"They can be used to make one of the two ingredients in thermite," he said absently.

The redhead paused. "You know, it's a little scary you know that. It's *always* the quiet ones."

"So you're saying I don't need to be worried you might be a closet psycho? Awesome."

Laurel gave him a blank look.

"The *quiet* thing," Jake explained. "I mean, *you* weren't quiet last night when..."

"That's different!" She blushed furiously.

"Just saying." He began dropping canteens into the cart as they moved down the aisle. "I know the walls in George's little fortress are thick and all, but..."

That earned him a tight-lipped grin. "I'll get you for that."

"I live in unbridled terror of feminine retribution."

"Oh, gods. Shut up," she said, rolling her eyes.

"Terror."

She cocked a hip and gave him a raised eyebrow. "You *can* be cut off, you know."

"Shutting up now," Jake said, brightly.

Laurel honestly tried not to laugh as she chased him to the knife counter, where they began picking out sharp, pointy things for the others.

CHAPTER THIRTEEN

George was visibly upbeat as he backed the multicolored pickup against the loading dock.

Evidently the aging fixer had circled north a couple of blocks before meeting up with Jake's party, to ensure he'd shaken any creatures that had followed. Most of the *Ram-tough* truck's cattle-pusher was coated in brackish gore, and bits of gelatinous tissue clung to its rusty, green hood when the fixer hopped from the cab.

"*Wow.*" Laurel stared at the sludge-covered steel. "What the hell happened?"

Foster smiled. "Not a lot. A dozen were on the street when I turned east, so I ran 'em down. Most of 'em just stood there as I rolled over their skulls."

"You ran them *all* down?" Maggie asked.

"Yee-up. That's potentially a dozen fewer shit-bags to deal with down the line." He lit a match on the truck's side mirror and brought the stogie between his teeth to life.

Allen was impressed. "Damn! That's...what? Twelve hundred points?"

The fixer looked at him blankly.

"GTA?" Allen helped Jake muscle the first cart off the dock and into the truck's bed.

"Wasn't that kind of dangerous? Getting into it with those things alone?" Laurel asked.

"Nah. I didn't even need to get out. Jus' backed over the few I wasn't sure about," George replied and tossed a tie-down over the cart to secure it.

Jake was giving the truck a leery once over. "Are you sure you didn't bust anything? The trip back is just over two miles. If we break down, or one of the tires was holed by a ribcage or..."

Maggie snorted as she looked over the aged vehicle. "Is this thing held together with bailing wire and bubble gum or what?"

George's face remained unruffled. "You could always jog behind it, gorgeous. I mean, you never use the treadmill. Too busy *pumpin' up*. I never get to see those guns of yours jig..."

"*Anyway*," the writer said firmly. "Back to the subject at hand? Are you sure this thing will make it back without breaking down? Since you decided to go all Road Warrior on the way here, I mean."

Foster smirked. "She may not look like much...but she's got it where it counts, kid."

There were varying degrees of laughter at that comment.

Then a group of zombies that had been slowly making their way south, began passing the mouth of the alley. One of the lead creatures noticed them and gave a deep, gurgling moan. The others looked in their direction, saw five humans, and thirty-one sets of rotting vocal chords joined the first, crying out for their flesh.

"Oh *shit*," Allen said.

Jake already had his hulking pistol out, as the others brought their weapons into play. The horrors started towards them and the smell of rotting meat wafted into the survivors' nostrils.

"Pick your shots," Foster said, pulling a SIG 716 assault rifle from the cab of the truck and taking aim at the creature in the lead.

They began firing on the pack. Over the last month, George had put them through intensive marksman training in the motor-pool beneath the safe house. Taking into account the utter failures experienced by the military during the frantic pull behind the Rockies, the fixer had bagged the center mass methodology and instructed them to aim only for the head. To insure they obeyed, he provided a single paper plate on a clothesline as their target and whoever missed? Well, just like when the aging sup had gone through basic training, they got to do push-ups. They got to do sit-ups. They got to run laps around the perimeter of the cavernous room. Needless to say, they were all in much better shape at the end of those forty-five days, along with being much better with firearms.

The ghouls began dropping at forty yards and not one of them made it to the twenty yard mark. The five humans decimated the stumbling creatures, sending explosions of body fluids and skull fragments back towards the mouth of the alley. As the last corpse hit the broken pavement with a wet splat, they all paused and swept the area, playing range-finder through the sights of their weapons. Foster had instructed them on engaging targets as a *unit*. Creating a killing ground that aggressors wouldn't be able to cross, without being torn to shreds by overlapping fields of fire. The process had proven itself now. The survivors hadn't hit with every shot they took. Some of their rounds went into necks, others into torsos, but they'd kept up a steady rate of fire. They'd alternated their shots, giving each other time to reload, while continuing to drop the hideous fucks coming for their flesh. George's face broke into a wide grin at their success and the show of controlled violence the party had displayed, in their first real engagement.

Or it could've been the smell of cordite hanging heavily in the air that gave his face the maniacal, stop-me-before-I-kill-again look of euphoria.

"Clear," Jake said.

"Clear," Laurel confirmed.

The others sounded off as well, ejected their partially spent magazines, and inserted fresh ones, making sure to chamber the first round to have one ready to go if need be.

"Did we really just do that?" Maggie looked a little shaken up after downing almost nine of the group with her MP4. Jake noted her hands were steady, despite the tremor in her voice.

"*That*, kids," Foster chuckled, "is what you call a successful *fucking* engagement. Good job. All of ya. I was a little worried about heading out before, but you all just blew any concerns right outta the water."

He began securing the last of the supplies they'd obtained— read: looted—in the bed of the pickup, while Allen moved up beside his friend to make sure none of the rotting things were still alive. Undead. Whatever.

"That one's twitching," Al said.

"Got it." Jake holstered his pistol and pulled the crowbar from its place between his tac-vest and backpack. He moved around the outside of the piled ghouls and spiked the twitcher in the temple with the weapon's chiseled end, stilling its spasmodically quivering limbs forever. As he wiped it clean on the thing's soiled, Oh-Aich-Eye-Oh jersey, Allen gazed around at the scattered bodies.

"It's a lot different."

Jake looked at his friend. "What is?"

Allen shook his head and let his weapon hang from its combat strap across his stomach. He looked around at the gore-covered cement and stinking meat-bags that, only a minute ago, had desperately wanted a taste of living flesh. "Shooting them. I loved those downloads you could buy for Call of Duty to turn all the characters into zombies? Thought it was a good time. It's not. It's not fun at *all*."

He turned and walked back to Foster's truck to help the old fixer secure the last of the straps over their supplies. Laurel strode to where Jake knelt, crowbar still held in his fist, when Allen turned away. She dropped the magazine on her Glock, replaced it with a full one and stood watchfully at Jake's side. The sexy redhead had downed seven of the creatures, and from the way she professionally held the pistol in a braced shooters' grip, George's training had taken a root in her as well.

She looked across the bodies and shook her head. "Al's a little messed up. Isn't he?"

Jake nodded, not knowing what to say about his friend's reaction to the firefight. "He's never actually shot at a person before."

"These things aren't people." Laurel said.

"They were. They were all someone's family. Parents, kids, uncles, girlfriends. They all had a history. Before." He came to his feet and looked around at the slaughtered dead. "Now? They're just shells. Hungry, biological, homicidal, robots that only know how to do one thing. Automatons that feed and feed and feed and won't ever stop, unless someone stops *them*."

She gave him a worried look. "Are you thinking about fighting them? Taking on every zombie we come across?"

"Oh *hell* no." Jake shook his head, laying his crowbar across one shoulder. "We're hopelessly outnumbered. There's no *way* we could just go around guns blazing, hunting down every maggot-head out there. I'm sure there's not enough ammunition handy as an army would need to fight all of them, let alone the manpower. If people are going to survive? Someone a lot smarter than I am is going to have to come up with a plan, real quick."

"So you're saying I could do it?"

Jake looked at her wryly from the corner of his eye and Laurel blew him a kiss. He sighed and shook his head. "Christ, I'm the Rodney-fucking-Dangerfield of the zombie apoc□"

He stopped, cocking his head towards the mouth of the alley and Laurel looked towards the street. They stood, listening silently for a moment. There was... something... but neither of them could place the sound.

The writer moved quietly to the mouth of the alley. He knelt at the corner, lowering his head to waist level to attract less attention and, ever-so-slowly, peeked around. His face paled. Pointing repeatedly back towards the dock doors, he backed away from the street and followed Laurel towards the group on cat-silent feet.

"Everyone?" Jake said in a hushed voice. "Keep quiet. We have a problem."

His friends looked at him with varying levels of nervousness. "There's a *big* fucking pack of those things moving this way."

"How many are we talking about?" Allen asked.

"Lots. A couple hundred, maybe."

The others, except for George, gaped at him in horror.

Foster spit and shook his head. "How much ammo does everyone have? Two, three mags, maybe?"

The others nodded and looked nervously at the mouth of the alley.

"We don't have enough to take on a crowd like that." The fixer scratched at his sandpaper-rough cheek. "No way. We'll have to circle way out. Maybe we'll be able to find a way around."

"I'm going to draw them away." Jake motioned for Foster's sidearm. "The rest of you head home and meet me at the back gate. Don't keep me waiting."

George tossed him his silenced Glock without hesitation, which Jake secured to his left thigh with two lengths of duct tape—use one thousand and three.

"Yeah, that's not happening," Allen said.

"Too *fucking* right it's not!" Laurel piped hotly.

"We don't have time for this." Jake removed his Alice pack and wedged it between the wall of the pickup's bed and the rest of their supplies. "I know you guys could keep up, but I need you to offload fast and be ready for me when I get there."

Laurel didn't move as the others got in the cab. "I'm *not* letting you go alone, O'Connor," she said, hip cocked, and looking pissed.

"I can do this, but not with anyone else along." Jake stepped close. "You've got to *trust* me."

"I do! But you can't expect me..."

Jake kissed her, cutting off the argument. When they broke apart, she looked at him, half-smiling, half scared sick over his crazy plan.

"I'm going to get you for this later," Laurel said.

He grinned. "Looking forward to it."

She pulled out the secure radio and shoved it into the left lower pocket of his Tac-vest.

"We'll wait for you ta call," George said. "Just in case any of those things are close by. Don't want yer radio squawkin' and drawin' em in."

"Are you sure about this, man?" Allen asked. "You know I run a lot."

"I've got a plan. Don't worry." Then Jake smiled tightly and jogged to the alley's mouth. Laurel and the rest watched as he crouched, and then ghosted slowly around the corner and out of sight.

"He's a little crazy, isn't he?" Maggie asked, locking her door.

"Hell," George rolled his window down slightly, so he didn't choke them with his stogie, "It'll be a walk in the park. What could go wrong?"

* * *

Jake's was fucked.

He was sure at that point that whichever little shit-head of a god was in charge of his life was so stupid that he was the one who handed out mints in the afterlife's bathroom. Probably due to the fact that none of the other gods wanted to be the one responsible for sending their moronic cousin to help out down in Hades. He'd break a pipe or something, then the underworld would flood with feces. So, said insipid deity was kept busy torturing Jake. That was the only explanation for how quickly his KISS (keep it simple, stupid) plan went from simple to FUBAR (fucked up beyond all recognition) so quickly.

He was going to make it a *point* to sucker punch the halo-wearing little shit, when he went to the pearly gates.

The writer used abandoned vehicles littering the sides of the street to stay virtually out of sight, as he approached the oncoming crowd. The things were slow as hell, but that didn't make them any less dangerous. Or frightening for that matter. When he reached the corner half a block south, the infected were just beginning to spill into the intersection from the opposite side, slowly making their way past the crosswalk. He sheltered behind a burned out mail truck and considered his options.

It didn't make sense to waste ammunition drawing the creatures. Counting the eleven rounds in George's pistol, he only had thirty-eight left and he needed to save them, just in case. After taking a quick look around, he scurried left to a silver Honda Civic and began smashing out its windows.

The crowd turned, almost as one, and he stepped a couple of paces into the street. "Hey, you ugly fuckers. Hungry?"

A hundred plus dead jaws dropped and let loose gurgling moans, sending a spike of fear up Jake's spine. He turned and jogged east, every now and then busting out a car's window or striking a light pole with his crowbar to cause some noise. The dead followed as best they could, shuffling awkwardly on unfeeling legs and reaching out in his direction. Jake sped up. He widened his lead to a hundred yards, leading the horde for two blocks, stopped at the far side of an intersection, and waited for them to catch up.

He wanted as many of the things as possible to see him cut north again, hopefully drawing them away from the noise Foster's pickup would make. That way, when the others reached the safehouse, the surrounding area would be free of the creatures. They could offload by the time he jogged back, so Jake could just pop in. As he watched the crowd move slowly towards him, he dropped the point of his crowbar against the manhole cover in the middle of the intersection repeatedly.

The dead kept moving onward and, judging by their speed, he had almost a good five minutes before he'd have to make tracks. Jake pulled the secure radio out of his vest and flipped it on. "You guys there?"

"*We're here! Are you all right?*" Laurel's voice was strained and full of fear.

"Don't worry, I'm fine. Just playing Pied Piper to a *really* messed up group of hungry rats." He watched the dead as they moved towards him up the block. "Tell George to head out. It should be safe now, since I seem to be so popular. I'll circle north. Be nice if someone was there to let me in, okay?"

"*We'll be waiting.*" Jake could hear the trucks engine come to life in the background over the mike. "*Be careful.*"

"Who me? Out." He killed the radio and put it back in his vest pocket.

As he secured the Velcro tab, glass shattered behind him. Jake spun around to find over a dozen infected pushing through the front window of a BW3s. Fully half of them were wearing employee shirts while the rest were ex-customers. They ignored the shards of glass that sliced at their grey flesh and crowded through the broken window. A couple lost most of their fingers from clawing at the sharp edges in their haste to get through, but the missing digits didn't affect them at all. He noted that the fingers didn't continue to move after being sliced from the creatures' hands, and then filed the factoid away for later consideration.

One of the employees, closer than the others—due to *not* tripping over the windowpane on the way out—moved slowly towards him, lips drawn back showing his blackened gums in anticipation of feeding. Jake considered the awful thing for a moment, strode forward and brought the hook end of his crowbar down through its skull. The zombie slumped bonelessly to the road and he kicked it in the face, jarring the weapon free.

"Sorry. I always liked Hooters' wings better. Their waitresses were hotter, too."

The rest of the group began rising to their rotting feet and it was time to go. He walked quickly north, sticking to the center of the road, watching every window he passed for signs of hungry occupants. Many had already been broken out. The few that hadn't were so covered in grime and gore, that there was no doubt the interiors of those storefronts were the last places in the world he'd ever want to see.

The B-Dub group was absorbed into the shambling crowd, once it reached the intersection. Even half a block away, the sight of that many hungry dead motivated Jake to move a bit faster. He started jogging, moving steadily north two blocks, then turned west for the longest leg of his return trip. Two miles isn't that great a distance really, but under stressful conditions (like say, zombies roaming around, wanting to *eat* your ass) it can seem much, *much* farther. Fear, adrenaline, and stress could steal your strength and cognitive abilities in situations like that, making it impossible to carry out even the most basic plan.

It was called *tunneling*. Seeing only what was right in front of you and never taking notice of the guy with the gun to your temple, three feet to your left. So, relying on training the old frog had drilled into him during his time with the SAS, Jake started to slow his breathing and carefully scanned his surroundings. He saw a few zombies along his path in the distance, but reasoned he could dodge them easily. While even one was enough to kill you, as long as he kept his head, making it to Foster's bolt hole wouldn't be too difficult.

So of course, half-way back, the gods began throwing speed-bumps in his way. As he came within thirty yards of an intersection, a *second* horde began trickling into it from the north. This one matched the group he'd lead away from the others and then some in numbers. There were so many that the creatures were almost shoulder to shoulder as they flooded into view. There wasn't time to take cover—read: hide—and many of them saw him right off the bat. Their moans were *terrifying* as they began stumping in his direction, yellow eyes focused on his flesh. Jake sprinted for the southern side of the intersection, staying just out of the lead ghoul's grasp as he cleared the corner at top speed. The hungry pack was way too close for comfort, so he made like a fugitive and fled for his life.

Minutes later, he turned east again, having left the creatures blocks behind. Feeling winded, he slowed to a brisk walk to catch his breath and checked his route again. A lone zombie lay in the middle of the street a few hundred feet further but, since it was missing one arm along with everything from its pelvis down, the writer discounted it as a threat and simply moved around it. The thing moaned feebly as he passed, but he didn't want to become distracted by taking the time to deal with it. The only thing *that* one would be eating in the foreseeable future would maybe be the odd, slow moving insect.

Jake moved east at an easy, distance-eating trot, conserving his strength. He was barely halfway back, less if you took into account the detour he'd taken. He could still hear the dead moaning out, far behind to the north, and their awful cries gave his legs new purpose. With effort, he fought down a moment of panic and concentrated on his surroundings again. A trio of infected were on his right, so he dodged left, leaving them to move slowly around an empty COTA bus he'd circled for cover. There was quartet a hundred yards farther on. Jake avoided them by climbing atop the flatbed of a semi and then quickly off the other side again. A pair of zombies shuffled from the door of a burned out, noodle shop. The writer shoved one into the other and jogged on as the dead duo struggled to rise, tangled up in the small doorway by each other's limbs. It seemed as if his plan had worked, due to the lack of too many large groups, which was a relief. It there had been more of the creatures, eventually they would wear a single person down and consume them. That was why his plan had been so dangerous, but also necessary. The risk was his to take, even though the others—Laurel especially—had been against it. That, and he was damned if he'd ask someone else to do something he wouldn't dare do *himself.*

Three *hours* later, after having to cut farther north (and doubling back on his route a few times) to avoid two more packs of the dead, Jake finally neared the cross street he needed to cut south. He felt good. Pretty scared and really sweaty, but good. Right up until he turned the corner, that is.

There were dozens of zombies in the street, but he had no other way to reach the gated lot at the back of George's building and no time to circle the block. Not with large groups of the dead to the east. Also, a few on the street had already noticed him and were moving slowly in his direction.

"Aw, *shit.*" Jake pulled away the tape on his thigh that secured the Glock Foster had given him and, tossing the remnants on the street, he chambered a round. He shifted his crowbar to his left hand, took the pistol in his right, and sped to the far side of the street. The dead oriented on him and began moaning. That caused more of the creatures to take notice, and he took a few deep breaths, steeling himself for a fight.

Using the cars as obstacles as best he could, the writer moved steadily down the block. He managed to get three-quarters of the way to the alley before he had no choice but to open fire.

A pair of zombies got close enough to smell. *Not* a pleasant experience. One had been a large man in a hat that read *Get her done*! and had a silhouette of a topless woman on the front. He was a full head taller than Jake's six-foot frame and had been quite a bit beefier. The other was what remained of a Greenpeace member presumably, considering she had *Save the Whales* emblazoned on the front of her now gore-smeared t-shirt. He stroked the Glock's trigger once, blowing the larger creature's brain out the back of its head, kicked the other in the chest, sending her skidding backwards across pavement, and he started running.

Jake slipped on the first creature's stinking brain matter as he entered the alley, but rolled to his feet and was off again in a moment. There were a few roaming the fifty-yard stretch of alley to the gate, but he took them out at close range, executioner style. He double tapped each one, making sure the miserable sacks of shit didn't get back up to come after him as he passed. Reaching the massive gate he yelled for the others to open up, but got no reply. He pounded against the thick steel with the flat of his hand and then the crowbar. Nothing. The dead began to filter into the alley, moaning thickly and heading for where he stood beating on the gate.

"Shit!" He knelt, dropped the crowbar next to his knee, then pulled the Hammer pistol from its thigh holster. He placed it beside the slim tool, along with the gun's two, extra magazines just to the left of his leg. If he could hold out for a few minutes, maybe...

Who was he kidding?

He was fucked.

The others weren't there.

Thanks to the broken glass Foster had cemented into the top of the wall when he'd had it built, there was no getting over it.

He only had three left in the Glock, twenty-eight for the Hammer, his crowbar and a...

He snatched the secure radio out of his pocket to find it had been smashed during his fall while entering the alley. Jake cursed loudly, hurled it to the pavement and took aim at the crowd of stinking creatures. He dropped the first one with a double tap, and then traded pistols. There was one left in the Glock and he was saving it for himself. He wouldn't let the zombies consume him. He took careful aim with each squeeze of the trigger, dropping creature after creature to the grimy pavement. After nine shots and eight kills, he changed magazines, dropped the slide and continued firing. He only killed seven this time, but the dead were having problems making it over the bodies of their fellows that littered the ground thanks to his careful shooting. He yelled for the others again as he slapped his last clip into the pistol.

I'm going to die here in this stinking alley, he thought, firing into the ghouls again.

He killed one with each round this time before the gun clicked empty. Jake looked at the Hammer and slid it back in its holster. He unscrewed the silencer on the Glock, tossed it to the ground and shoved the pistol into the waistband of his pants. Taking his crowbar in a two-handed grip, he watched the approaching dead. If he was going down, he was taking some of *them* along.

Some of the infected had moved past the fallen bodies and began to come for him.

"Goddamnit... I *hate* you," he said. "You took away everything. Everything but Laurel. So now you're gonna take me, but I'll make you *pay* for it."

Jake waited for death as it stalked towards him hungrily.

* * *

There were still pockets of resistance.

Some people, the ones who had prepared for a disaster, those with wilderness training, even the odd lucky schmuck in a bunker or nuclear launch facility still held out. They were few and far between, but they managed to survive. And not by drinking their own piss either.

Well, some did...

Many who had been the "undesirables" in the deep south; bayou trappers, gator hunters, even shrimp fishermen along the coast, managed to not only keep their families safe by vanishing into the Everglades, but also formed small, well-defended communities. It was nigh impossible for the dead to navigate the swamps, let alone find survivor colonies among the endless tributaries, waterways, and bogs.

Those who took up occupancy in the hidden refuges managed to live not only in relative safety, but also a fair level of comfort.

They did miss real toilet paper after a few weeks though...

CHAPTER FOURTEEN

Kat blew through the tenement's door and into the lot.

She ran as though Jikininki—evil demons her mother told her stories about when she was little—snapped at her heels.

The blue-haired pharmacy tech had been watching the building's exterior cameras, feeling surly and bored. She'd had to stay behind *again*, while the others had gone out to look for Jake. He was hours overdue and hadn't contacted them via the secure radio Laurel had provided him. So, out the four went—even though Foster thought it was a bad idea—to search for their missing writer. Or his corpse. Kat wouldn't believe Jake was dead, however. She wasn't even going to consider *that* idea, unless she actually saw his ravaged body...

Damn it, she thought, angrily. Pushing said line of thought firmly from her mind, Kat went back to looking at the screen.

She'd been watching a pack of the dead move slowly by when Jake streaked into view, running hard for the rear gate. She'd all but jumped down the flight of stairs, her Grandfather's katana in hand, calling out instructions to Karen as she dashed through the machine shop. Kat sent her after Leo, yelling for them to stay inside the safe-house to protect Heather and Gertrude. The hidden hatch in Foster's office cycled open and she was through in an instant. It took her forty-one seconds to get from the second floor, through the apartment building to the lot door, then another nine getting to the gate.

Too long! *Too long*! she thought frantically. *No time*!

She jumped up towards where the twelve foot wall met the building's edge. Bouncing back and forth between their surfaces—like a ninja out of a Jackie Chan movie—in four quick hops, Kat sailed over the broken glass embedded on its top edge and into the alley. Literally on the fly, she saw Jake fighting for his life against the remnants of a zombie crowd. A baker's dozen remained, but he was spending all his time and effort staying out of their reach in the narrow confines.

Her sword leapt free as she landed silently behind the creatures, just as he finally managed to crush a nearby skull. It blurred out and three more zombies dropped to the pavement, missing their heads. Jake would've been seriously impressed if he hadn't been busy stabbing another with the crowbar's chisel tip through the eye. Kat saw that his face was the picture of unchecked rage, and had his eyes changed color somehow? No matter. She didn't have time to look right then.

Two more infected turned in her direction and lost their heads to a flashing, horizontal slice. One of their disgusting craniums caused a third zombie to fall after it bounced under its feet, providing a gap for Jake to squeeze through, and he took a defensive stance beside her. The remaining five (and the one who'd tripped over the rolling head) followed them as they backed towards the gate.

"Tell me you have a gun," he panted.

"No chance to grab one," Kat replied. "I only have my sword because I'd been practicing, before I got roped into monitor duty."

"I can't make it over the wall, Kat. My legs feel like Jell-O." He looked at her and motioned at the gate. "Go! I'll keep them busy while you climb over."

"Forget it! I'm not leaving you out here with those bastards! We kill them all!" She took both arms off one that got close, and then kicked it back into the pack. "Use their numbers against them. Keep them off their feet!"

He smashed the nearest zombie's face in and stiff-armed it back into the others. It fell into two more and all three went down, allowing Kat to cut one in half from crown to clavicle, roll under another's grasping hands, then finish off the one missing its arms with a thrust through its temple. She pirouetted quickly to slice the grabby ghoul's head just above its eyes, sending the entire dome of its skull to the ground along with most of its brain. The things body hit the pavement and the rest of its brain matter (which resembled a repulsive-smelling, grayish-brown mass of mushy cauliflower) tumbled wetly from its skull.

The writer yanked the pistol from his waistband and put his last bullet between the eyes of one of the surviving trio. Dropping the Glock, he crouched, spun, and swept the legs out from beneath another, sending it rolling to the far side of the alley. The third was near enough to grasp his combat vest when it lunged at him, attempting to reach his neck. He was forced to grab it by the throat one-handed, just under its jaw and backpedal to avoid its snapping teeth. Kat jumped towards them, sword held blade-back in a reverse fighting grip, but she needn't have bothered.

Jake was *pissed*.

Dropping his crowbar, he caught the thing's hand with his own, and set himself. Then stepping close—too close, Kat thought—he extended his arm that gripped the struggling horror's throat, kicked its legs forward, and rode it skull-first into the concrete. The zombie's head pulped like a rotten melon, sending chunks of bone into its brains and said brains across the pavement.

She wasn't surprised by Jake's ability, but at the vicious grimace on his face as he killed the putrid thing. He was excellent when practicing self-defense, nearly a match for her—and Kat had been studying martial arts since she was a child. He'd never shown *rage* before, though. He was normally pretty controlled, if not calm, but now? The look on his face as he'd smashed the things skull in and fumbled for his crowbar was one of primal hatred. The last creature was just rising to its feet, when he spiked it through the nose. Rancid fluids exploded from its eyes and sinuses as the weapon penetrated, then it stiffened as the steel rammed onward into its brain.

"Chew on that, you miserable fuck." Jake put the sole of his combat boot against its chest, shoving the thing away. He yanked his crowbar free and allowed the body to fall back to the gritty pavement.

That was when the massive gate behind them cycled opened. Leo stood wide-eyed beside the inner control panel, awkwardly holding an assault rifle as the pair started towards him. It looked as if he'd been in the shower, because the cargo shorts the teen wore were nearly soaked and water was still beaded on his thin torso. The two blood-speckled fighters entered and he punched in the activation code again. The steel barrier slid shut, sealing off the gory scene in the alley and Jake almost went to his knees in relief.

"Holy crap! You guys kicked ass!" Leo said, seeing the massacred dead outside as the gate closed. "Jake, we were *really* worried! The others went out looking for you almost an hour ago!"

The exhausted man leaned heavily against the cinder block wall of the tenement, soaked in sweat and pale as a ghost. Kat glanced at him and said, "Leo, can you go radio the others and let them know Jake made it back? Tell George to expect some obstacles in the alley, too. We kind of made a mess."

"Sure thing." Nodding, he started for the door and stopped after pulling it open to smile at Jake again. "I'm really glad you're back. You gotta tell me what happened!"

Jake gave him a tired grin and a thumbs up as Leo hurried into the building.

"So..." Kat cleaned her sword on a rag from her back pocket, then tossed the soiled fabric into the gate-side dumpster. "How was *your* day, honey?"

"Oh, it was just *great*, sweetie, but traffic was murder." Jake's voice was strained and his body shook. He passed a hand over his sweaty face and pushed away from the wall. "That was way too close. Those things almost had me."

Kat sheathed the ancient katana across her back again, then set an easy hand on his shoulder and gave him a bright smile. "Are you kidding me? You did great. See? I told you having me kick the crap out of you daily would make a difference."

He turned his head to her and that serious gaze made Kat's heart speed up. "Maybe, but you saved my ass."

Oh man, she thought, *the things I give up for my roommate...*

"Yeah, well. Be a shame to waste an ass like that." Realizing her comment was taking their conversation into dangerous territory, she turned towards the door, expecting him to laugh and follow her. Instead, he caught her wrist, stopping her forward motion and causing her to look back. He stepped forward, pulling her around to face him again and cupped her face with his free hand. Those pale blue eyes of his spiked her like a butterfly on a pin. Kat couldn't make her mouth work as he moved so close that she could feel his breath against her lips when he spoke.

"You saved my life," he said. There wasn't any humor in his voice. "I'll never forget that. Thank you, Katherine."

Then he kissed her.

Kat eyes widened in surprise for a moment, then fluttered shut as she lost herself. Jake's kiss was warm with affection and very gentle. He didn't try to stick his tongue down her throat (which was a definite plus) and his hands didn't go roaming either. He broke it off after half a dozen heartbeats, and when she finally managed to open her eyes he grinned at her.

Her face remained blank. "That's a first."

"We *did* kiss twice before if you remember," he said, taking his hand from her face.

"Not that. You've never called me by my name." she replied quietly. "It's was nice."

"Oh. I never really... Laurel always calls you that. I just thought you preferred it."

She looked away. "I know. Sorry for being all girly right after we hacked up a bunch of zombies, but I've never let anybody see me like that. I'm just afraid you'll feel weird, now that you've seen me... kill people."

Jake looked at her worriedly. "They're not people. You know that, right?"

Her dark blue hair covered half her face as she shook her head. "You saw what I did. You *saw*. I'm *good* at stuff like that. It makes people afraid of me. Like it did with Allen after we saved Maggie and the girls. So I don't let anybody know about what I can do. I don't let them in." She looked at him sadly. "Once they find out..."

"What?" he demanded. "That you're brave and selfless and willing to risk your life for a friend? That you're one of the strongest people I've known since... well, for a long, damn time, and you shouldn't give a shit what people think? That you're intelligent and beautiful and funny and any idiot, *including* Allen, that can't handle it can go fuck themselves as far as I'm concerned?"

"You don't *understand*!" she said miserably. "I've never wondered why I couldn't keep a steady boyfriend. It's because I can't be some fragile, little, lotus flower."

Her grandmother had never forgiven Kat's mother for teaching her daughter the martial arts. She'd wanted Kat to be a *proper Japanese lady*, as she'd termed it. Quiet, reserved, and (like herself) concerned with nothing but pleasing her husband. The day Kat rejected that idea—her thirteenth birthday—during a visit overseas with her parents, was the last time her grandmother had ever spoken to her.

Her grandfather had been the polar opposite. He was delighted that she knew the family's secret techniques and had tested her diligently each morning, prior to her parents rising, in the family home's courtyard. Then every day the two of them went and had cheeseburgers for breakfast at *Oogata Midoriiro Tokage*, literally translated as the Big Green Lizard. If they'd called the place Godzilla Burgers, it would've been sued.

"I have to be me, but when I am, it drives guys away!" Kat explained. "I've tried to change, but I can't and that's just..."

"Bullshit!" Jake snapped, and gripped her arms, really angry now. "That's utter bullshit! I wouldn't change *anything* about you for the world. And just so you know. Me, personally? I think having an equal is a *lot* more preferable, than having a prissy, cowardly, drama-happy, prima-donna that I'd constantly have to protect!"

Kat started to pull away. "Sure. I've heard *that* before."

He jerked her forcefully back. There was something he needed to say. "Don't. Don't you *dare* compare me to morons who couldn't appreciate you. Oh, and for the record? A fragile, little, lotus flower wouldn't have been able to save me earlier. I'd be dead."

From the stunned look on her face, she hadn't thought about that.

"You're aggressive side doesn't scare *me*. If you want the truth, I think it's sexy as all hell. I needed *you* out there today. I want you to be strong and outspoken and fucking *deadly*, because we're heading west soon, and you've got skills none of the group can match. Myself included." Kat could only stare at him open-mouthed as he tore all her carefully constructed walls apart. "Do you understand? We need you, Katherine. *I* need you."

After standing there trembling for a few moments, she threw herself into Jake's arms with a low cry and locked their lips together.

This kiss was far more than their last. Their lips moved against each other's slowly, bringing a long, neglected void they'd both ignored to the surface. It was like walking for days through the Sahara, only to come across a glacier fed pool in the searing desert heat and the relief that diving headlong into its soothing waters would bring.

Kat's capacity for conscious thought fled the moment their kiss began. She clung to Jake, her hands grasping at the material of his combat vest, body straining to be closer than the limits of their skin would allow. He responded in kind by wrapping her in his arms, one hand pressed low over her spine, the other cradling her neck as he bowed her backwards slightly. It took her breath away. She gasped against his lips and moved her arms around his neck, fingers sliding through his unruly hair as her mouth pulled at him. Her tongue danced lightly against his, demanding that he match her need or be consumed by it.

Jake tried to keep a clear head, but it was almost impossible. Her hungry lips, her fingers that were locked in his hair, the way she felt with her body smashed to his, all threatened to cause him to lose control. Kat moved against him without inhibition, throwing off heat like a steam-driven engine with purpose. It was only a long-nurtured conscience that kept him from tearing away their restrictive clothing and lowering them both to the ground, right there. He wanted to bury himself inside her, make her writhe with pleasure, feel the score of her nails across his back, and hear her cry out as they coupled on the gritty asphalt.

But he didn't. He did care about Kat in a way he couldn't explain and felt drawn to the lovely, sword-wielding, half-crazy young woman, partially due to their daily sessions of *punch-me, kick-you* over the last month and a half. He and Laurel were definitely an item though, and Jake fully intended for them to remain as such. He had no illusions. He knew he was falling for her, hard, and that was a bad idea during an apocalypse involving the mobile dead. Or any kind of apocalypse really. But he didn't give a damn. Finding a woman like Laurel—smart, beautiful, and creative musically—was either a stroke of luck or just fate. She was passionate. Boy was she ever. Tough, good with a sidearm (again, zombie apocalypse) and wasn't the type to crush his heart like a jellybean when some guy with a thick wallet strutted by.

That was why he regretfully brought their kiss to an end. Kat released her grip on his hair. She could tell what he was thinking and smiled sadly. Closing her eyes, the lovely woman pressed his forehead to her own.

"So. In another world, maybe?" She asked, with a sad grin.

"Absolutely." He brushed Kat's indigo hair away from her face. "Somewhere in the multiverse we're on a beach together, drinking good rum, making love, and generally scaring the wildlife."

She cupped his jaw with both hands. "I'm not sure which is *worse*. Never getting to roll around in the surf, or the fact that you just let your geek-flag fly by using the term *multiverse*."

She kissed him briefly again then stepped back as he laughed and retrieved his crowbar from the ground. Kat kept his hand in hers though, and they started across the lot. She was sure if she let go just then, she would start crying. The *last* thing she wanted was for Jake to see her like that.

"You're awesome. You know that?" He squeezed her hand as he opened the door for her.

She grinned wickedly. "Just you wait. I'll be able to take down twice as many zombies next time. From now on? I'll be sure to keep a pistol on me. Since I know how to deal with them at close range now, those things won't be so tough."

He raised an eyebrow in her direction. "I'm not sure which is worse. How that comment would worry most people, or the fact that I'm really looking forward to seeing you do it."

Kat's smile was dazzling. "You ain't seen nothing yet, gaijin..."

* * *

The others got back about thirty minutes later.

Jake had cleaned up a bit by that time, changing out of his gore-covered Khakis into a fresh pair of army-issue, battle-dress bottoms—read: fatigues—and swapping his bloody tactical vest for another out of Foster's stores. He left it hanging over a chair-back at the table in the common room where Gertrude sat with the kids, sipping her ever present mug of Earl Grey.

Laurel was the first one up. She sprung from George's pickup almost before he brought it to a halt, ran through the abandoned tenement, past the access plate and up the metal stairs to the common room. Not saying a word, she almost knocked Jake over as she leapt the last ten feet into his arms.

He caught her mid-leap and her mouth sought his desperately. Wrapping one, long leg around his own, the other dangling an inch above the floor as he held her aloft, she hugged him so tightly that Jake was sure he felt his ribs creaking under the pressure. He said nothing, even as her strength hurt him, and continued to kiss her.

He wasn't really surprised at her reaction, until the redhead pressed her face to his neck. Laurel began to shake and clutched at him, causing the collar of his shirt to bunch under his throat, which severely restricted his ability to obtain much-needed oxygen.

* * *

Kat would've sympathized with her roommate's reaction at the sight of Jake, safe and whole, but she was upstairs in her room.

The ninja girl had told Gertrude that she needed to change out of her own blood-splattered clothing and headed up to the third floor. In reality, she simply needed a quiet place to cry for a while.

Her heart was breaking. When she met Jake, she believed him to be the type of person her roommate would connect with. That was why she'd set them up to meet. What Kat came to learn during the horror and chaos of the dead rising though, was that he was also the kind of man *she* connected with. Rugged good looks which—at least in her eyes—he had in abundance were nice, but largely unnecessary. He had an excellent, if somewhat nerdy, sense of humor, a caring personality, and those eyes...

But she'd set him up with her best friend, instead of keeping him for herself.

Stupid, she thought. *I'm so stupid.*

She was drawn to him. The way he spoke. The way he moved. The way he treated people, even when he was scared to death. Like in the alley, when he told her to leave him. The way he wanted her to save herself, as if she was *worth* more.

"Oh God. He's a *hero*," she moaned. "And I'm in *love* with him!"

Kat was horrified. She'd been of the opinion that there wasn't any such animal. Or if there was, they were an endangered species. Not believing there were heroes out there was far easier than knowing she would never find one for herself.

Worse, she knew full well that heroes usually didn't live to a ripe old age. More often than not, they came to a swift, bloody, and extremely messy end. The pain that realization caused felt like someone stabbed a rusty knife into her soul. It doubled her over, until she lay curled up on the bed, weeping hysterically into her pillow. She couldn't get her breath, and her heart pounded so hard it threatened to burst from her chest in fear. Jake was going to *die*. Kat knew it as surely as she knew she couldn't bear to continue living afterwards.

She could never tell him. It would make him avoid her; never mind the hurt it would cause Laurel to have her best friend attempt to cherry-pick her man.

Her chest hurt.

She could *never* tell him. The thought caused her lower lip to quiver and she couldn't stop trembling. She screamed into the pillow so no one would hear and tried to control herself. She failed. Kat sobbed brokenheartedly, pillow clutched to her chest as the pain shook her.

* * *

"Laurel, it's ok." Jake held her easily, rubbing his hands over her back. "I wasn't bitten. I'm fine. Really sweaty and ready to drop, but fine."

She didn't respond except to squeeze him tighter. Jake swayed back and forth, rocking her against his chest.

George, Allen, and Maggie made their way into the common room, all looking very thankful to be back inside their little haven. Heather hurried over to embrace Allen as he punched his friend in the shoulder.

"Man, the next time you wanna take a stroll? Let's not be anywhere *near* this city, yeah?" Allen said, after taking Heather into his arms.

"Fuckin'-A," George growled, plunking down heavily in one of the dining chairs. The old soldier looked beat after driving around in streets full of maggot heads for the last two hours. "That's the best, goddamned idea I've heard since all this shit *started*."

Laurel pulled back a little so she could see Jake's face, eyes still overly full and unwilling to loosen her arms from around his waist.

"We thought you were dead!" She said, raggedly fighting a storm of tears. "We thought they got you and... and..."

She hid her face in his neck again and started to sob.

Jake was a little disappointed by her lack of faith in his abilities, but he understood how Laurel felt. On the day of the outbreak, he'd been almost mad with need to get to her. She evidently felt the same way during the three-hour wait, while he'd engaged in a terrifying and exhausting version of Pac Man with hundreds of zombies. The difference was, as he'd slowly made his way back to Foster's hidey hole, she didn't have the slightest clue where he was. Maybe he'd been cornered or hurt somehow. Maybe he'd been *bitten*, then decided it was better to end it all away from the group so he didn't endanger anyone. Realizing how hard it must have been to watch him traipse off, stupidly playing the hero in an effort to keep the others safe, he was content to hold her until the worst of the storm passed.

"Don't cry. It took me a little longer than I thought it would to get back, but I didn't *really* have any close calls." Jake decided a comforting lie would be better than letting her know he'd almost become the main course for a rotting crowd, right behind the safe house. He'd talk to Kat, once Laurel calmed down, to make sure she didn't slip and mistakenly tell her about his brush with death. "Those things are slow as hell and about as mentally agile as a bag full of hammers. Out thinking them wasn't hard, I just had to..."

He wound down as he noticed Maggie and the two men looking at him wearing strange expressions. "What?"

"You came in from the north?" Foster asked. "Through the lot gate?"

"Yeah. I told you I'd..."

"He didn't see it," Maggie said.

They were all acting weird. Jake took Laurel's chin and brought her face up. "What happened?"

She got herself under control again and replied, "Out front. In the street. It's awful."

"Can you show me?" he asked.

She bit her lip and wiped her eyes with one hand. "I don't know if I can look at it again. I might not be able to handle it twice."

"It's alright. George can show me. Stay here with Gertie and the kids while..."

"*No!*" Laurel clutched his shirt tightly again. "You're not going out there again! No way!"

"We'll go up to the roof." Foster rose and put his work-roughened palm lightly on her arm. "I don't much feel like sticking my nose out there. Not now."

That worried Jake a bit. George had seen blood and death and horror in two wars across the face of the globe. If something made *him* uneasy...

* * *

There were bodies on all the roads. So many. In some places you'd think it was the road to Perdition, paved not with good intentions, but with the dead. The truly dead.
The damned, however, still walked...

CHAPTER FIFTEEN

Jake stood on the roof with Foster and Kat.

He stared at himself down on the street through a pair of binoculars George brought along. Well, it wasn't really him. It was a corpse *dressed* like him. Khakis, CBGB t-shirt, combat boots, the whole nine yards. It wasn't walking around, hungrily looking for someone to consume, for a couple of reasons.

One. It hadn't been killed by the zombies. They tended to *eat* their victims, not impale them with a crowbar just above their navel.

Two. It had been *crucified* on the rear of a tow truck, then tied to the wrecker arm with razor wire at its wrists and shoulders. A strand also encircled its neck, securing it vertically.

It was also missing a few things.

While it still had a head, everything from the bottom teeth up was *gone*. Like a gigantic ice cream scoop had taken it all away in one brutal swipe. If that wasn't bad enough, the front of the dead man's pants had been cut away from knees to waistband, and his genitalia had been brutally removed.

"What the *fuck*? How the hell did *that* get there?" Jake exclaimed, studying the corpse.

"It was waiting outside when we got back," Foster replied. "That's why Red was so panicked. Thought it was you myself, 'til I took a closer look. Gave me a hell of a turn."

"Did you see anything on the cameras?" he asked Kat.

She shook her head. "They don't cover that area. The only way to see it is from the roof. Or if you happen to be *running with zombies.*"

Jake rolled his eyes and passed her the binoculars.

"Whoever did this tied him to the crossbar while he was still *alive*. There's a lot of damage all along his arms, like he put up a struggle. Did you see the note?" She lowered the binoculars and pointed. "Behind him and to the right on the driver's side door."

He looked again and sure enough, a piece of notebook paper was taped to the window. "You're next!" he read.

"See the needle marks at the elbow?" Foster blew his nose on a red bandana he pulled from his back pocket. "Look *familiar* to anyone?"

"Barron," Jake said numbly. "We searched him before we taped him to the chair, after he and Nichole tried to drug Karen. He had fresh track marks along the veins at his left elbow. Are you *positive* it's him?"

George nodded. "I thought so when I saw those. I made sure. That stupid tattoo he'd show off on his stomach is pretty distinctive."

"Damn. *Nichole* killed him?" Kat folded her arms under her breasts. "I knew she was a crazy bitch, but this is a whole new level of nutso. Even for her."

Jake pulled out a cigarette, lit up with his Zippo, and stared at the slaughtered clubber, trying to work the scenario out in his head. It didn't add up. "If Nichole did this, she had help. I can tell you from experience after fighting those *things* out there; it would take more strength than she had on her best day to stick a crowbar though his gut like that."

"So, what? During all this...zombies...the end of the world, she found somebody as crazy as she is?" Kat frowned. "That's *really* fucked up."

"Well regardless of who's helping her, they obviously have one *hell* of a hard on at the thought of getting us. Whether for the supplies or our location or..." He broke off to glance at Kat and scratched at his stubble-rough cheek.

"Yeah. That's what I think too."

Jake nodded slowly, exhaling a cloud of smoke that wafted away in the breeze. "That's why they cut his package off. To send a message."

Kat looked back and forth between the grim faced-writer and the old fixer. "You're gonna have to explain that one to me."

"*You're next*. Me, specifically. Think about how they dressed him before they brought him here. Now take into account they castrated him." Jake flicked the butt of his smoke over the edge of the roof. "They're saying I won't be using mine anymore, once they get their hands on us. Maybe because they plan to do the same to me. Maybe because they've got plans for whoever I might be using it *with*."

They looked at Mike's hanging form for a few minutes before Foster broke the silence. "I'm gonna go give our ride the once over.

Tomorrow good for you?"

The writer nodded. "If you would, ask the kids to help Gertrude tonight and I'll tell Laurel. She said she needed a drink after seeing that, and I don't think she needs to know someone's targeting me. Not this very second anyway."

George gave him a thumbs up and went inside, leaving the two of them alone on the rooftop. Jake was looking intently at the message on the tow truck when Kat stepped close beside him. She was shivering, even in the warm July breeze.

"I've been having nightmares about something like that happening," she said finally. "Ever since the day of the outbreak."

He turned his head to look at her. "You never said anything."

Kat stuffed her hands halfway into the front pockets of her jeans. She could only get them halfway in because the pants were tight with a capital TIGHT. She shrugged, causing the torso-hugging, belly shirt she wore to gape around her midsection, providing him a brief glimpse of her flat stomach. "Not really something you talk about socially, you know? *How've you been handling the apocalypse, Kat*? Oh, I've been having nightmares about being chained to a group of other women and raped almost every night. When I'm actually able to get to sleep, that is. *Alrighty, been great talking with you, Kat. Gotta go. Write if you find work...*"

Jake stared at her, feeling like a brain-dead moron instead of someone who used to make his *living* through his powers of observation.

He turned, took her by the shoulders, and pulled her close. Her body was stiff at first, but slowly the tension drained away and Kat pressed her face against his neck, much as Laurel had done earlier. She had no way of knowing that, but he took note of the odd similarity.

She slowly passed her arms around his ribs, as if she were unsure how the gesture would be received. "Funny huh? I'm so good at taking care of myself, but I can't handle a few bad dreams?"

His arms tightened around her protectively. "I wouldn't let that happen."

She laughed. "I hate to tell you this, but I can still take you three out of five falls. Besides, I'm a big girl. I can take care of myself."

"I know. It's one of the reasons I like you so much."

Kat considered that for a moment. "But you're going to ignore me on this. Aren't you?"

"Sure am," he admitted.

"I can't let you to do that," Kat said.

"You don't get a say. Oh, and I'm a big boy. I can take care of myself. But I still needed *you* earlier in the alley," he replied. "I won't let somebody do that to you. I *promise*, Kat. I'll kill anyone who tries."

Jake felt her breath against his jugular as she sighed contently, warming the skin over his throat and sending a thrill up from the base of his spine. She settled closer in his arms and he wondered now why *he* hadn't asked *her* out when they'd met that day at the pharmacy.

Because you're a damn coward sometimes, his back-brain informed him. *You could've had her, but you were still pining and moaning over...*

He didn't let himself finish that thought and concentrated on the woman holding him. Kat was gorgeous, and he was human. It felt like every one of her body's curves found a corresponding niche against him, and he was finding it a struggle to keep his composure again.

"How did you ever stay single before all of this?" she asked, then went silent for a moment. "I can hear you. I can hear your heartbeat."

Of all the things she could've said just then, he found that to be both the most flattering and the most erotic. He looked down and saw her, eyes closed, one ear pressed high on his chest, listening to the sound of his heart speeding up. As he watched her, Jake realized something. He'd seen her scared, ticked off, half-blitzed, he even knew the mischievous look her face took on when she was playing the part of a goofy vixen.

But he'd never seen her content.

"Clean living with a dash of geekdom," he replied. "Come on, you've seen what I do for fun. Play with firearms, kill zombies, use quotes that reference obscure spatial anomalies."

Kat laughed. They stood together on the roof for a while, holding one another, and enjoying the breeze that *almost* swept the smell of rot from the air.

"So what do we do now?" she asked, snuggling closer as his eyes moved back to the grisly tow truck and what used to be a waste of flesh. Now, just wasted flesh.

"We're gonna take a road trip..."

* * *

The next morning, the small band of survivors left in the Screamin' Mimi.

They'd sorted, loaded, packed, and repacked supplies within the vehicle over the previous weeks, so nearly everything was already secured and stowed away. The group boarded the access ramp at the rear, meager personal belongings in hand. Maggie and the teens helped the aging Gertrude carry her suitcase even though she threatened to whip them silly with her cane. Leo provided himself as a target, taking her arm as she struggled up the incline, carrying only a photo album of her life with her husband until his passing. Jake awarded the teen a truckload of man-points for that.

He and Foster gave the common room a final once over, double checking that they hadn't left behind important items they might need during the trip. The only things George took were a large box of Cubans from beneath his desk in the second floor office and a ledger containing the signatures of all the soldiers who had passed through his safe house over the years.

"Have one with me, kid." George poured a pair of glasses with two-fingers each of Jameson's at the table. He passed one to the writer, took the other in his gnarled fist, and raised the light amber liquid skyward. "To the fallen."

"To a trip free of maggot-heads and psychos," Jake said.

They clinked glasses, downed the whiskey, and headed for the garage level. The old fixer left the bottle capped on the table next to their glasses, and then hit the lights on his way down.

The others were making themselves comfortable in the transport. Jake was impressed that a machine built for war, by the US government no less, would have anything resembling comfortable seats. Usually battle vehicles only offered two positions, a trait shared with most commuter airlines. Merely uncomfortable, and crippling.

That wasn't to say the interior of the Mimi was decked out like a millionaire's RV. Mostly, it was battleship-gray, armor plating over a naked, steel frame, hundreds of yards of wiring, power conduits, metal storage containers, weapons racks, and assorted ammunition boxes. The crew seating in the shorter drive module consisted of six, fully-adjustable, captain-style swiveling chairs, a driver and a navi-guesser, shadowing positions behind both (assumedly for the units commanding officer and subordinate,) and a pair of instrument stations set along the hull on the portside. On the starboard side was the vehicle's heart, the hydrogen cell power core. It gave off a barely audible hum, as its refining process separated H_2O into its base elements. The fuel tanks supplying it with water filled the gap to its right, leaving virtually no excess room in the cabin.

The secondary module held six more bucket-style seats just

through the foremost hatch and bunks for eight. The stores were beneath each of the crew sleeping chambers, packed full of firearms, ammunition, preserved meals, and other supplies needed to get them to the next hidden cache. The bunks—like the monitoring stations in the front—were recessed into the Mattoc's hull, running two high from front to rear, leaving a central aisle for crew movement. They weren't bunks but resembled Japanese hotel-style sleeping chambers. Or double-size coffins. Each one was equipped with a horizontal entry door which—as opposed to a pull curtain—could be secured by a simple locking mechanism from inside. Two people *could* sleep within each of the small enclosures, but they'd have to be mighty friendly.

The last module was mostly taken up by secondary storage for yet more ammunition, various tools, and the machine parts Foster insisted on bringing. Most were for maintenance of the hulking transport, but he'd also packed quite a few supplies used in maintaining their weaponry. The only obvious access point was at the rear of this module in the form of an enormous C130 style hatch, allowing easy loading of stores or just a quick retreat if needed. Most of the group's personal possessions, few that they had, were stored in the rear section as well, next to the ammo.

Maggie, Heather and the two teens had taken seats in the secondary unit, leaving the others to occupy the lead module with Foster, Allen and—oddly enough—Gertrude. George and the thin mechanic had already run the start-up sequence, bringing the hydrogen-cell core to life. According to him and the technical manuals, the Mimi could run for just over eighty-eight days before needing additional H_2O. Locating replacement fuel should be relatively easy. It was as simple as finding a nearby stream and a bucket.

"So how did they actually get funding for this thing?" Allen asked, as he and Foster activated the last of the transport's systems. The aging fixer had instructed the mechanic on its functions, ensuring that if something happened to him, Allen could keep the Mimi up and running as they continued their journey. "I mean the undercarriage and suspension *alone* are so far ahead of modern, automotive design it's ridiculous. Let alone its power source and the damn hull."

George flicked a gauge above his head with a thick finger and, satisfied it was registering correctly, glanced at Allen as he lit a cigar. "Think about it, kid. Six grand for a toilet seat? Two grand for a hammer?"

Jake chuckled and took a seat behind George. He thought Laurel would come up to join him, but she opted to sit with Gertie while the older woman ran through the Mimi's on-board computers. The aged woman accessed the systems easily, like a professional safecracker opening a five dollar combination lock.

"Your database is impressive, George," she said, "but you haven't updated your operating system in quite a while."

"Ya' do know what yer doin' there, don't ya?" Foster asked over his shoulder.

"Please," Gertie scoffed. "I've been selling hand-knit sweaters on eBay for years. Don't you think I know my way around a hard drive?"

"Alright, don't get yer bloomers in a knot," Foster soothed. "All good, boyo?"

"Got green lights across the boards," Allen confirmed.

"We're heading out," Jake called to the rear. "Everybody set back there?"

"Let's roll!" Maggie called, and Leo's hand moved into view giving a thumbs up.

"Start her up, George," he said.

"Already did." Foster grinned at Jake's look of surprise. "My baby's quiet, huh?"

The only sounds, as the Mimi began moving forward, were a slight hum from the hydrogen-cell and the occasional creak of its suspension. The massive, pink transport rolled effortlessly into the three-hundred meter access tunnel and up the long ramp towards the twelve ton security door. Foster brought it to a stop roughly ten feet from the steel barrier and began grumbling while he rooted around in the pack he had looped over the back of the seat.

"Where the hell is it? Thought I put the damn... Ah. Here we go." He pulled out an old, brown, 70s circa, Genie garage door opener.

"*Seriously*?" Allen looked at him in disbelief.

"What?" George asked.

Allen gazed pointedly at the remote.

Foster snorted in exasperation. "Look, do you have any *idea* how much paperwork I would've had to file to requisition a replacement?"

"Just tell me this ride wasn't put together the same way..." Jake's friend replied, waving his hand at the vehicle's console. "If that's the case, I think I'd rather stay here and starve."

"As a matter of fact, smart-ass, it wasn't," George growled, sourly. "This baby is two million, moving parts, put together by the lowest paid contractors the US Government could find. Don't you feel *safer* now?"

The fixer activated his remote and the immense door rose into the ceiling. George pulled the segmented vehicle through the opening and into the old "Ma Bell" complex's rear lot. The warehouse had been mostly vacant for years. A medical supply company had rented out its offices for a while, but after a massive restructuring moved overseas. Jake had a great view of the sprawling factory's remains from the portside window. He absently wondered if anyone had been curious as to why the government purchased the property, then left it to slowly deteriorate. Foster had informed him, when they'd planned their egress from the overrun metropolis, the sole reason for its acquisition was to provide a secure access point for the Mimi.

Six point two million for a garage door and people kept asking why politicians were always bitching for more money. *Our tax dollars in action*, he thought. Regardless, most could take solace in the fact that many of those same influence-peddling assholes were shuffling around somewhere, slowly rotting.

They rolled west onto Broad Street and began encountering the dead. Foster didn't veer or swerve or even slow down. He just drove right over them. Most of the creatures ignored the vehicle completely, which was very strange. When Jake and the others retrieved Laurel, every damn one of the things decided to stumble after his Jeep.

He mentioned it to George and the old fixer nodded. "Got a couple 'a ideas about that. Let's discuss it later, yeah? We need ta get out of the city right now."

Roughly a quarter of the dead took notice of the Mimi, turning their heads to watch as it rolled almost silently by (or even *over*) their decomposing forms. Out of those, perhaps a third dropped their gore-encrusted jaws and tottered towards the Pepto-colored transport. Some got close, trying to grasp its frictionless hull, only to have their fingers slip uselessly along its surface. A few were turned into putrid, abstract, road-art, messily squashed by the Mimi's huge wheels. Nearly twenty impacted against its solid plow-shaped nose as they made for the freeway, causing meaty explosions of body parts in varying intensities. George and Al judged each such occurrence, using the IOC (International Olympic Commission) ratings scale.

"Eight point four for that one." Allen watched a ghoul fly apart, after being cut nearly in half by the plow-shaped nose blade.

Another took a hit and tumbled over the roof of a pizza delivery car. Foster smiled. "Eight point seven. Impressive height and distance. Even without the spray."

"Five point two. He went under the wheel."

"Stupid fucker." George laughed. "Can't even get dismembered right."

"Oooo! That one was nice! Nine point three." The mechanic leaned left towards Foster. "Is that an ear on your window?"

"Yup. Here, I'll get it with the wipers..."

"You know you get bonus points for that, right?"

Jake struggled not to laugh.

Kat, Gertie, and Laurel all looked at each other, wearing identical expressions that said, *Men!*

"Um...George?" Laurel called. "You do know you're getting *on* the *off*-ramp. Right?"

"We're good, Red. Wait 'til you get a load 'a this." Foster chuckled. "Saw it from the roof when I watched Tweedle Dee and Tweedle Dumbass leave."

They started nosing down the north-bound ramp, on which they were traveling south, and saw that side of the freeway was utterly devoid of vehicles. The southbound lane, however, looked like a parking lot.

Or maybe a scrap yard.

Every foot of pavement was covered by useless, petroleum-fueled, art-deco sculptures, packed bumper to bumper. Some had been partially crushed or pushed up on other cars in the press as people attempted to flee the city. Some were still occupied by those who had been trapped during the initial outbreak. The expired drivers and passengers still sat behind fluid-smeared glass, slowly dehydrating. Here and there, stray zombies moved between the cars, seeking prey and making their way through the mess of tangled metal.

"Now *that's* interesting." Jake gazed intently out the starboard side window. "They didn't turn."

"What?" Laurel came to stand beside him.

"The ones in the cars. They didn't turn."

"No, look. Those two are moving." She pointed at a pair of creatures, still strapped in an overturned Prius.

Jake shook his head. "That's because zombies got to them. Its windows are busted out. See? The others, the ones that died in their cars, didn't come back again. Or reanimate. Or whatever the hell it is these things do."

Kat came forward to look too, so he took his seat again. That provided him with a truly uplifting view of two appealing rear ends as the pair of women shifted with the transport's movement.

"They weren't bitten," the lovely Asian said, looking away from the packed cars after seeing a Baby on Board sign in the window of a minivan. "I guess you can still die and not come back, unless one of *them* takes a chunk out of you."

"Thought that was how it worked," George said, as he drove them past the I-70 interchange. The fixer saw that creatures were more numerous on the highway below. "Huh. The eastbound lanes down there are all jammed and there's nothin' on the westbound. What? Nobody thought of drivin' on the other side of the damn *road*?"

"I doubt many of them had your sense of irreverence, George. Even during the Apocalypse. Face it. Not everyone's a super-spy with a warehouse full of goodies and a deep love of things that go bang," Kat said, returning to her seat.

"True," he agreed happily.

"How far do you think we can get in a day?" Laurel asked.

George considered that for a minute.

"Once we make it out of the city? Fifty, maybe sixty miles. Even with my baby here," he patted the console above his head as he steered around a lone, Chevy Blazer, "we're gonna have to search out routes through or around some pretty big messes."

"That's why we'll stick to the secondary roads," Allen said, while Laurel moved to lean against the back of Jake's seat, putting her hands on his shoulders. "There should be *way* less congestion away from major motorways. Fewer of *them*, too. If we're lucky."

"What if we can find an SUV or something to scout with? That would save a lot of time and effort, right?" Jake looked thoughtfully at the road ahead.

"Sure. Have to have some protection though. The maggot heads aren't really any stronger than you or me; they just don't seem to feel pain or care about takin' damage." George sped up a bit and stuck his Cuban back in his mouth. "Either that or somthin' fast and maneuverable. Like maybe a Harley or..."

"Let's *not* talk about motorcycles, okay?" Jake got the shakes whenever he thought about his *last* ride. Fleeing from the dead on a bike, while being shot at, was *not* an experience he was eager to repeat. "Maybe we'll find a military convoy. Or a dealership."

"Along with our other stop." Foster glanced over his shoulder. "Right?"

Jake nodded. "I haven't forgotten."

"What's this?" Laurel asked, still kneading Jake's shoulders.

"You didn't say anything about stopping somewhere," Allen said, frowning.

Jake motioned to George.

The fixer looked decidedly uncomfortable. "Uh. Yeah... See it's like this..."

* * *

"Hot Rod, this is Dead-eye. Over..."

Hot Rod turned to the shortwave on the worktable and grabbed the mic. "Go ahead Dead-eye."

"Check yer oil after the rally? Over..."

With a rush of excitement, Hot Rod checked the exterior cameras. "Yup. Have to change the plugs soon though. Two of them are bad and need replacements. Over."

"Not surprising. Our crew here did the same on almost a dozen haulers earlier this week. The boss pitched a fit today when they told him about it. Out."

Hot Rod dropped the microphone to the worktable and hurried to tell the others they'd soon have company.

* * *

Seventy two hours later, the Screamin' Mimi topped a rise on the isolated service road outside New Holland, Ohio.

Three days of monotonously, slow travel, much of it involving numerous traffic jams and having to retrace their route half a dozen times, had more than convinced the group they needed a scout vehicle. Foster drove the pink transport past what used to be a Mom 'n Pop garden center and stopped at the gate of a mid-sized junkyard. It didn't have a fence, per-se. It had a wall. Wrecked cars were piled three high and twice as deep around the perimeter of the seven acre lot. George brought out his Genie remote again.

"You've gotta be *shitting* me." Allen stared at the fixer, clearly in a state of disbelief.

Foster slowly turned to look at the mechanic and, holding the remote at eye level, pressed the enormous button on its face while sporting a malicious grin. The gate slid into the wall of cars, revealing that it was a *bus* with a steel plate welded completely over one side. For a moment, Jake felt like he'd been dropped into that old Mel Gibson movie, *The Road Warrior*.

When George pulled the transport through the gap, they saw that the only structure within was a three story, one-hundred by one-hundred foot, cinder block building that looked damned familiar. It was a smaller version of Foster's safe house. It touted the same, dark—probably fake—featureless windows, the same, anonymous, weathered paint job, even the same cosmetic guttering along the roof's edge. The only visible difference Jake could see, other than being smaller in size, as Foster pulled the Mimi to a halt, was a twelve by fourteen solid, steel door in the wall facing away from the gate.

"This is another cache, isn't it?" Laurel asked.

"Got it in one," the fixer replied as he and Allen powered the massive vehicle down. "Still manned, too. Been talking with its XO, Ray, for a year online. Nice guy. Real gear head. Ex-FBI. Never said why he took the post, though. Guess he had his reasons."

The group assembled their gear. The process had become second nature by then, thanks to Foster insisting they each carry a weapon—every waking minute of the day—for most of the last month. They made sure all their magazines were full and donned their tactical vests, double checking each other to ensure no one would be short on precious ammo. They then moved to the rear module. George punched numbers on the hull's recessed keypad and the massive hatch cycled open. They exited and it rose again to secure the Mimi.

It was frighteningly quiet outside, even more so than the city had been. Absent were the sounds of humanity. Jake heard birds in the western tree line, but other than the slight breeze moving through the branches all that broke the silence was the occasional, soft creak of metal from the junkyard's rusting, inorganic residents. After a cautious look around the area, they moved towards the large door of the safe house. Jake, Foster, and Kat took lead, with Leo, Maggie, and Laurel at the rear with the others sandwiched between. The fixer hit a button on an ancient intercom dangling from the cinder block wall and they stood waiting for some kind of reply.

Moments later, a distorted, static-muffled voice came from the tiny speaker.

"Hello?"

"Hi'ya, Ray," George replied. "It's me."

There was a camera above the huge door, which now turned towards their party. They heard the whir of the lens as it focused on them. Kat waved and blew it a kiss. Jake hoped fervently that whoever was watching on the monitor had a sense of humor. If not, they'd be getting back in their big, pink, zombie-crushing sardine can.

"Have any of you been bitten?" The voice asked.

Foster shrugged. "Not yet. At least not by any of them." He gave Jake and the redhead an amused look. Laurel pointedly ignored it, but the writer coughed uncomfortably.

"*Okay. Watch yourselves.*" The intercom crackled.

There was a muffled clank and the door rose smoothly into the wall above.

CHAPTER SIXTEEN

"I just want a shower," Heather murmured as they watched the thick, steel rise up into the wall. "I feel like somebody dipped me in a big, sweaty lake."

The others could identify with that comment. The Mimi was durable, almost beyond belief, and provided near bunker-level protection, but its ventilation sucked. It had nothing resembling central air. Thankfully, the two larger modules had a pair of three-foot movable panels (top front and rear) that its occupants could slide back to provide airflow. They could be controlled from either the lead unit or manual keypads located at the front hatches leading through the Mimi's interior. Upon opening, the spaces remained covered by a plate with half-inch holes punched into its entire surface, providing a broken view of the sky. While it wasn't the best, it was a far cry from creeping along in a metal oven.

The building's ground floor was taken up mainly by a machine shop. A pair of soldiers sporting black fatigues, web gear, and no-nonsense expressions waited ten yards inside. Both of them were young, mid-twenties perhaps. One was a tall, dangerous looking male, the other an equally tall blond female.

"Hey people," the woman said, stepping forward, "you look like ten miles of bad road. Anybody want a beer?"

Jake would've wept at the thought of a cold beer, but was too thankful to be out of the oven-like transport to bother.

"I'm Special Forces Sergeant Elle Pierce. This is Corporal Vincent Williams." Her companion didn't react. He just stood there, gun held loosely and vaguely pointed towards the group of survivors. "You understand, I have to ask if any of you are, uh... infected?"

"We're good, Sergeant. We haven't been out of the Mimi for three days," Jake replied.

She nodded. "Good enough. If not, you'd have turned long

before now. Let's get..."

"We're just supposed to take your word for it? How the hell do we know you're telling the truth?" The male soldier frowned and stared belligerently at their little group.

Jake looked calmly at the obnoxious Corporal. "You could just use your eyes. Are any of us coughing up black phlegm? Anybody's skin going grey and slimy? No? Why don't we dispense with the bullshit then?"

"Stand down, Vince. In case you didn't notice? They just pulled up in the ride that's going to get us to the land of surfers and sunshine," Elle snapped, causing Kat to hide a smile behind her hand. "You could show these people some gratitude. Or at least not act like an asshole."

Williams shifted slightly, his hand on the grip of a MP4. "This is a US Government installation, which means the military is in charge. Do any of you even have a security clearance?"

"We've been living in a cache a lot bigger and with more resources than this one, I might add, for almost two months," Laurel replied. "Besides, security clearance? Have you been paying attention to what's happened outside? There isn't any US Government left east of the Rockies. They're busy keeping a safe haven on the west coast. Who gives a damn what dirty little secrets we learn along the way?"

"Well, that's great," Vince snorted. "A stripper with a big mouth knows what the Armed Forces hierarchy's plans are, so we can..."

A second later the corporal's eyes widened. Jake's, huge pistol was pressed against his left eyebrow and the point of Kat's sword pricked him underneath the Adam's apple.

"You *might* want to rethink that comment," Laurel's blue-haired friend said softly. "No, you want to *apologize* to the lady." Jake's voice was colder than the dead walking about the world. He thumbed back the pistol's hammer, causing the soldier to flinch. "Or you won't have to worry about the zombies getting you. I'll blow your damn head off, *right now*."

"Elle?" Vince asked.

"Don't look at me," Elle said, raising her hands up above her shoulders.

"Everybody? Calm! The fuck! Down!"

With the exception of Kat, Vince, and Jake, they all turned toward the voice. An extremely attractive woman in her mid-thirties jogged down the metal stairs from the second floor. She had sandy brown hair falling over elegant features, high full breasts narrowing down to a trim waist, excellent legs beneath a pair of cut-off Daisy-Dukes. She glared disapprovingly at Vince.

"Corporal? Apologize." She strode up to where Jake stood, finger still on the Hammer's trigger.

"Sorry, Miss," he mumbled.

Kat took a step back and sheathed her sword. The writer stood unmoving for a few heartbeats, then thumbed the pistol's hammer forward slowly and took the bulky weapon away from the man's brow.

"Just so we're clear. These are my friends," Jake said evenly. "I don't know you. And for future reference? Personally, I think George there should be in charge of this group. But everyone foisted the honor on me. So you can either deal with it, or sit your ass right here and wait for the hierarchy to send a rescue to bum-fuck Ohio to save your hide. They should be here in a few years."

Vince grinned widely. "Sorry. Had to find out whether you were actually up to leading us across the mess this country's turned into. Gunny thought you were, but we had to be sure."

Jake looked at him quizzically. "You were testing us?"

"Nope. I was testing *you*." He nodded at the fixer. "You were right, sir."

"Well. All done patting each other on the ass now? Good." The model-beautiful woman stuck her hand out at Foster. "Hiya George, I'm Rae."

From the look on the old chief's face, her announcement caught him flat-footed. "*You*? You're shitting me."

"I know. The whole breasts thing throws *everyone*." She shook his limp and unfeeling hand. "Rachael Norris."

"But...but..." George stammered. "The radio! I *talked* to..."

Rae shrugged. "Voice modulator. Standard issue for caches, and extremely useful if you need to pass disinformation in hostile territory."

Foster looked at her narrowly. "What's the PSI rating for a radiator in a '62 Volkswagen Beetle?"

The woman smiled. "The '62s were air cooled. They didn't have radiators."

"Yep, you're him. Her. Uh..." He shrugged. "Nice to finally meet ya."

"Likewise." She turned towards the others. "Now, introduce your friends."

Laurel moved closer to Jake as George's online buddy made the rounds. Jake realized that Laurel was looking at Rae nervously as she slid an arm around his waist and he smiled to himself. It surprised him that a woman, who was so obviously drop-dead gorgeous, would be threatened by any other female walking the planet. To be honest, Laurel's need to stake her claim made him feel better.

He rubbed his hand along her shoulder blade as the fixer introduced Maggie and the kids. The redhead looked at him guiltily and he gave her a squeeze, earning one of her lopsided grins.

"You've got to be Laurel and Jake." Rae smiled at them as she shook hands with Allen. "George described the two of you perfectly. I'm glad to see you finally stopped pussy-footing around and got together."

Jake gave Foster a raised eyebrow, which the old fixer avoided while puffing his stogie. Laurel noticed the exchange, but she was too occupied with a sudden rush of relief.

"Anybody up for coffee? We've got a ton of Jamaican blend upstairs. Or showers?" Rae looked around. Naked longing for hot water and a lot of soap was plain on everyone's face. "Alright, who's going first?"

* * *

The women insisted that Jake and the other males shower first, because the girls would take longer and didn't want to be rushed. To be fair, Jake understood their point. Kat, Heather, and Karen all had hair down to the middle of their backs and Laurel could almost sit on the ends of hers. It would take them a bit to shampoo, condition, repeat, etc.

The men, on the other hand, were pretty quick. Hair, pits, crevasses, maybe a quick shave, and done. Afterwards, they ran fast hands through their hair, then went off in search of caffeine while the ladies started a long, steam-saturated session of girl talk.

An hour later Foster, Vince, Rae, and Maggie (who'd been relatively quick with her own shower) sat arguing the cause of the outbreak, as Jake leaned against the sink sipping sweet, sweet bean squeezings.

"I'm voting for aliens," Vince said. "It's their way to take possession of the planet without having to fight pesky humans for it."

"Doubtful," Maggie replied.

"How can you be sure?" George asked.

Maggie started ticking off reasons on her fingers. "No epicenter for the infection. There's no way to cover the entire planet all at once like that with a chemical weapon. Also, communications didn't break down until *after* it had been going on for about a week. An invading, highly evolved enemy would've taken out our satellite grid to avoid detection while they spread a biological agent."

Heather had already pulled Allen down the hall towards the closet-sized, sleeping rooms on the other side of the safe house by the time Kat entered the common area. The others were totally absorbed in their debate, so Jake moved into the kitchen under the pretense of refilling his mug as she bounced happily from foot to foot on the linoleum.

"Feel better?" he asked.

"Absolutely," she said happily, grabbing a mug of her own from the dish strainer. "I think I lost a pound or two just from rinsing off the dust."

He grinned. "New do?"

Kat's shiny, blue hair had been trimmed into a long pixie cut. The new style softened her strong cheekbones, and half obscured the right side of her face, accentuating her already dark eyes and mirthful gaze. Her hand went up to brush stray hairs back over her ear at Jake's comment.

"Like it?"

"You look *great*," he replied. "Very Keira Knightley. Why did you cut it?"

"Shorter hair should be much harder for one of *them* to grab." Kat sipped at her mug of caffeinated goodness. "Gertie's working on Karen right now, then she'll do Laurel's"

"Oh."

Reading Jake's expression, she smiled consolingly. "Don't worry. She's not lopping hers off, like I did." She stepped towards the table where the others sat, still arguing about the possible causes of the dead's reanimation. "Rae? Do you mind if I show our fearless leader here that monster you keep downstairs?"

The sultry woman glanced her way and nodded with a smile, as George explained the reasons behind their chosen route to the Southwest.

Jake followed Kat back down to the garage level, appreciating the view. It wasn't as if he'd be willing to start anything with her. A certain redhead was *more* than enough for him. She had a great posterior though, and he didn't feel guilty for looking.

Well... maybe a little.

She led him back into the bay beneath the walkway and he almost shit a square turd.

A Hummer was parked there. A real one, not the yuppie-yellow *look at me, look at me, I'm so rich and important, but I still feel the need to overcompensate* model. It had been heavily modified. Its exterior had been augmented with inch thick steel bars welded together in a crosshatch pattern, then bolted through the armored doors over its darkened, bulletproof windows. A heavy crash plate covered the front grill and someone had painted a large, fanged smile across it in yellow spray paint.

It was beautiful.

It was sensual.

It was an absolutely, fucking perfect, zombie-crushing, scout vehicle and Jake itched to get behind the wheel.

"How the hell did you know about *this*?"

Kat leaned against the awesome machine looking smug. "Talked with Rae while you boys showered. She and George have been chatting about automotive refab for almost a year. I mentioned how you've been looking for a scout vehicle and she said you could have it."

"Oh *yes*! And I thought my Jeep was nice! Damn! I can't *wait* to take this thing out." He ran a one hand over the hood, face thoughtful. "What should I call her?"

"How about...*Kat has the keys*?" She dangled said items from one finger, on a Hello Kitty key-chain. "Or perhaps, *if I ask really nicely, maybe she'll give them to me*. That one's good too."

"Funny. Can I have them now?"

Her expression grew impish. "What'll you give me?"

Jake new better than to answer a loaded question like that. "Are we negotiating?"

"Yep." She twirled the keys. "So?"

He eyed her warily. "What did you want?"

"Two things."

"Two? That doesn't..."

She pointed a determined finger at him. "Hey, you get the keys *and* a Hummer. It's only fair."

The writer gave a heavy sigh. "So?"

"First, I want a kiss," she said. "And not a sisterly little peck either. A *real* one. I'll tell you the second thing after."

"Oka-a-ay. You *do* remember our conversation in the parking lot, right?" he said. "Nothing's changed."

"Relax," she said with a smile. "I'm not going to ask you for a quickie in the backseat or anything."

He wasn't sure how he felt about that as she twined her arms around his neck. Relieved? Disappointed?

Once again, kissing Kat was an experience. The touch of her lips to his set Jake's spine tingling, and he had a mental flash of her lying on the floor of his apartment, clad only in that pair of Kamikaze panties. He caught himself wondering intently about what was under the jeans and t-shirt she wore now.

Pushing that thought firmly to one side—for all of a second and a half—he maneuvered her around until her shapely backside pressed against the quarter panel of the Humvee. He slid his hands down her ribs finally bringing them to rest around her hips. Then, gripping firmly, he jerked her quickly against himself. Her tongue flicked against his, and Kat pulled him deeper into the kiss.

Damn it, he thought, *why is it this woman can get me so worked up?*

His back-brain told him to shut up, then gave him some subconscious advice. Jake was a little surprised himself when he slid his right hand down over Kat's flank to firmly cup one of her buttocks. Her eyes shot open, then rolled slowly closed again as she moaned into his mouth. Her left leg curled around the back of his knee. Kat didn't seem to have any desire to stop and their embrace stretched out over the course of a few minutes, until he reluctantly pulled back.

She half lay on the Hummer's hood, out of breath as he reached for the keys. Kat was faster and down the front of her shirt they went.

"Um...Can I have those now?"

She folded her arms across her chest and shook her head, smiling. "The second thing."

Jake prepared himself as best he could and said, "Hit me."

"You have to *swear* that I'm your navi-guesser whenever you drive this monster out," she said.

He was a little taken back at that. "I was going to have Vince and Elle..."

"That's fine, but I'm still on the team," Kat interrupted. "I'm going crazy being cooped up all the time."

The thought of her risking her life out there with him every day made the unruly-haired man decidedly uncomfortable. "I don't think..."

"No." Her eyes flashed dangerously as she began ticking off reasons on her fingers. "The last couple of days have proven that we need a scout vehicle. Al and Gertie need to help George drive the Mimi. Maggie can't risk herself because she's the only one with medical training. Heather? Puh-leeze. The kids aren't ready for something like this. Hell, none of us are. That leaves me and Laurel. I *know* you don't want to take either of us along, and that's really sweet, but you need someone to watch your back. At least until Special Forces Ken and Barbie prove they can handle themselves."

Jake hated it, but she was right. Laurel was a darned good shot, but she didn't have a killer instinct. He couldn't have her out there with him, but he sure as hell didn't want to put Kat in that kind of danger either. Reluctantly, he admitted to himself that she *was* the only choice.

He just wished he didn't feel so damn happy about it.

"Alright."

She looked at him closely. "Swear."

Jake sighed. "I swear."

"See?" she said brightly. "That wasn't so bad, was it?"

He grinned amicably and motioned at her shirt.

Kat put her hands on her hips, turned her head slightly as she raised an eyebrow and took a deep breath. "Your fingers aren't broken."

Just get the keys, you wuss. His back-brain said.

Jake squinted at her thoughtfully. Kat moved her shoulders forward, pressing her breasts together and caused her neckline to gape even lower. After considering the problem for a moment, he carefully took hold on the bottom edge of her shirt, pulled it out, and caught the keys as they fell free. As he released her top, Kat fought to keep from smiling.

"You realize you just passed up a golden opportunity?" she laughed and straightened her shirt again, while he tried not to stare as she settled her various curves.

He was doomed.

* * *

Two hours later, Jake sat on the Hummer's tailgate, smoking contently.

He'd gone over the additions Rae had installed on the thing with Allen and learned the lovely woman wasn't just another pretty face. Her modifications were brilliant. The steel cage she turned the cab into couldn't be opened without the consent of the passengers or a cutting torch. Or maybe a couple of sticks of dynamite. It was a brick. A powerful, octane-driven brick. Short of the Mimi, a tank, or maybe the Batmobile, he'd never encountered a more solid vehicle.

Jake sat enjoying a cigarette, attempting to think of a way to keep Laurel from exploding. When he broke the news to her that she was going to be with the others in the transport, while he drove their new zombie-proof scouter around; she'd flip. There were sure to be quite a few choice words from his wild, wonderful redhead over that. Words like, *Bullshit* came to mind. Along with: *Are you out of your mind?* Or maybe even, *Oh, So you don't want to have sex any time soon, huh?*

"Hey, sailor."

Leaning around the edge of the tailgate, he looked back towards the main floor from the modified machine's recessed bay. Laurel sported her new haircut quite well. She'd gone for a longer style than her more adventurous, indigo-haired friend. It had been trimmed a few inches below her shoulders and was now all one length. Though it was no longer "barbarian maiden" long—almost down to her butt—as she sauntered towards him, Jake had to admit two things:

One. He'd never seen her look so sexy.

And two. He felt the abrupt need for pants that were looser in the crotch.

"Hello-o, nurse!" He gave her an innocent smile. "I'm ready for my sponge bath now."

She laughed. "Maybe if we try that at two in the morning, we *might* get away with it." Laurel joined him on the tailgate, hopping slightly to get her shapely rear end over the edge.

Jake took a final hit off his smoke and blew the cloud to his left, away from where she sat. "Tired?"

"You wish," she said, brushing her hair over to one side, baring the curved perfection of the spot where her neck and shoulder met. He felt the sudden urge to have his mouth there. "The door to the shower doesn't lock."

"Never stopped us before."

Laurel smiled and turned to crawl into the back seat. "Well, at least it's roomier than your last car. Even has that pine-fresh scent commercials always talked about."

"There's air fresheners under the seats." He rose from the tailgate and, hefting the metal slab up, secured it to the hull again. He walked around to the right passenger door and, while climbing inside, noticed Laurel's raised eyebrow. He pointed at the tailgate. "It locks from the inside."

"Uh huh." She nodded, clearly fighting a smile.

"And you tell me *my* mind is always in the gutter," Jake mumbled, sliding past her into the bed.

"That's because it usually *is*."

"This is a problem?"

"Not at all." Laurel rested her cheek in one hand and leaned against the seat back. "Maybe if you did it at inopportune times, *then* it would be an issue. I don't mind you looking at my boobs when other people are around, but groping me over corn flakes would be a bit much."

Jake chuckled and slid the triple locking bars in the body of the tailgate into place. While yanking on the hatch to make sure it wasn't going to pop loose, he heard the unmistakable sound of a door latching. He looked over his shoulder and found her grinning at him wickedly. Half crouched, Laurel slid into the rear, put a hand in the middle of his chest, and applied steady pressure until he was sitting in the bed, supported on his elbows.

"I'll take your word on the spectacular, structural integrity of this thing." She ran her hands over his shirt and straddled his lap. "There is one feature I *really* like though."

As he watched, she pulled the army-green undershirt up over her head and tossed it into the front seat. She drew her hands down his ribs, along the inside seam of her fatigue covered thighs, over her flat stomach, and finally up to cup her breasts. Jake's mouth went dry, but he managed to croak out. "What's that?"

"The privacy tint on the windows." Laurel slid her hands back down her torso and under his shirt. "Kind of risqué, don't you think?"

"Like having sex at the drive-in?" He leaned back against the surface of the bed as he moved his hands over her hips.

The redhead pulled his shirt off and, eyes dancing, bent over him until their lips were a breath away. "*Exactly* like that."

CHAPTER SEVENTEEN

The next day was spent reorganizing supplies.

With three people added to their group, Laurel and Maggie found it necessary to re-evaluate their food stores. The Mimi could carry thirty cases of MREs which, combined with their dehydrated supplies, totaled out to just over five weeks of food, at three meals a day, for thirteen adults. Laurel insisted on adding Rae's entire supply of black pepper—32 oz—two, 20 pound bags of rock salt, and six, 5 pound cans of Jamaican coffee beans.

Maggie was happy to see that Rae's small facility was equipped with a modest array of both topical and intravenous painkillers. Though George had been incensed, she'd kept everything worthwhile from the late Mike Barron's stash. She convinced him that even the cocaine might be useful at some point, but he'd been surly for days. The tall EMT also pulled together a fairly comprehensive trauma kit, because Rae had a set of basic surgical instruments. If they could find a surgeon, at least he (or she) should be able to perform basic medical procedures with a decent chance of success.

Allen, Heather, Maggie, and the two teens also cleaned weapons. Jake's friend loved it. Taking things apart to find out how they worked was what prompted Al's interest in his dad's auto shop as a kid. That being the case, he could appreciate the deadly beauty of Elle's 50cal in particular. The firearm was, to quote pop culture, a belt-fed, bullet-hosing, weapon of mass-fucking-destruction. Also, though Heather could barely support the weapon, when Allen told her she looked damn sexy with it strapped under her breasts she'd pulled him upstairs for a "noon-er".

Jake would've liked to do the same with Laurel, but had too much to do. He added a couple of days worth of supplies (food, water, ammo, and the like) to the Hummer, along with a basic med kit and a pair of highly, explosive surprises. He went out into the compound of junked automobiles with Vince, filling three, 10 gallon fuel containers to provide the Hummer with a full emergency supply, or in case they just couldn't find a convenient vehicle to siphon. He traced the southbound roads with George, mapping out the route least likely to have high concentrations of the dead. Though he trusted Rae's fabrication abilities, Jake wanted to put the Hummer through a dry run before taking on a large number of zombies.

Kat seemed determined to hold him to his word to take her along. She even went so far as to hang a small, stuffed Hello Kitty doll from the rear-view mirror of their SUV from Hell. When Jake curiously asked where she kept getting all the Hello Kitty stuff from, she just gave him a frank, sinful gaze, and raised an eyebrow. He decided he didn't really want to know at that point.

The following sunrise, after a night of bad jokes, some pretty darned good whiskey—Jameson's, courtesy of Rae's stores, which endeared her to Laurel—and a couple of discrete cases of, *I'm really tired, so I'll walk* (insert chosen partner's name here) *to their room, then see you all in the morning,* Jake drove the Hummer south down the service road. Kat had commandeered the navi-guesser position, so Elle and Leo sat in the back, fighting with the Triple-A road map. Both Allen and Laurel wanted to go, but with all the repacking still left to do in the Mimi, along with instructing Rae on how to run its various control systems so she could act as a backup, they were forced to decline.

Jake's friend understood. Laurel was rather upset.

"What the *fuck* do you think you're doing?" she screamed, as he turned the Humvee around in the machine shop.

"Taking a run south to Bainbridge," Jake replied, reasonably. "Rae said there's a motorcycle dealership outside the town, so we'll grab a couple bikes."

Laurel trotted quickly down the metal stairs, moved in front of the Hummer, and crossed her arms. Jake saw her hip cock out and sighed. It was going to be one of *those* conversations.

"Am I the only one who thinks that's a really bad idea? Because the *last* time you got on a motorcycle was so much fun?"

He attempted to pacify her, opening his door and running a hand around her waist when she stepped close to grip the frame. "We might need them as secondary scouts if something happens to this monster. I'd rather get them now, since we know where they are, as opposed to going anywhere near a large population center down the line," Jake explained.

Laurel had tried to think up an argument for that, but she

couldn't. She stepped up on the entry rail to pass her arms around his neck. "You have to *swear* you'll be careful."

"As careful as possible," Jake said.

She leaned around him, looking at Kat. "You make his life hell if he does anything *stupid*, alright? At least until you all get back here, so I can kick his ass?"

"Oh, *count* on it." Kat agreed, smiling widely.

Satisfied—if not happy—Laurel kissed him, climbed down, and closed the door. She and Foster watched as they rolled from the building, past the Mimi, and finally up to the massive gate. After making sure no zombies were around, George activated his Genie remote and the bus slid from the entrance allowing them passage. They needn't have worried. Outside Rae's hideaway, the surrounding area was as empty as a lawyers' soul. Neither human nor zombie graced the horizon in either direction.

* * *

The rural town of Bainbridge wasn't small, just rural. No high rises, no beautified welcome centers for mega-corporations, and no trendy coffee bistros hawking earth-friendly cups of soy-based, imitation bean squeezings. They had Rockwellesque storefronts, a feed store on the west side—complete with grain silo—and Gail's Diner touted *the best coffee in town.*

A pizza shop east of the square called "Mama Malscone's" was the only building Jake saw—as they surveyed the town from the northern ridge—that appeared questionable. It looked like the front windows had been covered with the establishment's oak tables. At least from what he could see from so far away. The windows were high enough to be a bitch to enter for a healthy, breathing human, let alone a brick-stupid ghoul that couldn't jump. It also appeared that whoever had (or was) sheltered inside had sealed the rear entrances, due to a length of rope hanging from a second story window that provided entry and egress. He wondered what happened to the survivor/survivors, and shuddered as a sudden flash of Mike Barron's butchered body derailed his train of thought. While the building *could* be vacant, Jake made a mental note to enter the small township from its opposite side. Just in case. Chances were whoever had stayed above the pizza parlor was lying motionless and rotting in the street somewhere along with the rest of town's population, but why take chances?

The drive had been pretty uneventful for the quartet, despite Laurel's reservations. There had been the occasional zombie shuffling along Route 41, but when they arrived on the outskirts of the little town, it seemed utterly devoid of activity. Jake, along with the blonde-haired sergeant, had carefully scanned the streets through binoculars from the ridge and pronounced it clear.

They took the Hummer through empty fields leading down to the rear of a Dairy Queen, circling the town's outskirts and finally out onto Main Street. There was evidence of previous human and zombie activity, but it was weeks old. Gore streaked down and across the walls of some buildings, most leading to a corpse lying on the sidewalk or close to a nearby pickup. There were some missing, judging from the nasty stains without bodies nearby. Jake reasoned that they'd gotten back up and wandered off again after reanimating.

"Wow. Hometown, USA," Elle said.

The dealership came into view four blocks later. It was fairly wreckage free, except for an overturned F150 near the entrance, and didn't appear to have been looted. That was a definite plus. Over two months of neglect had killed what little landscaping existed throughout the town, but the hardy fir trees edging the shop's lot seemed to be doing just fine.

"Huh. Blue spruce," Jake grunted.

"So?" Elle asked.

"If you pull a handful of needles and boil them into a tea, you get as much Vitamin C as you would from eating an orange." He noticed Elle giving him a raised eyebrow.

"I did a lot of editing for publishers over the last year, okay? Cookbooks, survival manuals, how-to guides. Hell, if we can locate the chemicals, I could make black powder, chloroform, thermite." Jake frowned thoughtfully as he brought the vehicle to a stop before the showroom doors. "Maybe even mustard gas or napalm. If we run across a swimming pool supply store..."

He killed the engine and readied the M4 that George insisted he carry. Since his near death experience in the alley, Jake had agreed. He was through fucking around. He'd started packing the semi-auto rifle, his monstrous Hammer pistol, a Glock 9mm, and (of course) his trusty crowbar secured in a tactical across his back.

It was silent outside, except for the sounds of nature, as the four made their way cautiously into the dealership. While jimmying the door (read: prying it open with his crowbar), Jake had an epiphany and pulled the front of the Hummer flush against the entrance as the others waited inside. He climbed through the top hatch and walked over the hood as his companions watched curiously.

"Just in case." He made sure the door was locked behind them.

"This way if any of those things show up, they won't be able to get in. If I have to, I can climb up to the hatch again, crawl inside, and draw them away."

"Or just run them over," Leo said helpfully. "*That* thing is bad-ass."

The quartet went about clearing the building. Thankfully, there were no signs of activity within. Not surprising, due to the lack of weapons or supplies in a motorcycle dealership. Elle wanted to take a couple of quad-runners, but Jake argued those would take up too much room in the Mimi's rear segment. They settled for a pair of Honda XR650 sport bikes instead. They were perfect for scramming off-road if the shit hit the fan. Also, with two of the same model, they could cannibalize one to repair the other if necessary down the line. Spare parts for everything were going to be very difficult to obtain in the foreseeable future, so having a backup was only prudent.

"Jake? Come up here for a minute?" Kat called from the second floor. It was a partial balcony, only spanning about a third of the upper level and was full of various riding gear—helmets, boots, and bandannas. All the necessities to keep you from turning into a stain on the pavement if you took a spill at seventy miles an hour.

He topped the stairs and his jaw dropped. Kat had somehow, in about a minute and a half, put her wardrobe through an upgrade. Gone were her ever-present jeans. She replaced them with a pair of black, leather pants which brought primal thoughts to Jake's brain almost immediately. She'd opted against a tac-vest when they'd left Rae's hideaway (which he thought was risky, but he didn't push the issue). She stated that lugging one around would only slow her down. Kat wore only a waist holster for her Glock, a thigh belt to hold four magazines for the weapon, a web belt with a small pouch, her grandfather's sword diagonally across her back, and a canteen. She also added a pair of steel-embossed, biker-style, arm bracers that came almost to her elbows. She wore these over a pair of police issue gloves they'd looted from Tim's Emporium.

Finally, being early summer, she opted to wear a bra—purple, of course—and a white tank top she'd trimmed from Foster's stores in the Mimi. It showed off the firmness of her flat stomach and hugged her torso like a second skin.

Jake caught himself wishing she'd passed on the bra.

"Do you think we should take some of these?" She pointed at the racks of riding pants and jackets. "They'd be decent protection, right?"

He broke off ogling her like a teenager with a quick shake. "Sure, but some of it would be damn restrictive, especially the jackets. Most people can't stretch their arms over their heads wearing one."

"True," She replied. Then, bending over at the waist, she collapsed her upper body forward, placed her hands flat on the floor, and slid easily down into the splits. Kat looked at him with her legs extended out ninety degrees to each side and slowly rolled her pelvis forward, then back, in a display of great flexibility. Jake managed to keep his eyes from bugging out, but he was forced to swallow against a suddenly dry throat. "I'm not most people."

"Good point. Take a few pair." He looked at the wall of helmets. "I'd say we should grab some of those too, but there's no traffic anymore. Besides, they'd limit visibility."

"I think you're right. I for one, feel the need to have a *really* good view of my surroundings with all those things walking around." The pretty Asian rose smoothly to her feet again and pointed behind him. "You'd look *totally* hot in those."

"Leather chaps? No way." Said items even had tassels on the outer seams.

"Laurel would agree with me," she said, mischievously.

"Changing the subject, *now*," he said firmly. "Let's go help the others."

They gassed the bikes from a pump in the dealership's maintenance area, then swiped a few five-gallon containers for fuel. They also managed to load both Hondas quietly onto a small, two-wheeled, motorcycle trailer on the showroom floor. As Elle secured the bikes with tie-down straps, Jake and Leo opened the bay door, backed the Hummer inside, and hooked it up to the trailer. Kat had been keeping watch at the door, Jake's rifle held loosely across her body, scanning the area for movement as the others finished. She was the one who noticed the anomaly.

"Um. Jake? I think you need to take a look at this," she called.

The writer moved up beside her in the doorway and followed the line of her arm to a house seventy yards to the south. There was something strange in the yard on the opposite side of the two-story. Something he couldn't make sense of from a distance.

That looks like... He frowned.

"Sergeant, I want you to stay here with Leo," Jake said. "Lock this door and keep searching the shop for anything that might be useful. We'll be back shortly."

"Got it." Elle punched the younger man in the shoulder. "Come on, kiddo. Let's see what we can loot."

"I'm not a kid," he replied, helping her yank the rolling door down.

* * *

Kat pulled her pistol, then she and Jake began moving cautiously towards the home. The lack of zombies in the area had been nagging at him. Granted, Bainbridge wasn't a large community by any means, but something seemed off.

As the two crept on, the almost ever-present smell of rot grew stronger. Its source was in the dwelling's front yard. A line of stakes ran before the face of the home, each topped with a human head in various states of decay.

The smell wafted towards them, not only from the hideous display but also from a large pile of charred furniture and, to Jake's disgust, bodies. Thirty of them if you went by the number of staked heads. The remains were just too obliterated to tell.

"What... in the hell?" Kat said, wide-eyed. "That's *gross*. I can understand killing zombies and all but taking their heads as trophies? Two words: Zombie goo. When exactly does getting that crap all over you become fun?"

Jake's eyes moved along the awful line, looking intently at each face in turn. "How do you kill a zombie?"

She gave him a quizzical look. "You destroy the brain? Duh."

He stepped forward and took her gently by the shoulders. "Do you see any trauma to even one of these heads?"

Kat looked past him, brow furrowing, then her eyes went wide. "But that would mean..."

"They were *survivors*."

Her dark eyes tracked across the yard. "Some of these are really small. Just kids."

Jake didn't trust himself to speak.

Kat's face went harsh as she looked back towards the center of town. "Do you think whoever did this is still around?"

"With this many stakes? Oh yeah." Jake followed her gaze, realizing they probably didn't even have to look very hard to find the murderer's hideaway.

Images of mayhem began flashing through his brain as they made their way back to the dealership. Even if it was the end of the world, there was just some shit he *wasn't* going to put up with.

"How are we going to find them?" Kat said quietly as they trotted across the grass-choked lot.

He smiled coldly.

* * *

"Now." Jake whispered.

He watched, with great satisfaction, as a rocket-propelled grenade streaked down into the large propane tank behind the pizza parlor. Elle had been very willing to climb the nearby rickety water tower lugging an RPG, and the enthusiastic explosion put a huge smile on her face.

The tank had been sitting approximately fifteen yards to the right of a quartet of corn-fed assholes, shooting at the corpse of a young man. They'd hung it from the lamppost behind Mama Malscone's. The fact that the four had been taking pot shots at it with their rifles *alone* had been enough for Jake to mentally sign their death warrants. The clincher had been the obviously restrained female forms he'd seen inside the restaurant on the forward looking infra red *or* FLIR.

George had insisted they take both a Jager Pro thermal scope, along with a pair of ATN starlight goggles, and Jake had agreed. Both could be worth their weight in gold under the right circumstances, and they didn't take up much room in the bed of the zombie-proof Hummer.

Jake experienced the brief but strong urge to pitch a grenade through the front door, when he saw the guard who was watching the women begin to paw at one of them. Both had been secured to tables somehow because, while the orange-toned female image struggled, her arms remained stretched out over her head. Jake refrained from pitching because not only would he have pulped the lone guard but also the prisoners inside. Flames shot up behind his eyes as the bastard started cutting away the woman's clothing, tossing it on the floor near the tables. By the time Jake made his way up the dangling rope to the restaurant's second-floor window, he was seething inside and abso-fucking-lutely ready to fucking kill the first fucking man he fucking saw.

After hoisting himself through the window, Jake pulled the massive Hammer pistol from his thigh holster. His M4 would've been bulky at best and noisy at worst, even during such a short climb, so he'd left it in their Hummer. The Hammer would do for close quarters. Loud, powerful, intimidating. Everything the doctor ordered for an afternoon of mischief and mayhem.

His low command signaled Elle to smoke the four out back. The explosion caused by the RPG rupturing and then igniting the propane within the tank was *loud*. They needed to wrap this little rescue operation up quickly, because dead for miles around were sure to have heard the noise and would come stumbling in. The enormous fireball shooting skyward was a bit hard to miss, too.

All the building's back windows blew inward, peppering Jake with sharp little chips of hot pain. He ignored cuts that opened on his arm, and the shallow one along his jaw line, as he sped down the narrow staircase to peek into the restaurant proper. Almost a quarter of the buildings rear had collapsed (what he assumed was most of the kitchen.) There were broken fixtures and glass everywhere. Even a few of the rearmost tables had toppled with the force of the explosion. Redneck Number Five was fumbling with his pants, as the blonde he'd been assaulting kicked at his legs and torso. Her friend was preoccupied with screaming her head off, too distracted to be of help.

Thumbing off the safety on his pistol, Jake slid towards the startled trio.

"Don't move, asshole!" he yelled.

The guard was too frazzled to deal with him and ran for the back door, firing his deer rifle wildly. Jake dove behind a pair of booths along the wall as the bullets tore up nearby padded bench seats, sending splinters and tufts of stuffing everywhere.

The guard's gun clicked empty, allowing Jake to roll out from the shelter of his booth and send a quartet of rounds at the man's back as the bastard ran. The writer had no qualms about doing so. The fleeing shithead had just assaulted at least one woman then shot at him. And a back shot was still a shot. His aim suffered as he rolled, so while one creased the outside of the guard's thigh and another passed close enough to his ear that he felt the heat of its passing, the man made it to the rear exit.

The would-be assailant got half a dozen strides through the door when a storm of bullets tore him in half.

Leo had driven their Hummer through vacant backyards, merrily murdering helpless yard gnomes, covered by the noise of the explosion. Pulling abreast of Mama Malscone's back door, he waited for Jake to flush the last man outside. The guard was smashed to the left as Kat unloaded on him with the M123 mini-gun, sending its projectiles through the cretin's body at two-thousand rounds per minute. She tore up quite a bit of asphalt around him too, but that was to be expected. After all, she'd only fired the weapon once in Foster's safe house.

Jug-band Casanova didn't even have a chance to scream as rounds chewed away flesh, shredded vital organs, and splintered his bones on their way through, tearing on to perforate the side of the Dairy Queen next door.

Kat released the trigger as what was left of the poor bastard finished skidding, mainly in two large and messy lumps, across the pavement.

"Yuck!" Leo called up from the driver's seat.

"Yeah, but effective," she replied. "Jake?"

"I'm good!" Ensuring the mini-gun wasn't pointed in his direction before stepping through, he waved out the door. "Leo, pick up Elle and get back here! Kat, help me with the survivors! Bring a couple pairs of those pants along!"

He jogged to the Humvee, snatched the bolt cutters from its rear toolbox, and sped back through the thickening smoke into the restaurant. Kat made sure she had her sword, pistol, and ammo clips, then grabbed the saddlebags full of biker wear before trotting after him. She paused momentarily, to spit on a smear outside the door that used to be human.

Upon seeing the two women, she fervently wished those men out back *would* rise as zombies, just so she could kill them again. From the sick expression on the writer's face, she could see he was thinking the same thing, and she felt a rush of heat that had nothing to do with the growing fire in the kitchen.

Bad Kat, she thought. *Burning building, remember? No time for heavy petting. Darn it.*

The nearest woman was a peroxide addict. An obvious bleached-blonde, who was too relieved to do much but repeat *thank you* over and over as Jake cut her restraints. He left Kat to help the traumatized woman dress and moved to free the second. She was also blonde, but without her friend's tendency towards all things Clorox. The woman watched him closely as he cut the shackles securing her to the pool table and attempted to cover her important bits when the tough steel finally parted.

"Who the hell are you people?" she demanded.

"No time to explain. Come with us if you want to live." He held out a pair of leather pants and a Harley Davidson tank top.

Kat laughed and Jake looked at her in confusion as the women hurriedly dressed.

"Where ees Sar-ah Conna?" Kat grated in her best Austrian accent. "Take meh too har... Now!"

He sighed and they all started for the back door.

Smoke from the kitchen was getting mighty thick. As he cleared the swinging metal doors, Jake noticed the paint beginning to bubble from the awful heat within. Then the group was in the parking lot where Leo and Elle waited in the Hummer, just beyond the circle of blasted pavement and the pyre of Mama Malscone's. Both relaxed as their friends hurried to the vehicle, with the two newcomers in tow. Leo hopped into the bed, allowing the blondes to share the bench seat with Elle. Jake slid behind the wheel again, and after insuring all its doors were locked securely, raced the

Hummer into the empty streets. Thoughts of zombies were looming large in all their minds just then, and it seemed like a good time to *get the fuck out of Dodge.*

"Everyone okay?" Kat began pulling water bottles from a cooler between the front seats and passing them back to the others. She opened one, handed it to Jake, and then grabbed another for herself, as the pair they'd rescued nodded.

"We are now," the less shaken of the blondes replied. Her friend was still a wreck, extremely pale and a little wild around the eyes.

"What are your names?" Elle asked.

The calmer of the two looked at the pretty soldier hesitantly.

"Unless you want us to call you Barbie One and Barbie Two?"

The woman gave an amused snort and downed half the water in the twenty ounce bottle before answering. "I'm Gwen Harker. That's Donna Blake with the day glow hair."

Said blonde waived listlessly.

"Are you military?" Gwen asked.

"Just survivors. Like yourselves." Jake turned onto Route 41 and accelerated up to a whopping thirty-seven miles per hour. That wasn't a high rate of speed before the outbreak, but now? With all the wrecked and burned out cars, abandoned roadblocks, and the odd walking maggot-head, it was about as fast as you ever wanted to drive on unfamiliar roads. At least if you didn't want to become a stain across the front of an SUV. Or end up wearing flaming fuel after ramming into the side of a gasoline truck. "How did Cletus and the Moonshine Brigade back there capture you?"

"We were spending a week at the cabin Donna's family owns... owned... just outside Shawnee State Forest near Blue Creek when it happened." The blonde rubbed her forehead and continued. "There were eight of us then. We lost the twins, Amy and Andy, that first day. There were six zombies down by the carports when we tried to leave. They were employees of the Lake Lodge down the road, I think. The things were all over Amy before we saw them. They started *eating* her. Her brother tried to help, but a pair of them ignored his punches and started biting him too. We ran back inside and locked the doors. Ryan, Josh and, Brandon... barricaded the first floor, then we watched from the loft while those *things* kept roaming around outside the cabin. "

"How long were you trapped?" Jake asked.

Gwen shook her head. "Not long. They wandered off five or six hours later. We kept quiet and out of sight, so I guess they just lost interest. Once they left, Brandon suggested we search for weapons and stuff. We found a few shovels and a pair of baseball bats in the maintenance shed next door. We had plenty of food at first, and there was a well out back. We all thought we could wait whatever this is out."

Jake shook his head and lit a smoke after cracking his window. He'd taken a few cartons of American Spirits from the dealership, and he was seriously stressed. After blowing up Corn-fed Red and friends back at the pizza parlor, he needed some sweet nicotine.

"How did you end up in Bainbridge?" Kat asked, short hair waving with the breeze. She'd dropped her window too, even though his smoking didn't bother her.

"We were running out of food, so we hiked through Rarden and up Route 124 earlier this week. We ran into a group of *them*, fifteen or so, just outside town at the bowling alley." Gwen's face displayed a *thousand yard stare* as she relived the event. "Ryan and Josh never made it back outside. Tammi kind of flipped out and just took off running. We don't know what happened to her. The three of us tried losing those things in town, but we kept running into more. By the time we decided to bag looking for a place to hide, there were over thirty of them following us. We were about to go cross country, up to South Salem, but..."

"But those guys found you?" Kat prompted.

Gwen nodded, her eyes harsh. "Yeah. They were waiting in the lot behind that pizza shop. When they started shooting, we thought we were saved. Then, after they checked the bodies, they turned their guns on us. Brandon tried to talk with them, but the fuckers ignored him. They started calling him *nigger* and telling us we were whores. One of the younger ones put the shackles on us, while the other three kept us covered. Afterwards, they took Donna and me inside. They made us strip down, to check for weapons they said, but they were just getting their jollies. We realized we were in some serious trouble when they chained us to the pool tables. Then they started on Brandon."

"They killed him," Donna said quietly. "They beat him for almost an hour. Then they shot him and dragged him outside. The one guarding kept chuckling as they hung his body from the light out back."

"They bragged about how they'd add him to their trophy collection," Gwen spat.

"Well, they won't be doing anything at this point," Elle chuckled, "except being used as prophylactics by thorny-dicked demons in the Ninth Ring of Hell."

The writer was at a loss over what to say after that comment. "Well. Uh. That's... um... graphic."

Elle grinned. "I've always had a way with words."

"Kind of comforting actually," Gwen said with an evil smile.

Jake got the feeling she'd left a few details out of her story, but he didn't want to push. Both women had been through a lot in the last twenty-four hours and needed a little time to wrap their heads around it all.

But that was life for you in the zombie apocalypse.

* * *

What had been Tracy Dixon was stumbling along down I-71.

The creature was in decent shape, considering. Even after months of being exposed to the elements, she would still be recognizable to someone who'd known her prior to the outbreak. It still had most of its skin, both its eyes, its limbs, even much of the once-pretty woman's clothing. The Manolos—even the unbroken one—were long gone.

Tracy had joined a pod moving south. They walked day and night. Sleepless, restless, stumping ever onward. Driven not by any higher purpose or will, but by the hunger that ruled them. Not one of them had anything resembling higher brain functions. The creatures were done with that. They moved purely on instinct.

A deeply ingrained need to find prey.

CHAPTER EIGHTEEN

A few miles later, Jake brought their Hummer to a halt.

Route 41 passed two-hundred yards west of Valley Vista Golf Course on their way back to Rae's cache in New Holland and, strangely enough, was cluttered with pockets of the dead. There was an unobstructed view from the sheer ridge, forty feet above the once immaculately-trimmed, eleventh hole. Since there was no way the creatures could scale the cliff, he'd decided it was time for a little target practice.

Something Foster had stressed, when he'd put their group through a last session of weapons training (was it only a few days ago?) under his safe house, was that marksmanship, just like any other ability, required constant practice. If you went too long between shooting sessions, your skills would deteriorate and when you needed them again, you wouldn't be able to hit that zombie you were aiming at. Then, you'd swiftly go from *survivor to lunch.*

So, any chance they got—especially since most of their weapons were either silenced or suppressed—the group had to put in some trigger time.

Jake estimated the pod, as they'd come to call large clusters of zombies, numbered in the low seventies. Plenty of targets for their purpose. He pulled over into the break-down lane out of habit, careful not to roll the trailer with their motorcycles too close to the edge, and turned the Hummer's engine off. The creatures had most certainly heard their approach, because they were grouped below the humans on the green in all their disgusting splendor.

"What do you think, Kat?"

She nodded, looking over the cliff side. "Looks alright. Nothing on the road, clear line of sight in both directions, and no way for them to get up to us."

He waved the others from the vehicle. Though their expressions were confused and wary, Gwen and the slowly recovering Donna followed him to the edge of the drop-off. Elle volunteered to keep watch and stood in the Hummer's turret, rifle in hand, scanning the road in both directions through her binoculars.

"Alright. I know the three of us," motioning at Kat and Leo, "know how to shoot. Elle was active duty, so she has a lot of experience with firearms. What about you two?"

"Do we have to do this *now*?" Donna asked.

Jake shrugged and made sure his M4 had a round in the chamber. "If we run into more creatures on the drive back, I want you girls to know how to handle a weapon. Not just for your safety, either. If any of us get hurt or killed, you might have to take our place. Once you know how to operate a rifle, you can substitute for someone."

Gwen nodded and seemed eager to begin. Donna didn't look convinced.

"Don't worry. We'll take it slow."

He proceeded to give them the rundown Foster provided their group prior to them ever touching one of his precious weapons. The old man actually *was* one of those people who was absolutely nuts about guns, so they'd all become fairly proficient with firearms under his tutelage. It took nearly fifteen minutes for Jake to review the basics on loading, securing, and firing the weapon, along with essential target acquisition, before handing the rifle to Gwen and telling her to squeeze off a few. He noticed that she insured the fire selection was set on single shot before taking aim at the creatures below. Then the attractive blonde took a shooting stance and began popping off rounds.

Ten shots later, seven of the creatures lay neutralized on the grassy field below.

"Nice!" Kat clapped and gave the woman an encouraging smile.

Gwen made sure her weapon's safety was engaged and passed it back to Jake with a frown. "I missed."

"Hey, I'll take seven out of ten. That's good enough for government work." He grinned, swapped magazines, then held the M4 out to Donna. "Let's see what you can do."

The pale haired woman shook her head, silently.

"Relax," the writer said. "Nobody expects you to..."

"I don't like guns."

Jake blinked. From the corner of his eye, he saw Gwen begin to massage her forehead. "Nobody *likes* guns... Well, some people do I guess, but regardless..."

"No, I mean I don't agree with them." Donna put her hands

behind her back and stepped slightly away. "I don't think they're needed in modern society. All they do is get people killed."

The others were silent as they absorbed that. Kat was wondering what Donna was smoking. It obviously wasn't anything that would've been considered *legal* a few months prior.

"So, let me see if I understand," Jake began slowly. "You don't feel the need to know how to defend yourself, because... why? Guns are bad?"

"They're not necessary," Donna insisted.

He gave her a level gaze and lowered his arms, allowing the weapon to rest against his torso. "I don't have time for this. Back in the Hummer."

They started towards the vehicle and Jake put a palm out at Gwen's politically correct friend. "Not you."

"What?"

"Guns aren't necessary, so why would you need to come with us? It's not like there's anything *dangerous* out here, right?" He looked pointedly down at the zombies at the bottom of the drop off. "You should be able to just stroll up the road to the next town and grab a room at the Motel 6."

"Just because..." Donna began.

Jake's patience had come to an end and he bellowed, "Because what? What? What *ridiculous* excuse is about to fall out of your mouth?"

Kat laid a hand on his arm as Donna stood there, wide-eyed. "I understand why you're mad. Bubble brain here needs a reality check, but..."

He shrugged her off and stepped back to the road's edge. "No. Not just no, *Hell* no. This one is going to come to grips with our situation, right now."

Jake pointed at the ravenous creatures on the greens. "Look at them."

Donna's arms crossed over her breasts and she kept her gaze at her feet.

"Look at them!"

Her eyes jerked towards the crowd of rotting evil below. Men and women of all ages, children even clamored for the flesh of the humans above. Gore coated hands reached for their party, and piss-yellow eyes stared unblinking from grey faces over snapping, jagged teeth. Falling into that horrid crowd would result in death, not reanimation. The creatures would dismember anyone unlucky enough to come within reach, devouring them in screaming pieces.

"Let's get something straight. The world you knew? It's gone." He pointed at the hungry dead as they continued to moan and jostle each other for position. "They *ate* it. Chances are everyone you've ever known is one of those fucking *things*."

He realized it was heartless, but Jake didn't believe there was any other way to impress upon her just how desperate their situation was. "Let me be frank, I don't give a damn about you, your infantile opinions, *none* of it. I've got people I care about depending on me to get them to safety if that even exists anymore. Now, you can either help us get there, which entails you growing the fuck up, and realizing nobody gives two shits about your beliefs, or you can strut your ass down the road. Oh, just so you know? All your dipshit, anti-gun, protester friends? They're shuffling around right now, looking for living people to eat. You'll want to consider *that* before you spew any more bullshit."

Gwen's shoulders slumped and she turned her head away from the awful horde below.

"You might think I'm being cruel, but I'm telling you this in the hopes it'll keep you alive," he pressed. "These creatures don't have anything resembling compassion or mercy. *They will kill you.* They'll eat or turn anyone they can catch, and I'm not going to let that happen to my people. If that means I need to kill a dozen of those things with my bare hands, or a few hundred by running them down in a fucking *tank*, that's what I'm going to do."

Donna stood there shamefaced as Kat and the others waited next to the Hummer. Jake watched as the frightened blonde absorbed his words, and he waited for her to respond. When she said nothing, he shook his head in disgust. "Just... get in."

Gwen helped her numb friend into the vehicle, and Leo joined them via the opposite door, while Elle continued to watch the road. Jake pulled another American Spirit from the pack in his vest pocket and lit up. He didn't know what more he could do. After over two months of zombie hell, he couldn't imagine how anyone would still have qualms about blowing the living—or unliving—shit out of one, given half a chance.

"She'll come around." Kat stepped up beside him to look over the edge at the dead below.

He shook his head. "She's a liability. Nothing's going to change her stupid, granola-munching views about firearms. I've seen the type before. Morons that walk into a hail of bullets, holding flowers and singing "Kumbayah." Jesus. That's cold. I didn't used to think that way. I hate this. Why did all of you put me in charge?"

"Because you hate it, of course," Kat replied.

"Mind explaining that one?" He blew smoke into the breeze.

"It's a mistake that a lust for power is the mark of a great mind.

Even the weakest have been captivated by it and, for minds of the highest order, it has no charms.'"

Jake gave her a sidelong glance. "Colton?"

Kat shrugged and gave him a vapid look. "I figured, 'with *great power, comes great responsibility*,' might be a little too obvious."

He snorted, shook his head and flicked the butt of his cigarette at the grey faces below. It hit one of them above its nose, the ember leaving an unnoticed blister between the zombie's eyes.

How long until they decompose, he thought ruefully, *a year? Two? Ten? They don't seem to decay like normal corpses do.*

The pair watched as the infected below continued their mindless dance, wondering now if there was any hope of humanity surviving long enough to reclaim its world. Everywhere their group had been, they'd encountered nothing but the dead. Well, the dead and people who had seemingly lost their minds. Jake felt the sudden and distinct need to hold Laurel.

"Let's get back on the road." Kat took Jake's arm, pulling him gently towards their Hummer. "I think we've done our good deed for the day, and we need to get back before dark."

* * *

Some days, things wouldn't go right if you put a gun to their head, Jake thought.

Halfway back to Rae's cache one of the tires on the trailer holding their new motorcycles ran flat on Route 138. After inspection, Elle insisted it was repairable, but she needed more time than they had daylight. Jake considered leaving the trailer by the side of the road and returning for it the following day with tools and supplies, but the pretty Marine convinced him what they had in the Hummer would suffice. If they could just locate a reasonably secure location, she could fix it in a few hours and they could roll on in the morning.

Luckily, they found an agricultural supply store five-hundred yards up the road. While the others watched the front, Jake and Kat scaled a drainpipe at the corner of the building. After breaking out a skylight, the pair carefully dropped into the stockroom via a length of fire-hose. There weren't any zombies inside and it was a simple matter to unlock the delivery bay door, allowing Elle to back both trailer and Humvee inside. After securing the bay again, Jake found a pallet-jack and moved a quartet of fully-loaded, topsoil skids to block the front door. Seeing that it opened inward, he was fairly certain, with almost four-thousand pounds of dirt blocking a solid steel door, that they could sleep in safety.

As Elle began repairs on the trailer's tire with Leo, Jake used their secure radio to check in with the safe house. It was no surprise the voice he heard on the other end was Laurel's. The redhead had been sitting beside her own radio waiting for their call, just in case. He relayed their situation to her, and she promised to let the others know they were safe. After a little chastising, she told him they'd better get their butts back by noon the following day because she had designs on his. He promised her it was a date, signed off, and shut down the radio to conserve its battery.

Kat then put together a surprisingly good meal with five beef brisket MREs and some dehydrated potato mix. Jake told her flat out he was impressed, as he shoveled plastic sporkfulls of bovine goodness into his mouth. She beamed at him. Afterwards, the women took turns using the employee bathroom while he searched the store for useful items. There wasn't much. At least nothing portable. Jake did manage to find three, full, five-gallon, propane tanks, which he secured in the rear of the Hummer as daylight faded.

Though safe temporarily, he still felt it best that someone stand watch. Elle and Kat both volunteered to spell him in three-hour shifts, but Jake declined. With his weapons and their Starlight scope, he headed for the roof. It had been some time since he'd had a moment to himself, and needed to reorder his thoughts.

After scanning the road in both directions, Jake proceeded to search the surrounding area. While there were a few zombies moving north along Highway 35, there was no evidence that the creatures knew of his group's existence. That suited him just fine. He didn't have the desire to play hide-and-seek with zombies in the dark. So long as no one made excessive noise, chances were good that their little group would remain unnoticed.

He placed the scope and his carbine on the roof's pebbled surface, sat Indian-style, closed his eyes, then began to slow his breathing. The lack of sounds normally associated with humanity helped. It was strangely peaceful, as long as Jake didn't think about how the all-encompassing silence had been achieved. His heartbeat slowed and he moved into a shallow meditative state. He'd learned the technique from a girlfriend in college and found it extremely useful over the years. An hour spent that way usually provided him with the equivalent of sleep.

Around eleven, after half a dozen checks of the surrounding area, he felt relatively fresh. Leo had relieved him for about fifteen minutes just before nine, allowing Jake to take a leak and wash the stink of smoke and cordite off in the bathroom sink. After changing into his only spare clothes, he was ready for a quiet night of utter boredom.

That was what he'd expected anyway.

Jake heard the hose leading down to the storeroom creaking, then Kat's head poked over the edge.

"Hey. You might want some company?"

"Sure. What are the others doing?" He watched as she flipped gracefully up to the roof.

"Oh, Leo and both the Barbies are crashed out, but Elle's still awake. Cleaning her weapons, as usual." Kat plunked down beside him. "That girl needs a hobby."

"I think that *is* her hobby." Jake rubbed the back of his neck with one hand.

"Mmm."

They sat in companionable silence, lost in their own thoughts. Jake rose to check the area by Starlight once more. "Can I ask you a question?"

"Hit me, gaijin." She leaned her head back against the three-foot wall circling the roof's edge.

"What do you think I should be doing differently?"

She frowned prettily. "In regards to?"

"Everything, I guess." He pulled out a smoke and, shielding his Zippo from the breeze, lit up. Jake made sure to keep the flame and coal-red tip of his cigarette below the level of the wall. No sense in advertising their presence.

Her face grew thoughtful as she considered it. "I think you need to stop worrying about every, single, questionable thing we have to do."

"Can you be a little more specific?"

"Killing those jerks today in Bainbridge, kicking Mike and Nichole out of the safe house for being a pair of drug-wasted deviants, not helping that poor guy who'd been bitten when we rescued Maggie and the girls. I know that was bad for you, but he was a goner," she told him gently. "No one expects you to handle *every* problem on your own, Jake. If you try, you'll just burn yourself out. Or go crazy. Everybody knows you're doing your best."

He grunted and took a deep drag from his smoke. "The problem is I don't know what the hell I'm doing. I'm a *writer*, Kat. What the hell do I know about leading people? And in the middle of the damn apocalypse? George would've been a better choice. I'm afraid I'm going to get someone killed."

"That's a risk we've all accepted. Nobody expects perfection from you. That's *my* job." Kat sniffed and Jake caught her bright smile even in the murky darkness, and it made him feel better. With man-made illumination now nonexistent, the nights were very dark. He had to admit, Kat's smile was the perfect ward against the gloom.

"What's the first thing you're going to do when we get over the Rockies?"

She seemed a little taken back by his question. "I... hadn't really thought that far ahead."

"Come on. There's gotta be something."

He watched as she considered it for a minute. Kat's face broke into a wry grin. "Well, I suppose getting a job as a pharmacy tech is out of the question."

He chuckled. "Maybe you could open a dojo, you know? Kat-San's Kick-Ass Kung-Fu and Center for Zombie Self Defense."

That caused her to choke as she stifled a laugh and slapped at his shoulder. He dodged away, and she scooted after him.

"Hey! Stop, will you? We don't wanna make any noise!" He tried not to laugh as Kat landed a couple of joking blows.

She ignored the comment and began poking him in the ribs with surprisingly quick fingers. "Kat-San no takey orders from smart-mouthed gaijin. Me smacky."

They spent the next minute grappling. Jake, attempting to keep from laughing aloud, Kat, attempting to make him suffer. More often than not, she managed to get a stiff finger past his defenses, but he kept from breaking down into a full-blown giggle fit. Finally catching her outside wrist, he pulled firmly and rolled Kat lightly across his hip and onto her back. She kept poking him with her free hand, until Jake got a hold on that one as well and pushed her arms flat to the roof's surface. Kat wasn't able to muscle free when he wrapped her right leg with his own, so she settled for smiling unrepentantly.

"That's better. You don't laugh enough, Jake," she said, slightly out of breath.

He grinned ruefully down at her. "Reasons to laugh have been a little scarce on the ground lately."

"Well. That's kind of insulting," she pouted. "You're alive and, mostly, thanks to me, well fed today..."

"I'll give you that one," he admitted.

"Don't interrupt," she continued. "You drive around in the baddest ride on the road, during which you get to spend lots of time with me. Again, a plus. You've got a pair of women lusting after your body like..."

"What??"

Kat rolled her eyes. "Laurel, *obviously*. Duh. Rae wouldn't mind taking you for a test drive, either."

"Rae?" Jake asked incredulously. "Why would you think..."

"Um, hello? Gave you a Hummer? No pun intended," she said. "Besides, she keeps looking at your ass. I caught her at it four times the day we arrived, for heaven's sake."

Jake was speechless.

The dark-haired, ninja girl smiled. "But that's because I stare at it too. Then again, I stare at everyone's ass. It's a cat thing."

He frowned. "I thought that was a dog thing."

"No, no, no. *Sniffing* everyone's ass is a dog thing. Cats watch."

He thought about that. "So...you've been watching me?"

"Of course," Kat admitted. "I *did* kind of promise Laurel, you know."

He looked at her narrowly, pushing her wrists up until her arms were extended over her head. "That's not what I meant."

His eyes had long ago adjusted to the darkness during his time on the rooftop, so he clearly saw the way Kat's face went blank before she answered.

"What do you think?" she asked, quietly.

Jake sank lower, until the lengths of their bodies were pressed together. He'd removed his tac-vest earlier and she never wore one, so he could feel her curves molding against him as her breath quickened. They were almost nose-to-nose now. Looking at Kat from less than a foot away, he clearly saw something hurt and broken move behind her eyes.

Something Jake was certain he recognized.

He hovered over her, watching as she swallowed and her lips parted, allowing her breath to brush over his face. He bent down, holding her eyes with his own and made hesitant contact with Kat's lips. The kiss was slow and cautious, like the way you would stretch a painfully tight muscle the day after you'd pulled it. Something stirred in his brain, and their kiss slowly deepened as her free leg curled over the back of Jake's thigh.

Releasing her wrists, he put an elbow to the ground to support his weight, while sliding his other hand down her arm. After gliding along her ribs, he continued over the skin of her waist and left hip. Kat sighed into his mouth as his fingers ran over the outer seam of her leathers to the bend of her knee, then pulled her thigh up over his buttock. Her lips continued pulling gently against him, while her fingers traveled under his shirt to take in the feel of his flesh. The muscles in Jake's back were solid smoothness, and she pulled his shirt up over his head so she could touch more. He allowed her to strip off the garment, and she ran her eyes over his upper body, followed closely by her hands. Then Kat wrapped her arms under his shoulders and drew her thumbs down the length of his spine, sending shivers through his frame.

He was starting to have problems remembering how to breathe. Her mouth was becoming more demanding and her fingers left hot trails across his back wherever they touched his skin. Jake worked his lips under her jaw, down her neck (no hardship there) and along her collarbone as she continued to run her hands over him.

Kat honestly believed her brain was going to explode when he pushed the straps of her cut off shirt and purple bra over her right shoulder. He didn't try to yank her top off, (*Like I just did to him,* she thought. *Oops...*) or attempt to bare her awkwardly to the world. Jake continued brushing her skin with his lips until he reached the place where her shoulder and upper torso met. He took the soft flesh where the mound of her breast began between his teeth, biting her lightly, which caused Kat to inhale sharply, and her hands moved to caress their way to the back of his neck.

When he began moving left along the top curve of her breast towards her sternum, she was losing her resolve quickly. Kat had promised herself that she wouldn't make a move on him. Both for his sake and Laurel's. With everything else they had to deal with—trying not to starve, murdering hillbillies, zombies, those kinds of things—adding an emotional triangle would just be too much. But Jake was right *here.* Their bodies were straining to come together and his lips moved to hers again and she could feel him under her hands and...

Oh, to hell with it.

She threw herself wholeheartedly into the kiss. If they died tomorrow, next week, next month, at least she'd have him once.

Jake knew he had real feelings for Laurel. What surprised him was that he was developing them for Kat as well. While he enjoyed the time spent with his red-haired firebrand, there was no question that he looked *forward* to spending time with the pretty and dangerous, dark-haired woman clutching at him now. Even if half the time he believed she was out of her mind. Jake couldn't complain, really. The other half of the time, he thought he was crazy too.

He pulled back and looked into the dark pools that the night transformed her eyes into. Kat's irises were dilated fully, either from lack of light or desire, and he kissed her again to keep from falling helplessly into them. She squirmed beneath him so he pushed himself up, thinking to give her room to move away, and got a surprise.

She was lost. The sight of him suspended over her, cords in his chest clenching visibly in the shadows of the rooftop...

Kat pulled her tank top off, and his eyes widened. Granted, she was still wearing a bra and he'd seen the twins on the night of the outbreak. He'd unknowingly walked in on her and Al, just before they'd engaged in some hot monkey lovin'. But he'd never had them aimed exclusively in his direction, prior to now. She sat up partially and brought her mouth to his again, as she reached a hand back to release her lacy, purple, Demi cup.

Jake realized if she managed to unhook that bra, there wouldn't be any turning back. He took hold of her wrist again as the first hook released and moved it down to the small of her back. Kat tried pulling out of his grasp, determined to free the last eyehook and send them both gleefully howling down the path to disaster. He also knew if he retained the hold on her arm, he'd end up hurting her before she'd stop, so he needed a distraction. He slid lower, avoiding her breasts, and bit her lightly along the line of her ribs.

Kat stopped going for the bra clasp and took a shaky breath through clenched teeth as her back arched. She moved her hands down to grip Jake's shoulders again, so he continued over the flat lines of her stomach. Her fingers twined through his hair as he ran his tongue through the hollow between her hip and oblique, causing her to shudder. Then Kat looked down at him and her eyes steamed.

Oh, that was the wrong thing to do, he thought.

Pulling him away from her stomach, Kat came to her knees and locked their lips together again. Jake wrapped her up in his arms as their tongues fenced lightly, and she slid her hands slowly down his back. Her fingers went under the edge of his Khakis up to her knuckles but, thanks to his belt, couldn't move any lower. She began sliding them around the line of his waist, inching her way forward, but was still unable to get her hands fully past the web belt and literally into his pants.

The situation was about to get out of control.

He pulled her tight against his body, trapping her insistent hands between the two of them, then slowly broke off the kiss and watched as she came back to herself.

"What's wrong?"

Jake sighed regretfully. "I can't, Kat."

She looked at him like he'd just grown a third head. Jake gave her a steady look, and she slumped against his chest, hands coming out of his waistband and settling lightly on his hips.

"I know," she said woodenly.

"I'm sorry." He took her face between his hands and brought her eyes up to meet his own again. "If you want me to be frank, I'm also reasonably certain I'm going to be kicking myself every day for the rest of my life for missing all the chances to let you have your way with me. I don't think you know how utterly *magnificent* you are. I blame every asshole you've ever dated, *ever* for that."

Those dark eyes of hers searched his face, then Kat grinned slowly. "So, I'm going to be on your mind for the rest of your life?"

"Um. Yeah." He brushed his hands lightly down the outsides of her arms. "I'd say that sums it up."

Her head tilted to one side as she considered that. The expression on her face made Jake decidedly uncomfortable, as her eyes roved over his body. Kat smiled, retrieved her cutoff shirt and donned it again. She caught him watching as she pulled the thin fabric over her head and her smile grew wider. He actually broke into a sweat when she passed her hands lingeringly over her breasts, smoothing the shirt to her appealing curves once more.

"I like the thought of that," Kat said, then kissed him briefly and stepped to the skylight. Taking hold of the fire-hose, she looked back at him over her shoulder. "See you in the morning, hero."

Then she slid easily down the hose, into the building, and out of sight.

"I'm not a hero," he called after her quietly, still leery of making noise that could attract the dead.

"Whatever you say," Kat replied, then her light footfalls faded towards the rear of the building.

Jake pulled his CBGB shirt back on and checked the surrounding area again through his Starlight scope. The distant ghouls still shambled north on Highway 35, but other than that all he saw were a few deer picking their way between the nearby trees.

Sitting again, his back pressed against the wall along the roof's edge, Jake decided he would never understand women.

CHAPTER NINETEEN

Elle relieved Jake at 4:00 a.m.

She'd made a very good case as they argued about him getting some sleep in hushed tones. He'd been going for better than 24 hours straight and he needed to be sharp when they hit the road in the morning. From the *don't act like an ass, sir* look on her face, the pretty, blonde sergeant wasn't going to drop the subject, either. So in short order, he was snoozing, stretched across a pallet of bagged peat moss down in the storeroom.

He woke suddenly, shocked awake by some sleep-borne terror that fled as soon as he opened his eyes. Try as he might though, he couldn't remember what the nightmare was about. The low light revealed Kat snuggled up against his left side, one arm wrapped around his waist, fast asleep. Her head was pillowed on his shoulder, face a picture of serenity. Jake watched her for a while, thinking fervently (again) that Allen was a damn fool. How could his friend have opted for Heather, pretty though she was, over this woman sleeping next to him?

Jake's fingers began itching to caress her face, and he realized he should get up off the pallet before he did something stupid. Again.

Cupping her head with his right hand, Jake carefully slid from under her arm. He grabbed a bundle of gardening gloves from the shelf and, ever so gently, laid her cheek on the rose-patterned fabric.

Kat stirred slightly. "Hhmm?"

He smoothed away hairs that had fallen across her face back over one delicate ear. "Everything's fine, Kat. Go back to sleep."

"Mmm-kay..." She sighed, nowhere near awake.

As he moved to stand, she murmured, "Love you."

Jake stood there with his mouth hanging open. No one had told him that in a *very* long time. Even with how close the two of them had become, Laurel had yet to actually say that. He stared at the dreaming ninja-girl, unable to speak if his life depended on it, in a state very near to shock. Finally, his brain reengaged. After donning his tac-vest, he grabbed a beef stew MRE from the Hummer and retrieved his M4 from beside the pallet where Kat still slept. As he entered the showroom proper, Jake could hear someone moving around in the bathroom while he opened the vacu-pack and began eating government-issue nutrition. Gwen came out shortly, hair damp and looking much better than she had the day before.

The trim woman wore clothes much like Kat's, sans the cut off tank-top, looking like a Roger Corman style, wet dream. Biker pants, *Born To Ride* shirt (four sizes too small, of course) with a cartoon pig riding a flaming Harley emblazoned on the front. The group had taken half a dozen pairs of the more expensive biker boots when they'd procured the trailer and the motorcycles. Kat insisted it was only looting if someone alive was actually there to loot *from*. Now, three months after the end of the world? It was termed, *salvage*.

"Morning," Jake mumbled around a mouthful of stew. He'd plunked down on a picnic display near the store's cash register. It was a textured plastic job, supposedly maintenance free and ugly as all hell.

Gwen took a seat opposite him with a brief smile. "Morning. Sleep well?"

He shrugged and finished off his meal. "Had some bad dreams, but that's been normal for about, oh, three months now."

"I know the feeling," she said, as he used his Zippo to light a smoke. "Those will kill you, you know."

He laughed. "I doubt I'll live long enough for that to happen."

"I don't think Kat would appreciate you croaking, after everything Leo tells me you've been through. How long have the two of you been together?" she asked, attempting to make conversation.

Jake shook his head. "We're not a couple."

"O-o-oh," Gwen said, wisely. "Friends with benefits. That's cool too. I had a guy back home like that for awhile."

"Uh. No," he replied. "Just good friends. No sex involved."

She gave him a skeptical look. "Really?"

He nodded.

"Wow...you must be the most unobservant guy on Earth."

The conversation was beginning to take an odd turn, causing Jake to shift in his seat. He wasn't comfortable discussing his sex life with a woman he'd just met the day before. "Why do you say that?"

"Well, duh!" Gwen rolled her eyes and gave him a look clearly questioning his mental abilities.

He blinked and settled for gazing out a narrow window providing a view of the crossroads outside. A lone zombie was passing south, wearing what remained of filthy coveralls and a pair of hip-wader, fishing boots.

Gwen pressed on. "I mean it's pretty obvious."

"Where's Leo?" He attempted to change the subject.

"Oh, he's up on the roof with Elle." The blonde shrugged. "They're still in the initial cuddle phase, so I think they were looking to get away from everybody for a while."

That was surprising news, to say the least. Jake had been sure young Salazar carried a torch for Karen large enough to be seen from orbit.

Everyone's libido is going into overdrive, he thought. I wonder if saying to hell with it and acting on your desires is a side effect of the apocalypse? Or maybe it's just because we're all stuck together every waking moment.

He knew people tended to form attachments with others they normally wouldn't associate with when thrown into highly stressful situations. Hell, he'd understand if that *were* the case. Before the outbreak, he would've been hard pressed to piss in his previous bosses face if the bastard's eyes were on fire. The man had been an egotistical snob and the way he spoke to his co-workers nearly earned him some high-quality ass-kickings from many of the other editors. Besides which, he'd been a complete horn-dog, and Jake believed anyone with *that* many paternity suits against him wasn't really the type of guy he needed to be having beers with.

I guess old Larry got off easy. What with the end of the world and all. No alimony payments due to Doomsday.

Tamping his cigarette out on the ugly picnic table, he looked outside again. A lone zombie was passing north wearing the remains of torn and filthy coveralls and fishing boots...

Wait a damn minute. Jake rose and moved quickly to the small window. Careful not to get close enough for anyone or anything to see him through the glass, he watched the creature stumble past their hiding place.

"Go wake Donna and the two of you stay quiet," He told Gwen, and headed for the stockroom again. Jake strode quickly to the pallet where Kat still lay sleeping, then patted her leather-covered knee.

The ex-pharmacy tech's dark eyes fluttered open and he placed a finger to her lips. "Something strange outside."

She nodded silently and grabbed her weapons from the same shelf where he'd found her gardening glove pillow. The pair scurried quietly up the fire-hose and onto the roof. There may not have been many infected in the area at the moment, which meant their luck was holding, but that didn't mean more of the creatures couldn't show up. That would turn their morning into an exercise involving lots of bullets and nasty body fluids.

Elle and Leo broke apart, rising to their feet as Jake reached down, grasped Kat's hand, and pulled her up through the skylight. He noticed that, even though they'd been involved in some *really* heavy petting, the pretty, blonde soldier looked totally at ease. Leo's expression displayed more than a little embarrassment, however.

Motioning for silence, Jake pulled the binoculars from his vest and targeted the stumbling ghoul. The awful thing was moving up the middle of the country road with purpose. He couldn't see it very well, due to the overgrown grass and trees, but confirmed that it was the same creature that had been heading south only minutes ago. Even with his limited line of sight, Jake could tell the zombie was in hunting mode. It was heading towards something that had tripped the rotten *dinner* switch in its dead brain. The creature's arms stretched forward in anticipation of latching onto prey with its grey, smut-coated hands. As Jake watched, he saw its jaw drop open to let loose with a moan and...

The pink, blade-like prow of the Screamin' Mimi caught it squarely in the chest. The force of the impact turned the zombie into instant, foul-smelling, flesh-toned goop.

"Oh, *fuck*!" Jake exclaimed and reached for his vest pocket where one of the Maritime distress flares George insisted each of them carry rested. Before his hand touched the launch tube, however, the enormous transport slowed and turned lazily into the Agri-Supply's gravel parking lot.

"You lovebirds keep an eye out up here, alright?" Kat said, moving to follow him, as he all but jumped down through the skylight to the storeroom below. "We'll find out what's going on."

"This can't be good," Leo murmured, as the blue-haired woman disappeared down the fire-hose.

Elle proceeded to check the magazine in her suppressed MP5. Foster had offered her one of his surplus M4s but, as with a .50 Cal, the buxom sergeant was most comfortable with her own weapon. Confirming it was full, she slapped the magazine home and turned a watchful eye to the road. "Don't worry, Jake will handle it. You just watch the other side of the building. That way, we can maybe continue the conversation we were having later?"

The younger man grinned, chambered a round, and turned towards the west end of the roof.

"I *told* you I'm not a kid," he called over his shoulder. "And I don't remember you doing much talking."

A smile warred on her face with an attempt at a stern look as she pointed to the far side. "I'll get you for that," Elle said.

* * *

By the time the Mimi's rear hatch cycled to the ground, Jake had pulled the skids of topsoil they'd used to block the Agri-Supply's door clear with the pallet-jack.

While he wasn't sure why the others had abandoned Rae's cache, he was glad they managed to find their way south to them. It was testament to Foster's skill at handling the mobile fortress that, even without a scout vehicle, the pink transport made its way through devastated areas containing zombies, wreckage, and whatnot.

He checked outside through the two foot window. Seeing none of the creatures, he unlatched the simple deadbolt and ran towards the Mimi. As its loading ramp settled to the pebbled earth, Rae, carrying what looked like a SIG 540 assault rifle, was the first one down its corrugated surface. Laurel followed close behind her. A little dirty, showing some smudges here and there, but to Jake she'd never been more beautiful. The growing tension in his chest released at the sight of her and, slinging his M4 across his back, he rushed forward to take her in his arms.

He held her tightly, lifting Laurel partially off the ground, until only the toe of one hiking boot remained in contact. The redhead responded to his relief in turn, gluing their lips together as Foster and Gertrude made their way to the rear hatch.

"What happened?" Kat asked, helping the older woman down the ramp.

"Don't fuss over me, dear. I've got my cane," Gertie chided.

Kat smiled and ignored her, continuing to support her arm until she reached the ground.

"We got caught with our pants down," George fumed. There was a cut along the side of the older man's scalp which had bled messily down the side of his face.

Jake kept his arms around Laurel's waist as he looked into the transport. "Where are the others?"

"They were taken," Rae said grimly.

"What?" Jake was stunned. "They're *dead*?"

Gertie put a hand on his arm, shaking her head. "No, dear. They're all still alive. But most likely they're wishing that wasn't the case right about now."

* * *

Jake got the full story during their return trip north.

He sent Elle and Leo in their Hummer with the two newcomers, then listened as Laurel recanted the events which had prompted them to flee Rae's safe house.

They'd been attacked mid-evening. Just a few hours after Jake had checked in over the radio. Foster and Gertrude had been familiarizing Rae with more of the Mimi's systems, insuring the statuesque woman was adept in their operations, just in case. While it was unlikely that George, Allen, *and* Gertrude would be out of action all at once, it wasn't outside the realm of possibility.

The three were hip deep in the *Official Operations Manual*, when Vince entered the transport. He told them that while monitoring the radio, he'd contacted another group of survivors. They stated they were convoying down County Road 25 at that very moment, seeking aid. The voice on the radio said their party had wounded and were in need of any assistance available, even if it was only a safe place to sleep for the night. Vince offered them shelter within the junkyard's thick walls, then let the others know they were expecting visitors.

Rae wasn't pleased, to say the least. Even though there was no point in worrying about national security any longer, she didn't feel the need to advertise her cache's whereabouts. Regardless, she absorbed the news that Vince had taken it upon himself to reveal their location to an unknown group gracefully. She told him he was a presumptuous ass.

George however, was absolutely livid.

The old soldier had given Vince a dressing down—reminiscent of a Master Chief breaking the spirits of new recruits on the first day of Navy SEALs training. There were pointed comments to the Corporal's inability to pull his head out of his ass, along with outright references to the man's pedigree. Being dropped on his head repeatedly as a child was suggested. Mental retardation was implied.

Laurel was reworking one of their food storage lockers in the second module, when she noticed the yelling. The redhead added another week of supplies to their vehicle's stores, even though she had to repack the recessed container twice. Upon hearing Foster preparing to *cut the Corporal's useless balls off*, she'd hurried to the rear of the Mimi in an attempt to keep George from *stomping a mud hole in his ass.*

When Rae told her why Vince was half a minute from embarrassing levels of pain, the object of Jake's affection reached for the Field Fighter knife on her hip. Giving the worried soldier a bloodthirsty look that spoke volumes, Laurel offered to help Foster *fix* him.

George, so angry he started repeating various curses, told Vince to go inside and gather the others in case the coming group was hostile. The corporal then hurried inside, making damn sure to shut the door behind him at Foster's full-throated urgings.

Which was when the bus composing the junkyard's entrance, was blown in half.

The force of the explosion knocked Laurel and George's lovely friends from their feet, while the concussion of the blast threw George against the Mimi's inner hull. That was how he received the cut on his head. Foster had still possessed the presence of mind to free his pistol and send a full magazine of rounds through the smoke, towards the gate. He was rewarded with a trio of screams, but the rest of his shots missed altogether.

A pair of armored trucks then busted through the wreckage, knocking chunks of debris aside as they pushed their way through. Each carried a quartet of armed men holding weapons ranging from pistols to AK47s, and the trucks headed without pause for the safe house. More vehicles followed. Half a dozen SUVs, an F150 pickup, and three racing bikes in all.

There hadn't been time for them to reach the safety of the cache. Foster was still groggily trying to keep his feet; Gertie was up in the drive unit...

Rae then made an executive decision. She'd activated the door mechanism, causing the Mimi's loading ramp to cycle shut. Laurel wanted to go out and fight the intruders (she'd become quite good with a silenced pistol), but George's female counterpart convinced the redhead to help her get him up to the front instead. At least from there, thanks to the transport's near-impervious skin, they could get some idea of what their options were from the bulletproof cabin.

As it turned out, they didn't have many.

The Mimi didn't have any offensive weaponry, so all the four survivors could do was watch as the attackers rammed one of the armored cars, rear first through the reinforced door of Rae's safe house.

Gertrude activated the external audio sensors (sneakily hidden in the hubs of the massive vehicle's wheels), allowing their group to listen to the assailants yelling for everyone to come out of the cache. They received a hail of small arms fire in reply. While Rae's hideaway was only half the size of Foster's, there were plenty of weapons within and the other members of their group were pretty motivated just then.

The driver of the lead SUV, a shaven-haired man in full skinhead regalia (complete with steel toed Doc Martins and suspenders over a white sleeveless shirt), began shouting orders. Two of the other attackers muscled a thirty-gallon drum of gasoline from the rear of the F150, and then rolled it over to the cache's door. They proceeded to break the top seal and upended the drum, spilling the fuel into the safe house and across the floor of the ground-level machine shop.

Lighting a road flare, Skinhead passed it quickly in front of the broken entrance, allowing anyone inside with a view of the door to see it and yelled that they had two minutes to come out, unarmed, or be charbroiled. That worried Rae. While her cache had been relatively tough (unless you rammed an *armored truck* through the door), the interior was far from fireproof. If the others didn't come out, they'd burn to death.

Laurel and Gertrude suggested—even though the older woman was obviously in no shape to do so—that they use the Mimi's large supply of weapons to attack the raiders. Rae and the still- groggy Foster had quickly convinced the two near-frantic women that would be not only futile, but suicidal. The attackers were simply too spread out, and there was no way they could mount any kind of successful counterattack to aid their friends in Rae's cache. The quartet watched, utterly helpless to aid Allen and the others, as the seconds ticked away.

Shortly, their companions filed outside. Allen and Vince were in the lead, then Heather and Karen, followed closely by the extremely pissed off looking Maggie. The four in the Mimi heard the attackers' leader ordering his men to cuff their friends, because Poole—whoever the hell *that* was—wanted them alive and unharmed. Skinhead had smirked, commenting that even though they weren't allowed to have any fun, he was sure the women would be useful in drawing the others out of the Pecker-mobile.

George scowled at Skinhead's comment, hand moving involuntarily to his sidearm, as they watched the attackers cuff their friends and move them up beside the drive module. After getting Allen and the others into position, their leader looked thoughtfully at Vince and pulled a battered notepad from his pocket. Leafing back a few pages, he'd then asked the corporal what his name was. Vince replied per military regulation with name, rank and, serial number. Skinhead checked his notebook and said, "Not one of them." The he pulled a police-issue Beretta from the shoulder holster he wore, and put a round through the soldiers head with all the emotion of someone swatting a bug.

The girls outside shied away as Vince's body hit the ground at their feet, his head bouncing off the grimy drive. Skinhead repeated the process with all his captives, nodding as each said their name, checking it against the list he evidently had in his notebook. Satisfied, he walked up to the Mimi, pounded on its hull with the butt of his pistol, and yelled for the others to *come out or watch a repeat of Mr. ROTC over there*, pointing at Vince's body.

Allen revealed then, that even though he looked like a geek, he had a mile of guts. The mechanic had burst forward, bellowing for Foster to start the transport and bug out. He nailed one of the men guarding them in the face with a roundhouse kick to the temple, and then caught the very surprised asshole next to him with a hatchet kick, breaking the man's collarbone with a loud, wet snap. Jake's slim friend then proceeded to stomp the first man into unconsciousness, continuing to yell for the Mimi to get under way. When one of the other captors moved to restrain him and got a two-fisted, sucker-punch from Maggie, due to the handcuffs they'd secured on her, the sound of the man's nose breaking was audible through the transport's sensors. Rae had given a cheer as the blonde EMT kneed him squarely in the testicles, lifting him a good eight inches off the ground.

As the other hostiles moved to secure the gleefully, rampaging pair, one of them bellowed in panic and pointed at the gate. A number of infected had begun making their way through the wreckage and, drawn by the short battle, were in full hunting mode. A few had already crossed the low flames, ignoring the way it burned their rotting skin, and set their clothes to smoldering. Long-dried gore coated their faces as they stumbled awkwardly towards the humans, and the sight of the crowd was enough to sober even the formerly-smirking Skinhead.

The attackers began firing into the creatures, dropping the horrible things as they approached the safe house, but there were more coming. The men finally got their two, unruly prisoners under control by butt-stroking Allen from behind, and a trio of them took Maggie to the ground. Heather and Karen were then shoved roughly into the lead armored car, followed closely by Allen's limp form, and the still-struggling EMT.

Skinhead started yelling empty threats for the Mimi's occupants to get out or they'd kill the others again, so Foster activated the transport's external PA and attempted to lie his ass off. He told the skinhead that their commanding officer was out on a scavenging mission and that for him to give up their vehicle prior to his return would contradict his express orders. George said it would be five days before his superior would get back with the rest of his strike team, and he would advise his commander to surrender the Mimi in exchange for their people, if Mr. Skinhead would give him the assurance they wouldn't be harmed prior to that time.

While this hadn't pleased the man, Skinhead told George their friends wouldn't be killed, at least not on the drive back to their camp. The longer it took Foster's superior to respond though, the higher the chances of someone getting *friendly* with one of their captives, and it would be a good idea for George to get him back. Fast. Then he proceeded to tell the fixer which radio frequency he would have to use to initiate contact with their stronghold. Foster assured Skinhead he'd pass the information along, and if there was anything else the man wanted to say before he, and the rest of the butt-bandits, scurried back to Looney-land. Laurel, sick with worry for the others, had slapped at the fixer's shoulders until Rae pulled her away. Skinhead turned and headed for the nearest SUV as his men continued holding back the oncoming ghouls, stopping only to shoot an angry look over his shoulder at the Mimi. The rest of the attackers then began pulling back to their vehicles, and in a move of pure spite, their leader threw his road-flare through the door of Rae's cache.

The massive *Whoomp* of gasoline igniting had turned the head of every creature in the area, as a fireball the size of an Escalade shot from the door of the cache, filling the junkyard with light pulled straight from perdition. The SEP-skin hull of the Mimi repelled the awful blast, while the raiders scurried to their rides and proceeded to roll out.

Some of the creatures plodded after the invaders, slowly walking back the way they'd came, but more made their way past Foster's pink behemoth and into the growing conflagration within Rae's hideaway. Drawn by flickering light and the growing roar of the flames, the dead had pushed against each other to enter the dying hideaway. Over a hundred of them shambled into the blaze, seeking the warmth of living flesh, and were turned into walking torches. For roughly two minutes.

The temperature inside the steel-reinforced building was more than sufficient to begin cooking a zombie brain almost immediately. The mindless things didn't have enough intelligence to realize that the flames would kill them. Dead, grey skin crisped with frightening speed. Eyeballs roasted in their sockets in seconds. The dead didn't feel fear, but from the cab of the Mimi, Laurel and the others had been privy to a ringside view of what Hell was sure to look like.

They left the junkyard shortly thereafter. There was no way to save Rae's cache. The fire was raging by then, destroying anything combustible inside. Flammable ingredients for use in a dozen different explosives obliterated the entire north wall, as George drove the Mimi through the gate. When he'd turned onto the service road, all the excess ammunition in Rae's armory expended itself. Thousands upon thousands of rounds went up through the second floor living area and the roof above to sail wildly into the night sky.

The four traveled south, detouring around several destroyed bridges and half a dozen now- impassible traffic jams, before meeting up with Jake and the others.

"How did you find us?" Kat asked.

Rae grinned smugly. "You don't think I'd let my baby out of my sight without a way to track her do you? I installed it in the chassis when I modified her. The system runs off an independent battery source that charges any time the vehicle's engine is running. It's got a month-long charge capability, and it's effective up to a hundred kilometers. "

Foster's eyebrows went up. "It's not GPS based?"

The stunning woman shook her head. "Nope, RF. As long as the transmitter in the search vehicle is within effective range, the beacon in the Hummer pings back the signal. That's how I extended the battery life. The beacon doesn't transmit per-se, it receives the locator signal from the primary vehicle and *absorbs* it. That causes a dead spot in the area which the sensors on the transmitting unit detects, translates into distance using ground radar technology, then gives you the location within two meters. Think of it as a post-apocalyptic On-Star"

Foster gaped at her in surprise.

Rae gave him an annoyed look. "Hello? Gear-head? At least I didn't rewire my TV remote to open my front door..."

"Moving on," Jake said firmly. You just *knew* some discussions weren't going to go anywhere productive. "How are we going to find the others?"

Now it was George's turn to look smug. "I guess you've never taken a real close look at yer vest, huh?"

That baffled Jake.

Foster snorted in exasperation. "Below the left pocket?"

Jake felt along the garment's edge. Something about the size of a pack of Wrigley's chewing gum and maybe half as thick had been vertically sewn into the seam. His eyes widened. "A locator beacon?"

George waggled his bushy eyebrows.

"When did you...?"

"Just after the Iranian Hostage Crisis," The fixer told him, steering around a wrecked Dodge Durango. The vehicle had what looked like chain link fencing screwed into the body covering its windows, giving testament that there had once been survivors in that area. The gore streaks along its dented quarter panels and bloody splatters on the interior of the windows were evidence that said survivors were long gone. "Carter believed in the *expandability* of covert operators. I was never big into leaving our guys to rot in some hellhole and get tortured. Maybe turned into some scumbag's fifteen minutes of fame on YouTube. Told the president to his face that he was a cowardly son of a bitch over that one, then had some fellas I was tight with in the NSA make locators for me."

"Tactful and, from you, completely unsurprising," Rae quipped.

Foster gave her a wry look. "This is why you ended up manning an installation in the middle of Ohio. Fer such a hot broad, your people skills really suck."

"Enough! I take it the Mimi has the capability to track the locators, right?" George nodded and Jake went on. "Do any of our people know about them?"

"Maggie does. Noticed it right off. Think it's because she was in charge of the equipment for the YMCA and her firehouse's medical supplies," George said.

"Do we have a direction?" The writer demanded, staring grimly through the windshield.

"Oh, yeah. Loud and clear, right, Gertie?" Rae asked.

"The signal has been stationary for almost two hours," she replied, hunched over in front of the Mimi's tech station, tapping away at the keyboard. "The interface is working perfectly, Rae. You should be proud of this. I must say, dear, its operating system is almost elegant."

Jake moved up beside Foster. "Let's go."

* * *

Gardner trekked ever northward.

He'd left Newport News, Virginia almost a month before and hadn't seen another living soul for far longer. He missed people. The last time he's been in contact with another human had been exactly sixty-one days prior.

The young man managed to acquire—read: steal—over a dozen automotive batteries during the initial outbreak. The small solar charger he normally used to keep his LED flashlight powered had kept them alive for a while, allowing him to use the short wave radio sparingly to talk with other survivors nearby. One by one, they stopped responding to his daily calls. He tried repeatedly to contact them but, eventually, the large bank of Die-Hards had been drained.

Unable to stand being cooped up—alone and barricaded in his third floor apartment—any longer, Gardner shouldered his pack and crept from the city under the cover of darkness. He moved slowly and steadily northward, avoiding towns and heading, hopefully, for Canada. He managed to remain unnoticed by the creatures by staying quiet, unseen, and alert, but every day seemed worse than the last. Every night seemed longer and darker than the one prior. Every fear seemed so much more terrifying.

Gardner kept moving doggedly northward.

CHAPTER TWENTY

Rae was becoming quite skilled at driving the Mimi.

Foster allowed her to take control around noon, as the transport continued west on a single-lane road, looping around Wilmington, Ohio. It had taken them most of the day to reach the town's outskirts after changing course repeatedly and avoiding jams of abandoned vehicles. Encounters with the creatures had been minimal due to the party staying off the freeways and keeping clear of larger towns. It was difficult to do in the urban sprawl of the Midwest, but not impossible.

Most of the ghouls that the survivors passed didn't even look in their direction, let alone try to claw their way into their vehicles. This was confusing to Jake in the extreme. The infected had been proven to search for prey through visual and auditory means, both of which two vehicles would provide. The only thing he was able to come up with was that—somewhere in their moldering brains— zombies recognized only the human form as a target. What it *didn't* explain was why some of them consumed any creature unlucky enough to be caught. Nor did it provide him any insight as to why some of their number (maybe one in thirty) not only noticed the vehicles but actively came after them.

Was there an undiscovered difference in the more aggressive creature's brain chemistry which allowed them to reason if only on the level of animals? Did their rate of decomposition influence their cognitive abilities? Was it a defect that caused them to recognize vehicles as something holding prey or a higher level of mental awareness? Jake didn't have the first clue. He'd been a journalist, not a geneticist.

Regardless, the Hummer had proven invaluable in finding their way through messes and even useful in dealing with the occasional aggressive ghoul. While the Mimi still set the bar when it came to splattering the nasty things all over the landscape, their new scout vehicle was more than adequate for ramming a few out of the way. Elle remained at the wheel, absently discussing where to start notching a body count into the dash with Leo, Gwen, and the still-silent Donna.

As they passed Route 73, Foster called Jake's attention to an airfield just ahead, past one of the town's discount Supercenters. It was once a hub for DHL, but had been shut down a few years back when the shipping company suspended domestic operations in the United States. George suggested they use one of its hangars to shelter for the night since the facility had been all but abandoned and there was little chance of infected presence within. The party could use their Longarm sniper rifles to monitor the perimeter fence, insuring there were no breaks to allow any creatures to enter. There might even be a few pairs of night-vision goggles in the airport's control tower they could acquire—read: loot.

Bowing to George's greater experience, Jake agreed that it seemed like their best plan. While the group *could* spend the night in the huge, pink transport, being somewhere a bit more open would give them a chance to decompress and plan their next move in relative safety. Rae turned the Mimi carefully towards the chain-link gate on the northeastern side, behind a row of warehouses, and brought it to a halt twenty yards away.

Leo hopped from the Humvee, clipped the ridiculously small padlock securing its chain, and pulled it open to allow them entry. After the vehicles passed through, the young fan of swordplay clipped a large carabineer into the links, securing it again and hurried back to the vehicle.

They trucked slowly across the empty airport, past the rear of the town's *second* Supercenter, to a cluster of small hangars near the north runway. Rae drove the Mimi past the partially open doors of the one farthest from the field's edge, then began to power the vehicle down while Jake, Laurel, and Kat exited through the rear hatch. The three ensured there were no creatures lurking within, prior to Elle pulling the door shut with their Hummer. Once she did, the only light within was what the party had brought along and the dim illumination leaking through the windows, three stories up the concrete walls.

The survivors were busy over the next two hours, insuring any standard-sized doors were secure, setting up a portable camp shower, and refueling the Hummer from the tank of diesel at the rear of the hangar. Elle and Foster (even though he grumbled the entire time) trudged up and gained access to the roof. They spent a good while checking the fence line and were unable to find any breaks for curious zombies to enter. Laurel put together a meal using MREs and a Coleman stove they'd taken from Tim's Emporium, and Kat worked on the blade of her sword in the traditional way, alternatively dusting it with fine powdered stone and polishing it clean with rice paper. Gertie busied herself helping Gwen and Donna acquire some sundries from their stores. Underwear, socks, that kind of thing. She was quite firm that they needed at least a few changes of clothes. Apocalypse aside, it was always an emotional boost to at least feel attractive. Or just *clean.*

It was well after dark, and Jake was in the transport's drive unit with Rae. George's female counterpart was walking him through the basics of her tracking system, explaining its hand-held unit. They were comparing readings coming in from Allen's locator to a map Foster brought along from his safe house, when Laurel found him. Her hair was still damp from using the camp shower and, as usual, that stray lock had escaped the elastic band at the base of her neck. It was half-sticking to her cheek, when she took a firm grip on the writer's shoulder and demanded that he eat.

Jake attempted to convince her that he was trying to figure out where Skinhead and the other attackers had taken their friends, but he was clearly not going to win that particular argument. The redhead's arms crossed over her ribs and one hip cocked out, letting him know said line of discussion was closed.

"Go, go." Rae waved him toward the rear of the Mimi. "There's nothing more we can do tonight. We'll be more apt to come with something feasible once we've all had some sleep."

Laurel smiled and gave him the *look.* The one that said: *See? Now be a good boy and march. It won't hurt. Much.* Jake sighed and, with his lovely female handler close behind, made his way out to get a bowl of macaroni and beef.

The two found some privacy at the other end of the hangar in a small office set against the exterior wall. That was the thing about the apocalypse. Any time you got the chance—in a safe place—for a little privacy, you damn well took it. Their party consisted of good and honest people, but if they all didn't find ways to be alone every so often, they'd start sniping at each other.

The lantern Kat's friend carried threw low shadows against the faux-wood paneling of the little office, as Jake grabbed a stray folding chair. He plunked down to eat with his plastic MRE spork and Laurel sat frowning next to him on the room's lone desk while he wolfed down the pasta. He looked different somehow. His face was unchanged. Jake still had the same serious gaze and strange, pale, sky-blue eyes, but they'd become shadowed. Not just from the weak light their Coleman lantern provided or the two-day's worth of stubble coming in on his jaw either.

"Do you want to talk about it?"

He shook his head. "Not really."

"Well, that's right out of *The Caveman's Guide to Life*." She raised an eyebrow. "You'll be speaking in grunts and looking for wooly mammoths to hunt next, I assume?"

Jake finished eating, pulled out a smoke, and lit up with a sigh. It seemed he had to explain his moods far more than he liked to everyone, ever since they'd dropped the whole *leader* thing in his lap.

"Laurel, this is my fault. If I hadn't wanted to go for those stupid bikes..."

She slammed the bottom of her fist down on the dusty desk. "What? You could've stopped it from happening? I don't think so. You would've been trapped in the cache with the others. Or maybe you could've been stuck with us in the Mimi, while they carted our friends off. Oh, I know! You could've been *killed* trying to keep that armored car from ramming its way into the safe house! That would've been so much fun, right?"

"Well, I could've... Hell, I don't know." Jake dropped his face into his palm and closed his eyes. "I don't know what I'm doing. I have no idea how to get our friends back. I don't know what..."

"No one expects you to be perfect." She said, gently.

Jake kept silent. Smoke from the coffin nail eddied around his unruly hair and he slowly exhaled. Sweat was beginning to form on his upper lip, since there was no ventilation in the small office. The power in the area had failed more than a month earlier.

She watched him brood for a few minutes, then decided to change the subject. "How did you pick up the Barbie duo? Kat told me a little about what happened, but she seemed pretty subdued, which for her is strange. I almost started searching the Mimi for body-snatcher pods."

He chuckled, and told her about the hillbilly-psychos and their awful trophy display, which had prompted their party to send said hillbillies to that big ol' hootenanny in the sky.

Laurel shook her head. "What the hell is happening? You'd think zombies would be bad enough, but it's like the people who are still alive out there have lost their minds."

"It could be many of the survivors snapped due to stress." Jake stared past his cigarette. "More likely, it's the instant gratification mindset."

"You need to explain that."

"People have always wanted things they can't have," he said.

"Say you walked into a music shop and found a guitar Pete Townshend played on tour, but you couldn't afford to buy it..."

"Which would suck," Laurel interjected. "The Who were one of the best bands *ever*. Right up there with Parliament Funkadelic, The Ramones, Butch Walker, and the Rat Pack."

Jake took a drag and gestured at her with his American Spirit. "While that comment proves, at least in my mind, that you have impeccable taste in music along with being the *hottest* redhead walking the face of the Earth, it's not my point."

Laurel smiled at him widely as he pressed on. "Think about what would happen if you could just walk in and take it because no one was there to stop you. *That's* what we're living in now."

She frowned again. "So... what? We're back in the Wild West?"

"Actually, that's a pretty apt comparison. The only law back then was what you could enforce at the barrel of a gun."

As she considered that, Jake stubbed out his smoke and lit another.

"What's worse, some people who were prepared for this apocalypse, or outbreak, or whatever you want to call it, *won't* be anyone you'll want to hang out with." He looked down at his boots.

"George was prepared," she reminded him, "and he's really nice. After you chip away all his BS and barnacles, that is."

"True. But remember, that's because he's a crusty, old-school sailor." Jake inhaled more smoke and blew it from his nose, as he'd learned to do with the SAS. It burned his nostrils and the small discomfort helped him focus his thoughts. "Foster spent most of his life *protecting* people like us and our country. He's nothing like the scumbags we're going to come across. Take those bastards that sacked Rae's cache..."

"Where?"

Jake realized she was trying to cheer him up and, though annoying, it was working. "They were *ready*. Unlike Jo-Bob and the Moonshine-Jamboree who captured Gwen and Donna, they'd been *trained*. That's the kind of people I'm worried about. Militias, white supremacists, cults. Hell, a determined chapter of the Latter Day Saints Harley-Davidson Club could ruin our day, real quick."

"Seen any of the last one's around?"

"Not for a couple of months now. That's what I'm talking about, though. There aren't any authorities left to stop the wack-a-doos." Jake worried. "The ones who'll rape and kill and enslave other people to survive. Or even just for fun..."

Laurel was silent as he finished his smoke. When the writer finally stubbed that one out on the floor as well, she took his hand and pulled him up from the chair. Jake stepped forward, allowing her to put her hands low on his hips to draw him between her knees. "You know what I think?"

Jake looked at her curiously.

"I think you try to take everything on yourself," Laurel said, hands sliding down the outside of his thighs. "You can't carry the weight of everything, you know."

"I have to try." He smoothed still-damp hair away from her face with one hand, "We're on our own out here. One screw up, one avoidable accident, and we could all get killed. Or worse. Our *lives* depend on me anticipating..."

Laurel's hands slid up Jake's thighs and took a double-handful of his buttocks. He jumped in surprise as she looked up at him, eyes dancing.

"Did you anticipate that?"

"Not so much," he admitted, stroking fingers along her shoulders, causing Laurel to shiver and take a quick breath. Her hands went up the small of Jake's back and took hold of his—now a bit ragged—GBGB shirt, pulling him close as her lips turned upwards.

She cranked up the heat as they kissed from slow burn to flambé. Laurel continued pulling him lower while she scooted her firm posterior forward, until she half hung off the desk's edge. The redhead proceeded to slide her legs up over his while nibbling at Jake's chin. Her hands caressed the skin of his waist lightly and she smiled as the sensation sent a shudder up his spine.

"I'm sorry I left you alone," Jake said softly, arms moving around her shoulder-blades. "If something had happened to you, I..."

Laurel silenced him with more kisses while releasing the clasp on his web belt.

It was *really* hot in the office anyway.

* * *

Kat was coming back from the only toilet in the—coed and ew—when she heard the moan.

Luckily, her eyes had long adjusted to the gloom, making it unnecessary to take one of their few Coleman lanterns along, so she wasn't *too* concerned with being seen. Moving stealthily in a low crouch, she pulled her Grandfather's sword free of its sheath along her back. The *ito* or flat cord that wrapped the stingray-skin covered hilt was far more reassuring against her palm, than the composite grip of a pistol could ever hope to be. Reversing the blade so it stretched back along her forearm, Zatoichi style, she crept into the darkness in search of the possible ghoul.

Kat *loved* the sword. It was easy to kill at a distance when you didn't have to watch the light leave your enemy's eyes, or get any arterial spray on you. Using a blade took *skill*. That didn't mean she wasn't competent with firearms. Her Native American father, a military lifer, had insured his daughter knew how to handle a weapon before she entered the sixth grade. She hadn't turned into a gun nut like Foster, though. She understood they were necessary (Hello-o-o? Apocalypse?). She didn't have *any* qualms when it came to putting a gunpowder-driven, copper-jacketed solution through the forehead of a hungry, dead problem. Or a country-fried would-be rapist. Whichever.

Padding along on silent, cat-like feet, she began to trace the source of the low sounds. She stalked forward and was just about to enter a small office at the far end of their hangar, when a barely-audible female voice murmured, *Yes!* A loud, breathy moan followed, letting Kat know that someone inside was about to take a trip on the "O" train.

She did *try* not to look.

Really.

Peeking around the doorjamb, Kat saw her roommate's wavy, red hair. It was half-sticking to her sparsely-freckled shoulders, as she and Jake moved against each other in the sweltering, little office. Even though his face was hidden on the other side of her friend's hair, the way he held Laurel was unmistakable. Cradling her upper body, he supported her weight with one arm as they rocked against one-another.

Kat's view was partially obstructed by a peeling, four-foot partition, causing her to curse mentally. She'd been trying to catch Jake in the buff. Unless she jumped, which would be a bad idea due to the possible noise her landing could make, all she could see was Laurel's back, the curve of one undulating butt cheek, and his upper torso. Jake and her friend were oblivious to their surroundings. The blue-haired young woman got the impression she might be able to enter the office without either of them registering her presence, but decided not to press her luck.

The muscles in Laurel's arms grew taut as she clutched at Jake and bit her lip in an attempt to keep quiet, but she wasn't able to hold back. She had to bury her mouth against the hollow of his neck as she cried out and writhed wildly.

Jake's supporting hand clenched into a fist and he shuddered. He managed to stifle a low groan but, though muffled, the sound sent a hot thrill up Kat's spine from the tips of her toes to the crown of her head. The ninja-girl realized she was breathing *really* fast as Laurel gasped and had to make an effort to calm down. Then Laurel cried out softly and threw her head back, her face the picture of bliss.

Kat slid away from the door. Sheathing her sword again with a shaking hand, she leaned against the outside wall, wrapping her arms around her torso in an attempt to get herself under control. The young woman felt extremely conflicted. She knew, without a doubt, that she should forget about Jake and those weird eyes and that smile and the way her heart raced when they kissed and...

Stop it. Laurel is your best friend. Are you really so low, so desperate, that you'd stab her in the back? Betray her trust? Ruin everything?

She didn't have an answer. She'd never intentionally hurt her roommate. She loved her like a sister and wanted her to be happy. Kat was overjoyed that her friend and Jake had hit it off. Laurel deserved him. She deserved someone who was sweet and strong and kind and honest and sexy and...

Stop it!

Kat heard their ragged breathing from inside the office and, against her better judgment, slowly moved to the doorway again. She knew she should go. This was private. Intimate. Something she had no right to see. She decided to turn around and go back to the others. In just a minute or two.

Her friends were still locked together, unwilling to let each other go as their bodies trembled and their minds reeled in the aftermath of the coupling. Jake remained hunched over Laurel, head down, chest working like a bellows, still holding her up away from the surface of the desk. Laurel gripped him tightly, face mashed against his shoulder as she panted, and continued running her hands over his back. She leaned against his arm, moving his face around again to meet his lips.

The kiss was slow and sensual, not a frantic demand. Kat looked on and her stomach fluttered. What she could see of Laurel's heavy-lidded face glowed in the low light and Jake's, while still tired, was content. Both were covered in a light sheen of sweat and still slightly out of breath, but she could tell there was real affection in their eyes. Her pulse sped up. Whether at the thought of her friend finding happiness in the writer's arms or the fantasy of him directing those pale, blue eyes her way as he wore that look, Kat couldn't tell.

Upon seeing the expression on Jake's face, an irrational surge of jealous lust flowed through her. Kat realized the silent vow she'd made wouldn't hold an ounce of merit if she were given half a chance. She wanted that. She wanted *him*. Unless Jake flat-out told her it could never, *ever* happen... she'd wait. Be there, quietly in the wings, in case...

Stop it, her intellect told her.

Screw. You, her heart answered.

She realized it was selfish. She also had no illusions as to how deeply Jake cared for her lovely, red-haired friend. The problem was any sense of self-control she had went right out the window when he turned those eyes towards her.

Edging away from the door, Kat listened as they whispered to each other. Though she couldn't make out her words, Laurel's voice brushed past her like a soft scarf, made of velvet smoke. Jake's followed in a murmur that stroked the base of Kat's spine and made her breath catch in her throat. She stood pressed against the wall, eyes closed, wishing desperately that she could trade places with Laurel to have that husky timbre against her ear. Then the pitch of his voice deepened and Kat heard her friend hiss with pleasure.

Again? Already? she thought, as Laurel's breathy moans floated quietly from the room. *Oh my God!*

Kat fled, unable to listen any longer, let alone dare to peek through the doorway again. She crossed the dark hangar's width, making sure to circle long-ways around the Mimi, and returned to the small circle of dim light emanating near the garish transport's rear hatch.

Rae and the Barbie duo had already sacked out for the night, locked away in the Mimi's coffin-like sleeping bunks. Kat didn't like the things. She never got much rest in them. It was *lonely* in there. Most times, she would just lean back in one of the seats, or stretch out next to the vehicle's rear hatch on a mummy bag.

Elle and young Leo had volunteered to share watch duty on the roof earlier, so only Foster and Gertrude, who was knitting *something*, remained awake. They sat on a pair of camp chairs looted from Tim's Emporium, sipping coffee brewed from an old-fashioned percolator, via their Coleman stove.

"Hey guys. Any more of that left?" Kat asked hopefully.

George tossed her a metal cup from the pack beside his chair. "Just remember ta wash it afterwards, huh?"

The pretty Asian stuck her tongue out at him and, using one of Gertie's knitted potholders, poured herself a cup of Joe. They didn't have any milk, only dry creamer and sugar packets, but after stirring both into the brew it tasted of Heaven.

"Do you know where Jake got off to, dear?" Gertrude looked around. "I haven't seen him in a bit, and if he's unsupervised for too long, he tends to do fairly heroic but *very* stupid things."

Think fast, Kat thought.

"I saw him with Laurel a while ago. They had a spat the other day and needed to work some things out."

"I know what they needed to work out." George waggled his eyebrows with a leer.

Gertrude rolled her eyes and went back to her knitting.

"What?" Foster demanded. "She's a knockout. He's a decent lookin' guy. You do the math."

Kat sipped her coffee and decided to keep her mouth shut. For once.

"No different than Leo and Elle up there." He waved a hand at the ceiling. "Or Al and that Heather girl, fer that matter."

George sobered as he mentioned Jake's skinny friend, then stated he had some numbers to run regarding the transport's fuel consumption rate. He folded up his chair and took it, along with his mug of coffee, up the ramp into the Mimi.

"He's very worried about poor Allen." Gertrude explained. "George is sure if we don't get to them in the next day or so, those awful men will probably kill him."

"Al's a lot tougher than he looks," Kat replied. "I'd have thought he'd be worried about Maggie and the girls."

Gertrude continued. "He is, dear. But unless something causes those men to become a lot crazier than they are, they'll keep our ladies alive. Allen may not be of any *use* to them if you get my meaning."

"Oh." Kat considered that. "Well, we'll think of something. There's no *way* Jake will let Al get killed. They've been friends forever. He'll figure out a way to save them and we'll go deal with those creeps. The same way we did with the men—and I use that term loosely—who captured the Barbies. "

Gertie was watching Kat's face as she spoke, and for some reason it made the ninja-girl decidedly uncomfortable. Gertrude put her needles aside. "Come here for just a moment if you would, dear?"

Frowning, Kat circled the camp stove, and moved close to Jake's neighbor. Gertie placed her mug on the concrete floor next to her chair. As she took hold of Kat's hands, she pulled gently until the younger woman went slowly to her knees in front of her chair.

"You need to talk, don't you?"

"Um. I'm not sure what you mean," Kat said.

Gertrude gave her a level look. "Alright. I'll just ask. Have you told Jake yet?"

Kat was surprised at that. "What?"

"That you're in love with him?" Gertie clarified. "Please, dear, close your mouth. It's very unattractive to have it hanging open that way."

Quickly pulling her slack jaw up off the floor, Kat's first instinct was to deny, deny, deny. "Gertie, I am *not* in love with Jake. I don't know where you would get that idea, but..."

"Really?" The aged woman asked in a droll tone. "The fact that you nearly tore through the wall of our safe house when he was fighting those creatures? That was a fairly good indication."

"I had to hurry! They were going to *eat* him!"

"And your kiss afterwards?"

Kat blinked. "How did..."

"The security camera in George's office."

"It-It was just relief!" she stammered. "I was glad he hadn't been bitten! He is my friend after all. Why *wouldn't* I be happy?"

Gertrude waved that argument aside. "And the fact that it's you, not Laurel, going out among the zombies with him in our Humvee? You kind of blackmailed that one out of him."

"I did not! Well... not *really*," Kat admitted. "Laurel's a good shot, but she doesn't have a vicious bone in her body. There has to be someone out there to protect him when things go all pear shaped."

"Mmm-hmm. Those are all excellent explanations, Katherine. Believable even. But I know differently." Gertrude patted Kat's hand. "Maybe my generation is simply more observant than... what would we call the current one, dear? Generation Z?"

"Gertie, it's late and..."

"When he's nearby, no matter what you're doing, your eyes keep going back to his face." Gertrude interrupted in a gentle but no-nonsense tone. "When he so much as stumbles, your hand twitches to reach out for him. I saw your face when the two of you kissed, dear. You looked like a love-sick teenager. You get that way every time he so much as glances at you."

"I do *not*..." Kat stared at the floor.

"Katherine, it's *obvious*." Gertie took her by the chin lightly with one hand and brought her face up. The younger woman's eyes were wide and frightened. "If you don't come to terms with it, you're going to end up falling apart."

A tear tracked its way down Kat's face, and when she spoke Gertie could tell she was fighting to remain in control.

"But Laurel...she's my *friend*. Besides, you said you *liked* her, and..."

"I *do* like her," Gertrude admitted, "but I never said she was The One. Or that she and Jake should start picking out china patterns. That remains to be seen. I want the boy to be happy too, Katherine. He's had *far* too much pain in his life, even before the last two months. Do you know for a *fact* that if the pair of you became romantically involved, you wouldn't end up being deliriously happy?"

"Just the opposite." Kat whispered, closing her eyes against more tears. "We have a lot in common."

"Then for heaven's sake, *tell* him."

Kat had trouble speaking. "I *can't*! He and Laurel... I don't want to hurt her. Oh, Gertie, what am I going to *do*?" She threw her arms around the older woman's waist, laid her head on her oversized, camouflage pants, and began to cry.

Gertrude held her as she sobbed quietly. She smoothed Kat's hair and rocking her slowly, as the blue-haired girl tried to keep the sound of her heart breaking from echoing through the empty hangar.

CHAPTER TWENTY-ONE

The next morning, Jake's group of survivors received a surprise.

Leo had thrown together oatmeal and dried fruit for breakfast, which wasn't bad, and earned him a peck from the sleepy-eyed Elle as she headed for the Mimi to change her clothes.

"So what do we do?" Kat was twining Laurel's hair into the braid her friend kept it in lately, while making a conscious effort not to look at Jake every few seconds. She double wrapped an elastic hair-tie on the end of the braid. "All done!"

"You're the best." Laurel smiled.

Don't look at him, don't look at him, don't look at him...

Jake finished his smoke and tamped the butt—*don't think about his butt*—out on the hangar floor. "Rae, has Al's signal moved?"

"Yeah," Rae replied, "about three meters. I'm thinking the attackers took our people straight to their home base. We need to scout it fast."

"Which means I'll be taking another trip in the Hummer." He stood and brushed the seat of his pants.

Do not. Think about. His butt!

"You sure we shouldn't just convoy?" George suggested.

Jake winced. "We might need to move fast and the Mimi's just too big to move through..."

He was interrupted by the sound of something meaty thumping on the hangar's entrance. It was basically a small hatch in the huge, sliding door at the southern-most side, allowing entry without cranking the mammoth slider open.

"Do zombies... knock?" Rae wore a confused look.

"Oh God, it's those *things*!" Donna exclaimed in a voice that made Jake's hair hurt. "They're trying to get in! They're..."

"Shut it!" Foster growled. "The damn things can't work a doorknob! She-e-it, woman. Long as we stay quiet and out of sight, it'll be fine. It probably..."

The low thumping sound came from the door again. The survivors looked at one another silently, and began reaching for their weapons. As the others waited at their vehicles, Jake, Kat, Elle, and Foster ghosted towards the door. There was another series of thumps as they approached, and the old fixer motioned for the trio to fan out around the entrance. That would allow for overlapping fields of fire if something nasty came through. After getting thumbs up all around that they were ready, George slowly unlatched the deadbolt and yanked the door open. Foster spun behind the steel slab as he pulled it from the frame to give himself some cover, but when none of them fired, poked his head out to take a look.

A short man in a pair of grey coveralls stood outside. He held a small .22 hunting rifle, thankfully pointed away from the group of heavily-armed and hard-faced individuals currently targeting him with automatic weapons, which was why he didn't get perforated. The newcomer had a small backpack over one shoulder and his well-worn, dirty but serviceable pair of Bates work boots were all but glued to the tamarack in shock. He also wore a fishing vest. Jake noticed that his left bottom pocket held a cheap two-way radio. The man's eyes widened as he saw them, weapons steady and locked on his face. He lowered his rifle to hang from its strap on his right shoulder, then put his hands in the air.

"Oh, shit," he said. "Please don't kill me. The world is really fucked up, but I'd rather not have to explain to the Almighty why I had to shoot my boss in the face just yet."

Foster took the man's weapon and motioned him into the hangar. As he entered, the stranger caught sight of the rest of their group standing near the Mimi. He gave them a good, long look and seemed to slump a bit in relief.

"Who are you?" Jake demanded. "How did you find us?"

The short man turned towards him. "Uh. Warren Jenner. I work here. Worked here. I saw you come in yesterday."

"Why didn't you approach us then?"

The stranger snorted. "Yeah, right. Maybe get my head blown off by somebody who got trigger happy? I'll pass, thanks. I thought it would be better if I came over once everyone was fresh in the morning."

Jake couldn't find any fault with that reasoning.

"Go ahead and put your hands down." He waved to the others and they lowered their weapons. "Look, we're not going to kill you.

Unless you turn out to be barking, shit-house crazy or something. In which case George here is going to take *great* pleasure in putting a hollow-point through your left eye."

Jenner looked at the aging fixer, swallowing audibly as Foster patted the Glock riding his hip. "Okey-Dokey."

"How'd you end up here?" Jake lit up and, seeing the look on Warren's face, passed him one as well.

Jenner took a deep drag, closed his eyes, and sighed with pleasure. "*Christ* that's good. It's been a month since I had anything but a crappy menthol."

Warren Jenner had been among the last to make it out of Dayton alive. Two weeks after the initial outbreak, it was evident that the city had become a deathtrap. Most major metropolitan areas east of the Rockies were written off by the powers-that-be, but many of the smaller ones had been relatively safe. For a while. That all changed when the National Guard units pulled out. At that point, hastily erected barricades of semi-trailers, overturned cars, and razor wire had been holding back the dead around Wright Patterson's 88th Medical Group's hospital. It had only been a matter of time until they broke through the Disaster Aid Center's defenses.

Warren, his boss Terrie, her husband Pete, Don, and a trio of film students they'd picked up at Wright State University, had watched from the roof of Myong's, a Korean restaurant a block away, when it happened. They'd been trying to determine how to get inside without being eaten, or shot by the Guardsmen walking the tops of the trailers, so they'd seen it all. There were easily hundreds of the things pounding on the barricade and the sight of all that hungry evil was enough to make Jenner believe his veins had suddenly been filled with ice. As they looked on, the eastern barrier failed and all hell broke loose.

The densely-packed dead had pushed forward on each other with such combined strength that one end of a trailer began inching into the sanctuary, away from the rest of its impromptu wall. The soldiers protecting the perimeter fired into the crowd, dropping zombies to the pavement by the dozen, but others continued their press onward. The guards began abandoning their posts when the first of the creatures slid around the trailer's edge. The gap in the protective wall widened, and soon the trickle became a river, then a flood. Warren and his companions watched in horror while the surrounding streets emptied and the refugee center turned into a killing field. Thankfully, they were too far away to see many details, for which the short man would be forever grateful. Distant figures went down, and the crowd began feeding on their victims' still-warm flesh. But most were lost in the press of corpses long before they ceased to scream.

"That was bad. The screams." Warren sipped absently at the coffee Rae had passed him. They were all clustered near the Mimi's rear hatch, listening as he recanted his story. "People calling for help while those *things* tore them apart...I'll remember one of them until the day I die. I think it was a kid, maybe eight years old or so. Kept screaming, 'Mommy! Mommy! Mommy!' then just cut off. I couldn't see where."

They all knew the infected had no conscience, but Jenner's story sickened them. A zombie's mental capacity was basically that of a Guinea pig, sans all the fluffy cuteness. A vicious, ugly, bloodthirsty Guinea pig that smelled like road kill and feces. The Mimi's occupants would, in all likelihood, encounter much much more horror of that caliber too, which did nothing to improve Jake's opinion of their chances.

"How did you end up here?" Jake lit a third American Spirit and passed Warren a second.

"I was a mechanic for DSL's executive fleet. Four planes make up a fleet. What a joke. Landed the job just after my stint in the Air Force. Terrie's husband Pete ferried their big-wigs around and told us Texas had a secure zone near Pecos. At least that's what the last broadcast said before the TV stations went belly up." Warren snorted. "Pete was sure he could get us down there in the Beechcraft King Air 200 he flew, because it had a seventeen hundred mile range."

"I take it he got dead?" Foster flicked the ash from his stogie.

"Jesus. Mr. Tact," Rae mumbled, shaking her head.

Jake knew the conversation wasn't going anywhere good. "Go on, Warren. What happened then?"

Jenner shrugged. "He got dead. A few of those things were inside the fuel farm. They finally broke out after Pete finished gassing up the plane. One of them bit him good. Tore a chunk out of his neck. Don and me managed to wax them with the baseball bats we brought along from Terrie and Pete's, but he bled out in two minutes. Terrie lost it. She was rocking him, covered in blood, when he reanimated then bit her. Don had broken his bat when we were dealing with the first three, so he stabbed Pete in the eye with this big-ass knife he carried. We had the kids stay with Terrie and hit the Supercenter outside the gate, thinking we could get supplies and stuff. Along with something to treat her boob, so..."

"Wait," Laurel interjected from where she stood, leaning back against Jake's chest, his arms wrapped loosely about her waist. "He bit her *boob*?"

"Damn." Kat uncomfortably crossed her arms.

"Told you it's not just me," Jake said smugly.

Fighting a grin, the redhead gave him a gentle elbow in the ribs. "Sorry. Little sidetracked for a minute. Go on."

"Well, Don and I grabbed some backpacks from the camping section, then loaded up with canned food, a few medical supplies, then we raided the sporting goods section and found a couple of .22 rifles. We would've taken more, but they only had a few of those paintball guns in the case, so the rifles and ammo were pretty much all we got." Jenner crinkled his nose at the memory. "There were a few of *them* in there. Five...no six. We took care of them, then pulled the security gates down, so even if there were more out front, they won't be able to see anyone inside. Don thought it would be a good idea because there's so much food in there. We rigged a quick rope ladder from a second-floor break-room window to the ground, since those things can't climb anyway, and came back to see what we could do for Terrie."

The short man scratched his head and took yet another long drag on his cigarette. "Terrie knew she was gonna turn. She'd jumped from the walkway of the control tower, while we were in the store. The next day, after we'd set up in the far hangar, she was walking around out front. She was really busted up, and I couldn't just leave her like that. I had to shoot her. "

Kat's face displayed a definitive pout. "I didn't get to shoot *my* boss."

"Moving on," Jake said loudly. "You said there are others with you?"

Warren nodded, passing his empty mug back to Rae. "Yeah. I had the kids stay in the maintenance hangar with the King Air. We talked it over last night and I convinced them it wouldn't be a good idea for all of us to come. If you guys had been like the people I heard about before the radio went down... Well, let's just say *finger lickin' good* has taken on a whole new meaning for some."

"Cannibals." Foster tapped ash off the end of his cigar again. "I told you all we might have to face things like that."

Most of the group looked a little green around the gills. Laurel swallowed and shifted a bit in Jake's arms, needing something to lighten the mood.

"We've been doing *that* since day one. It's just that none of them have a heartbeat any longer," Kat quipped.

"Good point," George said.

"Let's go reassure your... wait, you said the kids. What about that guy, Don?" The writer asked, frowning.

"He went out to look for help two weeks ago," Warren said. "I told him it was a bad idea, but he felt he had to try. Don't know what happened to him."

Jake nodded and, taking the .22 from George, handed the weapon back to Jenner.

"Elle, can you, Gertie, and Leo keep watch? Lock the door behind us, then move the Hummer opposite to it inside the hangar. Have Leo stay on the roof while you prep the mini-gun. Anybody breathing comes knocking before we get back, shred them. Don't bother opening the door, just shoot right through. If it's those things, so long as they don't get inside, let them be. We'll deal with them on the way back if we have too." He turned back to Jenner. "Sorry, just in case."

"Hey, I understand. Can't be too careful, you know? Zombies and all," the shorter man said.

"Everybody, suit up." Jake hefted his M4. He ejected the magazine, made sure it was full, reinserted it into the weapon, slapped it home, and racked the bolt. "Let's go meet the neighbors."

* * *

The young survivors were leery of their party at first, but warmed quickly.

The trio had sheltered with Jenner for over a month, without any word from the outside world. Kyle, Amy, and Beatrix were overjoyed at the sight of more living, breathing people. The latter went to pieces immediately when Foster entered.

"*Uncle George!*" She flew across the concrete to throw herself into the fixer's arms. Foster managed to secure his pistol before the girl thumped his chest, arms twining around the back of his neck.

"*Bee?*" He demanded, obviously in shock. Jake had never seen his old apartment sup show fear before, but now his weathered face was full of it as he crushed the weeping girl to him "Bee! Holy God, girl, what in the hell are you *doing* here? I thought you were in La Jolla with yer folks!"

Beatrix Foster was memorable. Twenty-two, the face of a naughty cherub, big blue eyes, hair dyed green and done up in two long pigtails Anime style, and (as Allen would've said had he been there) *smoking* fucking hot. If her measurements were anything but 36, 23, 32, Jake would eat his hat.

She didn't let go of her uncle as she filled him in on their escape from the overrun city. "I got a summer internship at Wright Patterson, so I stayed in Dayton! Kyle and Erin and I were at the dorms when... when *they* came. We'd been hiding out there for almost two weeks before Warren found us. We were trying to get to the refugee center when this Blazer skidded around the corner. We started running for it waving, you know? The others weren't going to stop, but Warren jerked the wheel from the passenger seat and almost wrecked the car, and they were all yelling at him and..."

George squeezed Bee again and held her as she babbled. His joy was evident when he looked at Warren. "I owe you."

Jenner shifted uncomfortably from foot to foot, rubbing the back of his neck.

When Foster was able to get a word in edgewise—once Bee finally took a breath—he told her about his safe house and introduced her to the others. She seemed somewhat underwhelmed with their group (especially Rae for some odd reason), until her uncle reached Jake.

"...and this is Jake O'Connor," George concluded.

"Nice to meet you," he said.

Beatrix took his hand, head turning to her uncle, eyes wide. "Wait... Jake? *The Jake*? The one you told me about?"

Now he looked to Foster. The older man glanced at Jake guiltily and nodded to his green-haired niece. "Um. Yeah."

She turned back, still gripping Jake's hand lightly. She smiled radiantly and took a half step closer. "Wow! Nice to meet you. My uncle's told me a lot about you, but he *didn't* tell me you were so hot. Pardon my drool."

"*You* just keep your drool to yourself." Laurel stepped up beside him and twined a possessive arm around his waist. Jake's went unconsciously around her as well, while he did his best not to smile at his lover's reaction to Bee's advance. She had to know there was no comparison in his eyes though, no matter how appealing George's niece may be.

"Have you seen many of the creatures since you guys got here?" Rae changed the subject before things could get ugly.

"Not really. We stick to the interior of the airport. Ryan and I go raid the warehouse about once a week and see a few. So long as we stay out of sight though, the things don't seem interested in this place," Warren replied. "Good thing too. We could last a couple weeks on the canned food we've stockpiled and water isn't a problem. Not with the potable tank in the back. But if lots of zombies showed up, they'd overrun us. I don't think the bay doors would hold a horde of them back."

"Is that the plane you were telling us about?" Rae pointed at a turboprop sitting just inside the hangar doors. There were several others within the stadium-sized expanse, but most of their engines lay open in various levels of assembly. The gearbox of a Piper Cheyenne II needed work, another had compressor problems, and a second Beechcraft King Air 200, with its landing gear in pieces, sat (probably forever) on the service floor, awaiting repair work that would never come. There didn't seem to be many qualified aeronautical engineers left.

"Sure is," Warren replied.

The rest of the survivors killed time making lunch with the help of some canned soup and Ritz crackers that Warren had looted from the Supercenter, as Rae and George examined the Beechcraft with Jenner. After three hours of tech-speak and evaluation, they returned to the others looking grim.

"Ya' want the good news, or the bad news?" Foster asked.

"The good news," Jake replied, pulling a cigarette from his tac-vest.

Rae wiped her hands on a shop rag she'd grabbed from a workstation on the walk back. "The good news is, from what I can tell, the Beechcraft is ready to go."

"I told you that," Warren protested.

"Trust, but verify," Foster's female counterpart said, sweetly.

Kat left off talking with Bee about their preferred brand of hair dye. "What's the bad news?"

Rae crossed her arms under her breasts, which Jake made a point not to watch too closely, and pursed her lips. "The plane holds fifteen. "

Jake put his face in his hands. "Goddamnit."

If they were able to rescue their missing friends, the survivors would be eighteen in number.

"What about if we take out the seats and interior fixtures?" Kat asked. That earned her a surprised look from Rae. "What? I'm not stupid, you know. I *was* a pharmacy tech before the world went to crap. Don't let the hair fool you."

Laurel gave her friend a huge smile.

"Point taken," Rae said. "If we removed all the seats, we might...*might*...be able to fit everyone inside the cabin, but..."

"We'd have to leave everything," George said. "Food, water, guns, ammo, all of it. Once we made it to Texas, we'd be ass-out for supplies, wouldn't have any way to defend ourselves and would pretty much be dependent on whoever the hell felt like helping us."

"What if...only some of us went?"

Everyone's eyes went to Jake. He'd walked away from the group unnoticed as the rest had absorbed Rae and Foster's assessment. He stood leaning against a steel, reinforced worktable, smoke from his American Spirit floating in an ever-changing cloud above his head and shoulders, as he kept his face away. Neither of the fixers answered. Jake turned around, eyes haunted, looking like he'd just been gut-checked with a sledgehammer.

Rae's eyes shifted up and to the left as she accessed the logical portion of her brain. Jake had seen that in many intellectuals over the years, but it was a little provocative when George's friend displayed said trait. "If you take into consideration supply space versus human ratio, even if we send along only ammunition, weapons, and an emergency supply of..."

"Seven people." Foster applied a match to his fresh stogie. "We can send enough food and supplies along for 'em to survive, defend themselves, that sorta thing. I can give them the access info and locations of caches in the area. That way, even if the zone is belly up, they'd have a bolt hole. Our route west takes us right by there anyways, so if something *did* happen, we could always detour an' pick 'em up. Though hopefully once they reached Pecos, the secure area will still be there an' they'd be fine. It's a gamble either way. Run the risk of getting eaten on the drive, which could take weeks or *months*, or maybe get eaten a little sooner flyin' down."

Silence reigned in the hangar as each of the survivors considered the news. To have a chance at salvation sitting right across the room on elegant wings, only to find that they might have to leave companions behind to die (or worse, become the mindless dead) was both frightening and sobering. Most of them were thinking of whether or not they wanted to throw the dice on a one-way flight to possible safety, but Jake only had one thing on his mind.

"We're not going to talk about this now," he said. "I know everyone wants..."

"Why not?" Bee asked

He tossed his cigarette to the ground and stepped on it with the heel of his combat boot. "Because unless we get our people back, before Skinhead and the others who attacked Rae's safe house do something permanent to them, nobody's going to be going to Pecos. *Maggie* is the only one that can fly. Something happens to her? The only way any of us are flying to Texas is if we jump off a bridge, flap our arms real fast, and pray for an updraft."

"Of course we're going after them." Laurel glanced at Kat.

"Damn right!" Her indigo-haired friend came to her feet, passing the strap of her sword over her shoulder.

Rae nodded. "I can track Allen's signal. It's coming in clear, roughly twenty miles to the southwest. From a town named Mulberry."

"Woah, woah!" Jake held his hands out for attention. "We're not going off half-cocked. George? You, Kat, and Elle are coming with me. Rae, you can navigate the Mimi, right?"

"Sure," she replied.

"Okay. You two," he pointed at Foster and Kat, "go let Elle know we're going hunting. George, make sure we've got the travel kits, extra fuel for the Hummer, and the fuel siphon."

The fixer snorted at him in amusement. "Yes, *Mom*. Anything else ya wanna remind me about that I already know?"

"Alright, alright. Kat? Have Elle help you with ammo and a three day supply of food." Jake frowned thoughtfully. "Make sure she brings a couple of her little friends that worked so well at the pizza parlor and grab one of the Longarms too. We leave in an hour."

He turned to Jenner. "I want you to pull anything unnecessary from the interior of that plane, except for six of the seats. Don't mess with the cockpit. Rae can help you to... No. Wait. Scratch that. Rae, I need you to show me how to operate that hand held, tracking unit of yours."

Rae glowered. "It'd be much easier if..."

"You're *not* going," Jake stated firmly, as they left Gwen and Donna to help Warren. It was definitely time to nip that idea firmly in the bud. "We can't risk both people who can drive the Mimi for this. Without George's baby, we'll never make the trip south."

Rae didn't like it, but finally (after quite a bit of unsuccessful wheedling) agreed, and stalked off to retrieve her portable tracker. Laurel stuck close to Jake as they trooped back to their hangar. Once inside, he made a beeline for the Humvee, opening the rear hatch to get at the Starlight and thermal scopes. After taking them to a nearby worktable, Jake began making sure the thermal was fully functional. He was sure they'd need it in the near future.

"I'm coming with you."

He looked up to see Laurel checking the battery readout on their Starlight. "I don't think..."

She gave him a hard look "I'm. Coming. *With*. You."

"We're just going to find the raider's base," Jake said, "not attack it. Rae will be monitoring the primary unit here in the Mimi, and I'll activate the tracker in my vest when we find them. Then she can bring everyone to meet us, and we'll decide the best way to rescue the others."

"Good. Then it won't be that dangerous and there's no reason for me not to go."

Jake was almost speechless. "No reason? There are *infected* out there! Tireless, flesh-eating zombies that want to tear us apart! You can't ask me to..."

"To sit with Rae in the Mimi, while someone I care about goes out in the streets full of tireless, flesh-eating, *fucking zombies*?" The redhead slapped her hand down forcefully on the worktable. "Is *that* what you were going to say?"

This wasn't going well. "Laurel, please! It's hard enough..."

She was having none of it. "Forget it! We had this discussion a long time ago. You *don't* need to protect me. I did pretty good before you and Kat and Allen showed up on the morning of the outbreak. Besides, I'm just as good as you are with a pistol. Better, actually."

That stung a bit.

"Now, we can get ready and go find our friends, or we can *continue* this line of discussion." Her hip cocked out and Jake knew he was in trouble. One eyebrow went skyward and Laurel seemed ready for a fight. His mouth went dry, and he felt the first twinges of panic as he tried desperately to think of a reason for her not to go along. One that preferably wouldn't get him killed.

"Cut him some slack, roomie." Kat came down the Mimi's ramp. She carried a Longarm sniper rifle over one shoulder and an ammunition box filled with AA11 rounds.

The look her friend gave her plainly said, you are violating the edicts of the female sisterhood.

Kat was unimpressed. "Look at him. He's scared out of his mind."

Jake swallowed audibly and went back to fiddling with the thermal scope.

"Of what?" Laurel scoffed.

"Something happening to you." Kat shrugged. "He just hasn't realized yet that he shouldn't be worried. I'm watching his back when we go out."

"Thanks a lot," Jake told her, obviously not pleased. That was like Kat telling him he needed a babysitter.

"Nope." Laurel shook her head. "It seems like every time he leaves my sight, he gets into trouble. Tim's Emporium, the alley behind George's safe house, the homicidal hillbillies..."

Jake didn't intentionally put himself in any of those situations. Mostly. "I can take care of myself!"

"Hey, don't kill the messenger. She made me promise, when she's not around, to look after you. Well, I do that. But you have to understand something. If you ended up hurt or worse, doing the stumbling-two-step, she'd be a basket case." The pretty blue-haired woman shrugged. "So, that said, when her ass isn't around, I watch yours and when she is, I watch hers. And that's not a creepy let's-all-hop-in-the-sack-and-get-it-on type of watching either. You're not into threesomes—for which, I'm sure Laurel's extremely grateful—and while I love her like a sister, I've got the only boobies I want to play with right now."

Jake and Laurel both looked at her with matching quizzical expressions.

"That came out *way* different than it sounded in my head. I'm gonna keep working on the Hummer. And that was no better. Shutting up now." Kat headed for the armored vehicle, humming to herself and doing little dance steps.

Watching as she moved away, Jake mumbled, "You know, sometimes I wonder about her. And sometimes I'm *sure*."

"You have no idea," Laurel replied. "Really. Remember, I *lived* with her?"

"She's right though." He looked down at the thermal scope in his hands. "My head knows you don't need me watching out for you constantly, but my heart has a different opinion."

She stepped forward to cup Jake's face in her hands. "I know you want to keep me safe; don't you think I want to do the same for you?"

Jake shut his eyes and reached up to stroke her fingers. "Swear you'll be careful," he pressed.

"As careful as I can be." Her lopsided grin he loved so much came out.

Then, they began preparations for war.

Chapter Twenty-Two

Jake looked down at the waste treatment plant through his binoculars.

It hadn't been difficult to locate where the raiders had taken their friends. The signal from Allen's tracker remained stationary and clear as they slowly worked their way southwest to the town of Mulberry. The pinging of Rae's hand-held unit allowed them to target the waste facility by midday, after which they wound through a residential neighborhood to park on Willnean Drive. It was taking them longer to assess the location than it had to find it. There hadn't been many of the dead walking the roads on the drive down either. In fact, their absence had struck Jake as a little strange. That said something about what people could get used to in stressful situations.

They'd taken a *somewhat* direct route to their current location, cutting miles to the south around the edge of the township to keep as much distance between them and the nearby suburbs of Cincinnati as possible. Though nearly ten miles from the outskirts, Jake knew full well there had to be an enormous number of the dead roaming the Cincinnati streets. It stood to reason the higher the living population was pre-outbreak for a given area, the higher the concentration of maggot-heads they were sure to encounter.

Once his party had gleaned their friends' location, they ensured the zombies gravitated to the car lot two miles distant by starting ten of the cars. Finding the keys to do so had been fairly easy, seeing how they'd been hanging in the dealership's filing cabinet, right behind the reception desk. Foster had suggested jamming a couple chair legs from the office between driver's seats and the steering wheels to keep the vehicles horns blowing, thereby drawing a greater number in from the surrounding area.

He argued the more that shuffled their way to the car lot, the fewer they'd have to possibly deal with later. Jake vetoed the idea, however, only because with the lack of man-made sounds, it was entirely possible the raiders might be able to hear all the car horns as well.

After his group vacated the dealership, easily hundreds of zombies came from all around. Grandmothers still in their nursing-home bathrobes, men and women in all manner of decay wearing hospital gowns, children still dressed in pajamas. Those freaked him out. The knowledge that the once-innocent five and six-year-old horrors would attempt to take great chunks out of his flesh if he gave them half a chance, not only sent a chill up his spine. It pissed him off.

The writer was truly coming to hate said feces-scented, puss-bags and wished he had a way to wipe every one of the things off the face of the earth so they couldn't walk about in death.

Hey, that's kind of catchy, Jake thought as they twisted their way through the housing development. *The walking de...*

"I see a couple ways to get in right offhand, but nothin' quiet." Foster gazed through the scope of his Longarm. "There's a trio of sentries up by the main gate and another walkin' back near the settling ponds. That one won't be a problem, but we'd have to take out the three in front at the same time or they could raise the alarm."

The facility below was fairly secure against intrusion. There was a ten foot wall encircling the grounds, for what reason Jake was unable to fathom. The only thing to steal from the place was, quite literally, shit. A trio of pumping control stations faced each of the ponds, but after examination with George's FLIR they had been proven empty. The primary and only occupied building was a three story, cinder block job, with heavy steel doors and no ground floor windows.

"These jackasses don't have the first clue." Foster laughed with amusement. "Look at the idiot in the hall on the second floor. He's leaning back in a chair and hasn't moved a muscle the whole time I've been watching. I guarantee he's asleep."

"Do you see the others?" Elle asked.

The fixer pointed to the second floor. "That's got to be our people, up there. Four heat signatures, adjoining rooms, and Mr. Snoozy in the hall. The other five are downstairs getting plastered. They keep passing what look like bottles around."

"Wanna bet the four stooges outside didn't lock the front door?" Elle said, watching the gate guards in the fading twilight. "Considering they all just keep walking in and out to take a dump?"

"No bet," Jake replied. A low, bubbling moan came from the road behind them in the distance. "Someone got that?"

"This one's mine." Laurel said. "You had the last one."

"I'm *still* mad about that," Kat mumbled. "Can't *believe* the ugly butt-head dodged the first shot."

"He didn't dodge it, he tripped."

"Still made me miss," Kat insisted.

"You can get the next one."

"Ladies, it's getting closer," George called, not taking his gaze from the view below.

Jake turned just in time to see Laurel put a bullet from her suppressed M4 through the creature's right eye. She calmly raised the weapon to her shoulder, sighted carefully just above the bridge of its nose and, with an easy squeeze of the trigger, sent a round forty yards through its grey skull. As the zombie slumped bonelessly to the surface of the dirt road, the redhead high-fived with her friend.

"Thank you," Foster said sarcastically.

Both girls stuck their tongues out at his back.

The fixer gave Jake a disgusted look. "Just had to bring those two, didn't you?"

"They'd have pouted if I hadn't."

"You'll pay for that later," they said, in unison and smiled at each other.

"So?" Elle asked. "How are we getting in?"

Jake shook his head. "I have no idea."

"We could blow the gate with one of the RPGs," the blonde sergeant suggested.

"Yeah. I think we're trying to avoid that if at all possible. I mean, there *are* only five of us and ten of them." Kat crossed her legs and leaned against the Humvee as she watched their rear. A dozen zombies had shown up since they'd begun their watch almost five hours ago, even though they'd been as quiet as possible. The noise made by the Hummer on their way into the housing development caused a few creatures to stagger in their general direction, despite the vehicles the survivors used to draw them away, two miles to the west. They needed to get inside, rescue their friends (without getting killed), then bug out before the area started swarming with the dead.

Jake sighed. "I'm open to suggestions here people."

As they considered the problem, Kat had time to absently drop another zombie coming up the road with her silenced pistol. "Today, guys?" she said. "I'd rather not have my ass bitten off by some creepy-smart ghoul while we stand around out here."

"Whoa! Hold it!" Elle gave the pretty Asian a nervous look. "Smart-ghoul? No one said anything about *smart* ones! Somebody forget to mention that?"

Laurel waved dismissively. "Relax, she's just bored. We haven't encountered any zombies that possess more brainpower than a turnip."

"Doesn't mean there *aren't* any," Kat replied loftily.

Elle gave Laurel a hesitant look. "So... we don't actually *know* if they exist or not?"

"I seriously doubt it," the redhead reassured her.

"It *could* happen you know," Kat pressed. "Physical deterioration works differently amongst living people, why not dead ones too?"

"Now you're just being silly"

Kat stuck her tongue out at her friend.

"That's mature," Laurel said.

"Ladies?" Jake could feel a migraine coming on.

"I'm just saying we shouldn't discount the possibility," Kat pouted

"Alright, but wouldn't we have run into one by now?"

Elle was looking back and forth between Laurel and the Asian as they debated the issue, still wearing a leery expression.

"Maybe we have," Kat insisted. "It's not like we try to talk with any of them before George turns them into Jell-O with the Mimi. We could've smooshed dozens of them for all we know."

"Can we *please* not borrow trouble? Talking about things like that has a tendency to make them happen." Laurel asked.

"That's ridiculous," Elle said.

"Yes. But it's true all the same," the redhead sniffed.

Foster had been looking intently at Kat since her *ass* comment. "Now *that's* a hell of an idea."

The indigo-haired, ninja-girl shot another creature that noticed them from four houses over through the temple. "George, I think you're great and all, but I'm not really into guys with so much hair coming out of their ears."

"It keeps 'em warm," the fixer replied, "and I wasn't talking about doin' the bed-sheet Lambada. How did you people survive the day of the outbreak? I swear, sometimes I think everybody in this group but me has fart-beans for brains."

"Care to enlighten us?" Jake asked, powering down the thermal scope.

Foster shouldered his sniper rifle and turned to Jake wearing a scary expression. "Think them guys down there have been on many dates in the last few months?"

Jake looked at him quickly. "Chief, that's a *terrible* idea."

George shrugged. "We got nothin' else, right?"

Frowning deeply, Jake didn't reply right away. After a minute or two he finally sighed and said, "No, you're right. Damn it. It's probably our best shot."

Kat looked back and forth between him and the grinning fixer.

"I'm *really* not going to like this idea, am I?" she asked.

Jake shook his head, looking extremely displeased, while George's face broke into a vicious smile.

* * *

The guards in front of the plant were shocked when a pair of hotties stumbled by the gate.

"Holy God look at that!" One exclaimed.

Kat and Elle looked like the answer to a lonely man's prayer. Laurel's blue-haired friend leaned on the blonde sergeant, one arm across her shoulders, faking a convincing limp. Kat had doffed her cut off tank top, keeping only her purple bra, leather biker pants, and boots. The minimalist outfit showed off her firm, flat stomach and a *lot* of skin.

Elle had—after taking a combat knife to her black, fatigue pants—created a fairly flattering, if slightly ragged, pair of shorts. She'd removed her tactical vest and outer cover, keeping only her form-fitting t-shirt, web belt, and jungle boots. She'd listened to Kat's advice and took her hair out of the utilitarian bun she usually wore, shaking it out into a blonde mane that softened her strong-boned face appealingly. Jake had been *very* careful not to show any appreciation for her toned legs when Elle finished her wardrobe modifications.

"Damn. We're gonna have to change it to the Barbie *Triplets*," Foster had marveled. "Shame the ground-pounders never had a *Girls of* calendar. Nice gams, Blondie."

Elle had smiled, blown the fixer a kiss, and given him the finger, letting him know he was number one in her book.

"I was thinking more along the lines of an 80s, hair-metal, video girl," Jake replied, and instantly knew it was a mistake. He noticed both Kat and Laurel giving Elle a pair of speculative (and slightly hostile) gazes. "Leo's eyes are going to bug out of his head if you let him see you like that."

A thoughtful look crossed her face, followed by a calculating grin. "I'll have to remember to toss my hair around a lot in front of him when we get back to the airport. That always seems to turn *older* men into drooling idiots, so it should work on Leo too."

The writer and George had shared a wry look, while the women laughed.

The disguise, such as it was, worked just as well on the guards.

"Artie, get the gate!" The second guard ordered, eyes wide and following the girls' shapely posteriors as they moved west along the road.

The third fumbled with the lock and asked, "Shouldn't we get the others?"

"Screw them! Do you wanna end up waiting your turn like we had to do with the other ones?" The first guard snapped, sliding through the opening. "We all saw how well *that* turned out, didn't we?"

"Hell no!" Artie replied, following the others hurriedly through the gate. "Dibs on the Asian."

They trotted after the girls, closing the distance quickly due to the "Asian's" limp. The pair heard the tromp of boots on the pavement and turned awkwardly to stare at the guards, as they approached. The men slowed their pace twenty yards away and strode confidently up to the pair, stopping just shy of arm's reach.

"And where did the two of you come from?" The first one asked. He was a burly, scraggly haired man, with a nose that had been broken far too many times. He looked Elle up and down, eyes traveling the length of her tanned legs.

"We were headed north and our Land Rover died," the blonde replied. "We had some friends with us, b-but those things got them last night. We hid in the Quickie Mart down the road all day until they went away again."

"I'm Donna," Kat said, with an obvious wince, "and this is Gwen. Are you guys alone? Do know anyplace safe?"

"Nowhere's really safe anymore, honey," Broken-nose said. "At least no place I've seen in almost three months."

Elle took on a frightened expression. "But Donna can't keep going much longer! She fell down the hill when we ran off the freeway and Jeff had our only gun."

"We could try one of the houses down the street," Kat suggested, looking like she was close to tears as she bit her lip. "Maybe there's still some food in one of them. We could hide until tomorrow night, maybe find some water and stuff. I might be able to walk better by then."

"Oh, you ladies don't have to worry about nothin' like that. We're holed up in the treatment plant here." Broken-nose jerked a thumb at the wall to his right. "You can come with us. We've got plenty of supplies and none of those things can climb the wall, so you won't have to worry about trying to find a place to wait out the day."

Kat's eyes went wide and innocent. "Really?"

"I don't know," Elle said, glancing at Laurel's friend. She thought Kat was laying it on pretty thick. Then again, the trio of morons was all but panting with anticipation at the thought of getting the two of them inside the plant's walls, so she couldn't really fault Kat for a convincing performance. "How can we be sure you're alright?"

"Hey, we're nice guys. Here, we'll help you get your friend inside, alright?" He waved to Artie, who moved to take the indigo-haired woman's arm from over Elle's shoulders. "It's kinda dangerous out here in the open you know? Those things are around. Not as many as in the city, but still enough to be trouble."

Elle faked looking around worriedly as Kat leaned on Artie. She moved to take Broken-nose's arm in hers and gave him a grateful smile. The skinny, shaven-headed man held Kat up, one hand around her back, entirely too close to the lower edge of her left boob for her comfort, and looked down at her cleavage as they took a step towards the gate.

"Ow!" She said and crouched towards her left foot. Artie went to one knee beside her as she bent down and grabbed her knee, just above the top of her biker-style boots.

"Damn it, Artie, get her moving." Broken-nose said, pulling Elle away towards the entrance. "We have to hurry or t... *Gulk*!"

The last was forced from the man's mouth involuntarily, as Elle punched him squarely in the throat. His eyes went wide as her blow crushed his trachea, closing off his airway and he released her arm, hands rising up to claw at his neck. She followed up by grabbing the back of his head with one hand and smashing her other elbow into his nose.

As Elle ruined her man's night, Kat drew Jake's eight inch Field Fighter knife from the top of her left boot and stabbed Artie smoothly through the chest. The fixed blade passed easily between his ribs, slicing open one lung on the way through to puncture and still the raider's heart forever. He was dead before his brain registered the glint of the knife's edge. She jerked it free and shoved his slumping form away.

Elle had just finished driving her raider's broken nose into his brain, when the third man finally recovered from his surprise at their vicious attacks, and raised his carbine in Kat's direction. There was no way she'd be able reach him before he could unload on Laurel's friend. He was at the edge of the road, ten yards towards the entrance, and well out of reach. Elle watched the guard flick the safety off and...

A shadow rose from the ditch behind him. Before the man could squeeze off his first round, a sludge covered hand yanked the muzzle of his weapon away from Kat and another took a crushing grip on his throat. Whatever the thing was, its strength was incredible. The raider couldn't budge the foul-smelling fingers from around his neck and he panicked, realizing he was about five seconds from death. He tried to pull away, only to lose his grip on the Styer semi-auto he'd carried and watch it arc over the dark figure's shoulder as it was tossed away.

The guard punched at the thing, thinking to throw it off balance and maybe get a lungful of air. That plan flopped miserably. The shadowy muck-man blocked his clumsy swings and hit him in the gut with a hooking punch, stealing his breath. The raider couldn't even cry out for the guard at the rear of the plant, as his diaphragm knotted painfully and he dry heaved. As he bent over, the awful shape took his jaw in one hand, the back of his skull in the other, and forcefully spun his head almost one-hundred and eighty degrees to the rear. The move broke his neck, severing his spinal column, and the man dropped to the ground like a two-hundred pound sack of shit.

Jake spat on the raider's body while checking to make sure the other guards weren't going to cause them any more trouble. The ladies had taken care of them both, almost without a sound. Then they ran the hundred yards back towards the abandoned school bus east of the plant to retrieve the girls' clothes and weapons. As they reached it, he held one fist in the air and faced the north. Up on the ridge behind the plant, a dim, red flashlight flicked on and off twice. Then twice again. There was a short pause then the light flashed four times and didn't return.

That was the signal that Foster had taken out the remaining sentry with his Longarm sniper rifle and the outside of the facility was clear for the moment. They decided once Kat and Elle drew the trio in front outside, George (with Laurel watching his back from the turret of the Hummer) would take the rearguard out. After their companions moved inside—making sure to lock the gate behind them—Laurel and the fixer would keep watch until Jake's group retrieved the others. Although a little miffed she wasn't going along, the redhead didn't really mind remaining on the ridge above. From that vantage point, she'd be able to watch for any hostiles (dead *or* alive) and could warn the others, via the secure radios she and Jake wore.

The fact that only five of the raiders remained within the building, had prompted the writer to change plans. Waiting for the rest of their party in the Mimi to arrive would only give the raiders more time alone with their friends. Jake and Foster had discussed it and come to the decision that, even though outnumbered, he and the two girls should be able to surprise the half-drunken hostiles and make hamburger out of them. They'd all had basic room-clearing training—Jake and Kat via Foster, and Elle by way of the United States Military. So down into the belly of the beast strode and crawled the three survivors.

It wasn't fun, quietly slithering through *two hundred yards* of drainage ditch, especially the drainage ditch of a *sewage* plant, but Jake had done it. It had been the only way he could get close enough to back up the girls without being seen. There was a large field, sans anything resembling cover, between the ridge where they'd scouted the plant and the area they'd planned to neutralize the guards. While he might not have been seen if he just crouched over, Jake wasn't willing to risk Elle and Kat's lives on a maybe. So, an hour prior, he'd crept into the ditch just inside the tree line, and struck out through the soggy mess at the bottom. He'd only had to think about all the fun he'd had training with the SAS, and the greasy, rot-infused muck covering the lower third of the ditch hadn't seemed too bad. For the first sixty yards anyway. After that, the slime had taken on the distinct (and much more potent) aroma of death and, well, crap.

Oh yeah. Become a civilian combat journalist, Jake thought, as he'd slid quietly through the foul-smelling gunk. Live a life full of glamour, fame, and excitement. More like mud, shit, and fucking terror. I should've been a dentist...

As the girls dressed and donned their weapons again, Jake moved towards the sewage plant's gate, scanning the inner grounds carefully for any sign of movement. By the time Kat and Elle approached silently, he was sure there wasn't anyone (or thing) lurking in ambush, so the three moved into the facility proper.

Jake went first, followed closely by the Kat, with the blonde sergeant playing rearguard. They paused and gave Elle time to snap a master lock through the gate's bar, securing the courtyard and preventing anyone from fleeing the area, then made for the primary building's side door. When they reached it, she used the thermal scope to check the space beyond. The last five raiders were all on the opposite side of the building in what looked to be the motor pool. Also, there was a block of offices inside between them and the trio seeking to gain entry. As long as they were *quiet*, Jake and the women had a damn good chance of catching their friends' captors unawares.

Kat knelt before the door and pulled a lock-pick set from one of the pouches riding her web belt. She inserted one into the nob with her left hand, probing the lower part with her right using a needle-slim rod. Her eyes closed in concentration and her tongue stuck out from the side of her mouth, while she gently worked the lock's innards. Jake was both amused, and hit with a sudden wave of genuine affection, while he watched the play of emotions on her face as she attempted to gain access to the building. He was half expecting to have to pry the door open using the crowbar riding the length of his spine, but it only took her about twenty seconds to unlock it. After replacing the tools, she grinned at his raised eyebrows and silently mouthed the word *Ninja*.

Jake rolled his eyes and they stacked to the right of the door. He'd learned the "stacking" technique overseas, when the crusty old SEAL had drilled his training brick over and over and over again, until they could, *Fucking perform the fucking process fucking properly*, as the older man so eloquently put it. The entry team lined up on the same side of the door. The second man put his hand on the first man's shoulder; the third man put his on the second man's and so on and so on. The last man in the stack readied himself, and then squeezed the shoulder of the one in front of him. Moving up the line, each man gave the one to their front the signal, until the lead man felt the squeeze on *his* shoulder. Then, knowing the team was ready, they entered the room. The first going left, the second right, on down the line, until the entire group was inside (preferably in three seconds or less) and they proceeded to decimate any opponents within. He took a few deep breaths, made sure the fire selector on his M4 was set on three round bursts, and waited. A few seconds later, when he felt Kat's hand squeeze his shoulder firmly, he pulled the door open, crouched and hurried inside.

It was pretty dark in the offices, but not so much that they couldn't see to maneuver. Avoiding a half-full water cooler, the trio moved slowly down the hallway towards the far side of the building. A slim ribbon of faint light shone under the edge of the motor pool's door. It wasn't fully closed so once they reached it, Jake slowly put an eye to the gap to view the room beyond. Sure enough, a group of five men sat around a propane grill on chairs they'd removed from the offices the three had just passed. Each had a firearm, resting either against the arm of their chair or on the ground beside them, but not a single one held anything but a bottle. A couple of them were dead drunk, already passed out in their chairs.

"So, why are we holding on to the skinny dink?" One asked.

"Hostage," Another replied. "Poole thinks we'll be able to use him later to get their spiffy ride."

"We got the broads for that. Besides, that guy has a big mouth. Bastard wouldn't shut up, even when Artie and me worked him over this morning."

His companion laughed. "Heard him. Wha'd he call you? A *limp-dicked, shit-gobbling, cock bandit*? That was pretty funny."

"Fuck you. I made the little bastard bleed for that one."

Jake had heard enough. Using hand signals in the low light of the hallway so the bastards in the other room wouldn't hear them, he let Kat and Elle know what they were going to do. Both girls nodded, looking pretty pissed in their own right. The raiders' voices carried and they'd heard the comments about Allen. The three readied their weapons and began to stack at the door.

"Any luck with the blonde bitch?"

"Nah. After what she did to Pete, nobody wants to try her again just yet." The first one said, taking another pull on his bottle of Jim Beam before passing it to his companion. "Looks like she's gonna be a tough nut to crack."

His friend laughed. "Oh, I've got a *nut* for her. Pete was stupid. As long as Poole doesn't come back until day after tomorrow, I'm gonna..."

Nostrils flaring, Jake felt Kat's hand tighten on his shoulder. He nudged the door open and slowly edged into the room. The men were sitting facing away from the offices, which was good news for Jake's party. One of the three was so blitzed that he was looking at the ceiling singing badly to himself. The others were engaged in their conversation, so they didn't notice the newcomers until they were only thirty feet away.

One man froze in surprise. The music fan smiled at the pretty girls. The third reached for his Bushmaster rifle.

Jake's M4 gave a triple huff. The raider and his rifle hit the floor, one unfired, both now unseeing. The two sleepers jerked awake at the sound of their companion hitting the concrete, fumbled for their guns, and caught a trio of rounds from the women's weapons in their chests. The music fan and Mr. Nutcracker went for their rifles as well. Jake dropped another and then the last with quick bursts to the center mass as they attempted to rise, then swept the area again, just in case.

The only sound was the labored breathing of the first raider he's perforated. The man lay in a growing pool of blood, unable to speak due to the holes in his abdomen, trying to keep his insides from spilling out.

Jake had never been a fan of cruelty, but there was no way he was going to waste his time trying to save this asshole who'd just bragged about working over his best friend. Stepping up beside the mortally-wounded raider, who looked at him with a mixture of fear and pain-fueled hatred, he put another three-round burst through the man's skull. The women who had been checking the other bodies, insuring none of them were just playing possum, paused as Jake executed the dying man. He turned to look at them, face filled with disgust, motioning for them to continue. He didn't need to think about what he'd just done, at least not until they'd rescued Al and the girls. There would be plenty of time to battle with his conscience later.

They all swapped out their partial clips for full ones and began moving to the stairwell at the rear of the motor pool. When they reached the door, he signaled for a halt. "Elle, check the thermal."

The blonde let her weapon hang against her stomach on its sling and scanned the second floor. "Looks like our sleeping friend in still in Dreamland."

"Good. Kat, do you think you can take him alive?" Jake asked.

The ninja-girl gave him an inquiring look.

"I want some answers," he said.

"As long as I can get close enough. You two might have to wait in the stairwell."

"Let's go check. You take lead. If you think it's feasible, you deal with the guard." He gave them both cautionary looks. "I know you're both careful, but watch where you shoot if it comes to that. We don't want one of our people taking a stray round."

The three crept up the dim stairway to the second floor and stopped outside the door. Kat crouched and, ever-so-slowly, pulled it open to peer down the hall. The sentry was still leaning against the wall, snoring softly. A single, gas-fueled Coleman lantern, set on low, sat beyond him in front of the nearest man to the door. Kat gave a double thumbs up and pushed her MP5 into Jake's hands. He began to take her arm, wanting to find out what her plan was, but got his answer as she pulled her sword. Elle was watching their rear, so she missed Laurel's friend smile and blow Jake a kiss before ghosting into the hallway.

Jake watched as Kat crept onward, her back not quite touching the wall, not making the slightest noise. He didn't hear a thing. Not a breath, not a footstep, nothing. It was almost like she wasn't physically there anymore, but only an image in the form of a very appealing wraith, creeping closer to the slumbering raider. Once again she reversed her sword so the blade stretched out behind her shapely posterior, then continued stalking forward. Laurel's friend moved within arm's reach of the guard, and Jake hoped fervently that the man wouldn't stir. He had the raider in his sights. He would've killed the man without hesitation had Kat not set off herself, then struck the guard expertly behind the ear with the pommel of her sword. The raider fell to the floor with a quiet thump, a large knot already forming on the side of his head.

Jake rushed forward, turned the man face down, and proceeded to frisk him. His vest held only a bottle of Tylenol, a small flask maybe half full of cheap vodka, a wallet, a partial pack of Camels, and a disposable lighter. He didn't have a firearm, or any other weapon. Not even a shitty folding knife. That was a bit strange, but Jake wasn't going to look a gift horse in the mouth. He pulled a trio of zip-ties from his Tac-vest and secured the raiders hands behind his back. Once he was sure the guard was restrained, Jake retrieved the Coleman lantern from down the hall, and Kat set about picking the lock on the first door.

Seconds later, Kat swung the door open to reveal Maggie and Allen resting together against the far wall.

The buxom woman held Jake's slim friend's head on her lap, smoothing his hair back from the mess the raiders had made of his face. One of Al's eyes was swollen completely shut and looked like it pained him, even in his sleep. There were numerous dark contusions covering Allen's face and his lips were split in several places, giving testament to the extent of the raiders' beating. The mechanic's nose was, thankfully, not broken and he wasn't missing teeth, but Jake had seen zombies that looked better. Maggie had a *lot* of blood in her hair that trailed down the side of her face, half soaking her shirt, and even from the knees up on her green fatigues. He thought she might have a nasty scalp wound, but the only obvious damage she'd taken was the red and quite swollen left side of her face. It looked like someone had popped her a good one, or given her a truly, harsh slapping. Her eyes were full of piss and vinegar as the three entered, however, and she gave them a bloody-toothed smile.

"Am I ever glad to see you guys! I'd kiss every *one* of you on the lips right now, but I don't want to get blood on your mouths," she said.

* * *

Tracy Dixon's slippers were wearing away.

Her pod still moved southwest. They'd been walking for weeks, slowly heading away from Columbus proper into the rural countryside.

She hadn't taken much damage during the outbreak, unlike

some of her impromptu companions. Not that any of them would care. Many displayed gory, painful wounds that would've killed normal humans outright. Bullet holes, stab wounds, missing limbs, torsos void of internal organs, all filled with fecund body fluids and maggots.

The fly larvae were having a tough time of it though. For some reason, they seemed to be having a hard time digesting her flesh.

Chapter Twenty-Three

Though Jake badly wanted to help his friend, they still had to free Heather and Karen. "Elle, get Allen downstairs and check him out. Make sure he doesn't have any internal injuries. Mags? Are you together enough to give her a hand?"

The blood-splattered woman nodded and helped Elle carry the semiconscious Allen gently from the room. When they'd disappeared through the stairwell door, Jake turned to find Kat already down the hall, deftly working on the other door's lock. He hurried toward her, wanting to call out but worried about the noise. Even though all the raiders were currently assuming room temperature, they were still in an unfamiliar place, in a hostile area, and needed to leave soon. He'd almost reached her, when she finished working her magic on the lock, put her picks away, stood, and pulled the door open.

A pair of half-dressed raiders stood inside. It looked like they'd been asleep and had woken suddenly at the sound of the survivors talking in the room next door. The two men began to swing the muzzles of their weapons around, towards where Kat stood at the door.

"Oops." She raised her eyebrows.

Jake never stopped his forward motion. He grabbed her around her waist on the fly, snatching Kat from the doorway and spinning them away against the far wall as the raiders fired their first rounds. Bullets began chipping away at the opposite side of the hallway, knocking silver dollar size chunks off as they shattered on the reinforced concrete.

Sheltering Kat with his body, Jake stretched around the door frame with his M4 and, hoping for a lucky shot, loosed half the weapons clip in quick, three round bursts. He swept it from side to side, trying to cover as much area as possible and cause the pair within to take cover. Another hail of bullets forced him to yank back with a hiss as one creased the top of his forearm. It wasn't a bad hit. The round had carved a shallow groove in his flesh, and it felt like someone had hit him with a white hot poker, but Jake managed to send another burst through the door before pulling back.

Kat twisted against his arm, fumbling at the pouch on her belt and something metallic hit the floor. The sound of it bouncing was almost lost in the gunfire from within the office, as she leaned towards the increasing flurry of lead coming in their direction. Jake looked down to see her lips moving.

Oh no, he thought, *is she...counting?*

At four, Kat hurled the frag grenade into the room and firmly kicked the door shut with the sole of her biker boot.

The explosion that followed blew the heavy door off its hinges. It slammed against the opposite wall, displaying an inner surface now perforated with dozens of holes from shrapnel released by the grenade, before falling flat to the floor with a resounding clang.

Jake was still shielding Kat with his body as he stood, ears ringing from the blast, holding her away from the wrecked entrance. Leaning cautiously around the edge of the door with his weapon leading the way, he peeked into the room. Two ruined forms that used to be raiders were splattered messily across the far side of the office. Maggie and Elle were yelling up the stairwell for them, voices strained with worry, so he called back that everything was fine and they'd be down in a minute. Jake let his M4 hang down his back beside the crowbar from its combat strap, as the smoke flowing out of the room began to clear.

They were still trying to catch their breath when Kat asked, "So... was it good for you too?"

He would've laughed, if the image of her being turned into a hundred plus pounds of hamburger wasn't so terrifyingly vivid in his head.

"That was *dangerous*, Kat."

Jake's voice was so angry that Laurel's friend looked at him in surprise. He still hadn't let her loose from the protective, half-embrace and his eyes were closed. Kat didn't know it at the time, but he was trying to rid himself of the terrible image of her blood-covered body that hovered in the forefront of his mind.

"Hey, relax!" she said jokingly, and tried unsuccessfully to turn towards him. "We all thought it was Karen and Heather in there, so there's no way I could've know about Eek and Ook with the semiautomatics. Besides, they weren't quick enough to nail me. I mean, hell-o-o? Highly trained, butt-kicking, ninja-girl here? You should know by..."

Whatever she was going to say next was lost, because as Kat began to move away Jake yanked her firmly back again. His arm was still wrapped around her from behind and—something neither of them had noticed until that moment—his left hand was fully cupping her right breast. He'd been too worried about the bullets coming their way and she had been too afraid he'd catch one protecting her (hence the frag grenade), to realize how intimately they were entwined.

"That's not funny," he said quietly, becoming even more infuriated because the woman was taking how she'd almost died far too casually for his liking. Said fact caused Jake's hand to tense slightly and she tried to squirm away.

"Um, Jake? Your hand?" Kat said half-jokingly, patting his arm, expecting him to snatch it from her boob while stuttering a blushing apology. Like normal.

Instead, he caught her other wrist with his blood covered right hand, brought it down against the outside of his thigh and didn't release her breast. He gripped it *tighter*.

Kat gasped and let her head fall back against his shoulder, her fingers bunching the fabric of his pants as they curled into a fist.

"You need to be more *careful*," Jake breathed against her ear. "If you don't, your luck is eventually going to run out. Do you expect me to handle that?"

"You'd be fine," Kat said unevenly, turning her head away, "Laurel..."

His arm jerked, yanking her skyward roughly. Kat's back arched, causing her buttocks to tighten against his groin, as a high whine forced its way from her throat. Her hand, previously gripping his pants released and spread its fingers painfully wide, as her other pulled at Jake's arm in an attempt to relieve some of the pressure on her breast.

"Promise me you'll be more careful," he demanded. His hand squeezed tighter.

Kat was trying to come off the ground, straining as she rose from one tiptoe to the other. Her eyes skewered shut and her teeth clenched. While Jake couldn't tell through her shirt and bra, her nipple had tightened painfully, causing her breath to come in short gasps as her body quivered.

"Jake, I... I can't..." Her brain couldn't make her mouth work properly. His hand gripping her breast was absolutely maddening. "Jake..."

His grip tightened further. "*Promise. Me.*"

She was almost panting, either with pain or desire or both. The only thing in her world just then, was the feeling of Jake's hand on her, his arm around her, his breath in her ear. Kat could wheedle, threaten, finagle, pout and (in a pinch) kick-ass with the best of them. At that moment however, if he'd asked her for... well, anything. A kiss, to strip, for sex, for oral. *Anything*. She would've obliged him, willingly.

"I promise, okay? I promise!" Kat gasped, desperate for him to let her go before it prompted her to take action. Action like ripping his goddamn *clothes* off, shoving him to the ground, and seeing how many positions they could experiment with before the others came upstairs looking for them.

The writer slid his hand away and she couldn't decide whether to feel relieved or disappointed. While Kat tried to puzzle that out, Jake passed both arms under her ribs and held her. She reached back over her head and ran her hand through his unruly hair, taking great pleasure at feeling him tense when she bumped her buttocks backwards against him.

"Damn it, you're complicating my *life*," he grated out in exasperation. "Why do you do crazy things like that?"

"Just keeping you on your toes," she replied smiling. "I have to remind you I'm here every so often, so you don't take me for granted."

Jake snorted. "Yeah, like *that* could ever happen."

Kat smiled and ran her hands along the outside of his arms. He didn't react as she accidentally passed over the shallow wound across his forearm, but she felt the moisture and her hand was soaked red when she lifted it for a look.

"Shit, you're bleeding!" she exclaimed, pushing his arms from her waist and raising his hand. The wound ran diagonally from the outer edge of his wrist up over the meat of his forearm. Her eyes widened as she watched blood drip slowly off and join more on the concrete floor beside his boot. "Aw, man. Laurel's gonna *kill* me."

"I'm fine, thanks," Jake said wryly.

"Don't be such a baby." Kat took a handful of his vest and started for the stairwell. "Let's go see how Al's doing and get Elle to wrap you up. Did you hit your tracker? "

As they hurried down the stairs, Jake activated the beacon in the left seam of his Tac-vest. Since they'd brought Rae's hand-held Geiger counter sized tracking unit, they'd come up with a way to call for the Foster and the redhead, sans using their radios. Secure or not, there were forty (or more) of the raiders roaming around out there somewhere, and while killing five or ten of them was one thing, eight times that number would present something of a problem. George and Laurel would see his signal activate on Rae's monitor, load into the Hummer, and head for the front gate to pick them all up.

The two hurried down to where Elle and Maggie helped Allen painfully regain consciousness, and the slim man gave them a swollen-lipped smile.

Well, at least none of his teeth are missing, Jake mused.

"Hey," Al said weakly. "How's my hair?"

Jake laughed. "Good, but you've got something on your face. Oh wait... it's your face."

"But my hair's good?"

Allen was sitting with his back to the wall with Maggie on one side, keeping him upright. The blonde EMT had a hand around his slim shoulders supporting him, as Elle applied butterfly bandages to the cuts on his face.

Jake crouched beside his friend. "You look like shit."

"Yeah, but at least I don't *smell* like it." Allen replied. "What did you do? Go for a swim in a Port-a-John?"

"Close," Jake said ruefully. "I take it from your oh-so-flattering knuckle facial there, you were your normal, charming self?"

Al gave a dismissive sniff. "No big deal. That bunch were pansies. Every one of them hit like a girl."

"You should've seen it. They were so pissed off when Allen wouldn't tell them anything. He just kept cracking jokes about their mothers. And their sexual preferences. I thought the one that beat on him was going to have a stroke." Maggie put her other hand lightly to his blood-splattered shirt. "Funniest thing I've ever seen in my life. And the bravest."

"I'm so jealous," Kat said, trying to take the slim man's mind off Elle closing up yet another gash in his forehead. "*I've* wanted to slap you around for months."

"Thanks." Allen chuckled and winced.

Elle finished smoothing the last bandage on his face. "We can move him to the Hummer once Laurel and Foster get here. I'm *pretty* sure there's no internal damage."

"Nurse? Why does it burn when I pee?" Allen quipped.

Elle rolled her eyes and started packing up her med-kit.

"They took Karen away." Jake turned to Maggie. The muscular woman's face was filled with worry and self-recrimination.

"When?"

"Early yesterday morning," she said, her eyes haunted. "It was just after... just after I killed one of them."

She was clearly uncomfortable talking about *that*, so he let the comment pass for the moment. "What about Heather?"

Both Maggie and Jake's friend went silent.

Allen was the one who eventually told them the news. "She tried to run. They only tied Maggie and me up when they took us, after their attack at Rae's. When the convoy got here, she just jumped for the door of the armored car before the guards knew what was happening and headed for the tree line to the south. They were yelling for her to stop. Some tried to catch her, but thanks to Foster's boot camp he put us through she was leaving them in the dust. She could *run*, man. The one in charge, that Skinhead bastard, he's the one who told them to shoot her."

The slim mechanic's sad eyes were miles away as he relived the moment. "At least, it was quick. Half the convoy opened up on her. Probably hit her a dozen times in the first second. She didn't even have a chance to cry out. They sent a man out to check her, but Heather was already dead. They just left her where she fell. The raiders joked about some of the creatures roaming around out there last night. I... I don't think we should try to bury... there won't be much left."

"Al, I... God-fucking-*damnit*." Jake stared numbly at the floor.

"It's not your fault," he croaked, wiping blood away from his mouth. The split on his bottom lip had opened again prior, when Elle applied some topical disinfectant, and was seeping slowly as he spoke. "I know you came as soon as you could. Hell, I can't believe you came in to get us at *night*. With all those things around? Always said you had big ones, pal o' mine. Now, *brains*? That's another story."

"We set up a distraction." Jake closed his eyes and tried to keep his voice from shaking with rage. "There aren't many left nearby now, so..."

Allen grabbed his friend's arm with a bloody hand. "Exactly. You found a way. The raiders are the ones responsible for Heather's death. Not you."

Maggie stared coldly at the bodies strewn around the camp-grill in the motor pool. "And they're the ones that paid for it. I hope the bastards have fun in Hell."

Jake, still feeling like he'd failed completely, helped Allen to his feet and supported his friend as he stood wobbly. Kat took the lead as they moved through the building again and back out into the grounds. Even though they knew all the raiders to be dead, the party moved carefully until they took position beside the entrance and waited for the others to arrive in the Hummer. There were sure to still be creatures in the area. No matter what kind of lure they devised, nothing would be one-hundred percent effective at drawing them away. That had been evident during the wait (and the wet, disgusting crawl), prior to rescuing their friends. Even with the cars running two miles distant at the abandoned dealership, the sound of the Humvee motoring through the empty streets had been enough to draw the odd zombie to their location. The survivors had found it necessary to put almost thirty of the creatures to rest, before engaging in Fosters reckless rescue plan. The things would be a constant danger regardless of location, until Jake and his friends could make it to the hopeful safety of the Rockies.

"Is that the field where...?" Kat didn't finish the sentence, but stood instead staring out at the overgrown expanse holding her MP5.

Maggie nodded. "That's it."

Anger, rage, unreasoning hatred, none of them described what moved through the writer, just then. Jake waved for Maggie to take Al and told the others to stay by the gate. Then he went back into the offices.

The Humvee was bouncing up the road when he reappeared, carrying the bound raider Kat had neutralized from the second floor. As the others loaded in and helped Allen climb stiffly through the rear passenger door, Jake had Foster drop the vehicle's rear gate and shoved the unconscious man in beside the supplies. He wasn't gentle.

"What's with that one?" George asked, as he helped him secure the tailgate again.

"I'm going to find out where they took Karen," Jake said hotly, "and then, we're going to get her back."

Laurel rounded the corner of the Hummer carrying a pair of fatigues and a black T-shirt (surprising how many of them he seemed to go through), so Jake stripped off his slime-coated, garments and quickly rinsed off what he could of the muck with water from his canteen. Foster and Laurel watched the area while he dressed again, telling them quickly what happened inside the facility, but no zombies made an appearance.

Jake missed Kat hiding a smile as she watched him change in the passenger side mirror. She could only see his back (half of it anyway), but even that much set her heart racing. Her hand clenched on the pommel of the sword resting across her legs and itched to touch him. If there was ever a time that Kat envied her red-haired friend, it was at that moment.

She stayed where she was while George slid into the driver's seat and brought the Hummer to life again. Jake and Laurel hastily climbed into the turret to hold onto one another, and the safety rail behind the mini-gun, as Foster set the vehicle in motion.

It was a little cramped with seven people inside so, since the two were going to snuggle together at *some* point over the return trip anyway, they'd opted to enjoy the late-night air above. Besides, Jake still had a bit of an aroma about him, from his crawl through the ditch.

Laurel couldn't have cared less. She simply breathed through her mouth.

Between kisses, that is.

* * *

Jake's rescue party almost made it back to the safety of their Wilmington airport refuge.

Even though angry-looking cloud cover had moved in as they'd retrieved Allen and Maggie from their captors, their spirits were high. When the front finally began spitting rain down against the Hummer's windshield, they'd all been understandably upbeat. Jake and Laurel even remained standing in the vehicle's turret, ignoring the warm rain as it quickly soaked their clothing and upper bodies. It seemed that finally, even though they were hip-deep in the apocalypse, their luck was beginning to improve.

They really should've known better.

They should have remembered the first rule when it came to dealing with the hungry, mobile dead.

Nowhere was safe.

Foster had backtracked their route, eventually winding east around the township and had just crested the Rombach Road overpass when he slammed his foot down on the brake pedal. The old warrior's hands clenched white-knuckled tight around the steering wheel as he fought their ride into a controlled skid along the wet pavement. The vehicle's all-terrain tires slid noticeably as its wheels locked and it skewered sideways, slamming Elle, Maggie, and Kat against their seat-belts. Allen, now blissfully unconscious from his injuries and a liberal application of Morphine, was tossed roughly about on the floor where he lay.

Jake and Laurel still stood in the Hummer's turret, enjoying the rain and the offsetting warmth each provided the other. When Foster suddenly braked, Jake managed to spin his redhead away from the roof's lip, but his lower back bore the brunt of their impromptu halt as it smashed into the thick steel. There was a moment of impact, followed by a sudden and nauseating amount of pain. Jake managed to retain consciousness, but it was a near thing. He felt as if someone had smacked him across his back with a metal plate, which was basically what had just occurred.

Gritting his teeth against the pain, Jake gently pushed Laurel away a bit and quickly checked her for injuries. While dazed and rattled by the sudden stop, she seemed a darned sight better than he felt. Jake silently wished for some Morphine himself, then decided he'd have a *very* pointed talk with George about the necessity of Warning Your Damn Passengers Prior To Sudden Stops.

"Oh, shit," Foster growled, staring out through his door's half-lowered window.

Elle leaned forward to get a look at the road ahead over his shoulder. "Oh, shit?"

"*Oh, shit!*" Kat's eyes bugged from their sockets.

Jake turned and, gazing over the vehicle's roof saw Zombies.

Hundreds and hundreds of zombies.

The stumbling horrors were packed almost shoulder-to-shoulder as they shambled along, moving towards the gawking survivors in what could only be termed a fucking *massive* pod of hungering evil. Jaws dropped open across the leading rank of creatures and dark, brackish drool fell from their lips as they anticipated feeding on fresh human flesh.

"Back-back-back-back-back!" Jake pounded his fist on the Hummer's roof, emphasizing haste. Ignoring the sharp throbbing along his spine, he drew the hulking pistol at his hip, took aim, and obliterated the nearest creature. Fetid grey matter splattered the surrounding corpses with stink-infused rot as the zombie's head disappeared, pulverized by a .12 gauge slug hurled from the barrel of Jake's Hammer repeater.

Others began stumping towards them on uncoordinated feet as George fought with the gearshift. The older man let loose a truly vile string of curses, popped the clutch, spun tires on the wet asphalt before gaining traction, then sent the Hummer roaring into reverse.

"Christ! Where did they all *come* from?" Elle already had her rifle in hand and racked the bolt, insuring a ready round waited in its chamber.

"Who gives a shit?" Foster snapped, driving by the rearview mirror on the Humvee's windshield. He cranked the wheel left, sending them into a tailgate-leading power slide. "No way we can fight through 'em, an' there's no alternate route to the airport's rear gate! We sure as hell can't lead these things back to the hangar and our people, either! A group that size would knock our perimeter fence flat in no time an' we'd be screwed right in the ass! Fuck-fuck-fuck!"

Jake's thoughts were moving at warp speed. Noting the

nervous expression on Laurel's face as they shot back the way they'd come, he wracked his brain for some kind of plan.

They could call Rae and the rest of their group, tell them to bug-out and join up somewh—

No, that wouldn't work. They couldn't afford to leave the airport. The creatures would doubtlessly notice the Mimi long before it reached the fence line, making it impossible to secure the gate again. Jenner should have the King-Air prepared by now and getting his friends to Pecos would be impossible without the plane.

Wait! Rae could use their massive, Pepto-pink transport to mash the crowd flat and...

That one was a wash too. Even though the Mimi was zombie-proof, the creatures would still undoubtedly enter the airport. They'd lose possession of both their temporary hiding place *and* the King-Air until they'd eradicated every last straggler of the horde, and who knew how long that could take? Or if they could even attempt to fight the possibly-overwhelming number of left-over maggot-heads that would be wandering around inside the fence line?

No, they had to lead the enormous herd of mobile dead away from the airport gates to insure their hiding place wouldn't be attacked. For that they needed...

"Ah, crap. Here we go again," Jake mumbled, shaking his head in resignation. "Maggie, pass me my rifle and hand me up some of those spare magazines from the ammo box under your seat."

"What are you thinking?" Laurel asked, and sent a few rounds into the mass of bodies from her own M4. One merely blew the arm from one of the creatures in a messy explosion of bodily fluids, but her other two shots entered skulls and dropped a pair of them in their moldy tracks. Kat leaned out from her own window beside the navi-guesser seat, aimed carefully through her Glock's sights, and eradicated another as Foster accelerated away from the slowly perusing crowd.

"Something pretty damn dangerous." Jake took the quartet of magazines Maggie thrust at him and stuffed them into his still nasty-smelling tac-vest.

"Wanna share?" said redhead demanded, letting loose with a double-tap at the dead.

Jake ruefully noted she killed another zombie with those rounds. Not too shabby for shooting under stressful conditions, let alone from the turret of a moving vehicle.

"George, slow us down a bit," he called out against the wind.

"Why the hell would I wanna do that?" Fosted demanded.

Oh, *this* idea would go over almost as well as a fart in a

spacesuit.

"Because I'm going to get out and lead them away," Jake replied, levering himself up onto the roof of the Humvee.

There were various, emphatic protests from his companions. The most pertinent and vocal of which (naturally) came from Laurel.

"*Are you out of your fucking mind*?" she yelled hotly. Laurel's face was the picture of towering rage.

"Believe me, the last thing I wanna do is have a rerun of 'Dodge the Zombie' like I did back in Columbus, but..."

She cut him off, took hold of Jake's belt, and yanked him unceremoniously back towards the turret hatch. "Sometimes, I swear you're a goddamn lunatic! Where *exactly*, inside that bone-filled block you wear on top of your neck, do suicidal-*fucking*-ideas like that come from? Do you *have* a death-wish or..."

Jake grabbed his raging lover by her shoulders and the look on his face brought her tirade up short.

"We can't fight that many!" he snapped, shaking her slightly and glancing back at the awful crowd slowly coming after them, "We can't lead them back to the others, either! So somebody has to wait until the rest of you are out of sight, then draw them off! It's the only way!"

"But why does it always have to be *you*!" Laurel screamed. She knew his reasoning was sound, but that meant Jake was putting himself in the cross-hairs for them, and her, again.

"Because, whether I like it or not, I'm the leader of this dysfunctional little group. That means it's my call, my *responsibility*." He smiled wryly, gave her a warm kiss, then climbed over the roof's edge to stand outside the driver's side running board.

As Foster swerved the Hummer around an abandoned Chrysler 300, Jake told George his plan.

"Head back the way we came until you're well out of sight. At least two miles," Jake said, readying himself. "I'll draw them back into Wilmington proper a ways, try to lose them in the side streets and alleys, then hole up somewhere. It will likely take a while to lead off that many, so give me a full day before anyone starts panicking. I've still got one of our radios, but I'd rather not use it in case more of those raiders are in the area. If I land in the shit..."

"You get your ass back ta' the hangar, soon as you can. Once these pricks," George motioned behind them at the horde, "are clear. Don't worry. I'll get everyone ready to come runnin', just in case you need savin'."

"I'll be fine, Chief."

Foster stuck a thick index finger in Jake's face. "Don't fuck around with me on this, boy! Too many people'd miss your sorry ass for you to get eaten. You make me come lookin' for you, I won't care if you've been zombified or not. I *will* whip your ass."

"Understood." Jake shot the older man a nervous grin. "Try to keep Laurel from flying apart worrying about me. You know how she gets."

Foster snorted. "Forget that, O'Connor. Your girl starts gettin' all weepy or somethin', I'll foist her off on Gertie. She's good at dealin' with that kind'a thing. My job's killin' stuff."

"You're a sexist dick sometimes, George." Laurel sniffed, then glared at Jake around Elle from the rear seat. "And *you* better come back safe. You hear me?"

"Do my best." Jake tensed and readied himself as Foster began to drop their speed.

"Don't sweat it roomie, I'll keep our hero out of trouble."

Jake started, almost losing his grip on the steel re-bar crisscrossing the Humvee's window in the process, and looked up. Kat stood on their bouncing vehicle's roof, hands on her hips, short hair whipping in the lessening wind, absently retaining her balance with all the ease of her namesake.

"What are you *doing*?" he demanded.

The pretty Asian laughed. "Coming with you of course. Duh! Like you'd last ten minutes without me watching your back?"

"No you're fucking not! I'm...!"

"We don't really have time to debate this." Kat crossed her arms under her breasts, tilting her head in amusement as a smile brightened her exotic features. "Our smelly friends back there are still pretty determined to catch up with us, and between you and me? They don't seem to know when to quit, so I doubt they'll stand around while we argue. Worse than Jehovah's Witnesses."

Laurel bit her lip. Kat tagging along would improve Jake's chances of survival a thousand-fold. While she had a tendency to make odd (if not bubble-headed) comments occasionally, Kat *did* possess a prerequisite set of ninja skills. Stealth, acrobatics and, if the situation called for it, a totally ruthless attitude. Laurel would have both of them to worry about now.

"Take Kat along!" Laurel called, "She'll be able to help you avoid those things! If she can focus on staying alive and not on every little shiny object she passes, that is."

"Love you too!" Kat flipped from the Hummer's roof as Foster brought it to a brief halt, and paused as Jake leapt from its running-board. "And don't worry, this is gonna be fun!"

"Great. Just great! Can you be serious and help me figure out how to live through the next few minutes?" Jake fumed, watching as the others reluctantly roared away in Rae's Army-green machine. "I was thinking we'll head south first, loop around into the center of town, and try to keep those things moving west. That way, maybe they'll just keep walking in the same direction and not decide to turn around once they lose sight of us."

"Sounds good." Kat trotted easily beside him as they jogged into the streets of Wilmington. "What do we do about a hiding place? I mean, there can't be many safe locations here. If there were, there'd be survivors around, right?"

Jake considered that. "Good point. Damn. I hope you're wrong."

"Well, let's narrow it down a bit." Kat glanced back. Yep. The zombies were still following. "We know a few places that would be out, right off the bat. Police stations, firehouses, government buildings..."

"Hospitals too. We don't want to go anywhere near those. Dead in the surrounding area would most likely be thick as flies on a fresh dog turd."

Kat wrinkled her nose. "Well, thanks for that image. So basically; we need a building that's easy to secure, that's not anywhere near what we consider hot zones, and someplace people wouldn't normally go."

"You got it. Considering we know virtually nothing about this town doesn't help either. Remember, we just happened on that Agri-Supply?" Jake scanned the street ahead. There were no suitable locations he could pick out. "Just have to keep our eyes open. Besides, we have to draw our friends back there off first. Then we'll look for a hiding spot."

They circled south around a previously well-maintained Williams Memorial Park, crossed Fife Avenue, turned south through a small subdivision, then continued east on Elm Street. Jake thought it ironic that the two of them would most likely be eviscerated (and eaten) on a street once famous for a fictional, movie serial killer with a weakness for knife-fingered gloves.

He and Kat began looking for an opportune place to ditch their necrotic followers, just after passing the town's YMCA and the local college. There were all manner of abandoned homes and businesses along their path, ranging from cookie-cutter single-family pre-fabs to century-old stone and mortar constructions. Wilmington would've been a picturesque Midwestern town, prior to the zombies rising. Somewhere you'd have seen local firefighters handing out candy to kids during the hokey parade, before everyone headed to town hall for the yearly 4th of July ox roast. It irked Jake that even if the impossible happened, and someone found a way to eradicate every zombie currently walking about the world, the days of small town barbeques and pie eating competitions were likely gone for good. People born after, or during, the global apocalypse they were currently struggling to survive would never feel completely safe. Children of the next generation would never have the oh-so-precious security of youth. The knowledge that, as the song went, *everything is gonna be alright*. They would never have an innocent childhood, free from fear of the dead.

Realizing if he continued navel-gazing he wouldn't be around to see next week, never mind the next decade, Jake shoved the morbid thoughts away and focused on his surroundings.

They were miles from their refuge now, so George and the others would be able to enter unmolested and, more importantly, unnoticed by zombies. It wouldn't be safe for Jake and Kat to return until well after nightfall, however. They still encountered the occasional roaming ghoul as they jogged along, so all the creatures within the town weren't part of the pack trailing them. These odd maggot-heads, while still deadly, weren't much of a threat for the jogging pair. To save their ammunition, the survivors opted for their melee weapons. Jake slung the M4 across his back, pulled his crowbar from the modified shotgun sheath along his spine, and Kat drew her grandfather's sword. Any creatures that got uncomfortably close either lost their heads (quite literally) to the edge of Kat's blade, or had their brains splattered across the landscape by Jake's motivated bludgeoning via crowbar.

While the pretty Asian seemed to be enjoying herself, Jake was torn. Every zombie *had* at one point been someone's family member. They'd had people who cared about them, spent time with them, loved them, maybe even missed them now that they were dead. A sharp twinge of guilt punctuated his swings as he buried the crowbar's hook end into dead skulls. This was offset by a dull, but swiftly increasing, anger over the awful things. They scared him. That was normal. Who *wouldn't* be frightened when confronted by a real zombie? What he felt wasn't fear, though. It was disgust at the very thought of a mobile, hungry corpse. He found their existence offensive. As if, even though he knew the belief to be irrational, zombies as a whole thumbed their noses at the natural order of the universe. No, the slow-burning in his gut wasn't fear.

It was hate.

Hate that burned away at him like a small, hot ember of

charcoal, fresh from the campfire.

Jake came to that epiphany as he crushed yet another creature's skull. This one, in life, had been one of Wilmington's Sheriff deputies. The thing staggered from a side street as they passed, its tan uniform coated with long-dried blood and bits of its face that had rotted away. Jake paused and took in the vacant-eyed thing. The gore-incrusted star it still wore on its chest, the comically-tilted cowboy-style hat covering its flaking scalp, the empty holster at its hip beneath a right arm that had been gnawed off at the elbow. The way its face took on a hellish, hungry expression as the zombie stumbled at him, one-remaining hand stretched out to clutch its prey. It pissed him off.

Swaying back to build momentum, the fuming writer smashed his crowbar mightily down upon the crown of the creature's skull. The tool's chisel tip smashed its way into the zombie's head easily and turned the horror's brain to mush. The thing dropped without a sound, and Jake yanked the hook free to jog after Kat.

She'd just dealt with another zombie in their path with a devastating side kick. The power transferred up Kat's leg from the swaying fulcrum of her leather-clad hips as she skipped forward, smoothly shot past the hinge of her fully-extended knee as her foot went vertical, shot out through the sole of her heavy biker boot, and caught the creature in the point of its jaw, cleanly knocking its head free from its neck. Jake's eyebrows went up as the zombie's still-snapping head sailed over a nearby mail truck, bounced into an open manhole, and disappeared.

"Woah. *That* was hot," Jake was impressed. "On a side note: remind me not to piss you off."

Kat beamed at him.

While amused by his companion's antics, in Jake's opinion it was high time to ditch their carnivorous fan club and go to ground, so the pair put on a burst of speed and made for the next intersection.

"What now?" She asked, as they skirted around the corner of Douglas Street to turn north on College.

Jake shook his head and ran on. When they passed the Sheppard A. Watson Library, Kat grabbed his arm and pointed across the lawns. "What about there?"

Following her gaze past the roadside parking lot, Jake saw a large, brick building, half-hidden by the overgrown trees and ground cover. It was a four-story affair with steel doors and barred windows set far too high for even the most determined zombie to gain access.

"That could be just what the doctor ordered. Let's look"

They raced across the lot and into the trees. Upon closer inspection of the plaque on its door, Jake learned they'd found the "Old Hall" or College Hall. Built originally in 1865, said structure housed the Admissions and Academic Affairs offices of Wilmington College, as well as a few classrooms and the president's office.

"This is perfect!" Kat hopped up and down in excitement.

"Not really, but it'll damn-sure do until tonight." Jake doubted there were any consumables inside. Not knowing how long they'd have to flee the horde, Jake hadn't brought his pack along and Kat steadfastly refused to wear one. All they had were their weapons, a full canteen of water each, the few items in Jake's tactical vest, and whatever the pouches on Kat's belt contained. Not much in the way of food, to say the least. "Let's find a way in."

They ran for the Hall's far side, desperately hoping for a back entrance, but the only door seemed to be the one out front.

"Well, shit." Jake grumbled, "So much for complying with the state fire code."

"Check it out." Kat grinned and pointed overhead.

Jake looked up to see a newly-painted fire escape, set high on the exterior wall. "Okay? That doesn't really help us gain access to..."

Kat ran at the wall, leapt high, planted one booted foot on its brick face, jumped skyward from *there*, and caught the bottom rung of the fire escape's ladder with one hand. As Jake watched open-mouthed, she pulled herself up, climbed to the platform and began working the ladder release.

"Crap! They painted over it!" She yanked repeatedly at the latch, but it wouldn't budge.

Jake checked the area. While no zombies were visible yet, he could hear the pod coming from the corner of Douglas. The chorus of gurgling moans was a dead giveaway.

"Break inside and get to the front. I'll go around and you can open the door for me."

After considering that for a moment, Kat shook her head emphatically. "Yeah, forget that idea. Now get your tush up here!"

"How?" Jake demanded, looking back towards the sounds of approaching zombies.

Mounting the ladder again, Kat sped down to the second step, sat down on it, and lowered herself head-first. Gripping the rung with the backs of her knees (like a trapeze artist about to catch another midair), Kat stretched out her hands to Jake. "We don't have all day, you know?"

With a resigned shrug, he slid his crowbar quickly into its

scabbard, crouched and jumped with every bit of strength in his legs. His hands smacked against Kat's forearms and she firmly gripped his own as Jake swung gently beneath her.

Oddly enough, as he dangled there momentarily, Jake noticed gravity had a rather appealing effect on the female form. At least, it did when a woman was pleasantly endowed and hanging upside-down. Kat's tank-style belly shirt gaped quite a bit normally, because she liked showing off her firm stomach and the lines of her slim midsection. Now, Jake was treated to a view of Sir Issac Newton's discovery acting upon a world-class set of breasts beneath said shirt as she bore his weight.

"Are you gonna hang there all day or what?"

Reluctantly shaking off his reverie of her anatomical attributes, Jake began pulling himself higher. Kat's toned shoulder muscles tightened as he rose to latch onto the bottom rung, insuring that if Jake slipped, he wouldn't go tumbling back to the cement path below. Once he had a grip she motioned him upward, pulling on his tac-vest.

"Too dangerous for me to squirm around to let you by. Go up past me."

Jake gave her a raised eyebrow.

Kat rolled her eyes in exasperation. "Just climb."

"Alright, alright. Jeez."

Powering up by the strength of his biceps, Jake managed to gain the next rung. Kat aided his efforts by pushing him up from below (by way of shamelessly taking a firm, double handful of his buttocks) as he slid against her. She could have simply retained her grip on his vest, but where was the fun in that? Besides, he'd been looking up *her* shirt. Fair was fair.

Once they were both safely on the platform, Kat pulled the lock-pick set from the top of her boot and swiftly opened the nearby window. Both of them scrambled inside past the blinds and secured it tightly again. None too soon, as it turned out.

The horde came abreast of the parking lot next door and began moving past their hiding place. Breathing heavily from their acrobatic exertions, Kat and Jake watched through a small gap in the blinds as first dozens, then hundreds of zombies shuffled by along the street.

"I know I said this would be fun and all," Kat panted, her lips so close that a thrill of pleasure danced up Jake's spine at the feeling of her breath against his ear, "but damn, there's a *lot* of them."

He nodded and glanced around the room. They sheltered in a small office, most likely the Financial Aid counselor's if the grant information adorning its walls was any indication.

"We should check the rest of the building. Just in case." Jake reached for his crowbar.

"Give it a minute," Kat urged quietly. She absently wrapped one arm around his waist and continued observing the dead outside, "Let's wait until they move on, okay? If there *are* any zombies in here, dealing with them might cause enough noise for others out there to notice."

Jake couldn't fault her reasoning and remained where he stood. After a few minutes of watching the horrific parade slowly move along beside the Hall, he put one arm lightly around Kat's shoulders. She in return stepped against him and twined her hands together at the small of his back. There was no intentional sensuality in their movements, simply the need to touch and be touched by another living person in the face of all that death.

"I wonder if we'll ever be safe from them," Kat murmured, and her fingers gripped the fabric of Jake's CBGB shirt. "I mean, I'm sure we'll make it to the west and all..."

Jake didn't take his eyes from the creatures outside. "You're more confident about it than I am."

"Don't interrupt," she said crossly, still looking through the blinds. "It's rude. What I mean is do you think things will ever be normal again? Dance clubs, crappy movies, celebrity antics on really stupid reality TV shows, that kind of stuff?"

Not wanting to depress her, Jake kept his true thoughts to himself. "People are resilient. Look at our history; world wars, volcanic eruptions, hurricanes, terrorism... None of it ever put us down permanently. Eventually, we'll find a way to come back from this too, somehow."

"Do you *really* think so?" She turned her face towards him and Jake's heart rate sped up.

Kat didn't become serious often. Truth be told; many of their group believed that, save for when she was actively engaged in something dangerous, the pretty young woman had long ago fried her brain with all the blue hair dye. Jake knew differently. The way she acted was nothing more than a defense mechanism. At least, he was fairly sure that was the case.

"Probably. Maybe. As long as there are smart-mouthed, ninja-girls around to keep everyone honest. And supplied with 'Hello Kitty' items."

That caused Kat to stifle a laugh. She turned away from the window and the zombies beyond, hugging Jake warmly as she buried her face against his shoulder.

"Thanks for that." Kat pulled back after a minute and wiped at her eyes as they teared in uncontrolled mirth.

Jake touched the tip of her nose with one finger. "Anytime. Now, how about we check the rest of this place out, huh?"

She nodded and, staying on his heels, drew her sword as they neared the door. "Guess we should. Granted, if we run into more zombies in here we'll need to deal with them *really* quietly. We draw attention from that group outside, and I'm going to run like fun for the nearest horizon."

It was Jake's turn to stifle a laugh then. Setting his ear against the door's face, he listened intently. Hearing nothing, he turned the knob and slowly pulled the door open. When no drooling horrors raced into the room, Kat followed him into the echoing hall outside. To their relief, nothing broke the silence on the second floor. Moving cautiously, crowbar in hand, Jake led them further into the hall. Empty rooms were all they encountered and, upon reaching the stairwell, he decided to clear the first floor before proceeding upwards. It wouldn't do to have a zombie (or ten) coming up the stairs behind them, cutting off the only escape route.

Moving with exaggerated care, the leery duo descended the dimly lit ground level. Kat noticed a thin layer of dust coating the floor, revealing no one had been inside for some time. After pointing this out to Jake, they moved into the foremost room.

Kat twirled her sword and smiled. "Well, this is a nice change. No zombies, nobody shooting at us. You're going to spoil me if you keep bringing me to such nice spots."

"I'll risk it." Jake strode quietly to one of the windows and carefully looked through the small gap around its edge. "Let's see what our friends outside are up... Oh, *shit*."

Kat hurried to look over his shoulder. Outside, the grounds were slowly filling up with zombies. The horde, after squeezing through the narrow Wilmington streets in pursuit of the two fleeing survivors, had not simply kept trudging north on College Street. The creatures had spread out.

College Hall was surrounded.

"I don't know if even I could get through that many unseen," Kat whispered against Jake's shoulder. "This is bad."

"What's worse, we can't call the others for help. If those bastards who sacked Rae's cache are around, they'd know exactly where we are. They could even trace us back to the airport." Jake turned away from the disturbing view and sat down, allowing his back to slump against the interior wall.

Kat joined him and set her sword across her lap. Taking his hand she quietly asked, "So, what do we do?"

"I have no idea," Jake admitted.

Outside, the dead continued to move tirelessly around the Hall.

THE END OF BOOK 1

About the Author

For over a decade S.P. Durnin crisscrossed America seeking the perfect pint of Guinness while developing a love/hate relationship with the idea of hungry, mobile corpses. He has lived in Montana, Texas, California, Colorado, Washington, and New Jersey.

In his younger days, S.P. was known to keep a "morning after" backpack in his trunk (in case he woke up in a strange place) right next to his crowbar, but in recent years took the next logical step, upgrading to a bug-out bag.

He now resides in Ohio with his family, one spoiled cat, and two dogs, until the inevitable zombie apocalypse.